Mage Riders
- The Recruits -

Dedicated to:

TO MY BEST FRIEND
TO MY ONE AND ONLY LOVE
I COULDN'T HAVE DONE THIS BOOK WITHOUT YOU
MY ROGER
NOW AND FOREVER AND THEN SOME!

Table of Contents

Prolog

Osiana Issi q tenarala involcate
(Walk in the light of Osiana)

From her bedroom balcony, her beautiful violet eyes focused on the moonlight bouncing off the massive Viamar Sea. *What a wonderful sight,* she reflected. *Theror has created a delightful world.* Her slender long arms reached out as if embracing the entire scene. The sea breeze played with the woman's long silvery curls, caressing her perfectly exquisite face, hugging the flawlessly curved body as the wind welcomed her divine touch.

Strong arms encircled her slender waist as her lover drew her warm welcoming figure to him. "What are you thinking?" the man whispered gently in her ear. "Will you not share your thoughts with me?"

"I was appreciating the sea. I'm thanking our moons for sending down their golden beams to light the waves for me to view the night's beauty." She turned, folding nicely into his strong body. "I wish you could stay forever and share it with me."

"Yes, I would if I could, my dear, but time is of the essence," he passionately kissed her delicately shaped pointed ear. She smelled of freshly cut flowers, sweet and innocent.

"Let me go with you," she nibbled at his lower lip teasing him to stay longer.

"I need your wisdom here," he whispered. "As my most powerful ally, you must be careful, watch your back. I have cunning enemies that will try and undermine my efforts." He went to the balcony's railing gazing out over the extensive fortress gardens to the large body of water beyond, which seemed to stretch forever. "What I must do is something I alone must take responsibility for."

She nodded her head, "The signs are good that your efforts will succeed although there is a darkness that surrounds the six of them. A thick fog clouds my thoughts. My sight is blurred." She held onto his hand squeezing his strong fingers. Her mauve eyes seemed to glaze over as if gazing to a far distant place.

"Your vision has given me courage, but I fear for the six of them also. If they were not the hope, the only hope for the kingdom, I would gladly abandon the plan." He lowered his head. Sadness filled his handsome young face.

"Our time together is drawing to an end, my love." The gorgeous woman once more caressed him.

He grabbed her tightly, "Don't say that." Her laughter encircled him as if dismissing his fears. "Theror has promised me that we could be together. He promised no interference," the handsome man forcefully assured her.

"And we have been together," her full lips kissed him lightly. "Theror did not promise forever."

"I will bargain with him again." He vehemently raised his fist to the heavens.

"Theror will not be so fooled this time," she countered. "He wants me to return, he wants his daughter back."

"Well, he can't have her!" He held his lover tightly as if he'd not let the God take her from him.

"Let us forget the future, just for tonight," she snuggled up to him. "Come to bed before you leave."

And he gladly did.

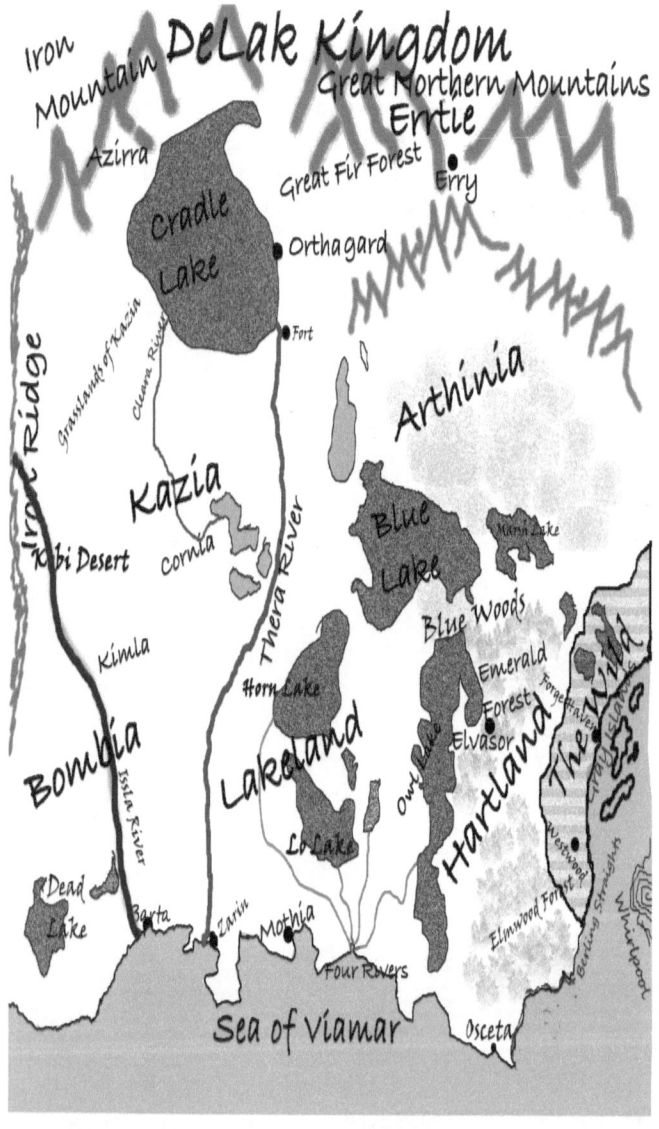

Chapter One
The Young Lord

The sun was filtering through the wooden slats of the windows. *Dawn already!* flooded his mind. Marth sat up stretching his long legs under the table that ran the length of the castle's extensive library. He pushed his book away giving it a good disgusting shove across the polished oak surface. How he hated the subject of medicinal herbs. Yet the young lord could not ignore studying the restorative spells, it was his one weakness. Unlike almost all magic that came easily to the young mage, healing did not. *How ironic, he thought, I did not get any of my mother's boundless healing talent.*

The thought made his inner mind smile as her memory clouded the reflections of his long lost childhood. His face, however, showed not a hint of amusement as his expression always had a half frown. His whole being radiated the attitude of a serious young student mage. Young Lord Marth had dark bushy eyebrows with shadowy almost black eyes below. Onyx black curls swung around his ears and down to his neck. The youthful scholar was not like his mother who had been fair haired, amber eyed and delicate, a typical Kazian. He took after his father, an Arthinian - tall, strong, and dark and with a foreboding manner. That thought made his mind grimace. *No, I'm not like him,* he rebelled against the image. Yet deep down the truth stung.

"Osten!" he spoke the word clearly, as he grabbed onto his wooden staff and pointed it at the lengthy floor-to-ceiling set of windows on the wall in front of him. The wooden slats opened, letting the beginning of the day's light come flooding in. The mage sarcastically thought, *The sun rises over the distant hills bringing a new day to the Plains of Arient in the glorious Barony of Arthinia once more. Yet it offers me no warmth! I want nothing more than to open my eyes to see the Viamar Sea, to be among my peers at Mothia.*

Marth shook the dark thoughts from his reflections and instead again picked up the book and glanced at the words, not really seeing them. His mind was miles away thinking of Mothia, the home fortress of the mages.

Hopefully he'd soon be there being tested and taking his place among those who wielded powerful magic. He'd studied his entire eighteen seasoncycles of his life for the chance to be among those that commanded the words that mattered, words that actually made a difference. Unlike his father, he did not want his magical talents for power to rule but for the good of everyone. The kingdom's mages offered only help and wisdom at their fortress on Mage Bay.

A low rumble brought his mind to the figure at his feet, his wolfhound, Gorg. "I'll get your breakfast soon, just let me get this one last chapter done," he patted the large bushy head that lay against his foot. Marth had found Gorg as a puppy, a runt of a farmer's liter who would not last long among the other wolf pups. The two had bonded, an unusual occurrence for the shy baron's young son, who was already known for his reclusive ways. Perhaps he felt the runt pup and he had something in common as Marth had always felt inferior to his domineering and overbearing father.

Whatever the reason, whether it be happenstance or destiny, the two bonded to where each easily read the other's thoughts. As both boy and animal grew up they grew closer together. Marth kept it to himself, the talent was rare and considered dangerous to have "wolf powers" - the ability to communicate directly with the barony's sheep herding animals. The Arthinian hillpeople had long ago tamed most of the multitude of wild black wolves to be their guard dogs, always keeping them well fed. The wolfhounds were protective guards against the other wild animals that roamed the Arthinian forests and lower hills. A good wolf dog was a prized possession. The weakest pups were often culled, thus Gorg's farmer was glad to be rid of the runt.

Marth's pet, to everyone's surprise, had grown into a full massive hound, bigger than most and extremely protective of the boy. The baron's son had gotten many an offer to breed his canine, but after consulting Gorg, his pet refused every offer. The dog's thoughts came crashing through from under the table, *Do not consider tying me to one of those farmer's lap dogs. They shunned me once. I'll have nothing to do with them. I'll find my own mate, thank you.*

Marth snickered, his pet definitely had his own mind and the animal had strong opinions. "I'll not push anything on you Gorg, although be careful with the wild wolves. They do not like my kind." He got a grunt from the big dog as the only reply. Marth knew that his wolfhound snuck out to the higher deep forest glens, finding the wild gray wolves more to his liking than the tame sheep herding hounds.

The sound of small feet running caught his attention. He looked up to see his young sister, Lilith, come skittering into the library, still wearing her nightdress. Like their mother she was a delicate blonde figure with bright inquisitive ocher eyes. She would be a beauty someday, tall and lithe, a duplicate of her mother, Lady Maria Kaz. Although not even nine yet, the child's healing abilities were already blooming. She was always helping heal the sick hillpeople and their many farm animals in the barony. Already the farm people prized the young girl for her capable restorative healing hands. The young lord knew that it rankled his father that Lilith was popular among his subjects.

"Marth, were you in this stuffy room all night studying?" she stood defiantly before him, one hand on her hips, the other hand shaking her tiny finger at him. "Not again! You study too much! Why? You're already the best mage in the whole castle. You'll ruin your eyes, not to mention your health." She looked so young, so cute chastising him - the spitting image of his mother. His sister was the only one who could get him to smile.

Gorg stuck his head out from under the table. Lilith immediately hugged the big dog with her thin little arms not quite reaching around his neck. The wolf gave her a big lick on her delicate perfectly shaped porcelain face.

"I've been here all night studying herbs, that although they come quite easy to you, dear sister, the plants do not come easy to me! Those damn herbs do not speak to me like they do to you!" Marth slapped his book shut in disgust.

Her laugh filled the room with airy lightness. He could almost breathe in the luxury of it. "Coralla is taking me out this morning to look for ashroot, bomberry and laoric. Come with us, please Marth." She pulled affectionately on his arm, "If I find them all she'll take me to Farmer Orchie's to see the new filly that was just born! It is supposed to be a beauty..."

Her voice trailed off and her eyes grew dark and scared, her small slender body became rigid. Marth didn't have to turn around to see what had frightened the little girl. He knew immediately that his father had entered the room. The whole atmosphere of the library became dreadfully heavy, as if a thunderstorm had entered.

"What are you doing here Lilith? And in your nightdress!" Their father never raised his voice. He didn't have to; his words were strong - every last one of them. "Coralla!" his words now aimed at the library entrance.

"Yes, Sir," said an older woman with a full head of white hair that although was always tied back in a bun had strangles of curls escaping. The strands framed her pudgy friendly face.

The nanny tentatively edged into the room. Despite her obvious advanced age, her amber eyes were young and sparkled with intelligence. Her hands were gnarled with age, which she dutifully clasped in front of her aproned burgundy dress - a sign of Arient Castle servitude. She had come from Kazia with her mistress Lady Maria and now looked after Lilith.

"Why is she not studying?" the baron's voice commanding an immediate response.

It was Marth that answered him before his sister's tutor could respond. "Lil was studying with me." He held up the book on herbs for his father's view.

"I'm SURE she was," the baron's voice was full of his usual sarcasm. "Her name is Lilith - use it!" he stepped around them, standing in front of the windows. His foreboding stature was outlined in the dawn's light. Their father had obviously been outdoors as he lowered his gray robed hood, which was wet from the morning dew. The ruler had probably been falcon hunting. He had the meanest biggest birds, not only in his own barony but also in the entire kingdom. Even the king paid handsomely for one of Lord Thard Arient's hawks.

His father's scarred face frowned at them, but then Marth could not remember a time that his father was not frowning. Besides Lord Thard's face having burn scars, the baron had one long red scar that ran from his nose to his throat that everyone tried not to stare at but failed miserably. When the baron pointed his finger at his daughter, his exposed arm also was covered with nasty burn scars.

"You will take her to her room and make her write the properties of the top twenty herbs that are prevalent in Arthinia. There will be no breakfast and if she is not done by lunchtime than no lunch. Am I clear?"

"Yes, Sir," Coralla dutifully answered. Lilith ran to her tutor and they both scuttled as fast as possible out of the room.

Despite his rising anger, Marth said nothing. He'd long ago learned it only made matters worse to disagree with his father. Baron Arient demanded total control, total obedience. Being one of the strongest mages in the DeLak Kingdom, he got it from everyone. Even King DeLak tread lightly around him.

He looked up at his father's damaged face concentrating on the black eyes that could scare anyone's soul to the depth of their being. Yet, the son's gaze did not waver, to show fear only fed the baron's cruelty. Thard Arient pounced on weakness.

To Marth's relief his father's gaze turned out to the windows. "You are probably wondering why I am here." The young lord was indeed wondering, considering he rarely saw his father, but he said nothing. The baron went on without a reply; he had not expected one. "I have heard from King DeLak."

Marth could not contain his excitement, "Has he sent for me? Am I to go to Mothia?" The young mage had been waiting for the summons since his eighteenth birthday a mooncycle ago.

"Don't be ridiculous!" the baron's words were spat out in disgust. "Why would the king bother with you!"

Marth felt his heart sink; of course, the message would have come from the Mages' Council, not the king. He heard Gorg growl. The wolf had no love for the baron.

"Keep that hound of yours under control," Thard reprimanded. "You will get rid of that animal before you go."

"Before I go?" Now Marth was totally confused.

"War may be coming, although I have my doubts that the Bracaard Kingdom is strong enough to attack us. Still, there is concern. The king feels the need to build up his army. You have volunteered."

"I am no soldier," he stood up. Gorg's anger filtered into his brain, but Marth ignored it. "I have my studies, I'm to be tested soon!"

"The king has requested that the noble houses all contribute. You will go!" his father had turned from the windows. Thard's black eyes were wide and angry. "You will do as I order!"

"I…" Marth grasped his staff, for once the mage apprentice was so angry he automatically grabbed for his strength, his magic. The wooden shaft quickly turned into a broad sharp sword.

From the doorway came a flash of light. His sword became so hot he dropped the blade back onto the table. The magical weapon returned to its regular staff. "What have you been telling the boy!" drifted over. Marth turned to see a bent over figure hobbling into the room wearing the gray robes of

Mothia's wizards. In the ancient mage's hand was an ornate long staff that exuded ancient powerful magic. The formidable man's intense gaze looked ageless; curly shoulder length white hair with a matching long beard. Bright grayish mauve eyes peered out at the two of them, no nonsense eyes.

Marth immediately bowed. "Master Yanith," wishing he had put on his own brown apprentice robe.

"Thard, what have you told him? I told you to wait for me!" For once the baron seemed unsure of himself. Yanith was the only mage that was as powerful as his father. The leader of all of Mothia's magical entities wielded great authority, but it was tempered with wisdom and compassion - something his father sorely lacked.

"There is not much he needs to know. The boy will go where he is told." Lord Arient scowled at his son. It was a warning for his offspring to say nothing. "I fought in the Coorish War, he can do his part!" His father rarely talked of his years fighting the Bracaards. It was a forbidden topic. Thard's extensive scars were a testament of the battles the baron had fought.

The old man turned to Marth, "The king has need of you, son, the kingdom has need of you. Unlike what your father said, it was I that chose you. We need soldiers. War is coming. We need strong intelligent warriors that can lead our army."

"I am not a soldier, not a warrior, never mind not a leader. I am a mage, a scholar," Marth blurted out forgetting his manners of not interrupting his superiors, especially the leader of all the kingdom's mages.

Unlike what his father would have done, Yanith smiled. "That is the problem, they should not be exclusive - one or the other. You are not a soldier, but you will be!"

His father spoke up forcefully making his point, "You are leaving the barony and will not return until you are given permission from the king to return. If you do not survive or if you run away, either way you'll not return."

"Thard, do not frighten the boy for god's sake. Marth," Yanith warned, "the training will be until you have acquired the skills that you will need to fight. Your instruction will be extensive, but I have no doubt you'll do fine. Then you may return and I will personally see to it that you are tested by Mothia. Just remember, *Do as you are told.*"

"How long?" Marth managed to get out despite his dry throat and shaking hands. These two powerful men were shattering his dreams. Did they not realize how devastated he was, how hard he had worked?

"Perhaps a seasoncycle or perhaps longer." Yanith pointed his arm and Marth's staff went flying over to him. The old mage deftly caught it. "You will not need your magic. No one is to know who you really are. You will be just another recruit."

"If you break the rules you will not return, do you understand!" his father once again interjected himself.

"Thard please!" the old wizard frowned at the ruler of Arthinia. "Someone will be here after dark to escort you, son. Only you. What you require is in your rooms. Take nothing else with you. You'll need nothing. Meet your guide at the West Gate at sunset."

Gorg deeply growled. *You cannot go without me.* The angry thought plunged into Marth's mind. Then suddenly the wolf's views were gone. The young Arthinian knew his ability to talk with his dog was gone, gone as his magic left him.

"You must leave the wolf behind," Yanith had a sadness in his voice. "You will go alone. Make arrangement for your pet. Any questions?"

"Do I have a choice?" Marth put as much venom in his answer as he could.

"I'm afraid not. Good luck." The old wizard turned to his father, "Come Thard, I have something to discuss with you."

Holding tightly to Marth's staff, Yanith left with Baron Arient following close behind. As his father reached the door he turned back. The tall dark man glared at his son - no goodbye, no wave, nothing. Just a harsh mean threatening glare, then the barony's ruler turned and left.

"Sire, I have everything for you in your chambers," a burgundy uniformed servant announced from the back of the library. "If you will just follow me." It was more of an order than a request.

Even the servants were commanding him. Marth was already not young Lord Arient. He knelt next to Gorg. "You must leave the castle. My father will do you harm if you stay. Go to Farmer Orchie's, he'll welcome you. Do not go to your wildwood wolf friends. You'll be hunted there. I will return to you, I promise." He hugged his pet, his boyhood friend. Gorg whined loudly. "Go!" He watched his wolfhound slowly leave just as Lilith had. For the first time since his mother's death he held back tears. The ex-mage quickly stood up, hurrying over to the servant who was waiting to show him to his quarters.

He walked into his rooms and the door was immediately shut and locked behind him. The loud click of the lock resounded deafeningly in his ears.

Being the baron's son, he'd been given a suite of luxurious rooms, but he rarely spent time here. The mage apprentice often was found studying in the library or spent a lot of time traveling the barony, studying what nature and what the local sheep hill farmers had to offer. His father would not get him decent tutors and the few castle mages were so cowed by Thard that they steered wide of Marth, knowing the son had his father's displeasure. The young lord had been forced to teach himself. Fortunately, magic came easily to him. Perhaps his parentage helped.

Despite this disadvantage, Marth had become a top-notched wizard. At twelve, he had passed the pre-test when the council had sent a Mothia mage to the castle. He was cleared for the testing when he would reach the age of 18; now his dreams had been dashed, destroyed by the whims of two older powerful men.

The young lord doubted he'd survive the warrior training. Despite being large, like his father, he'd never been coached in the rudiments of martial arts. As his father had told him when it was time to learn self-defense like all the young men of Arthinia - he was not soldier material! The son had not argued, his father's decision meant more time for his studies. Besides, Marth had his magic to protect him, the staff's sword was more than able to safeguard against any enemy. Now he had nothing, nothing. Stripped of his talent, he was now openly vulnerable. The ex-mage felt naked without his magic.

Laid neatly out on his bed was a set of rustic clothing. Coarse dark brown buckskin britches that reached just above his knee with a thick rope tie belt; a twill gabardine pull over shirt that was worn in places with a ram skin vest. He guessed the outfit was a farmer's son's hand me downs. The stockings, however, looked newly made out of thin-woven wool. A tall pair of deerskin lace-up boots lay nearby. It was all peasant's clothing, probably obtained from one of the county's abundant sheep farmers.

Also upon the bed was a sturdy pigskin knapsack. Inside he found an extra pair of socks, undergarments and another worn shirt. That was it, nothing else. He scanned his rooms. Everything was gone. The rooms were stripped bare; his favorite books, his everyday outfits, all gone. Every drawer had been emptied. Obviously, this had been well planned. As Yanith had told him, *take nothing with you.*

He went over to his balcony that overlooked the distant Arient hills. The morning sun was still low on the horizon. The balcony was not that high, perhaps he would jump, *I could escape, go to the hills, live among the vagabonds that dwell there.* The baron's son had made friends with the barony's outcasts who he had met in his travels. His mind reeled as his rebel thoughts reminded him that he would be giving up any chance of ever getting his magic back. Escape was not an option.

With nothing to do, he lay on his bed trying not to think of the future. Having not slept, the young lord soon fell sound asleep. When he awoke the sun was low on the horizon, sunset was not far off. Marth shook himself awake and got dressed in the peasant outfit. The clothing fit him decently; his nose smelled the stink of sheep. The outfit was certainly not tailored as his castle garments were, but with the rope belt everything stayed in place.

As darkness approached he heard the lock on his door being lifted. Marth opened the door - no one was there. The hallway was empty. He headed toward the west entrance gate - the servants' entrance. Even the kitchen was empty. As he reached the outside door, his ears heard the patter of little feet. He knew it was Lilith.

"Marth!" she ran up to him, grabbing his leg tightly. "Don't leave me, they say you are going away!"

The young lord knelt down, letting her arms encircle his neck. Her hot tears streamed down on him. The small girl stepped back. "You smell of farmer Orchie's farm, are you going to his farm?" she urgently asked grasping his hand forcefully.

"No, Lil," he had to fight to keep his emotional turmoil out of his voice. "You need to go back before father catches you here." He looked up as Coralla stood behind her charge. "Take her back."

"Come Lilith, you got to say goodbye." The older woman took hold of the little girl's shoulders. "Good luck, Lord Arient. Come home soon."

"I will," he reluctantly let go of his sister. "Coralla, please check on Gorg. I have sent him to farmer Orchie's."

"We will, my lord, we promise." The nanny literally had to drag Lilith away. The little girl kept turning back, her arms reaching back for Marth. He unenthusiastically reached for the western door. The night was now dark; the moon had not come up yet.

He followed the gravel path, past the delivery entranceway toward the western gate. Being night, the large iron entranceway was padlocked closed. During the day, it was normally busy with heavy trade of fully loaded carts delivering the castle's supplies. To the one side, leaning against the adjacent stonewall, was a short stocky man, barely visible as he was dressed in dark clothing with a good-sized broad sword on his belt.

"About time ya get here lad. Give me ya knapsack," the man crossly directed his words at the young lord. His accent was one of the Lower Mountain peoples. Some called them men, but many called them dwarfs. They dwelled in the shadows of the far northern Great Mountains. They often came to the castle selling their intricate metal wares. Marth slung down his backpack, which the man quickly grabbed.

"Here, watch! Ya tie this bedding to the top with thee thick rope ties. Also, here is a beaker, plate and spoon." The dwarf stuffed the utensils into Marth's knapsack and handed the bag back. "Take this," the short man handed him a good-sized knife that was in a leather sheath. "Be careful, the blade be sharp. Don't go cuttin yaself. Tie it to ya belt."

"Where are we going?" Marth asked. "Why don't I get a sword, like yours?"

"Can ya handle a sword?" the guide pointedly asked.

"No, but…" Marth stumbled over his words.

"I guess that answers it, doesn't it? Wese not time fer questions. Dangerous eyes be everywhere. Quickly, follow me." The stocky figure took off running along the wall. Marth was out of breath when they stopped. Without a word, despite his short stature, the man sprung upward grabbing the top of the wall and lifted himself up. Marth looked on in wonder. "Come on, lad. Jump up!" When Marth didn't respond, his guide shouted down, "Mar jump up!"

Marth tried, but there was no way he could reach the top of the wall. The short man jumped back down. "What has Laren got me into?" the dwarf loudly sighed. "Come stand on me shoulders, at least yee be tall. Grab the top of the wall, stretch!"

Standing on the small man's broad shoulders, with some effort Marth clumsily reached the top of the wall. He followed his guide by jumping down but hit the ground hard and a loud moan escaped his mouth.

"Quiet, ya fool!" the stout bulky figure spat out.

"My name is Marth," the young former mage angrily told the darkly outlined figure.

"Ya name is now Mar son of Roth; a regular peasant name. Youse must remember it, practice it. Ya have a couple of days to get used to it! Ya ain't no lord no more! AND I'll call ya anything I does want. Get used to it, recruit." And with that said the dwarf took off at half run with Marth trying to keep up.

"Hey, wait up," the newly named Mar breathlessly called out.

As his short escort doubled back, showing no signs of being out of breath, the undersized man heavily moaned, "I'm gonna kill Laren if I don't get me self kilt first. Sends me on a jester's errand he did."

The town of Arianta was close by with the castle situated just above it. His guide avoiding the street lanterns, kept in the shadows, running down alley after alley, passing closed up merchant shops. The dwarf was constantly glancing backwards, slowing down when Mar fell behind. When the two finally stopped, they had reached the southernmost part of the city. It was where the Arthinian capital lay on the outskirts of the Blue Woods. His guide did not hesitate, but rushed into the cover of the pine trees that brushed harshly against their clothes.

Marth knew all the forests of Arthinia. The baron's son had traveled many of the roads and paths through the Blue woodland. His guide instead chose to traverse the cumbersome heavily treed wilderness. The pine and scrub trees grew thick in this area. No one came here. With it being high summer-season, the evening stars could not be seen through the canopy of the heavily leaf-laden branches. Mar completely lost his bearings. His body ached from being whipped by the low branches. Yet to his credit the Arthinian kept up with the small stocky man, who was having an easier time being able to duck under the tree's hanging limbs.

When they came out on to a wide beach, Mar finally recognized the area. They had emerged on the shores of Owl Lake, named for the many gray owls that lived near its banks. He wasn't sure as to what part of the lake they had stopped, but he guessed the northern tip.

"Get some firewood, not much, mind ya. Just enough sticks for a wee fire," his guide instructed. "I'se goin to scout around." And with that the burly stunted man quickly disappeared, melting into the woods without a sound.

Despite being totally fatigued, Mar did as he'd been instructed gathering a small pile of branches. The two moons had come up. At three quarters, the orbs bounced their light off the lake. His young eyes couldn't help but admire the tranquil setting. Suddenly, the new recruit felt a knife in his back. The Arthinian lost his breath as the blade pinched his skin.

"Ya could be dead, ya fool. Ya should be watchin the camp, not galagoppin around," the familiar voice of his guide floated to his ears.

He quickly turned around, but the short man was already by the pile of branches. "Here light the fire while I get us some grub." The dwarf threw two stones at Marth.

"What am I supposed to do with these?" the recruit looked at the sturdy figure silhouetted by the night's moons.

"Oh, for god's sake, it's flint," as if the guide's words explained everything. When the dwarf saw Marth didn't know what he was talking about, the exasperated man grabbed the two stones. "Watch, ya strike them together, the spark lights the wood."

"I was never…"

"Yeah, yeah," the mountain man held up his hands, "wese don't dwell on the past. No one cares for yar privileged life disadvantages." His sarcasm rang loudly, "Keep yee previous coddling to yaself, MAR. It ain't no longer relevant. Me name is Tillman son of Yethman, they'se call me Tilly."

"I didn't mean…" but Marth shut up as Tilly again put up his hands. Now that the fire was going, the Arthinian could make out the features of the mountain man. He had guessed right. His guide was from the lower mountains situated in the northern part of the DeLak Kingdom just below the Great Northern Mountains, the home of the dwarfs. Tilly had bright almost red fuzzy hair, a typical short and stocky body, but there was nothing "soft" about the man. His broad shoulders and big rough thick-fingered hands took center stage, as did his bulbous nose, bushy eyebrows and bristly straggly beard. His small goatee only emphasized his large lips. His features were topped by large pointed thick hairy ears.

Marth brought to mind everything he'd read about the lower mountain peoples. They had inter-bred so much with the dwarfs that they had taken on many of their northern neighbors' characteristics - short, stocky, bushy red hair. Yet they clung to their taller human ancestors, claiming alliance not with the dwarfs but with his father's barony, Arthinia. It was a sore point with the Dwarfs, who believed they should belong to the Upper Great Mountain Barony, Errtie. They were a proud people thinking themselves as a totally separate race. You called them *half-breeds* at your peril.

"Get yar grub stuff, the beans are just about done," Tilly stood over him with a steaming hot pan. The food did not smell that enticing.

"I'm not hungry, just tired," Mar told the man although the Arthinian hadn't eaten all day and his stomach was growling.

"Ain't yar choice," the mountain man scowled, "Youse learn quick enough that a soldier eats what he can when he can. Hold out yar grub mug."

Marth did what he was told and his cup was filled with what looked like a bean soup. His nose told him he didn't want to taste it.

"EAT!" Tilly demanded as he handed him a piece of dry bread. "Youse will get used to it and youse'll learn to be grateful for whatever ya get."

Marth took a sip wondering if he'd embarrass himself by gagging. To his surprise, his mouth welcomed the hot warmth and his stomach was grateful. The young lord hadn't realized just how hungry he was. He eagerly dipped his bread in the rustic brown soup; the broth made the dry loaf more palatable and relieved his hunger pains even more. When his mug was finished Tilly refilled his cup and this time Mar didn't hesitate, but ate the whole second helping.

When the former mage had finished, the new recruit looked up across their small fire to see Tilly half smiling. "It aren't bad is it?"

"No," Marth answered wiping his mouth with his sleeve, something he'd never considered doing before tonight. "No, it wasn't. I don't suppose you'll tell me where we are going?"

"Wese going to the training camp. The encampment isn't a known place so it won't do any good to tell ya where. Just know wese are going south, all ya need to know. Now wese have to get an early start so get some sleep. I'se take the first watch."

"We are still in my father's lands. The area is safe here. There is no need to keep watch," the Arthinian tried to explain.

Tilly cut him short, "Get something straight lad, no place is safe for ya."

"What?" Marth thought the man mad. Arthinia was his home, but before he could pursue the subject further, Tilly had put the fire out and was gone. His guide probably was scouting.

He unwrapped his bedroll making a pillow of his vest. Despite not being used to sleeping on the ground, the young lord found himself sound asleep as soon as his head hit the padding. Late into the night, Tilly awoke him with a kick. "Time to watch, keep sharp," the mountain man harshly told him.

Mar shook the clouds from his brain. Every part of his body ached. He leaned against a tree trying to figure out what hurt the most, his feet, legs or back. The moons were low. Dawn wasn't that far off. The air was crisp with a morning cold to it. He put on his sheep vest, glad of its warmth.

Marth heard the forest's noises. An owl hooted sporadically, the crickets sounded like the bugs were everywhere. The cool wind played with his black hair, flinging his onyx curls in his eyes. Everywhere was the soft sound of the rustling of the leaves. It was mixed with the scurrying of small rodents which hurried between the tall lake willows. The Arthinian tried to concentrate on being alert, for any woodland sounds that did not belong. His ears heard nothing unusual. Normally the ex-mage would have called on his magical abilities to enhance his hearing to warn him of any dangers, but there was nothing now to call upon. Mar felt empty, vulnerable.

Get over it, he thought, *it is what it is. Do what you have to do and get home.* Still despair hung close by.

Suddenly, his ears did hear a noise. Before he could yell to Tilly, four shadows emerged from the woods near the white sandy beach. Even in the dim light he could see their gleaming sharp swords. Marth yelled a warning, but the mountain dwarf was already up and confronting the intruders. The small figure fiercely kicked one of the aggressors, sending the attacker sprawling while he tackled a second one. The other two men headed towards Marth, swords held high to strike.

Mar grabbed for his nonexistent magical staff that usually was stuck in his belt. He yelled *Pithatra Attaco,* at the same time. Fear consumed the ex-mage, as the Arthinian realized how helpless he was as his hand came up empty and his magical words meant nothing. Instinctively his body ducked as one of the men swung at him and the sword hit the tree behind his head. Thankfully the weapon was deeply stuck in the wood. The other assailant charged. Out of the darkness a big black animal jumped and landed on the second attacker. Gleaming sharp white teeth sunk deeply into the man's sword arm.

Marth's second assailant screamed, dropping his weapon. The first man turned to help his shouting companion ignoring Marth, sensing the animal was the bigger threat. The first attacker's sword was still stuck in the tree. In his hand appeared a long dagger. He charged the wolf that had his fellow comrade by the throat. Mar, however, jumped on the man's back, keeping his arm tight around the fellow's throat. The two twirled in circles, the man choking as Marth increased the pressure. Both finally fell, tumbling unceremoniously to the ground. Unluckily the young lord was no match for the large man, who quickly pinned him down on the soft beach sand.

"I'm gonna slit your throat," the man's guttural threat was full of hate. "You young spoiled magic wielding pansy."

Suddenly the man was off him as the wolf pounced, knocking the attacker sideways. Marth's hand found his knife. Unsheathing the sharp weapon, he stabbed the man's arm that was fighting with the large animal. A screech came as the man rolled up, throwing the large animal to the side. The assailant got up and ran. The man didn't get far, however, as Tilly's knife careened through the air catching the evil aggressor in the chest. The villain fell quickly to the ground, dead.

The mountain dwarf came over to his charge, "Yar okay lad?"

Marth could only nod, but managed to jump up and ran to his wolfhound. Gorg was standing over one of the men growling. *Stand back,* he told his pet, but then realized he no longer could think his thoughts. "Stand back," he said out loud, "good boy." He hugged his dog.

"That's the biggest wolfdog I've ever seen," Tilly remarked.

"I raised him since he was a pup." Mar looked around. The first two attackers lay dead on the other side of the beach and the third had been killed by Tilly's knife as he had tried to flee. The last one was alive but was wounded.

Tilly grabbed the man by his collar. "Who sent ya?" The dwarf wildly shook him. "Tell me, or I'se finish what the dog started. I'se cut yar throat."

The attacker spat in the guide's face, "Scum, you king's scum,"

Dawn was pink in the sky. Marth saw the man's scruffy appearance, his dirty vagabond clothes. The other three men looked the same, paid assassins. *But why?* Marth wondered.

Tilly again grabbed the man putting his knife at the man's throat. Blood began to appear. "Alright, I'll tell you," the paid murderer relented. "It was that Duke."

"Which Duke?" A shocked Marth also grabbed the man, disbelief entering his brain, "which Duke?" he repeated.

"That Duke over in Shallotown." The assassin almost choked as Tilly pressed the knife even further. Fear filled the attacker's eyes, "Duke Hilstow," he reluctantly forced out between his rotting teeth. His breath was rancid with whiskey adding to its odor.

"Hilstow," Marth couldn't believe his ears. "He's my father's closest advisor."

"Yeah, you're a dead man," the scum sneered at Marth. "He did it on orders from your father."

"You're lying," Mar, filled with rage, once more grabbing onto the man's rag dirt ridden shirt. Tilly pushed his charge back.

"Don't go use up yar energy, lad. This villain ain't worth it," his guide disgustingly told him.

The attacker, seeing his opportunity, scrabbled up and started running. "Stop," Tilly yelled after him, "Or I'se will kill ya."

The assassin turned and threw a long knife at the Northman, who quickly ducked. The deadly blade flew past him into the lake. The mountain man's knife once more careened through the air, catching the fleeing man square in the throat. The last assassin fell dead to the ground.

"Get yar stuff," his guide yelled at him, "wese gotta get out of here. The'se sure be more around. Send that wolf home."

"I won't, he saved our lives. The dog comes with us." Marth's anger made him bold. He had had enough of being ordered about.

"Ya was told by Yanith to bring nothing with ya." Tilly pointed his finger at his charge.

"I did as I was told. I didn't bring Gorg. He brought himself. The wolf comes with us." Marth stood his ground. He was not going anywhere without his wolfhound. "For god's sake, he saved our lives."

"That he did, lad, that he did," Tilly conceded. "It be on yar shoulders when wese get to the meeting's place. Ya can deal with Laren then."

"Fine. I will." Mar gathered his knapsack and repeated, "I will."

To Mar's surprise Tilly headed them north along the lake's sandy shore. Their boots made deep indents. About half a league up the shore his guide headed into the forest. They hadn't gone far when the dwarf reached a deep-set thicket. "This ain't gonna be pleasant, but follow me, lad."

The three of them went through the thicket. Thorns tore at their clothing and their arms got several long scratches. Poor Gorg's fur was covered in thistles. Finally, they came out the other end. "Now take off your boots," Tilly ordered. "Follow me lightly." They headed back south with Tilly taking a branch and erasing their light stocking footsteps. When they came back to the lake he instructed that Marth remove any stockings and to roll up his trousers. To Mar's surprise, they headed into the lake, but not before Tilly made sure not one sign of their footsteps appeared anywhere. "They'se not be able to track us this way," the mountain man explained as his guide waded down toward the south. Gorg followed along the shoreline; his paw prints mixing in with all the other animal marks.

The three went on, keeping to the lake, until the sun had fully come up. "Wese can't keep out in the open much longer, too many foul eyes," the dwarf explained and headed toward a rocky outcropping, climbing up on to the higher ground. Here they put their stockings and boots back on and headed into the thick foliage. The trees, once more, grew thick and tall. For several hours, the two kept a fast pace continuing south with Gorg right at Mar's feet. When they finally stopped the Arthinian was exhausted. They had left Arthinia behind and were now entering the lower Hartland forest of the elfs.

"How far are we going?" the young lord hardly recognized his own voice. His words came out raspy and dry. They hadn't even stopped to take any water. "We aren't supposed to travel through these woods without Baron Falsteff's permission. The elfs are very strict about that. They will frown on my wolf's presence."

Tilly laughed, "Like I'se told ya - wese got more things to worry about than the elfs, lad. A lot more."

After they all took a swig of water from Tilly's bladder jug they began their trek again with the mountain man once more taking the lead. Marth just followed, realizing his fate was no longer his own.

Chapter Two
The Princess

"My lady, I have set your clothes out for you," the frilly-aproned uniformed lady-in-waiting bowed deeply. They are drawing your bath."

"Yes, yes," with a wave of her hand Danella dismissed her servant. "I hope you put out that new red gown I just had seamstress Molly make," the royal princess yelled after the woman.

"Ah, no," came drifting back as the servant turned around. "The low neckline, your mother…"

"Oh, for goodness sake," she yelled at her servant. "My mother treats me like a little girl. I came of age over two moons ago. I can wear an adult gown. Go get it! Count Moliff will be here this evening for dinner." Princess Danella smiled at the thought of the count's enjoyment of her new outfit. It was time the court thought of her as a grownup, not simply the king's youngest child.

Her mirrored vanity reflected a pale, finely shaped face with large green eyes. Her curly auburn hair was at the moment tied back highlighting delicate features; a perky nose, small flat ears and luscious pink lips that needed no shade enhancement, but often contained a pout, especially if she didn't get her way. Even in a simple loose fitting yellow morning frock, her figure appeared slim emphasizing a small waist and slender hips, but like her mother, the princess would bloom as she aged, filling out nicely.

Her eyes drifted to her balcony doors that lay open revealing the beautiful extensive castle's gardens below. Beyond, on the horizon, lay the foreboding marshlands and to her right was the massive Viamar Sea. To her left, she caught a slight glimpse of Four Rivers, the royal capital city. Perhaps tonight she'd take Count Moliff for a leisurely garden stroll. Of course, her mother would probably insist on accompanying them. *They treat me like a child!* Her long tapered shaped nails tapped the table's polished surface in annoyance.

Danella's hand went to her staff that was always conveniently close by. *Vienanu*, she commanded. The staff disappeared. A large yellow-jeweled necklace encircled her neck. Her long slim fingers lightly touched the exquisite large gem. The magic flowed; reminding her of the unique powers the jeweled chain gave her. *I am the only one in our immediate family who can command it.* The thought brought a rare smile that for just a moment dressed her face. It really was more of an amused smirk.

"Perhaps today would be good time to wear your brown robes," came from across her room. "Rumor has it that Master Yanith is here visiting."

"Ugh," escaped her lips. "Whatever is Mothia thinking of making its mages wear those ugly garments? When I am a tested mage I will not wear such garbage."

Danella frowned at the tall gray robed figure that blocked her apartment's entranceway. "I hope you are not here to give me a lesson? I'm in no mood for learning spells and potions." She turned away, ignoring the thin, scarecrow figure of a man.

"You are never in the mood, my lady." The Mothian slowly advanced into the room. The old mage carried a long staff that he used also as a cane, limping slightly as he came to stand next to his pupil. "You're to be tested soon. You may be a naturally talented wizard, but I'm afraid that is not enough."

"What will the council do, fail me? I think not. Those old men would not dare fail the king's daughter." Danella dismissed his comments with her well-manicured hand. "And I'm not going to Mothia, they can send their tutors here."

Master Tobus laughed lightly, "I'm afraid, your highness, that will not happen. The council shows no favoritism. You will have to do your apprenticeship at the Mothia fortress, like it or not. You will hopefully pass the test and wear the gray robes of a full-fledged mage someday."

"We will see Master Tobus, we will see," she coyly smiled at him. The king's daughter had no intention of bending to the will of the Mage Council with their ridiculous rules. Rules did not apply to the monarch's family.

"We need to go over the different baronies and their weather patterns." The magic instructor sat down on one of her apartment's ornate plush cushioned chairs. The young spoiled princess glared at him. The mage had not asked permission to sit. Her manner softened as the princess realized the old man was in some pain. His body, although quite tall, was bent and broken perhaps by age or perhaps from injuries he had sustained during the Coorish War. She softened her attitude, not something the young woman did often. Tobus had been her major tutor all her life and she was really quite fond of the old man.

"Really Tobi (Danella had nicknamed him when she had been a young child), I'm quite busy today. I have only a few hours before my father's dinner party for Duke Moliff." She glanced over at her luxurious canopied bed. The red gown now lay neatly on the bedspread with matching silk slippers.

"I'm afraid, I must insist," her tutor waved his staff, *Approcho,* he commanded - an ancient looking scroll appeared on his lap. "I got this from the Mothia archives. It contains some very old spells that are still used today to help control the kingdom's winds. You are most fortunate that permission was given for me to borrow the valuable manuscript."

"Oh, for god sake, how can that possibly be of help to me?" Danella shook her pretty little head. "I have no need of such spells. I will not be a simple weather wizard."

"I think your father would heartily disagree, my lady," the tired mage frowned deeply at her. "King DeLak would not rule for long if the kingdom's crops failed and his subjects starved."

Danella looked alarmingly at Tobus, "Really, I think you exaggerate…"

She didn't get any further as one of her father's attending golden uniformed servants had unceremoniously entered her rooms and rudely interrupted the conversation. "Excuse me your ladyship."

How dare he, anger filled her thoughts, *I will have to talk to my father about this servant. The rude man will be disciplined!*

But the servant ignored her glares continuing, "Your father would like to see you immediately."

"I'll be there shortly," the king's daughter angrily quipped, but again the servant ignored her.

"His Royal Sire said IMMEDIATELY," his voice became a few octaves higher, the urgency of his request forcing itself forward.

"Very well!" she stood up stamping her foot, "I'm coming!"

Danella followed the servant down the hallway. Being used to the castle's opulence, the princess paid no attention to the rich wall tapestries or the crystal covered chandeliers hanging from the ornately painted ceilings. The opulent carpeting and the many standing-at-attention golden uniformed sentinels went unnoticed. All that consumed her thoughts was annoyance at being summoned.

To her surprise, the servant brought her to the king's throne room and not to his private living quarters. It took her off guard. The young woman hesitated at the carved massive doors leading into the huge room. She was not dressed for an official audience. Two soldiers stood at attention, their hands saluting her quickly.

She turned to Tobus who had been closely following her. "Something is going on," Danella quipped to her tutor. "Why would my father be in the throne room now?"

"I'm sure we will soon find out." Seeing her hesitate, the old mage took the small arm and led the hesitant daughter into the high domed ceiling official hall. The great vaulted room always intimidated Danella as the chamber reminded her of her father's importance, of his omnipotent rule. The large meeting hall was not a "family" room.

The whole room was surround by tiled walls depicting the many battles that lay in the kingdom's history. Some were of the Coorish Wars that had happened when her father had been a young prince. Some of the pictures were gruesomely realistic and not pleasant for her to see. The monarch's daughter cared little for the past. Life was calm and prosperous now. It would always be thus. Borest DeLak was a good king, a peaceful king.

Only a few of her father's scribes were with the king and queen. Another surprise came when Danella not only saw her father sitting stiffly on his throne, but her mother sat dutifully next to him. Both were dressed in their formal velvet robes and had their jeweled crowns upon their heads. This was obviously a formal meeting. She stopped and stared.

"Mother?" the royal daughter looked surprisingly at her "mum" as she informally called her. Danella could see her mother's red eyes - the Queen had been crying. Her normally composed, proper female parent didn't even look in her direction. "Mother!" she loudly again said.

Tobus pulled on her sleeve, he was kneeling. The stunned daughter came out of her stupor and genuflected next to the old man. "Sire," bowing her head the princess managed to get out as her eyes stole another look at the distressed queen.

"Danella, you may rise," her father's stern voice drifted down to her.

She couldn't stand it any further, "What is wrong father? Is Miklelaus alright?"

"Your brother is fine," her father waved his scepter, dismissing her concern. As if he'd heard his name, her older brother came walking into the room. The young prince immediately went down on one knee, bowing his head low, then slowly rose.

"Sire, I am here as you commanded!" Her brother always was a showman. Being heir to the throne, the king's oldest child liked to play the part. Despite his pompous attitude, Danella was fond of Miklelaus. When he wasn't caught up with being the heir, the handsome man was fun and a great jokester.

Her brother, like her father, was of a sturdy build. He was striking in a roguish way. Miklelaus was much taller than his sister, but like her he had curly thick auburn hair that flowed down to his shoulders. Her brother wore well-tailored stylish clothes that befitted his station. Yet, the lad was no dandy preferring rugged well-woven hunting attire. The women at court fawned over him, each vying for his attention.

Miklelaus also noticed his mother's distress, "Mother..." he started to say, but King DeLak angrily stomped his scepter.

"For goodness sake, your mother is fine," the monarch yelled down at his children.

Danella, although she was in awe of her father, did not fear him. "Well mother doesn't look like she's fine," the royal daughter barked up at him.

"Danella, please," her mother said, her words pointedly aimed at her daughter, "I'm fine, I just, just..."

The king cut in, "She's having a hard time saying goodbye to you, Danella."

The princess stepped back in surprise, "Saying goodbye?"

"Yes, I have called your brother here so Miklelaus too can give you a farewell," her father's voice was cold, unlike his usually doting paternal voice. Danella stood dead still, trying to let his words sink in. His next statement really shocked, "The kingdom needs recruits. You will be joining the army."

"I'm what?" she stuttered. Tobus grabbed onto her arm as his student quivered on the brink of fainting from the words coming from her father's mouth.

King DeLak ignored her. "Scribe, read the decree," he commanded the court's transcriber that stood at attention at his sovereign's side.

"*I do here declare my daughter Danella Louisa DeLak has volunteered to serve in the royal army for an undesignated amount of time to be determined by her commanders.*" The scribe loudly droned on, "*We are proud that our daughter will be joining the other royal baronies in contributing to our kingdom's defense. Her mother and I will miss her, but know that she will return to us a ready and competent soldier in the end.*"

"I, I…" words got caught in her throat.

It was her brother that spoke up, "Sire, I do believe this is extraordinary. Truly, should I not be the one going?"

"Don't be foolish, Miklelaus," the king sounded annoyed. "I will need you here."

"I refuse!" Danella managed to get out. "I will not be a stinking soldier."

"But you will be," came from behind her. The princess caught a glimpse of her tutor, Tobus, turning and bowing next to her.

"Master Yanith," the tall figure managed to get his bent broken body in a low bow. Her tutor touched Danella trying to get his pupil to bow also, but she shook him off.

"Do you have something to do with this, Yanith!" she demanded turning to face the ancient looking mage. Her eyes glared at the white haired, long bearded master wizard. His long staff lay in his left hand. The rod seemed to brightly shiver, reminding everyone of its immense power. Danella, however, was too angry to notice anything but her own misery.

Before she could say anything further the head of the kingdom's mages at Mothia half smiled. "I have everything to do with it my dear," the powerful wizard looking directly at her confirmed. He withstood her glare, his deep violet-eyed gaze never leaving her. "A guide will meet you on the Northern Wallgate just at sunset. You will go with the guide bringing only the things that have been provided for you."

Danella turned back to the throne, "Mother, help me. This is madness."

"I can't," her mother's voice became stronger. "You will do as your father commands. I wish…"

The queen got no further as King DeLak sternly said, "Stop it Rochella. Say no more!" Her mother lowered her swollen red eyes to her hands that lay trembling in her lap, saying nothing more.

"I refuse to go!" Danella stomped her foot and pointed at Yanith, "He can't tell you what to do father, and this is ridiculous."

"I have to agree," her brother came to her defense.

"Be quiet!" King DeLak uncharacteristically commanded his heir sternly, "I brought you here to say farewell to your sister. Do it and go!"

Her brother nodded and curtly left, not saying anything to her. Danella could feel his intense anger.

Yanith, however, ignored her complaints explaining further, "You will not let anyone at your training camp know who you are. When I feel you have successfully completed your warrior training, you may return. You'll not use any magic!"

The Mothia wizard held out his hand. Danella felt her necklace fall. As it returned to being a staff, Yanith deftly caught it in his left hand. To her amazement, the feeling of magic left her. The princess lost her breath, falling to one knee. "How dare you, you pompous weasel," she screamed at the head mage.

"Danella!" Tobus put his hand on her shoulder, "You cannot talk to him that way!"

"Leave her alone, my old friend," Yanith told the mage. "She has every right to be angry."

"You will listen carefully, Danella Louisa," King DeLak interjected loudly. "If you do not do as I have ordered or if you do not succeed in this task, you will be banished from court. Yanith has assured me that should you pass this training, he will personally see to it that you get tested at Mothia. Your magic will be restored."

Danella just stood there, frozen in time, trying to awake from her nightmare. The king's daughter stared at her mother, but she could not even get the queen to look at her.

"Come, my lady," a servant announced behind her. "Follow me please."

Somehow the broken princess turned and shadowed the servant. At the door, she paused. She heard her father talking to her mother, "Listen, Rochella, was it not you that bemoaned the fact that our daughter was just a pawn to be married off to the highest bidder? I have just given her the chance to up her worth, to have a say in her future. Stop whining."

Her mother's distressed voice reached her ears, "I don't understand Borest, why are you doing this? Our army does not need her. It is ridiculous!"

"You are wrong," came from Yanith who now stood next to the royal couple. "If I am correct, war will be upon us soon, we will very much need her. Lady Danella has more strength than you give her credit for."

"I cannot ask the other baronies to send their sons and daughters and not send my own! You forget I am not only King but also the Baron of Lakeland in my own right," King DeLak forcefully reiterated to his wife. "I do not relish sending my own daughter to the army but then neither do the other nobles. This order is my will! Let none question me!"

"Come, my ladyship," the servant gently nudged Danella back to her royal quarters. Numb, she mutely followed. The minute she entered her rooms, the door was locked. She turned the handle, trying to open the huge wooden doors but to no avail.

Danella pounded on the door until she was hoarse. "Let me out!" her voice screamed, but the lock stayed closed. "I need to talk to my father!"

The royal woman was furious, throwing a vase holding a bouquet of gorgeous garden flowers, smashing it against the wall in anger. It was then that she noticed how bare her surroundings were. While she had been in the throne room arguing with her father, the room had been stripped clean of all her possessions. Not one servant, not one, laid waiting for her commands.

The princess ran into her dressing room. Not a stitch of clothing was anywhere in sight. Her collection of gorgeous gowns was gone, her massive selection of silk slippers gone, her jewelry box completely empty. No decorative hats, gloves, or belts lay nearby for her choosing. The room was nakedly absent of her presence. She went back to the main bedroom. Her vanity table was stripped spotless, not even a comb or a jeweled barrette, nothing.

The princess looked over at her canopied bed where her newly beautiful red gown had been laid out. In its stead were peasant clothes, neatly folded, ready for her to wear. In her disdain, she threw them on the floor, stomping on the garments; her anger flowing to her feet. Danella had exhausted herself, finally falling on the bed, crying.

"I won't stand for this," she wailed. "They can't do this to me!" Her thoughts went to her options. *My father must have lost his mind,* coming to grips with why it had happened to her. *What can I do!* Tears flowed easily as her predicament became quite clear. *Damn that meddling Yanith, that decrepit old mage!*

"I won't stand for this!" Danella yelled despite it falling on no ears. Jumping up the small woman paced her room in self-pitying resentment. "Aunt Lucia will not stand for this!" her words bounced around the empty room. Her brain focused on her father's sister, Aunt Lucia. Her favorite aunt had been married to the Baron of Kazia. Danella had visited her several times on the beautiful estate in the distant farmland barony of Kazia. Her aunt would help her; make the king come to his senses!

How could she send her aunt a message? Besides there being no parchment anywhere, nor any writing sticks, no one would send the note either even if Danella managed to write one. *I must escape myself* came floating into her brain. *I will escape to my aunt's until my father comes to his senses. But how?* That was the immediate problem.

Her eyes went to the balcony. Observing down below, the king's daughter noted the guards standing within sight of her windows, but the sentries were not close and were pointedly looking outwards. Her mind reeled with what to do. *Should I escape, could I find my way to the capital city Cornia in Kazia? I'd be safe at Baron Kaz's castle.*

She returned to her vanity. Sitting, her hand opened the center drawer. *Motio panel,* she whispered the magical words. Nothing happened. The princess moaned, she had no magic to open her secret compartment. Her fingers tried to pry open the back panel, but all she managed to do was break a nail. "Damn", Danella looked furtively around. The broken vase lay scattered on the floor.

The royal picked out the biggest shard and came back to the vanity. She wedged the piece in the drawer's backboard and pulled, cutting her finger, but the sharp glass did the trick. The panel sprung open, revealing several coins and some fine jewelry. She smiled at her forethought to hide these treasures. The idea had been a childhood fantasy that had stayed with her.

Next, she picked up the peasant clothing that smelled of goat. Holding her nose, she put them on. To her surprise they fit quite nicely. They were more young boys' clothes. *Good,* she thought, *no one would be looking for a peasant boy.* The king's daughter put her long tied-back auburn hair under the pull over cap that had been included with the clothes. The faded tan chamois shirt was too long. The crude undergarments were too big. The pants were slightly over sized so she could tuck the excess shirt in at the waist making her look bulkier. The coarse thick rope belt kept everything in place. The wool stockings fit nicely as did the deerskin brown boots.

Glancing in her vanity mirror she couldn't help but smile at the irony that reflected back at her. Danella looked like a young farmer boy or even worse, a dwarf. *No,* she thought, *I'm not ugly enough for that!* Either way no one would recognize her.

Also on her bed was a pigskin bag with a sheepskin vest laid on top. She looked in the bag, nothing but an extra set of clothing including another set of rustic wool handmade underclothing. *Please,* she scowled at them, *who would wear those!* She quickly put on the vest. The coat would hide her sex, making her look more like a boy. Despite it being summerseason, she may need the warmth in Kazia. The barony was colder there.

She used the broken glass from the vase to cut a small bag from the bottom of her pillowcase. Here she stuffed her precious coins and jewels, then tied the small bundle to her rope belt and then tucked the treasures inside her shirt. Danella would have to find a way to trade the valuables for passageway to Kazia.

Then the princess went out to the balcony. The sun was getting lower, but sunset was still some ways off. Thank goodness, this part of the castle was in deep shadows. It would help hide her. Taking a deep breath, the disguised woman slipped over the side of the wrought iron railing coming on to a small lip that lay right below. Her tiny foot fit nicely, but still she made the mistake of looking downward and almost lost her nerve. For long moments, the escapee held her breath. *I can do this,* slipped into her thoughts, *think of the alternative, a stinking soldier!*

Her foot moved as her hands grabbed onto the thick ivy vines that covered the castle's exterior. She crept slowly, wincing from the pain of the vines cutting into her soft delicate hands. She held tightly from one vine to another until reaching the next balcony. Her hand grasped the railing and her foot clung to the balcony's overhanging floor. Climbing over, the small woman ripped one of her stockings. A long red scrape now dressed her right leg. Danella winced, but tears of relief at having made her escape flowed down her cheeks.

The princess entered a room she knew quite well, the library that the king's daughter shared with her brother. Her sibling's rooms lay on the other side. Tobus often dragged her here for the magical studies the mage thought so important. To her relief, her tutor was nowhere to be seen. It was rare that her brother spent any time here. As her elderly teacher wanted concentration, none of the servants bothered them here.

Danella crossed quickly to the door. Peering out, she saw no one. The hallway was deserted. Slipping out, the ragged looking peasant boy headed down the corridor. Afraid someone would still recognize her, her hands grabbed a vase of flowers, holding them in front of her face. She headed to the western wing of the castle. This part of the building was the servants' wing.

Several parlor maids hurried past her. The servants said nothing, obviously thinking her a hired castle urchin returning a vase for new flowers. Only when she got near the kitchen did someone speak to her. "Boy, where ya goin?" a rough voice asked. The large stocky woman was dressed in a flour covered apron, obviously a cook.

"Taking flowers to the gardener. Need new ones." Danella said the only words that came into her head. The spoiled noblewoman had no idea how to act but quickly added, "Ma'am." As princess, she often heard the word between her own servants.

"What's wrong with ya, boy?" the cook pointed down an adjacent hallway. "Youse ain't allowed here. Get yar puny ass down to the supply delivery door. Gardener Malta be workin in the south garden."

Feeling her cheeks redden, she turned quickly down the indicated hallway. As a royal sibling, Danella was not used to servants talking to her thus and the words irked her, but fear of discovery thrust her anger inward. *Think of escape,* her brain cautioned her. *Think of nothing but getting to Aunt Lucia in Kazia.*

The servant's delivery entrance was more of a loading and unloading dock. Its double doors were wide opened letting the merchants' carts back right up and dispatching their wares easily. She'd never come in contact with the various farmers and peddlers that made up the castles everyday suppliers. Her nose was assaulted by the countless smells. Sharp vinegar pinched her nose as barrels of pickles and cabbages were rolled past her. Containers of local ale lay waiting their turn on the dock; pungent and sweet. Her stomach did flip-flops, her mouth suppressing a gag.

The disguised king's daughter rushed down the stairs, then passed several waiting carts full of large pumpkins and other local crops. One dray was full of bright orange corn, a delicacy at the castle's table this time of year. Open barrels of green apples filled the last wagon. Scruffy looking peasants dressed the carts, another rare sight for her. They were hearty stout men and women, plainly clothed in frocks and loose-fitting pants. Many wore big floppy hats that protected them from the sun, although it was now late afternoon. All ignored her as Danella hurried alongside the carts.

Her perky nose scrunched at the odor of the large muscular draft horses. The smell of hay still lingered from the wagons making her even more squeamish. *How can they stand it,* she thought? Danella was so busy with the different sights, she ran head long into a man who was standing next to the last wagon.

The male peasant farmer cuffed her, sending what he thought was a small boy's body sprawling. The vase of flowers flew, smashing on the ground. "Youse tryin to pick me pocket, boy?" His voice was dangerously gruff. His rough callused hand went to his crude knife that hung low on his belt, a very long knife. Fear overtook the frightened woman as the ruffian advanced. Despite her angry indignation, Danella scrambled up, running as fast as her legs could move. She fell several times, scraping her knees. To her relief the man did not follow after her but only yelled obscenities in her direction.

The gravel road was full of more wagons, waiting their turn to unload. There were guards, but the sentries were more interested in directing the two-way interchange as empty carts were also trying to leave. Danella followed the departing carts to the merchant's Westgate. The huge sturdy wrought-iron dwarf-made gate was wide open with not only wagons but also people on foot, both entering and leaving.

She had almost made it through; the guards were paying no attention to those on foot, especially those leaving, when someone grabbed her arm. "I'm glad you finally got here," a feminine voice in a strange dialect assaulted her ears. Fear gripped her as the royal slowly turned around.

A tall slim woman stood before her. The female had dark brown skin and wore loose fitting pantaloons and a smoky gray colored laced up shirt with inlaid shiny beads decorating around the collar. On her slim waist was a light tan wide cloth belt. She also had a matching colored scarf that was intricately wrapped around her head. A bright red jewel was stuck on her turban just above her forehead and a white feather was stuck into it.

The princess, startled, stared defiantly into the dark tanned face with slanted light gray eyes. The woman was quite exotically beautiful with luscious full lips. On her exposed ears were dangling delicate earrings with a matching gold chain that sparkled in the near sunset glow. Still, despite the fancy clothes, the woman exuded ruthless danger. On her belt lay a long rapier; her leg contained another knife holder. Even more, on her laced-up deer skinned boots; the hilt of a third knife could be viewed.

Danella's scream got caught in her throat. "Why are you here? This isn't the Northern Wallgate?" the princess managed to croak out, stepping back a few steps.

"No, it isn't, is it?" Once more the princess was struck by the woman's rich dialect. She searched her brain, who had come to court with that foreign accent? Her mind reached back to the visit of the Bombia ambassador from the desert drylands of the far-west. The woman's full lips curved up in a shrewd smile, showing beautiful white teeth, "Let us say, I know you Dani."

"My name is Danella, you will talk to me with respect!" the king's daughter stood her ground. "Do you know who I am? I'm, I'm…" she couldn't get the words to come out. Her words froze on her lips. *Damn Yanith,* she thought, *what has he done to me! What spell has he put on me!*

"Your name is Dani daughter to Yorith. Get used to it peasant girl. If you need to, practice saying the words. Your life depends on it!" the Bombian woman warned, kneeling down to her own bag. "You may call me Sari." Reaching in, the woman came up with a crude dented mug, a cruder type of spoon, which the woman placed in Dani's bag. She also handed Danella a rolled-up rough blanket. "Tie this to the top of your knapsack. This is your bedding. Hurry, we need to get going or we'll miss the ship."

"I'm not going anywhere. I going to Kazia, to my aunt's castle," her hands went challengingly to her hips. She stomped a booted foot on the gravel emphasizing her defiance.

"Suit yourself, *your ladyship,*" the tan complexion woman dismissively waved her jeweled hands. "It is a long way to Kazia and you have no funds. You may return to your father's court, but he'd only throw you out."

The woman's smile grated on her. Danella looked defiantly at her keeper, after all, the royal had her secret stash bag. The jewels would buy passageway to her aunt's. Her hand went to her belt - nothing was there! "Someone stole my bag!" she screeched.

"Well that's too bad now," the woman's smile again exasperated Danella. "Come with me, or not. You'll find the world, outside your pampered castle life, can be dangerous and confusing. The slavers are always looking for young attractive inexperienced women. You'd be sold for a high bid. But then, suit yourself."

With that said, the woman turned and started toward the gateway out of the castle grounds. Danella stared after her. Her emerald pampered eyes glanced back at the castle. The gruff man who had pushed her earlier was making his way back toward the exit. Before he saw her, her booted feet scooted after the retreating exotic figure. "Wait," the princess yelled. "Please, wait!"

When Dani had caught up with the woman, she was beside a wagon that was loaded with empty barrels. "We need a ride to the other side of the city," the Bombian was talking to the wagon's handler.

"Cost ya a ducas," the peasant crop trader sneered at Danella's guide.

The Bombian woman held up two pieces of copper coins. "One for each of us, old man. It's more than you'll see this seasoncycle. What do you say?"

The farmer grabbed the coins, "Get in the back and be careful of me barrels. Ya break one and youse pay for it."

Her guide jumped on the back of the cart, "Come on," she motioned to Dani.

The princess looked at her. There was no way she could jump up on the wagon. The wooden bed was too high! The Bombian realizing the princess' dilemma just shook her head. "I hope Laren knows what he's doing!" the woman exasperatingly jumped down and then pushed Dani up onto the bed of the wagon.

"Who's Laren?" Dani asked. "Where are you taking me?"

"You'll find out soon enough," her guide took the seat next to her charge. "New recruits don't get to ask questions, they only take orders. Get used to it."

"How dare you talk to me that way!" the princess replied as her anger increased.

"Like I said, get used to it!" Then, the woman lay down in the wagon's hay filled bottom. "Wake me when the wagon gets to the end of the city!" The Bombian immediately fell asleep.

The dray bumped along the city streets. The heady stale smell of the cart's hay made Dani sneeze and her eyes water. The city passed by. Rarely had she made it to Four Rivers. The few merchants she'd dealt with, the seamstresses, the hat makers, the shoe cobbler, came to her at the castle. The royal's view of the kingdom's capital usually came through an elegant, cushioned enclosed carriage. This view was up close and personal.

They passed down the main street where a myriad of shops were closing as nightfall was approaching. Merchants with brooms were sweeping the wooden sidewalk out front of their stores. Many were rolling in their barrels of goods. The wagon passed bakeries, clothing shops, and various general goods shops. The colorful outside vendors were closing their canvas canopies. To her inexperienced eyes it was a wonder, a sight of bright paints and unimaginable astonishing sights not to mention the many new smells and confusing noises that assaulted her other senses.

As they passed further along, saloons and inns took center view. Then came the houses that lay side by side with little balconies with women hanging out clothes. Urchin children played in the streets. The kids were loud and boisterous, their playful laughter making her smile. One of the children came too close to the wagon. The driver yelled and lashed out with his horsewhip, catching the little girl on the backside. "Get away ya street rubbish," the crude farmer yelled and raised his whip to strike again.

Dani yelled out in indignation. Angry, the royal stood up and went to the front of the wagon's bed, half stumbling, holding on to the barrels for dear life. "Stop that, how dare you hit that little girl."

The farmer turned briefly, his yellowish-brown teeth, grinning at what he thought was a dirty boy urchin. "Perhaps ya'd like to take her place, ya filthy scum."

Suddenly an arm reached around Dani. The whip was forcefully yanked out of his hand. The curse that started to leave his mouth abruptly stopped when her guide's knife poked him unceremoniously in the ribs. "Maybe I'll slit your stomach open to see what kind of filthy rot you are filled with." The viciousness that came from the Bombian was quite evident.

"I'ds need me whip," the vulgar man cried, but shut up when the knife pressed slightly into his shirt.

"I'll give it back when we get off," her guide told him. Sari grabbed Dani's arm pulling her back to the rear of the wagon. "Was that compassion? Well, there is hope for you after all, princess."

Danella said nothing. She watched wide-eyed as the Kazian cut the farmer's whip leaving only the handle. "I told him

I'd give it back to him," she snidely remarked. "Come on its time to get off."

Dani looked at the moving ground. "I can't jump, we'll be hurt for goodness sake."

"Okay, I'll go first," the Bombian woman told her. But, as the woman jumped, she pushed the princess off also. Danella rolled as her body fell to the ground. She was winded and covered in ground dirt, coughing as dust filled her nostrils.

"See, that wasn't so bad now, was it?" her guide gave her a hand up. "Come on, let's get moving. We're already late. That captain had better not leave without us or I'll skin that skipper alive."

The woman was crazy. Dani was following a crazy person. Yet what choice did the princess have? They were indeed near the end of city. Farm fields could be seen in the distance. The houses here were larger with well-manicured lawns. The well-to-do lived on the outskirts of the city. People were better dressed, even the children were well decked out.

The exotic Bombian picked up the pace, doubling back to confuse any followers. The two were soon again back in the city proper, but now they were coming upon the Viamar Sea. Taking back roads they passed a lumberyard, a blacksmith and a tool and weapon store. Her guide headed toward the water. The city's docks with a host of ships came into view. Facing the ships were the fishmongers' shops. Most were closed since the catches came in early morning and were sold by early afternoon. Dani held her nose as the smell of the fish permeated the area. Her chaperon seemed not to even notice.

"Come on, the ship is still here. Thank goodness, Captain Arber doesn't like to miss paying customers. Hurry!" The woman picked up her pace. When the two women got to the gangplank, Dani stopped. The desert woman looked annoyingly back. "Hurry up!"

"I can't go on this ship. I get seasick." Danella pleaded. "Honestly, I tried to go with my father, I get sick! Can't we go another way?"

Her guide came back, standing in front of her charge. "Listen, unless you want to take four days to head up shore, you'll get on this barge. On foot will take four days of traversing through the marshes, miles of hiking through mud and rain with those pampered feet of yours. Not to mention the biting insects! Think hard girl!"

Dani closed her eyes. The thought of the long trek turned her stomach. Danella took one step after another until her feet reached the deck. Her stomach was already retching.

The captain stood at the top of the plank. "You're late Hass, I should charge you extra." The skipper was a broad-shouldered man, his hair peppered in gray, a long stingy mustache circle above a cruel thin mouth.

"Yeah, sure Arber, and I'll deduct some of my coins after we taste your cook's rotten food. Just show us to our cabin and the quarters better be clean."

"And who do you have with you?" he leered at Dani. "Kind of young, isn't he?"

Danella didn't even see her guide draw her knife, but it was pointed at the captain before he could even finish his remarks. "This is my servant. You and your crew will leave him alone. Am I clear on this?" The knife drew closer, almost touching the captain's uniform.

"Of course, Hass, of course," the skipper held out his hands in submission. "No one will bother him. Come, I've given you your usual cabin."

The two followed the boss man to the back of the good-sized freighter. It must have had its hulls full as the boat was hanging low in the water. Dani caught the name of the ship, *The Fire Goddess.* The name perhaps came from the rusty color of the old barge's sides. The name was painted in bright red letters. The freighter was clean and tidy, but the crew looked rough and mean. The two travelers saw no other passengers. Yet, despite a few stares, none of the crew bothered them. Their cabin had stacked bunk beds and a small locker.

"Stay close to me," her guide instructed. "Despite the captain's assurances, the crew is a bunch of rag tag scoundrels. Mean bastards to boot. The scum would like nothing better than to harass and steal your clothes and your boots. Just stay close."

"Hass? Who's Hass?" the princess ventured.

"It's one of the names I use. Just ignore the captain, he'd rob his mother if it would make a profit." Sari looked over the Viamar Sea, her thoughts far away. "Just stay close," the guide again sternly reiterated.

Dani had no inclination to leave the Bombian's side. They heard the departure bell and went up on deck to see the sailing. The city was just about in darkness. As the ship gained speed from the opening of the sails, the wind picked up rustling their clothes but also bringing some relief to the summer-season heat.

"Well, we are off," Sari said, but Dani didn't hear. The princess was too busy running to the ship's side, throwing up and already feeling quite miserable.

Chapter Three
The Twin Elfs

The arrow soared through the air - *Swish. Thud.* The sharp metal spearhead slammed into the center of the target marked on a huge maple tree. "Aha," Ausanwel raised his arm in triumph. "Try and beat that, Lauranna!" he joyously laughed. Being an elf, his celebratory voice sounded like a well-tuned lute, quite pleasant to the ears. He quickly ran over to the tree, pointing at his perfectly placed arrow.

The crowd of watchers all yelled their encouragement. "Good shot," his best friend Theawel clapped. "You'll not best him now, Lauranna!"

Ausanwel's twin sister raised her light wooden intricately carved yew bow, easily bringing back her fingers with her protective deerskin banded arm that lay perfectly straight and still. The arrow was exactly parallel to her chest. The elf's beautiful long lashed violet eyes did not blink as the tall well-shaped Hartlander woman sighted the target.

"Hey, wait until I can get clear of your shot. I don't want an arrow sticking out of my butt!" her brother lightly teased. The friends of the young elfs made the forest sparkle with their own lyrical mirth.

His female twin, however, ignoring them, immediately let her arrow fly. To everyone's amazement the shot split her brother's arrow in half. Quickly, deftly, reaching back into her elk skin quiver she let two more arrows fly, each splitting the first one. There was awed silence then boisterous clapping. "She did it," their cousin Horalilana yelled. "Lauranna did it!"

"So, she did," her boyish roguish looking brother said shaking his long fair-featured head in disbelief. Giving a big shrug, his tall slim yet muscular body leaned against the targeted maple tree, as the forest wind played with his long silvery fine white strands of hair wrapping around his well-shaped thin pointed ears. His long fingered strong hands pulled the arrows out of the center mark. The elf's dark purple eyes focused on the two cut-in-half arrow shafts, "Perfect, your shots split them right down the middle! You've beaten me again!"

His sister smiled, "Maybe next time you'll win. Pay more attention in Master Lilianana's class and maybe, just maybe someday you'll triumph over me. Well, maybe come close at least." His female sibling's eyes shined in triumph.

"My magic skill will never beat yours," her twin quipped as the male elf picked up his bow and quiver. *Vienanu,* he commanded and his bow became a thin flexible long staff that fit nicely in the palm of his hand.

"True," Lauranna teased him, "after all I was born first."

"You two aren't fighting again?" Theawel slapped Ausanwel on the shoulder. "She's right, you know. No one is going to beat her. She's Master Lilianana's favorite pet student."

"You're just jealous," Lauranna quipped to her brother's best friend as she removed her deerskin leather archery gloves. "We will see how we all do come the testing. I shall wave to you all as I leave for Mothia."

"We will see, sister, we will see," her brother laughed. "Your prideful boasting will someday get you in trouble, mark my words. The Mage Council is full of pompous old men that don't often compliment nor do they give up their rule easily. Just ask our father! He has to deal with them!"

"Lady Marianna is now on the council. She'll keep them in line," Lauranna said as the female elf took her bow in hand. *Vienanu,* she sang the word and a thin yew magical staff, shorter than her brother's, now was held firmly in her right hand.

"She's on the council just because the woman is Yanith's wife," Theawel interjected.

Lauranna glared at him, "Your wrong! The lady is the most powerful healer in the kingdom!"

"We're going to be late for class," their tall willowy delicate cousin Horalilana had joined them. Her bright indigo eyes were always full of laughter, though the girl was a stickler for guidelines. She was Baron Falsteff's daughter. It was expected of her to hold the barony's rules.

"Ah, come on Horalilana, lighten up. It's Midsummer Festival time," Theawel complained. "Old Lilianana will understand. She must have been young sometime!"

"I'll let you explain to her then why we are late," Horalilana pointed a warning finger at him.

A look of horror came over Theawel. "We'd better go," the elf suddenly changed his mind. Their elderly mage teacher was not easy on her students and most lived in fear of her extensive powers. The Hartlander instructor towed the line with every one of her students. No exceptions.

"I'll race you," Lauranna pushed her brother playfully. "Whoever losses has to get the worms for Boris and Hilda."

Not waiting for a reply, the thin lithe female elf took off. Ausanwel raced after his feminine twin. The Elmwood Forest was crowded with huge oaks, majestic maples and slender yews not to mention the various thick barberry and elderberry bushes that lay at the feet of the massive tree trunks. There were also sharp thorny bramble bushes that jutted out their ligneous long threatening branches, waiting to snare someone.

Running between them took skill, but being elfs, it came naturally easy to navigate the maze of trees. Just like their herds of elk, deer and gazelle, the elfs were nimble woodland creatures. Their tall thin but muscular legs were made for running long distances and agile enough to conquer the woodland labyrinths. Soft deerskin boots also made them silent travelers even on the thick crunchy underbrush forest carpet. Their elfen heritage made the elfs crafty talented hunters. They were the best huntsmen in the Kingdom of DeLak.

Both twins raced toward Falsteff Castle, which lay at the Elmwood Forest's northern tip with the city of Elvasor located just below it. The immense wooden/stone structure was the home of Baron Falsteff, their uncle. They went to the well-built elf stronghold almost every day for mage classes. Their own father's estate lay not far to the north in the Emerald Forest.

The twins were known not only for their blossoming magical abilities, but they were the best runners and hunters among their generation of woodland elfs. Despite his sister's head start, Ausanwel was gaining on her. Suddenly he lost sight of the slender fleeing figure. *Damn,* his mind focused hard, *she's using her magic again. I should have stipulated no magic.*

As Ausanwel passed a big oak tree, he saw too late a leg jet out, tripping him. Losing his balance, the elf went flying forward. The young man was agile enough to roll and jump quickly back up. His sister, however, had gained ground and was now several trees ahead. Her teasing laughter rolled back to him. The tall limber youth doubled his efforts. As he raced down to the valley leaving the forest behind, the twin knew it was too late, Lauranna was waiting at the bridge that led to the castle's garden entrance. Her large cocky smile said it all.

"You cheated," he accusingly pointed at Lauranna. "You used magic to win."

"Stop being so gullible, Ausanwel," she laughed. Her arms went into the air taking in her surroundings. "We are elfs. Magic is as important as our breathing."

"Don't let the baron hear you," he chided. "Remember we are not pure elfs."

That brought a huge frown from his twin. "He's wrong. I will prove him wrong!" his sister spat out. "Just because our mother was part human, that does not make us less elf!"

Their friends were catching up with them. "Beaten again!" Ausanwel heard over and over again. *She beats me in her magic ability, not to mention she's more cunning then I'll ever be,"* his inner nature moaned. The two had been in competition with each other ever since they had been born eighteen seasoncycles ago. Yet the siblings were close, having grown up without their mother. The twins had clung to each other since their father was often off traveling as the baron's ambassador.

"Stop pouting," Lauranna punched his arm. "Just remember Boris and Hilda's worms," the winner coyly reminded him.

Hearing their names, two large gray owls floated down to sit on each of their shoulders. Hilda on Lauranna's and Boris on Ausanwel's, both birds affectionately rubbed against their masters' cheeks. They were magnificent creatures, not usually seen during the daylight hours being night predators, but for the twins, the birds made an exception. Their pets were often on the two elfs' shoulders even during the daytime.

Ausanwel reached into his pocket retrieving a small leather bag. Two wiggly worms quickly disappeared into the owls' beaks as they gratefully took their treat. "Boris tells me that the peregrines have had their chicks." The male owl often let its thoughts enter Ausanwel's mind. Communicating with his pet was the one talent that he alone did not share with his sister. Although the female owl, Hilda, was close to his sister, the bird did not "talk" to her.

"We'd better go a different way home if we don't want to get attacked by those hawks. They'll be very protective of those chicks for at least a mooncycle," Lauranna conjectured, looking to the north, the direction of their home. The twins usually went through the lower Emerald Forest where the peregrine flocks were in abundance.

The twins followed the group of young elfs as they headed toward their class with Mistress Lilianna at the base of the ancient massive oak tree that lay at the center of the castle's garden. Their teacher had taught several generations of young elfs their magic spells and potions. Despite advancing age, the female elf "*walked in light*", the feeling of enchantment filled the air around her willowy tall figure. Their tutor was still elegantly beautiful and none doubted her powerful magic.

Some said that their teaching mage had valiantly fought in Coorish War many seasoncycles ago, but their tutor would never talk about it. She seemed so peaceful and calm, delicate in her features, strict but not easy to anger. Yet, those that underestimated her did so at their peril. Lilianna wore her silver white hair in a tight bun woven with sparkling pink rubies that matched her bright lilac eyes. When irritated her hair flew around her perfectly shaped face as if a storm was brewing with her sparkling eyes turning a bright purple color, her long pointed ears rapidly twitching.

The budding mages sat at her feet. The colossal oak tree's branches above seemed to frame their teacher as Lilianna began her lesson. "Can anyone tell me why the elfs were considered the "chosen" by our goddess Osiana?" The instructor looked down at her sitting students. None but Lauranna stood. "No one else? Why is it always Lauranna that answers?" The mage sounded exasperated.

"Because she's likes to show everyone up," Theawel snidely remarked which brought a frown from their teacher.

"Perhaps you could use a little of that, young elfin," Lilianana scolded. She nodded at Lauranna to speak.

"Our Osiana, the goddess of all magic, is herself an elf, mistress. Her enchantment fills our barony and is why every Master Mage at Mothia has been elfin. That is until Master Yanith."

"Your answer is correct, except remember Master Yanith is mostly elf, although not of pure birth, he nevertheless has a long elfish ancestry. He is the strongest mage in the kingdom, some say the strongest ever…"

"He is just like Lauranna and Ausanwel," a voice interrupted from the crowd of students. There followed a moment of embarrassed silence, as the twin's birth was a topic mostly avoided. Although their mother was only partly human, they were of the royal Falsteff blood through their father and thus considered noble full-blooded elfs. Some Hartlanders, however, disputed their claim to "pure" elfhood.

"Which makes my point that elfin blood is strong and need not be 'pure'. All Hartlanders should remember that the Kingdom of DeLak was founded on elfish blood. Even the king has elfin origins. All the people of the realm are kin to us. Many share our slanted eyes and pointed ears. Do not let your prejudices blind you to this fact," the aged female mage instructed them all.

There was a loud murmur among her students, but she held up her hand and silence once again reigned. "The elfs were once alone in this world," she explained. "They became weak with their own self-importance. Osiana bowed to the will of her wise father, Theror, and created the other races that now inhabit our kingdom. The humans, the hillpeople, the dwarfs, the drylanders, the mountain people all were created from elfin blood."

"We are the oldest of the races," Horalilana had found her voice. "Hartlanders should rule the kingdom not the human monarch at Four Rivers. It is the will of Osiana that her elfin people should sit on the throne!"

Everyone knew that Horalilana espoused the words of her father, Baron Falsteff. The barony of Hartland was strongly divided on the topic. The young elfs erupted yelling at each other, some agreeing, some not.

"Quiet!" Lilianana raise her arms. A bright light surrounded her. All went quiet. "Theror has decreed that the elfs will be the barony with the most intensive magic, the most powerful of magic. There is not one elf, unlike all the other races, that does not have the gift of some magic. Hartland itself is magical; its forest, living creatures and rivers. Do not again fall into the mistake of being *self-important* or Theror will take that privilege away!"

The students were silent. There was no arguing with Mistress Lilianana. "Remember the Bracaard races. The blue humans, the weaselworts, the border trolls, the orange-eyed lizardpeople and the demon mages were not of Osiana but of her evil brother Kortis, who defied his father. The boastful god made the Bracaard races against his father's will. They have evil spirits and use the black arts of hatred. It is only through our union with the other DeLak races that we keep their evilness from our lands."

"The king's army beat them eons ago!" Horalilana spoke up, once again espousing her father's words. "The elfs do not need to fear our enemies. The Bracaards are way across the Viamar Sea, beyond harming us! The other western races, especially the Border Trolls, are stupid and weak and cannot cross the Iron Ridge. The eastern far northern trolls are afraid of us."

"You are wrong!" their tutor's voice carried across forcefully to the young elfs. Her hair flew wildly around her head, "The king's diligence keeps the evil at bay. Do not let your guard down nor let your prejudices cloud your judgment." The tall imposing figure paced in front of them. "We have gotten soft with so many generations of peace. The young have forgotten the sacrifices our ancestors have made for us!"

The male owl, Boris, entered Ausanwel's thoughts, *she is right, the female mage is right!* The bird ruffled his feathers against his master's neck. Hilda fluttered on Lauranna's shoulder following suit as if she agreed with her owl mate. Boris continued, *Evil, once again, stirs from the sea, the seagulls have been warning us,* the bird's irritated thoughts forcefully entered in his master's mind.

Stop being such a worrywart Ausanwel chastised his pet. *You owls are such worrywarts.* The majestic birds were considered wise and the "birds of the gods", the young elf thought, but he did not share that with Boris. The owl already believed himself superior, no need to add fuel to his sometime haughty nature.

Mistress Lilianna did not get to finish as a green uniformed servant interrupted her from behind the group. "My apologies, my lady, Baron Falsteff would like to see Lauranna and Ausanwel Falsteff in the audience chamber."

Their tutor nodded. Both the twins followed the servant down the garden path past the myriad of colorful sweet-smelling flower beds. They continued toward the large intricately carved double timber doors that led to the main entrance to the castle. Massive sturdy stonework graced either side of the entryway. Dwarf masons had made the strong structure when the Coorish War had ended as a thanks to the Hartland Elfs' war sacrifices. Before that, the Elfs were a disjointed barony with its inhabitants living in elaborate tree houses. Many Hartlanders still lived in the trees, but more and more were building stone and wooden houses on the forest ground.

The castle had several slim delicate turrets that mimicked their willowy woods and had elaborate carved statues depicting their various woodland creatures. These decorated the outside stonewalls; large antlered elk, gentle deer and the slender quick horned gazelles looked down from high above. The smaller forest inhabitants of fat hares, fierce boars, squirmy squirrels and even the tiny chipmunks were interspersed along the walls. The elfs held on tightly to their woodland origins.

On the top of each turret were huge carvings of the great gray owls. Wings spread wide, the birds seemed to warn all that entered Falsteff castle to remember the elf's wild heritage, of their hunting prowess and cunning nature. Both the twins' pets took off, soaring high above in just seconds. *We will see you later,* drifted into Ausanwel's mind.

As they walked down the main corridor, Lauranna turned to her brother, "Why do you think the baron wants to talk to us? Did you and Theawel get into more trouble? The baron always blames me too!"

"No! It may be about father. We haven't heard from him in over a mooncycle. He was in Bombia last time we heard from him."

This thought caused both twins to hurry their steps, passing by the stately leading servant who yelled after them, but they paid no attention and rushed to the entrance of the audience chamber. The two hurried in unannounced.

Both came to an abrupt halt as not only was Baron Fraulwel Falsteff awaiting their arrival, so was their father, Lord Eranwel Falsteff. Both men were loudly arguing, each pointing accusingly at the other.

"You promised me, Fraulwel! You promised me that if I became your ambassador, my children would be protected and on equal footing with your own offspring." Their father's voice was angry and even somewhat threatening. Rarely had Ausanwel and Lauranna ever heard their diplomatic father in such a state.

"I have done all I promised," their uncle answered. "They have been allowed to attend all royal classes, including

Mistress Lilianana's classes and gotten all the elfen training the others of noble birth have had. It was your indiscretion that put them at a disadvantage to begin with!"

"I would not call my wife an indiscretion!" their father yelled.

"Then what would you call an *impure* royal marriage - prudent?" the baron loudly barked back.

As both twins came to a running abrupt halt, the two brothers looked up noticing them. Both men immediately shut up but did not stop glaring at each other.

"Father!" both daughter and son ran over to their parent. The Hartland ambassador hugged each of them. Remembering where they were, both the twins faced the baron and bowed their heads, "Your Lordship," the twins said in unison.

"Thank you for sending for us. It is great to see our father!" Lauranna just about exploded with excitement. Despite their father's frequent absenteeism, they loved him deeply and were closely attached.

"I wanted your father to have a chance to say his farewells," the baron was an elf of few words, always being blunt and to the point. The tall yet sturdy elf ruled Hartland the same way. The ruler did not elaborate any further.

"Where is he going now?" Ausanwel asked, reluctant acceptance filled his voice.

"Your uncle was not referring to me," their father pronounced rather sharply in the baron's direction. "You have been volunteered for the king's army. King DeLak has sent out a decree for the baronies to send more recruits, including those from the noble houses."

Both twins stood silent. Neither of them comprehended what their father had implicated.

"When am I to leave," Ausanwel was the first to speak up as the words sunk in.

"No!" his sister almost screamed her denial. "It is I who should go!"

Baron Falsteff held up his jeweled hand. "You're both going!"

Silence fell as the twins looked to each other. "Both of us? Is Horalilana and Boraliwel going?" Lauranna asked her uncle.

"Of course not!" the baron snapped back, "I need them here."

"I find that rather unfair!" their father almost shouted at his brother. "You have no right to exclude your own children and endanger mine!"

"Baron Falsteff did not chose them, I did," Yanith had entered the chamber. He hobbled forward on his beautifully carved staff. The master of Mothia had arrived silently. The old mage seemed to suddenly appear. "It is my choice to include your children, Ambassador Eranwel, not your brother's."

The twins bowed low as the master of the kingdom's mages came over to their father. "I do not do this lightly, my old friend." He leaned heavily on his staff, a great sense of sadness filled his grayish lavender eyes. "Eran, you have been all over the kingdom, you of all should know that war will be upon us. We need leadership from our noble barony houses."

"Then let me go," Eranwel said. "Let us that served in the last war do so again. It may have been a long time ago, but I remember what it is to fight."

"No, it is for the young to take up the responsibility now." Yanith response was strong, not to be countered.

"But, do you need to take my best students?" came from the doorway as Mistress Lilianana pointed her finger at Yanith. "Do I have a *NO* in this!"

"No, Lil, no you have not a say in this," the old mage shook his head regretfully. "It is my decision and mine alone."

Before anyone could say another word, there was a commotion by the door as a rather rotund dwarf pushed his way into the chamber. Several guards and servants were trying to detain him, but he pushed them all aside entering the room rather unceremoniously. "Get out of me way!" his gruff deep throated voice yelled.

"Leave him be," Yanith told the servants. "He is here because I invited him." `

The disconcerted look on the uniformed domestics was one of startled amusement, but no one dare challenge the powerful mage and all backed away letting the dwarf enter.

"Good grief, Yanith, ya didn't warn me that I'd be attacked before I even got started!" The short man looked the typical dwarf; undersized in stature with a long beard that was tucked into his wide jeweled iron chain waist belt that was supplemented by big wide suspenders; all supporting his bulging stomach. The lower Iron Mountain inhabitant wore rustic sturdy worn rawhide trousers, a thick plaid waistcoat and leather vest. He wore a typical miners cap with curly bright red hair hanging down over his thick furry ears. In one of his pudgy jeweled ring fingered hand was a good-sized ax whose blade looked dangerously sharp. The most memorable part of his face was his large protruding rosy nose yet it was his bright shiny dark blue eyes that you finally settled on.

"Well, if you weren't late, Mathie, I'd have walked you in," the mage chuckled. "Let me introduce you to Mathew son of McDonol, from the lower Red Iron Mountains to our north. He will be the guide taking Lauranna and Ausanwel to their training camp."

"A dwarf!" the baron's disapproval rang loudly in everyone's ear. It wasn't that the elfs looked down on the dwarfs, they in reality looked down on everyone, but still, Iron Mountain dwarfs were rarely seen in Hartland. These dwarfs were considered as uncouth, rowdy, ale drinking laborers that came to do iron and stone work and then were encouraged to quickly leave.

Yanith ignored the baron, talking directly to the twins. "You will not take anything with you. No one is to know who you really are. Being elfs, you will have the advantage of being able to survive in the wilderness as elfen youth are well trained in hunting. Still you have much to learn in the art of being warriors. If you successfully finish your training, you may return back here."

It was Lauranna who angrily spoke up, "This is totally unfair. We were to be tested at Mothia. I have worked hard…"

Yanith interrupted her, "If you choose not to do this, you forfeit all chance of going to Mothia, but if you successfully finish the training, I will personally see to it that you are tested." That said, the powerful mage raised his free arm and both of the twins' staffs were suddenly in his grasp. "You may not use magic. You are soldiers now, not mages."

Both the twins gasped as they felt the magic leave them. Ausanwel grabbed his sister as she started to fall.

"Come lad, lass and follow me," Mathie waved to them. "We have a long journey and you need to get ready."

"Father!" Lauranna ran over hugging her father. Her brother, Ausanwel, just stood there stunned even when his father came over and hugged him goodbye.

"Come back to me. I have great faith you'll both do me proud," he told his children. "I say that not because I'm your parent, but because you have your departed mother's strength and intelligence. You will make her proud too." A tear slipped down the ambassador's cheek.

"Come on!" the dwarf pulled at both of them. "Ain't good to just sit around dallygaggin."

The pair followed him. Their tutor, Mistress Lilianana, looked stricken as the twins passed her. Their ancient wise mage instructor raised her arms, "Osiana, Issi a tenarala involucate" *walk in the light of Osiana* her words followed them out.

Mathie led them down into the castle servants' quarters. This part of the castle was rustic, lacking the opulence the rest of the royal apartments had. The dwarf stopped at two plain-planked doors facing each other. "Youse things are in there. Leave everything behind. Hurry!" the short figure pushed his charges forward.

Ausanwel went into a small almost bare room. Window-less, it contained a small cot, small closet and nothing else except on the bed was a set of strange clothing. There was a pair of hand-sewn brown breeches, a worn out gray shirt, a thick rope belt, wool stockings, homespun underclothing, and a pair of side tie-up deerskin boots. The twins had been to the hill country of Arthinia on one of their father's travels; he'd seen such clothing on the sheep farmers. The apparel even smelled of livestock.

Leaning against the bed was a pigskin knapsack. Inside were an extra shirt and one more pair of underwear. Also included was a woolen vest that looked worn. For long moments, the elf just stared at the clothes. A pound on the door and a "HURRY UP" brought him out of his stupor. *Stop feeling sorry for yourself,* he came to the realization that pity would do him no good. *It is not the first time that we've been dealt a bad hand.* A picture of his beautiful departed mother came to mind. His family had not had it easy at court, but his family had not only survived but also thrived. He could do this too!

Grabbing the clothes, he dressed. His nose did not like the smell the outfit emitted, that of a barnyard. *You'll get used to it,* Ausanwel chastised himself, *you have a lot more to worry about.* The male twin took up the knapsack and headed back to the hallway where Lauranna, dressed as he was, sorrowfully waited with the dwarf.

"About time!" the northern guide stomped his foot. "I'se wanna get ya down Owl Lake 'fore nightfall. Wese need to get to the lower Elmwood, better coverage there."

"Why in the god's name are you so spooked? Our forests are safe!" Lauranna demanded. "Can we head to our estate first? I have several things I need."

The stocky plump dwarf let out an exasperated sigh. His bulging nose seemed to become even redder, "Youse better get it into yar head lass, ya ain't goin home, youse are now a marked target. There be many a Mothia enemy that would like to kill the plans that Master Yanith has. Never mind those that would undermine King DeLak. So, let's get movin."

Ausanwel laughed, "It will be you dwarf that has trouble keeping up with us." The male twin looked at Mathie's short stubby legs and his protruding belly. The twins, with their long legs, could easily out hike the northerner. The idea was most laughable.

"And," Lauranna added, "it will be us who protects you, dwarf. That small ax you carry will do nothing to fight off an enemy. Let me get our bow and arrows at my father's farm and no one will give us any problems. We can grab our blades while we are there."

They had reached the fork in the road that led either to town or to their forest. The dwarf quite exasperated turned to them. His stubby fist went to his sides in an irritated stance, "Look, both of ya, as far as the army is concerned yar no longer elfs, just new raw recruits, dumb new recruits! Ya gotta lot to learn. Youse is now Ash and Lura - new names, new people. Get used to it!"

Both stood stunned watching the dwarf head down the forest path. He turned around. "I said, COME ON!" Mathie shouted back. "I thought ya elfs were supposed to be smart. Did ya not understand me?"

Ausanwel, now Ash, felt his face reddened. How dare a dwarf chastise them - a dumb dwarf! Lauranna, now Lura, grabbed his arm pulling him reluctantly down the road. The three had not gone far when Mathie led them off the road and into the thick treed forest.

"Wese best keep out of sight," the dwarf waved the twins on. "Wese be headin toward the Owl Lake. Know where that is?"

"Of course," Lauranna dripped with disrespect. "Unlike you dwarf, we know our land."

Mathie ignored her sarcasm, "Good, if wese get separated, I'se meet youse there." The dwarf abruptly stopped, facing them with a serious face. "Take these two blades, keep the blades ready. Don't hesitate to kill, this ain't for play." When Ash went to tuck the weapon in his rope belt the dwarf grabbed him, shaking the male elf strongly. "I said keep it ready! That means in yar hand, dunce!"

"How dare you, take your hands off my brother," Lura screeched, her voice losing its lyrical quality in her anger. The female elf stood with her slender knife pointed at the dwarf's belly.

"So, you think ya can fight me?" the dwarf actually laughed. "Come on female elf pup, let's see ya try." Mathie stood with his ax casually in his right hand and a long sharp dagger in his left.

Lauranna waved her knife before him, "I'm more than a match for you, Iron Dwarf, you puny little bully."

Ausanwel immediately took his place beside his twin. "You'll have to fight both of us Mathie," he pointedly announced.

"Fine, I can take ya both with one hand tied behind me," the northerner growled as he threw down his dagger and gripped his ax with both hands.

"Enough of this foolishness!" came from the forest as another dwarf emerged from the trees. She was taller; women dwarfs are taller than the men, and broader of shoulder. There was no cap on her head and her red orangey hair was tied back with a yellow ribbon showing her large fuzzy ears with big earrings hanging from them. She wore knee high pants, but a linen yellow colored smock hung down over her sturdy knees with a wide yellow woven rope belt at the middle. Tall rabbit furred boots finished her off. There was a fierceness about her; the stout woman radiated a battle-ready air.

Like Mathie, the female northerner had a large nose that was slightly less red than his, but her eyes were bright light blue. In her fancy woven belt was a small ax, but her shoulder also carried a large bow with a quiver full of oversized spear arrows. Her large stumpy hands were bedecked with beautiful gem rings. Her wrists were encircled with spiked iron bracelets. The dwarf was not someone to mess with.

"Magdalon," Mathie moaned. "Now ya show up. Where was youse earlier?"

"I'se was draggin these supplies around, McDonol." Her voice was rough, with a crusty low accent. "Get ya fat ass over here and help me." Mathie assisted her slog a large bag over from the forest. The female dwarf had obviously been carting the sack around with her.

From the carrier, she took two sturdy bows and quivers full of arrows and handed them to the twins. The female dwarf also gave each a watering pouch, some very rustic utensils that were more like iron sticks and a dented wooden bowl. "Keep yar knives ready and yar bows at hand," Magdalon strongly instructed them. "Mathie is serious about the dangers wese is comin into."

Both twins clutched the bows, though not made of elfen ash, the weapons were nevertheless sturdy and well finished. Lauranna immediately strung it, let out a sigh of meeting an old friend. "This is more like it!" the elf lyrically laughed.

"Don't go thinkin ya is good with that!" Mathie tried to warn her. "Get close before shooting those arrows."

"I know how to shoot a bow, dwarf!" Lura frowned at him. "I could teach you a thing or two. We've been trained well in the martial arts."

Before the male dwarf could reply, the female interrupted. "Leave them be Mathie, she'll learn. I've trained their kind before. They are elfs, hard to train because the mages don't realize they are starting all over when their magic isn't available. It takes awhile for their cockiness to go away."

"Fine, Maggie, I'se let ya deal with them." Mathie grabbed his backpack and headed into the woods again.

"I'm Magdalon McDonol daughter to Connel from Ryland in the Red Iron Mountains. Call me Maggie.

Are you Mathie's sister?" Ausanwel asked.

"No, I'm his wife," she laughed. It was a hearty rich laugh full of merriment. "Youse will get used to him. Ya not find a fiercer fighter. Ya are lucky I came across ya when I'se did. Youse have not bested him, believe me." With that said, the dwarf gathered the depleted bag, which became her knapsack and followed her husband into the woods. The twins quickly trailed behind her shaking their heads in disbelief - *fierce fighter,* Ash thought, *more like an undersized fat troll.*

To the twins' surprise, the two dwarfs kept up a rapid pace throughout the afternoon. The elfs actually had trouble keeping up with them. The dwarfs, being shorter, had an easier time going under the low hanging branches and the two short guides seemed only focused on where the four were going. When they reached the soft beach of Owl Lake on the northern section of the wide water's shores, both Ash and Lura were exhausted.

To their amazement, the two dwarfs foraged into the woods bringing out two small canoes. "Good, the boats are still here. Come on ya two," Maggie yelled at the twins directing each to a craft. "Wese need to get down lake by nightfall."

Ash climbed into the first light canoe with Mathie while Lura sat in the other boat with Maggie. Unlike the elfs, the dwarfs were heavy causing the boats to ride low in the water. Their guides took up the oars and started paddling along the shore keeping within the lakeside's hanging tree branches.

"Where are we going?" Ash yelled back to the rowing Mathie.

"Be quiet!" Maggie urgently urged him from the other boat. "There be unwanted ears everywhere. The forest talks."

Ausanwel felt his face flush; of course, the male elf knew his own land. Elfen trees did indeed magically talk with the Hartlanders, but the forest would not betray them. These woodlands were friendly. He was going to reply there was nothing to worry about, but Mathie turned back to him.

"There be others that hear the forest voices, lad. Others not friendly to either elfs or dwarfs."

Ausanwel was taken back; he could no longer hear the whispers of the elms, maples or ash trees. The oaks were now silent to him, their voices all gone with his magic taken from him by Yanith. The twin suddenly felt totally empty, friendless. He didn't even have his owl to consult. Maggie was right, the two of them were now on their own. Elves with no magic were adrift in a deep silent world. Ausanwel wondered if his sister felt as he did - vulnerable.

Into late afternoon, the boats headed south down the lake until the four reached the narrows that led into the beginning of the lower Owl Lake. Upper Elmwood Forest was left behind and the Lower Elmwood, an area with many more outcrops of rocks, began. The lower Owl Lake was much narrower. The shoreline was compact and full of large rapids. The travelers took turns paddling, pushing against the flow, keeping close to the sides until nightfall was almost on them.

When their guides finally pushed over to a large sandy beach, all four voyagers were tired and hungry. Still the dwarfs pushed them further into the forest until they were well away from the shoreline. The sun was low and the shadows of evening were upon them.

"Keep the campfire small," Maggie warned. "Set up yar bedrolls close to the fire. The flames will keep the wildones away from us."

"I don't think we need worry about the boars." Ash slumped down near the heat of the fire, glad to have the warmth as the deep treed Elmwood was much colder than home. "They never attack elfs."

"The fear of yar magic keeps the beasts at bay," Maggie said, reminding them of their lack of magical talents now. The pudgy northerner stirred a pan full of beans for the evening supper. Mathie had disappeared into the woods some time ago. "It is their masters that worry me more. It is rumored that bounty hunters have been raising and crossbreeding the large boars with wolves to be their attack mongrels."

"What!" Lura's face was pale and frightened. "Bounty hunters? What bounty hunters?"

"The marauders are men being handsomely paid by the enemies of King DeLak. They have aligned themselves with the Bracaard scum and would see black evil return to all the DeLak Baronies." Making the elfs get their rustic bowls out, Maggie filled each with a type of bean soup and handed out stale hard bread.

Both twins looked at the stew with great disdain, frowning deeply at the smell. Neither one of them touched it.

"Eat!" the female dwarf cook demanded. "Tack beans are all wese have for several days. Even elfs can't last long if they don't eat!"

Each twin took the dry bread and dipped the slice in the bean mixture. The bread made it more palatable. Ausanwel had to admit that after he'd finished, his stomach felt better. He noticed his sister seemed less pale.

Mathie came back shaking his head, "Everythin is quiet, too quiet! No sign of any woodland life. Somethin has got them scared."

"I'se take the first watch," Magdalon stood and paced within the small light of the campfire. "Sleep while ya can elfs, wese be up before dawn."

Lauranna put her blanket roll close to her brother's. "Do you think we are in danger?" the elf whispered.

"I don't think so," Ash lay down pulling his bedroll over his head. "Our uncle would have heard if there was any danger coming in from the eastern sea, but keep your knife and bow handy just in case." The male elf was so tired, he hardly got the words out before the twin fell fast asleep.

Someone urgently shook him awake. Ausanwel looked up to see Mathie putting his finger to his lips. His wife was over by the fire feeding it more wood. Ash sat up, looking around, trying to shake the cobwebs of sleep from his mind. Lura was already up and had her bow strung, an arrow already poised at the nearby trees. It was then that the elf saw the shining white eyes of the wildone staring intently at their camp between two trees.

Both dwarfs were facing the other way. Bright eerie eyes seemed to circle their entire area. Ausanwel jumped up grabbing his bow in one hand and tucked his knife in easy reach on his belt.

"Don't let them separate us, lad," Mathie warned. "Keep close to the fire." The dwarf had his axe held in front of him and a large lit branch in his other hand. The light of his torch reflected off the eye sockets of the boars."

The wildones came out of the protection of the trees; huge mangy horned beasts with large sharp pointed teeth showing through their drooling mouths. The animals crept forward on big legs with claws extended, crawling forward on all fours, squealing loudly.

Suddenly one of them jumped. Maggie swung hitting the animal square in the face. A yelp, then the creature lay dead on the ground. The dead beast set the rest of the pack howling, loudly howling. The loud screeching sent chills down Ash's back. The wildones now more cautiously advanced.

Lauranna sent an arrow toward the biggest of the boars. To the she-elf's horror, it missed.

"I told ya Lass, wait until they'se are really close!" Mathie yelled at her.

"Do as he says," her brother told her. "You don't have magic to guide it. You'll just miss."

The largest of the wildones attacked Lura. It reached her in three long jumps - eyes blazing in hate. Ausanwel saw the mangy beast coming and jumped it from his crosswise position, knocking the large creature sideward. The monster just missed his sister. The big wildone, however, was up facing the male elf within seconds. Lura screamed and threw her knife. The blade hit the half-wolf in the top flank shoulder. It turned and snarled at her, but quickly turned back to her brother.

Ash held his knife up, but the elf knew his small weapon was going to do little to the massive animal. His sensitive nose could smell the boar's musky matted fur, felt its rancid breath as it attacked. The male elf braced himself for the impact. It never came. Out of the darkness two large owls attacked, pulling the animal sideways. Mathie had rushed over striking the beast with his ax. There ensued a battle as the half-wolf fought for its life.

The dwarf and the wildone rolled on the ground. It was hard for Ausanwel to see who was winning the struggle as the campfire's shadows blurred the two. Lauranna was over aiding Maggie, the she-elf was using her bow at short range and the wildones were yelping as arrows pierced their bodies. The female dwarf was hacking away with her ax, felling several of the other half-wolves that made it beyond Lauranna's bow. The two owls were fiercely attacking on either side of Lura. Both birds were clawing at the eyes of the beast helping Magdalon finish the last of the hoard.

Ash took his knife and jumped over the two struggling dark figures. The male twin grabbled fur and pulled, bringing his blade straight down. The beast screeched. Suddenly the struggle was all over with Mathie plunging his ax deeply into the head of the large wildone leader.

Both Ash and Mathie stood up over their kill. They were soaked in dark red blood. Beyond the other side of the camp-fire, Maggie and Lura were standing in the middle of a hoard of dead animals. "Thanks for the help, lad," Mathie sounded winded.

Ausanwel just nodded. He was astounded at how fierce the small dwarf had fought with his deadly ax. The male twin walked over touching his sister's arm. Lauranna seemed in a stupor. She finally looked up at her brother, "I never realized how much I depended on my magic." Her voice was strained and stricken.

"It's alright," Ash tried to comfort her. "You'll get it back."

"It'll never be the same," Lauranna said, but straightened and went to collect the arrows.

Her brother went to help her, but Maggie grabbed his arm, "Leave her be, son. She'll be all right. Your sister needs to be alone right now."

"I found a stream not far from here," Mathie came over wiping the blood off his ax. The dark red stains gave Ash the shivers. "Let's get washed up, rinse our clothes. The smell of blood will attract more. We need to get out of here before more show up and even worse, their masters."

"Where'd the owls come from?" Maggie said as the two large white birds settled on the twin's shoulders.

"They are our pets," Ash informed her. "I will order the birds home as best I can."

"Don't bother, lad," Mathie shook his head, "ya can't keep them away. Laren will know what to do with them."

"Laren?" Lura asked.

"You'll meet him soon enough. The general is the com-mander of the camp," Maggie interjected. "Wese all answer to him. Wese best get out of here!"

The four quickly put out the fire, picked up their things and headed out, following their guides once more. Ash looked back at the carnage thankful that the night was still too dark to view much of the battle. The male twin was glad to see that his sister was keeping up. *Yanith was right,* he thought, *no matter what we will never be the same.*

Chapter Four
The Dwarf

    CLANG reverberated loudly around the room as the huge
hammer hit the still piping hot iron that lay pressed against the
anvil. Sweat poured down Hoffler's brow, down his face and
ended up soaking his shirt and even his long, rough canvas,
dirt-stained worn out apron. The dwarf didn't even notice, so
intent he was on getting the right shape out of the sword han-

dle his hands were pounding into submission. *Ousta fromista, the mage apprentice* chanted as he grabbed tightly to his heavy iron mallet. First his eyes scanned his work then his mind searched the piece of metal on the table. No weak spots, cracks or misshapes appeared.

"It looks good," came from his mage teacher. Yuthiala had been standing over him. "You've made good progress in *feeling* the essence of the metal."

"Aye," Hoffler replied, "now I need to join the steel blade to it."

"In time, young Lord, in time," the mage straightened his tall frame. Not being a dwarf, but a lanky beanpole of a human, he found himself bending over a lot. The ruler of the Errtie Barony had recruited the Mothia mage to teach her son. There were only a few dwarfs that could wield magic, thus the southern human mage had come to the Great Northern Mountains to teach one of the few dwarfs that showed true magical promise.

"It won't be long now and you'll be off to Mothia for the testing and can start your true apprenticeship," his teacher wiped his own dripping brow. The forge room was hot, dirty with scraps of several types of metal and broken farm equipment in need of repairing. Not a typical classroom.

"Vienanu," Hoffler chanted. The heavy mallet that had so effectively shaped the iron sword handle, became a short thick oak pole. The sturdy rough feel of his intricately dwarfian carved staff felt good in his stubby short fingered hand. Power flooded his body, cooling him off.

"We need to go over some of the weather spells," Yuthiala reminded his pupil, "and you need to meet with Guthermuler on the old elfin spells. You know Mothia will test you on those." Old Guthermuler was one of the few dwarf sorcerers that had actually passed the testing.

"I'm sick of elf this and elf that, damn pompous pansies. How about he gives me a lesson in dwarfian spells?" Hoffler grumpily remarked.

"I'm afraid there are not many of those," Yuthiala responded. "All magic comes originally from the elfin Hartland. Some speculate that all the iron in your surrounding mountains here keeps the magic at bay. Magic thrives on living things -

trees, plants, animal life, waterways. Thus, your barony does not have many mages."

"My lesson will have to wait. I have a meeting with my mother. I'm already late," Hoffler explained as the apprentice took off his forging apron.

"Oh, that's right. Your wedding is coming up. Will Natalia go with you to Mothia?" Yuthiala let out a big sigh. The tall southern sorcerer was also looking forward to heading back to the mages' stronghold on the kingdom's southern Mage Bay near the Viamar Sea. He could not get used to the mountain's cooler northern temperatures. The coming winter hurt the Mothian's aging joints.

"Well, aye, if I pass the testing and get to go down south," the dwarf sounded unsure of himself.

"Stop worrying, you'll do fine. We've been intensely studying for over two seasoncycles. Even Guthermuler admits you are better than he ever was and Gutie holds great respect in Mothia. No one wields iron and wood better, not even the elfs. So, have confidence in yourself." Yuthiala went over to one of the tables and picked up an exquisite ruby ring. The piece of jewelry was intricate and finely carved, set in a perfectly shaped round wooden setting with an outer ring of gold. The tiny dwarf carvings set in the wood were superb, emphasizing the big ruby jewel that sat neatly in the center. His teacher held the band up to the light. "Natalia will love this."

"I'm showing it to my mother today. If there is anything not right, the baroness will point the flaws out to me. She's very fussy and extremely critical of anything I do. If it passes her inspection, I'll give it to my future wife tonight at the festival."

"Hoffler!" came from the iron works' door, "Yar late! Ya know how the baroness hates youse being late!" His friend Franler stood with his fisted hands on his waist. "She'll not let ya go to the pub tonight, come on! I brought ya a change of clothes, youse don't have time to go to yar rooms and change!"

"I'd better leave," the mage apprentice told his teacher, "Franler's right."

"Damn well, I'se right. Let's go!" His best friend's short stocky figure stood waving to him with Hoffler's change of clothes in his hand.

The mage apprentice quickly changed leaving his sweaty clothes behind for the servants to wash and put on his fancy court garments, more fitting to being the barony ruler's son. His mother was hard to please, so the royal dwarf made sure everything was in its right place; his silk shirt was tucked neatly in his finely woven wool pants, his dark velvet purple vest buttoned properly, his best boots shined brightly. Hoffler smoothed out his tightly curled orangey hair and bristly red full beard the best he could. His fingers on his left hand pulled on his right ear's ruby earring for good luck and the dwarf then followed behind his best friend.

Both young dwarfs headed toward the castle which stood just down the hill from the forges. The huge structure glinted in the morning sunlight, the sun bouncing off the complex carved stone pillars that dressed the entrance into the barony's dwarf mountain fortress. The whole castle had been sliced out of the Errtie mountain ridge. It lay against the background of the huge impressive mountain cliff as a reminder of how important the metals that lay within the Great Mountain range were to the dwarfs. Even the sturdy-featured stocky dwarfs were a reflection of the ruggedness of their surroundings, of the harshness of their cold climate and barren rock landscape.

The castle was built as two large carved out, high-windowed levels. The rooms were a small part of the huge cliff, but the structure's width seemed to go on forever. Vast large openings dressed the entire front, bringing in much needed light into the dark mountain interior. Outside, long stone porches ran along the front side of the upper rooms. The castle looked down on the town of Erry which lay at the base of the ridge.

The two dwarfs, as they headed towards the castle, walked down the main street that was wide and precisely paved in immense, carefully placed granite blocks. The broad lane allowed heavy mineral wagons to easily traverse to the forges from the mines that lay nearby.

The streets were full of male and female mineworkers heading toward their respective caverns. The many shop owners on either side of the street were just opening up. The deliciously aromatic bakeries were full of Erryians getting their breakfasts of sweetbreads and biscuits covered in brown buffas gravy. Hoffler felt his stomach growl and started toward his favorite pastry shop. Franler, however, grabbed his sleeve.

"NO! Youse already late!" his friend strongly reminded him. "The baroness will blame me!"

Hoffler reluctantly turned away and hurried once more up the street toward the castle. Several dwarfs waved and yelled out to him. "Hey, see yee tonight at The Crossroads," some of the townspeople shouted as the two quickly passed down Main Street. Every time the mage apprentice went to stop to talk (his favorite pastime), Franler pulled his friend away.

Finally, they passed the castle's stables where the livery workers were hitching the mammoth workhorses to the well-made steel clad durable wagons that would soon be filled with mountain ore. Several of the drivers yelled out to him, "Hey Hoffler, bring yar largest mug tonight!"

He laughed, waving, "I'se be there!" The baroness' son stopped as his eyes rested on the weathered face of an older female driver. Despite Franler pulling at him, Hoffler shook him free and strolled over to the fully tacked wagon. "Stella, how is it goin? Have ya seen Natalia this morning?"

The woman stepped down from her wagon perch, "No Hoffler, I think she has her gown fitting today." The female dwarf was taller than him making him look up into her sun-burnt leathery face. Although much older than his fiancée, Stella had befriended Natalia when his fiancée had first come to Erry from the far away mountain village of Azirra. The wagon driver was his first cousin and had taken his intended under her wing. The older woman dwarf had been a great help in letting the young female dwarf assimilate to city living.

Hoffler reached up petting the snout of one of the large draft horses. Stella was Errtie's top breeder and draft horse trainer. The whole mountain region came to her for expert equine advice, which the stable owner freely gave.

"Come on!" Franler screamed at his best friend.

"See ya tonight," Hoffler gave one last pat to the im-mense horse's thigh; the coat felt soft and silky, a credit to Stella's care. It was a welcomed feeling as the dwarf used to ride every so often with Stella, helping her tack and care for the mammoth animals. On their journeys, he had learned of the lives of the miners as they made their trips from the nearby caves. Hoffler missed the easygoing life, but lately court duties were calling more and more on him.

The mage apprentice passed through the stone archway into the courtyard proper. Hoffler was almost at the vast wooden doorway, which lay open this time of the day, when he bumped into his older sister. Of course, she was dressed in her guard uniform with tons of stars and award stripes as befitting her status of heir to the barony. Her other title was 'head general' of her mother's army which radiated in every fiber of Gertrude's being. The woman was a soldier's soldier. He mockingly saluted his sister - Hoffler had teased his sibling since their early childhood days.

"Humpf," Lady Gertrude growled, "yar late. Her baroness is not pleased."

"Unlike yee, Gertie, I can't be everywhere. I'se to be tested soon, I need to study!"

His sister hated him not using her formal name, Gertrude, but Hoffler didn't care. She was Gertie to him, always would be. "Remember to talk proper king's language to the baroness. You know how she hates you talking like a peasant," the female soldier reminded him as the Errtie general changed her own tone. His sister turned around walking him to the Grand Room where his mother kept audience. Soldiers lined the way saluting their commanding general as the two went by.

Both his parents were there on their formal "thrones" Hoffler jokingly called the big wooden seats, although only the king was allowed a formal throne. Both Errtie royals were in their official dress. The seats were ancient, ornate, huge cushioned chairs made of dark oak. It was not his parents, however, that caught his attention. The high wizard, Yanith, was standing next to them in deep discussion.

The mage apprentice quickly bowed, "Master, what a great honor to see you." His staff tingled with being so close to such immense magical power.

Yanith turned to him, the old mage slightly bowed. "I have heard great things from your tutor. You have impressed him with your mastery of our arts."

"If my son could only learn to manage his time," his royal mother dryly cut in. "Perhaps a stint in the king's army will teach the boy that discipline."

Hoffler stared at his mother, what in Theror's sake was she talking about? He heard his sister's guffaw behind him, "He wouldn't last a minute in the army."

Her laughter was cut short by the baroness' sharp retort, "Shut up Gertrude, we did not ask for your opinion."

Yanith sharply interrupted, "Please, let us not argue. This is not a pleasant situation for Lord Hoffler, let us not make the situation worse."

"What are we talking about?" Hoffler felt his heart pounding. His staff was pulsating with his fast beating heartbeat.

His father, Sir Bertran, broke the tension. The royal consort had put a hand on his wife's arm as if to tell her to remain calm as the red faced Errtie ruler was angrily tapping her foot. "Son, King DeLak has sent word for the need of more recruits to join his army. He feels that the royal barony families should do their part. You have been chosen…"

His sister interrupted the father, "That's ridiculous, your baroness, I should be the one going. I can choose those that will come with me. If rumors of war are true, Mother, why are you sending Hoffler?"

Again, his father was the one who spoke up, "My dear, Gertrude has a point. We do not have many mages here in the north. The smithies really do need our few mages to help manage the forging…"

"It was not the baroness's choice," Yanith authoritatively announced leaving no doubt of his strong, no-arguing power. "I chose Lord Hoffler."

"I'm not a soldier. I'm not going to join some stupid not-needed army! There are only unsupported rumors of war! I'm to be tested soon. For Theror sake, I'm to be married soon. I refuse!" The baroness' son stood his ground facing the old mage, grasping tightly to his staff.

"I'm afraid you have no choice, son," the powerful head sorcerer replied. Hoffler felt his staff leave his grasp and it flew neatly into Yanith's hand. "I understand this is not what you want, but if you are successful and survive this task, I will personally see to it that you are tested immediately upon your return."

"And if you refuse," his mother's command came drifting over to him, "you will be banished from Errtie. Do you understand?"

Hoffler glared at his mother, "And what of Natalia? It is not fair to her…"

"Do not worry about her," the baroness sat back down with an annoying huff. "I will compensate her mother and will assure her that once your brother, Koristh, comes of age, I will send for Natalia then. She'll still be marrying into our royal family."

"What!" Hoffler shouted, but from behind him the ex-mage heard a loud gasp. The dwarf turned to see his fiancée, wide-eyed, pale and with astonishment filling her gorgeous green eyes. Natalia looked so lovely in her pastel jade colored velvet gown. Her blonde hair was braided with yellow flowers intertwined. The decorated curls were piled high on her head. Once a bumpkin Azirran, the young female dwarf had transformed herself from a country girl into someone comfortable and accepted at court.

Natalia had come to be his wife against her own will after being ordered to do so by her chieftain mother from the far away northern village of Azirra. The union was seen as quite an advantageous marriage that would help Azirran trade. To the female country dwarf's surprise, she had fallen in love with Hoffler and they both now looked forward to settling down in Erry. She was one of the few dwarf females that was comfortable at being a mage's wife; magic not being totally acceptable by most northerners but instead slightly feared. The mage apprentice had fallen completely in love with this country dwarf and now couldn't imagine life without her.

She met his eyes. He saw her anger and the hurt that his fiancée dare not express openly to the baroness. Like Hoffler, the Azirran's fate was not her own. At the realization that the ex-mage had no choice but do as Yanith commanded, he turned back. "And how long do I have before I leave?"

"You are leaving immediately. You will not tell anyone who you are or that you were a mage apprentice," Yanith bluntly told him. "You need not know any more than what is told to you by your guide and you must follow orders exactly! *Remember to do as you are told.* Now, bid your parents goodbye."

Hoffler already knew his magic was gone. The minute his staff had left his hand, the dwarf had felt empty, almost disorientated without the magic's strength. He couldn't bring himself to say anything, but turned and followed the powerful head master of Mothia out of the now silent room. He heard Natalia's soft sob and the beginning of an argument between his sister and his parents. The new recruit closed his mind focusing on keeping up with Yanith.

They hadn't gone far down the hall when two tall shadows stepped out of a darkened corner. One he immediately recognized as Yuthiala, his tutor, whose sad face told Hoffler that his teacher knew of his pupil's ill fate. The other human male was even taller than his magic instructor. The man had a rugged weather-beaten tan face, reminding him of his cousin Stella. The towering slim guide obviously spent a lot of time outdoors. He was definitely human, but his yellow eyes hinted of some Kazian ancestry. His whole demeanor was one of fierce determination, definitely not someone to challenge in a fight.

It was Yuthiala that introduced him, "This is my son, Schaller. Please trust him, I hope he will be as good a teacher as I was but in the art of defense. He is a good soldier. I will sorely miss you Hoffler. I look forward to your return. Please come back to be tested at Mothia."

The ex-mage dwarf could not find any words; his emotions were all stuck in his throat. Hoffler grabbed the hand that his tutor held out and felt one last tinge of magic.

"Good bye, sir," Schaller saluted his father and then bowed to Yanith, who just nodded. "Come follow me," his guide pointedly said to Hoffler as Yuthiala's son hoisted a heavy knapsack onto his broad shoulders. You are late, we have a ship to catch."

They had not gone far when Natalia stepped in front of them. "You cannot leave me," she pleaded. Tears were running down from her high cheek bones to her cute little full rosy lips. Hoffler could not help but think his love quite beautiful.

He grabbed the outstretched small hands drawing her close. "I'm so sorry," he whispered to his ex-fiancée. "My mother is right, it is unfair to keep ya bound to me. It may be awhile before I return, if I return." Hoffler reached into his pocket bringing out the exquisite ruby ring and the dwarf put the jewelry in her hand. "Remember me, but move on. I love ya too much to ruin yar life. Neither one of us can live in banishment."

"I could," Natalia passionately whispered to him.

"I do not want that for ya," Hoffler let his one true love go and followed Schaller as the two headed toward the east outer door, the servants' door. The baroness' son felt Natalia's eyes following him, but Hoffler didn't look back. His heart was breaking.

As the two left the castle the once mage apprentice, now a soldier, again didn't look back. The dwarf couldn't bring himself to admit the reality of what was happening. Schaller had said nothing but kept up a fast pace. Once out of the town of Erry, they hugged the Errtie Mountain Ridge keeping to the cliff's shaded overhangs. "Keep close to the rock's edge, there are overhead eyes I wish to avoid," his guide firmly commented.

Hoffler looked up but saw no one, just the mountain hawks and other large birds of prey. There also appeared to be a large flock of falcons circling. His guide stopped and seemed to be concentrating on something in the high mountains to the east. Suddenly, a contingent of large bald eagles came rushing into the overhead sky. Hoffler stood amazed at the skyward battle that was taking place as the eagles attacked the falcons.

"Come, hurry!" Schaller shouted at his charge. "The eagles will keep them busy for a while." His guide started running along the ridge. Hoffler ran as fast as he could, but keeping up with the long-legged human was not easy. By the time they stopped, the dwarf was winded.

"I can see we need to work on your endurance skills," his guide matter-of-factly commented. Hoffler was going to comment on his short legs, but Schaller had already anticipated the excuse, "I don't want to hear that it's because you're a dwarf. We have many dwarf soldiers that are faster than I am."

Hoffler said nothing, but followed the tall human into the beginning of the Great Fir Forest that lies to the west of Erry, giving the much-needed cover that Schaller so wanted. The huge trees grew so close and tall that the sky was non-existent. Despite the summercycle, the air grew much colder and the dwarf wished he had his big fur coat. The ground was covered in a thick layer of pine needles making their footing precarious.

Still, the human seemed not to notice, almost elf-like he glided smoothly over the squishy ground while Hoffler struggled with his footsteps sinking into the soil. He almost collided with his guide who suddenly stopped. To his amazement a white raven was sitting on Schaller's shoulder. The lank harsh featured man seemed to be talking to the bird.

The hawk flew majestically away, his wide wings swishing upwards. *A rare white raven, no one sees them during the day, Hoffler thought. The bird is a night creature rarely viewed at all!* The dwarf's mind raced, *was this magic?*

"The hawk tells me that there are enemies to the west of here, let us go via the North Mountain Trail. We will have to hurry as that way is the longer trek and we still must make Cradle Lake before nightfall. There is a ship to catch at Orthagard.

"Are you a mage?" Hoffler ventured a question. The rough-edged soldier was hard to question. His no nonsense attitude did not encourage conversation.

The man actually laughed. The gesture changed his whole face and Hoffler could see in that moment the resemblance to his father, Yuthiala, who often smiled. "No, I'm not like my father. As a matter of fact, I get my talent from my mother who was a Kazian seer. I inherited her ability to talk with avian wildlife, although I did not get much else from her."

There was bitterness in Schaller's voice and the dark rough foreboding man returned. He waved Hoffler on as they set a fast pace. The two followed the North Mountain Trail that led to the upper Cradle Lake, which appeared late afternoon. Being summer, the freshwater was only slightly ice-covered; during the winter it froze solid, making the entire lake unusable to boats. The lake's one and only city, Orthagard, was situated near the lower part of the large body of water. Being more south gave the city almost three seasons of trade before winterseason's ice cover shut their harbors. The two travelers followed Cradle's shoreline, heading downward.

The closer the travelers came to the city, the more people appeared, especially mountain dwarfs. Ages ago, the mountain dwarfs had interbred with the western lower mountain human settlers thus the inhabitants tended to be taller than Hoffler's Erry population. Some called them dwarfs, some called them humans. Still the Cradle Lake inhabitants were loyal subjects to his mother and were able fighters in her army. Gertie had several commanders from this part of their barony. Just below Orthagard was a large army fort, on the Thera River, which housed even some of King DeLak's soldiers. Both Errtie and Kazia claimed the fort, being on the border of both baronies. They jointly operated the fortress, although not always harmoniously.

Small farms grew to bigger farms; mostly raising buffas and elk herds. Wild grain and corn farms also popped up near the city, as the climate was more conducive for agriculture. The winters here, though, were harsh. His guide, Schaller, fit right in with the Orthagard dwarfs who also were rugged and no-nonsense people. Their fearless miners dug deep into the Great Mountains finding rare jewels bringing prosperity to their city and the barony.

Hoffler had visited Orthagard numerous times with his father, Lord Bertran, who came several times a year to meet with the city's chieftain, Fagalusga, on behalf of the baroness. The city's leader was a tough, big built muscular dwarf that ruled her domain with an iron fist. Her daughter, Helstag, was married to Hoffler's oldest brother Laghar. His wife was twice the size of him and extremely over bearing. They lived with her mother, the chieftain, and helped manage the city's trade. Despite Hoffler cringing at Helstag's domineering manner, his brother seemed happy. *Thank goodness Natalia isn't like that,* entered his head before the dwarf realized it no longer mattered.

As they approached the city, the roads became wider. At the edge of Orthagard the two followed the well-traveled, neatly kept avenue that led to the city's docks. Swarms of huge wagons with all types of cargo were either loading or unloading the immense freight ships that were berthed at the lake's shipyard. The Orthagard harbor was one of the few means of quickly getting goods to and from the northern Errtie barony.

His guide, however, did not head to the ships, but took a right onto a street that contained a prosperous crowded tavern. All sorts of people were going in and out, many of them rough looking dwarf sailors. Instead of going into the main entrance, Schaller skirted around to the back where a large stable was conveniently located.

The smell of horses filtered into Hoffler's protuberant dwarf nose. Memories of his cousin Stella's castle stables came flooding back. Oh, how the Erry dwarf wished he was there, helping the older woman hitch up the wagons to go to the mines. He was already homesick.

"Okste, where are you?" Schaller yelled.

The largest man Hoffler had ever seen came trotting from the rear of the stable. Hoffler stepped back, instinct making him grab for his staff, but of course there was nothing there. The man towered over his guide and was twice as wide. Although he'd never seen an Okian tribesman, his intuition guessed this giant was one of the barbarians from the far Western Mountain Range that bordered the kingdom's distant, mostly inaccessible, high mountain boundary.

The Okian tribes people kept to the northwestern mountain cliffs, rarely leaving despite the king's effort to recruit them into his army. The tribesmen were so fierce; some said un-trainable, more like animals then people. The men sported full black beards despite having blonde hair. Their eyes had a wild desperate look that seemed always on the verge of some rage. Large hands, large feet, immense ears, large everything characterized their every feature. Even their big yellow widely spaced teeth scared Hoffler.

Schaller began talking to the giant in a language the Erryian had never heard before. The behemoth answered him, the Okian's voice ragged and deep. Still, though Hoffler didn't understand the words, the dwarf could tell the tribesman was evidently angry; his voice full of guttural growls.

"What's he mad at?" Hoffler squeaked out, wishing he were anywhere but here.

"Okste isn't mad, he's just saying how he was worried that we are late." His guide pointed to his dwarf charge, "Huff, name Huff son of Thorman."

"Hoffler," the dwarf reminded his guide, "My name is Hoffler."

"NO," the tall man looked sternly at his charge, "You are Huff now, don't forget it." The words were forcefully said and meant that there would be no argument.

Yanith's words came flooding back to him; *do, as you are told, nothing else.* So Hoffler said nothing but nodded. His name was now Huff. "This is Highbeard Oklanka, you can call him Okste."

"I don't think I'll call him anything," Hoffler responded. "I've heard how dangerous they are."

Schaller laughed, "Fine. He's our bodyguard. I'm not asking you to socialize, but don't go far from him." Okste with his immense hands handed the soldier a knapsack which in turn the guide handed to Hoffler. "Go into that stable and change, leave those fancy clothes behind. You stand out like a sore thumb. Hurry, we're late."

Inside the bag the ex-mage found rustic miner's clothes. The outfit, including the roughly stitched undergarments, smelled of raw mining ores. The dwarf quickly changed; the pants were tight as was the thick rope belt. Hoffler could hardly tie it. He vowed to lose some weight. The miner's boots, however, fit perfectly as did the gingham pull over dirt stained shirt. The cap was just a tad too big, falling down over his large ears. The sheep's vest fit fine.

When Hoffler hurried out, Schaller shook his head in approval. "Let me do the talking on the ship. Your language is too Erryian for a lowly cave digger. This is the only ship I could find that would take us down river. The captain and crew haven't the best reputation so keep a low profile. We aren't worth their attention. I know how to handle them. Understand?"

Hoffler, now called Huff, obediently nodded. The Erry dwarf followed the two men to the docks where his guide headed down the wharf to the last ship, which was a large older cargo freighter. The ship had a dilapidated rusty appearance. Several dwarfs were loading big barrels up the large ramp. An acid sweet smell invaded their noses as they dodged the barrel laden dwarfs that were loading cargo and entered the wide pine tar sealed deck where the captain was yelling orders.

"About time ya got here," a gruff scruffy looking bearded Orthagardian dwarf greeted them. "Yar lucky we're running late or youse be left on the dock." The skipper turned his attention to the loaders, "Get those pickles down into the hold. The smell is making me sick! Make sure the cannon powder for the fort is up front. Those barrels gets unloaded at our first stop!"

"Sorry we are late," Schaller contritely answered, obviously placating this ugly bullying antagonizer. "We got lost finding the dock."

"Ain't too bright, are ya? Just keep that barbarian out of the way," the captain laughed pointing to Okste. "He's gonna cost ya double." The grubby man, although complaining about the pickle smell, reeked pretty bad himself. The grungy captain turned Hoffler's stomach. Although taller than the ex-mage, the man was a scraggy mess of overweight fat with droopy eyes and runny nose. *He's inherited the worst traits of both humans and dwarfs,* Hoffler mused with disgust.

The three of them headed down the deck. The regular crew was priming the ship for undocking. The captain looked respectable compared to the roughness of the unkempt sailors. Schaller was right though; no one paid attention to the three passengers. Huff noticed the large curved knifes each deckhand had on his belt. He gladly followed Schaller to the farthest point on the rear deck where only a few sailors were stationed.

"We have only one day on this sad excuse for a ship. We get off at the fort. Let's keep back here. Even the privy is close by, the least we see of the crew the better. They'll be afraid of Okste. The scum should stay clear of us." The big Okian tribesmen just sat down, his back against the ship's side railings. He took a huge ax from his bag and laid the weapon on his lap. Hoffler supposed it was a warning. *The oversized scary weapon works, scares the hell out of me,* Huff thought as the dwarf slid further away from the barbarian.

The ship glided clear of the dock. The ride was amazingly smooth. *Probably loaded down,* Hoffler thought. Schaller had fallen asleep. The sun was hot, even the spray from the lake couldn't cool the dwarf off. His mouth felt dry and crusty. The Erryian watched the sunset as the ship entered the Thera River. The water looked clear and cool, making his thirst even more pronounced.

Huff turned to Okste. Using his hands, the dwarf tried to mimic drinking. The barbarian at first just looked at him as if Hoffler was crazy. "I'm thirsty, you dumb ox!" he shouted at the giant. He repeated the drinking gesture with his hands. The large man finally got the idea. Nodding, the tribesman produced a large water skin bag. Hoffler gratefully took a big drink.

The new recruit noticed that the group of loading dwarfs was on the other side of the front of the ship. Huff guessed the loaders also didn't want to mingle with the crew either. Most were sleeping.

Darkness brought a little relief from the hot sun. He drifted in and out of sleep. There wasn't any moon so his vision couldn't see much of anything. His large ears could hear the swoosh of the water as the frigate passed down the river. Sleep had finally come when suddenly one of the loading dwarfs violently shook his arm. "Fire!" reached into his drowsy mind bringing the Erryian wide-awake.

Okste also jumped up, the deck bounced from the man's weight. The barbarian obviously had heard the dwarf deckhand and was yelling loudly, waking Schaller with a kick.

Again, Hoffler's hand went to the nonexistent staff. The ex-mage was now fully awake and could smell the smoke. "The gunpowder!" he yelled at his guide. "It will explode!"

"Get into the river!" Schaller screamed. When Huff didn't move, his guide yelled, "Now!"

"Are you crazy!" Hoffler screamed back. "I can't swim!"

The dwarf felt himself lifted off the deck. The huge barbarian threw him overboard. Huff yelled all the way until his feet hit the water, "I c-a-n-'t s-w-i-m!"

Despite it being summer, the water was cold. Hoffler felt like someone had hit him with a brick wall. Under he went, his mouth filling with water before his brain realized to close his lips. Down he went. The dwarf flailed his short pudgy arms, awkwardly kicked his feet. His head surfaced, but started to sink down almost immediately. *I'm gonna die,* his mind angrily belched at him.

As his head started down again, someone grabbed his arm and pulled hard getting his neck above the water. "Hoffler, kick yar feet!" a voice yelled in his waterlogged ears. He immediately did so but then realized the voice!

"Natalia," he gasped in astonishment. "What..." his mouth tried to speak, but water again filled his throat shutting him up. Huff felt her arm again raising him above the water.

"Grab onto Okste," Schaller had come up beside him. "Hold onto him, he'll take you to shore."

"Where's Natalia?" he managed to sputter out.

"Okste got her too, now kick your feet and give him a hand!" Schaller screamed in his ear as the night lit up - the ship blew up behind them. Pieces of the frigate rained down just missing the struggling swimmers. A wave of water flushed over his head. Hoffler clung desperately to the barbarian. The Okian tribesman headed toward the shore as the ship burned behind them. It seemed forever before the swimmers reached the river's edge. Huff staggered up the riverside beach collapsing on the sand. His mouth gasped for air as his legs pushed him further up the shoreline.

Hoffler grabbed onto a small willow tree pulling himself upright. "Natalia!" he yelled.

"I'm here," he heard from behind him.

"Thank god ya know how to swim," he sputtered. There was something to be said for being a country girl. There were no places to learn to swim around Erry. "What are youse doin here?"

"I followed ya. I got on the ship as one of the loaders. I ran over to warn ya of the fire." She crumpled tiredly onto the sand next to him. "I'se didn't think wese were ever going to make it ashore."

Hoffler looked over to Schaller who was kneeling near Okste. Even in the low light coming from the burning ship, Huff could see the worried look on his guide's face. "What's wrong with him?"

"He was hit by the exploding ship's debris," Schaller told Huff. "His arm is hurt badly." Natalia jumped up, going to the fallen large man, putting her hands on him. "What are you doing!" the soldier pulled her back.

"I can heal him," the female dwarf said. "I'm a healer."

"YOU'RE WHAT?" Schaller and Hoffler shouted simultaneously.

"Just let me try and heal him," she calmly told them both. "It can't hurt."

To Hoffler's surprise, she touched Okste's arm then started chanting words he'd heard Yuthiala try to teach him. The mage apprentice hadn't had much interest not being a healer himself, only learning enough to pass the testing. Okste groaned and then sat up rubbing his arm that was no longer bleeding.

"Youse never told me…" he started to say, but the female dwarf cut him off.

"My mother forbade me to mention my healing as she felt yar mother may have changed her mind. It was hard enough in our village for me to find a dwarf willing to marry me. Magic, especially in our area, is frowned upon."

Sitting up, Okste let Natalia wrap his arm in a rag that Schaller had handed to her. "It's a little wet, but it'll keep the wound clean," the guide told her.

"Thank you," the barbarian nodded to her. "My lady has a great talent from the goddess Osiana. May she bless you."

"Youse talk the king's language! Why ya…" Huff sputtered at the large man.

Schaller cut him off, "It's your own ignorance that is to blame, Huff. The Okian tribes are both intelligent and friendly. Do not always believe the false rumors. We need to move on down river. Whoever set that fire will not be far away. The fort is not much further. Say goodbye to your dwarf friend and let's get going."

"I'm not going to leave her here. Natalia saved our lives, for Theror's sake. Look what she did for Okste!" The dwarf stood his ground. "We'll be leaving her to whoever set that fire or if she goes back my mother will punish her! If ya don't take her with us, I'm leaving ya right now!"

Schaller threw up his hands, "Laren is going to kill me. Fine, she can come and YOU can deal with the general. He is not going to be happy!"

That being said the dark ominous man headed down stream not looking back at any of them.

Chapter Five
The Drylander

Larandar knelt on the hard, dry soil filling his hand with the drifting sand that easily passed over the ground. The wind driven dust slipped through his rough suntanned fingers reminding him of how fragile life really was. His youthful light gray eyes lifted, looking from the high bluff to the vast hot desert not far away. His magical senses drifted to the distant horizon. Sunrise was beautiful as the golden rays filtered over the wind-driven sandy dune wilderness. He took his long scimitar knife from his wide rawhide belt which was inlaid with sparkling decorative jewels. He pointed the knife directly at the sun. Powerful magic flooded his mind, showing him where the enemy was heading. He could feel the blood-sucking trolls; smell their stink, feeling their evil as they marched northward. He also felt an overwhelming blackness among the group.

The raiders must have a shadow-creating sorcerer with them! No wonder the band of trolls had snuck into Bombia without anyone knowing until it was too late! All the magical barriers the Bombia mages had set up were for naught, over-ridden by the invading fiends' wicked demon mage. The red skinned horned creature's wards were too strong for an apprentice like himself to penetrate.

Although the landscape looked barren, Larandar knew better. The desert teamed with life; strong virulent life that had to be resilient to survive such a harsh climate. The wilderness was the essence of what it was to be a drylander.

"They are heading across the Kobi," he commented to a tall, dark-tanned, rugged fellow Bombian soldier who stood right behind him.

"Yes, the trolls know we are tracking them and the bas-tards are trying to cover their tracks," Hasibar answered as his finger pointed westerly. "There is a sand storm coming and the trolls know it. Our troops will lose them for sure, my lord, if we get caught in that tempest."

"They have to be heading toward the Kobi Pass. If we follow close to the ridge we could cut them off before they get through the gap." Larandar stood up brushing the sand off his long tunic shirt whose light wool cloth threaded with camel hair was densely woven to protect against the desert's weath-er. The clothing reached down to his buckskin pants' knees and lay just above his soft desert buffas' tan-hide tall boots. The young lord placed his attached shirt's hood over his tur-ban.

The drylanders called his turban a sacred kaffiyeh or blessed headscarf. It was intricately wrapped to protect his bright blonde colored hair. The head covering just barely let his large thick pointed ears peek out. An accompanying cloth could be lowered to protect his face when needed. The desert could be harsh, especially on the eyes. His hand went to his small silvery goatee beard that covered his chin and extended all the way up to his ears.

"I'll get everyone up here, we will ride right to the ridge," Hasibar said as the soldier put his hands together and bowed to his baron's youngest son. Larandar just nodded touching the giant white hawk feather that lay in his kaffiyeh, a sign of his birthright as his first lieutenant went to get the rest of the scouting troop.

When his best friend left the bluff, the desert man felt a stirring in his left tunic pocket. "Come out and take a look at the sunrise, Bishi," he commented. A small black snake slithered up to his neck, affectionately curling around from one of Larandar's pointed thick ears to the other. The serpent was extremely shy, never mind extremely poisonous, frightening those that saw it. Yet it was his favorite pet, often his only companion in his treks through the lonely desert.

Larandar softly spoke *Vienanu* and his scimitar became a long thin staff. He held it out as Bishi curled up on it. "You are right, the trolls are headed north toward the cliff pass. We will be hard pressed to catch up to them, but we will try," he told his snake, getting a nod from the serpent's head as his pet put its slotted nose to the air - the reptile had extra sensitive hearing and sense of smell.

The snake quickly slid into his pocket again as Hasibar came running up the slope, "My Lord, a horse approaches from the south. The rider carries the baron's mark."

"I'll come down and meet him," his voice carried concern as it was not a normal occurrence that his father sent anyone after him. The Bombian lord went down to the lower ridge and from there he could see the dust rising from a short distance away as a rider wearing the gold uniform of his father approached. Larandar's seven fellow soldiers waited impatiently. Even the horses pranced nervously, anxious to get following the dangerous intruding border trolls. Time was of the essence.

The rider scampered up the first bluff. His horse was covered in sweat as if ridden hard and he had a second horse in tow. When the messenger was close he quickly dismounted, falling down on one knee in front of Larandar and bowing deeply. "Sahib, iextis itll it…"

"Speak the king's language, as my father has decreed," the Bombian snapped at the golden dressed soldier. "We now pledge allegiance to King DeLak!"

"My apologies, Lord," the servant corrected himself. "Baron Bombia has sent me to tell you that your presence is needed at court." The heavily accented words were broken but understandable. It was proving hard to get the drylander people to leave the old customs behind and to join in becoming part of the DeLak Kingdom. "I have been looking for you for two days, Sahib. I have brought you an extra horse, you must hurry!"

Larandar let the *Sahib* go as the lord was more concerned with why his father would call him home. "What is so important? I will return as soon as we track down these killing trolls!" the drylander spoke harshly to the messenger, his irritation getting the better of him. "My father knows how important it is to catch these marauders. The trolls wiped out an entire caravan, killing every man, woman and child!"

"I am sorry, Sah.., my, my lord," the messenger stuttered, "but your father said *immediately*! The baron means *immediately*." His hand held out a rolled scroll that he gingerly handed the young lord.

The Bombian noble briskly unwrapped the parchment, anger filling his long slender strong fingers. It was a message with the seal of his father ordering him home *immediately.*

Hasibar interrupted his thoughts, "Go my friend, we will follow the evil ones and catch them! It must be important or the baron would not have sent someone after you."

Larandar grabbed onto the scout's forearms and bowed, "May Theror go with you!" and his fingers touched his white feather. "Horate," he yelled and his huge white horse was at his side. Not many could ride the huge steed that had been with him since the animal was a young colt and he a young lad. Tucking his staff in his belt, Larandar jumped up on the massive white stallion. The horse needed only a cloth saddle and soft bridle.

"Do not try and keep up with Horate," he told his father's messenger. "You'll only kill your horse trying to maintain his speed." With that he kicked his legs lightly in Horate's sides and they were off down the butte.

It was not long before he had left the scouting party far behind and was heading into the southwestern part of Bombia. Here the land became rocky with small boulders and dotted with scrub brush and huge cacti. Small green islands of scrubland grass slowly appeared with flocks of lambs and sheep grazing as the night came slipping in. It was almost completely dark when he reached the Issla River; Bombia's only water source.

Larandar rested several hours, quickly falling deeply asleep, his scout training forcing him to rest. When the young lord awoke, he took a long drink of the river and quickly prayed his thanks to Theror. Water was precious to drylanders unlike most of the rest of the DeLak Kingdom that had a multitude of lakes and rivers dotting its landscape. The sky was pitch dark. Dawn was still distant, but he just had to follow the river to come to the capital Kimla.

Late afternoon, the young noble met several nomad tribes that were moving their tent cities as was usual for this time of seasoncycle. Although the summercycle was still at its peak, the heat was becoming bearable. Autumn was approaching and the cattle were grazing on the last of the blooming grasses awaiting the winter rains.

The closer he came to Kimla, large permanent tent towns appeared with the smell of the barony's spice crops permeating the air. As usual Larandar breathed in deeply. Spices were the barony's livelihood. Bombian seasonings were in such demand and the crops were so important to the kingdom that his father was allowed to bargain for almost total autonomy in his ruling of the king's new barony.

Yet it was not completely total rule. The drylanders now had pledged their allegiance to the king and owed the kingdom its loyalty. Baron Bombia felt he needed to assimilate his people to the customs of the overall kingdom while maintaining what was most important - their free desert nomadic identity. The rumor that the trolls were preparing for war made the security of the king's troops a necessity. The Bombia soldiers could not fight an all-out war with the trolls and weaselwort tribes that lived on the other side of the Iron Ridge which was their western border, not to mention the even farther distant Lizardpeople.

The nearer he got to Kimla, the great looming table butte that marked the capital's location stood starkly out in the mostly flat land. It was here that the large Theror and Osiana temples were located. His father's impressive permanent tent castle was also situated close by. His heart pounded as the plateau loomed ever closer. Larandar couldn't imagine why his father had so urgently sent for him. Whatever the reason was, it did not bode well.

Many of the city's inhabitants recognized him. The large white stallion, Horate, made him easily recognizable. Many bowed and waved as he passed the many city bazaars and open shops. He rode up to the hard-packed circular entrance leading to the temple and led his stallion to his father's side stables; one of the few wooden buildings visible. The Bombian lord passed in front of the carved stone pillars that led into the temple proper. It was ancient, his ancestors many seasoncycles ago had carved the stone temple into the plateau's base as a tribute to both their main god Theror and his magical daughter Osiana. It was an immense structure towering high above him.

Larandar turned and faced the great limestone statue of Theror that graced the entrance between the pillars and he bowed deeply at the scowling domineering serious faced god; in one hand a beautiful desert lily, in the other a long-pointed sword. Larandar quickly crossed the courtyard to his father's vast construction of permanent billowing tents. In keeping with their nomad society, the barons of Bombia had made their castle look like the tents that so dotted their desert land. The huge imported ebony wooden beams held the many interconnected billowing white canvases high above. The tents were strong and sturdy, easily able to handle the toughest sand storms the nearby desert could throw at them. They also allowed for the cooling wilderness breezes of the Iron Ridge to filter in.

As he entered the opulent entranceway, intricately woven tapestries and large palm trees decorated the sidewalls. Jeweled candle chandeliers hung overhead. Figurines of the various desert creatures from snakes to lizards to buffas spewed out scented incense made from the various spices that grew so abundantly in the dry Bombia soil.

Servants in the baron's multi-layered flowing golden silk uniforms rushed forward bowing lowly offering wine and fresh melon fruit. He drank the wine offered, but declined anything to eat; his stomach was churning in nervous anticipation. He quickly downed the rich thick drink. Larandar hadn't realized how thirsty he was. The rich woody tasting dark drink tasted of a hint of cinnamon and mint. It was a Bombia belief that those two spices added energy. After the long hard ride, the young man desperately needed it.

"Please follow me." His father's main servant seemed to have been waiting for him. To his surprise, when he was led into his father's largest meeting room, his mother was the one that greeted him. She was such a delicate figure dressed in flowing colorful silk layers, beautiful, petite and exotic not to mention highly intelligent. He could understand why his father had only this one wife and had proclaimed further baron's also take only one. Alisan had given his father five strong sons. Larandar was her favorite being her youngest. Larandar also knew she so wanted a daughter, but her childbearing years would soon be behind her. His oldest brother's wife was pregnant, perhaps she'd have a granddaughter.

Larander knelt before his mother, bowing his head. "Most beloved mother," he looked up into her large lovely gray slanted and decorated eyes. They were sad. She'd been crying. "Mother, is something wrong with my brothers? Are they here too?" he urgently asked her.

"No, no they went south to see to a colitatu. It seems the monster was dropped down from the ridge by the trolls and is killing all the sheep and calves it can. They could not wait for your return so they took Caliar as their scout."

"A colitatu! Those bastard trolls!" He was shocked. The large snake was at least six times the size of a man. The reptile was raised by the trolls that lived on the other side of the ridge, raised for troll food. It was their 'cattle' but a highly dangerous creature. It usually did not attack a human unless cornered; keeping to mostly sheep or small calves, as that is what the trolls fed it.

Alisan pulled him up into a strong embrace. "I missed you. You spend too much time wandering among the desert creatures." Again, he felt her strong hug. "I feel great anger in you, my son. Let it go, we now belong to the kingdom. You must accept that." She hugged him again. For such a small delicate woman, she had amazing strength, but then so did most Bombian women. The necessity of desert life had taught them resilience and fortitude. "The thought of not seeing you again is most painful…" her voice choked into a sob.

Before he could get his confused thoughts in focus, her small tapered jeweled covered fingers grabbed his hand. "Your father is in the temple, I'm to bring you there." She again affectionately squeezed his hand.

Out of habit, he saw her reach for her veil, but her hand fell as she realized the cloth was no longer there. His father had degreed that all women open their faces like all the rest of the DeLak Kingdom's women. They were now fully part of the kingdom, no exceptions. It was not popular, but his father's word was the rule of the land. Larandar understood the reasoning for it, but the young Sahib in him did not like it. He had great pride in his Bombian traditions, of their independence from the king. Yet, one did not argue with Baron Elandar Bombia except perhaps the king and Mothia.

Mothia entered his mind. Perhaps he was being sent to the mage's stronghold to be tested. He was ready! As an apprentice, he studied hard under the Bombia mages' tutorship and they had pronounced him ready! *At last,* he rejoiced, *it has to be the reason why I've been called home. After all I am now three mooncyles beyond my eighteenth seasoncycle.*

He followed behind his mother as she led him out to the courtyard and toward the temple. His spirits were lightened. The wind played with his mother's flowing silks and played with his white kaffiyeh hawk's feather, almost as if congratulating him. He felt Bishi stir in his pocket. He'd completely forgotten about his pet. Coming up on the temple's luscious gardens, he reached into his tunic's pocket and put his snake on the ground. "I'll be back," he told his serpent and watched as the black snake slithered into the bushes.

Both mother and son lowered their heads to their god at the entrance and then entered into the dark interior of the temple. After the bright sunlight outside, the lighted torches seemed dull. They once again bowed deeply to the foyer's great marble statue of Osiana. She was almost as big as her father's statue. Given the darken interior, the white marble figure seemed almost self-illuminated.

The beautiful goddess of all things magical had her arms stretched out in a welcoming gesture. From between her breasts flowed a majestic waterfall - water, the life-giving substance of the desert. Larandar held his staff high and once again knelt, feeling the magic surge through him from the enchanted figure. Inside the temple, white robed mages and vestals were busy worshipping. Incense filled the air. The temple's servants bowed low as the two royals passed.

As they approached the sanctuary entrance to the cathedral's main altar, voices raised in anger filtered down to his ears. Holding tightly to his staff, he softly said, *casusa verti.* His father's voice resounded loudly in his ears - "I am not happy that the king takes one of my most precious resources from me. We have need of our mages. They are the life line of our spice crops and their magic keeps the evils from our land."

"Do not blame the king. Do you think I would ask for you to sacrifice your son if Mothia did not think it was most important? I ask no more than I have asked any of the other baron families. It is you that wish to be a part of the kingdom or do your words mean nothing?" The second voice held a bitter tone.

Larandar turned into the large domed ornate stone walled room. Despite the beauty of his surroundings, depicting all the beautifully carved Bombia gods circling the altar, it was the figures of his father and of the mage master Yanith that caught his gaze. The energy of Yanith's magic filled the air, his own slim wooden staff warmed to the feel of it.

"Master," the apprentice knelt, bowing his head. "It is an honor to see you. I am not worthy that you have come yourself."

"Don't be so honored, my son," Baron Bombia barked. "He has come at the order of the king and those pompous Mothia mages. You are to become a soldier in his special army."

"What?" Larandar was stunned as he stood up and stared at the white haired, long bearded master mage. "What army? I'm ready to be tested. I'm an apprentice mage, not a warrior."

"The king has need of you son. I am putting together an elite company of soldiers. You will be trained to fight and you'll represent your family. All the baronies are sending their close family members. It is not fair that the king asks for more recruits and the royal families do not contribute. You will not need your magic."

With a wave of the old man's hand, Larandar's staff flew from his own hand into the old mage's grasp. Larandar felt as if someone had hit him in the gut as the magic deserted him. For a moment he lost his breath, falling to his knees.

"I'm sorry son. You will not tell anyone who you are and *will do as you are told*. If you survive this service that you do for the king and Mothia, I will personally see to it that upon your return you will be tested. It just means putting off being a mage for a while."

If I survive? roared into his brain. He found his voice, his anger forcing itself forward, "I'm needed here. We have trolls crossing into our lands, killing our people. My brothers depend on my magical abilities to track these murderers. You cannot do this!"

"He has done it, son." Elandar Bombia's authority loudly rang in Larandar's ears, "If you refuse I will banish you from these lands. You will obey me! You will make this land proud! Be the best soldier you can. You are already the best mage scout we have. Your brothers will miss you."

"How long before I leave?" he stood facing Yanith with as much defiance in his stance as the ex-mage could muster. His eyes could not look at his mother; her sadness he felt in his very being.

"Now," Yanith pronounced definitively. "Please follow me." The old mage headed back to the sanctuary, leaning heavily on his staff. Larandar silently followed not even looking back, it was too painful.

The temple suddenly seemed deserted. There were no white robed mages, they had all disappeared, and no white silk covered vestals with scented candles praying, filling the incense containers. It was Yanith and himself; alone with their two powerful god statues. Larandar was full of resentment. His dreams had been shattered. The ex-mage was now a new recruit for the king. He did not bow to Osiana or Theror, but yelled his anger at them.

"Do not be foolish," Yanith said to him. "Do you think me so unwise as to squander one of my most promising sorcerers? Have you learned nothing of what Mothia is about? Being a blessed sorcerer means sacrifice and hardship. You are not ready to join Mothia if you have not realized this. The special force I'm putting together is the only hope I have that the kingdom will survive the upcoming war with the Bracaards. Please do not let your anger hurt that hope."

"War?" Larandar stood staring at the Mothia leader. "How does this one group so change the war?"

"You must trust me..." Yanith started to say when a small figure came strolling toward them. The woman was about half Larandar's height.

"Isn't he ready yet?" the high-pitched lyrical female voice interrupted. "We need to get going. I have arranged for us to join a spice caravan as it leaves the city." Her impatience and irritation was extremely evident. The woman was dressed in trader leathers with a long rapier attached to her belt. She wore a black cape that almost reached the floor. She sported a large floppy hat that put her face in shadows, but her long delicately pointed ears still stuck out as did white wispy curls hanging around them. The most striking feature was her height of only three feet.

"Larandar, this is Loriala. She will guide you to the training camp. She'll protect you along the way. We must be very careful. I do not want our enemies to know Bombia is involved in this endeavor."

"This woman is going to protect me? She's a child!" he bitterly laughed looking at the soft attractive curves appearing in the woman's short stature, and of her cool pink colored eyes. "Do you mock me, Master Yanith? More likely I'll protect her." *She's a child dressed like a warrior!* He disgustingly thought.

"Please listen to her," Yanith ordered. "Remember your father's barony is at stake. Bombia's role must not be known! Your newly formed barony is not ready to confront the enemies of DeLak. Let everyone think that Bombia will not participate in the upcoming war. Remember to *do as you are told* and tell no one who you are." With that Yanith disappeared, literally disappeared - leaving an astonished new recruit.

Was only his spirit here? Larandar wondered as the drylander stood with his mouth open in total surprise.

"Come on big boy," the woman sarcastically teased as she threw him a pig-skinned carrying bag. "Change, you need to look and act like everyone else. You're not a prince any-more."

He looked in the bag. Rustic non-Bombian clothes filled the interior. He glanced around to where he could change. "Hurry up! Just dress here." He eyed her as if she was crazy. "What do you think, I haven't seen everything you got - now change! Here, I will look the other way, does that satisfy your male modesty?" With that she turned her back on him. Blushing profusely, he quickly dressed.

When she turned around, Loriala looked him over from head to foot. He looked like a regular hill peasant sheepherder that had Bombian ancestry; a muslin shirt that was a little too tight, it did show his tough muscles. There was also a pair of woolen jerkins tied by a wide woven rope belt, again, a little tight at his muscled upper thighs. His treks through the desert showed well on him. His worn deerskin boots were laced up to his pants and fit perfectly. In the bag was an extra set of clothes and a sheep vest that fit nicely. Also on the bottom were roughly made utensils.

"Leave the turban," the short figure insisted. "That's a dead giveaway." She almost sang her words. He wondered where the woman was from.

"I can't, my head gear is part of my religion," he told her.

"Don't care. Do you want to protect your barony or not? Trust me, Theror could care less, especially after you just cursed him out." The tiny woman eyed him, chuckling softly. Her light lilac defiant eyes glared at him, daring him to argue with her. Yanith's words rang in his thoughts, *do as you are told.*

He unwrapped his headdress, leaving it with his former clothes. His guide also tied a simple bedroll to the top of his bag. When she turned to leave, he quickly grabbed his turban with the white hawk feather, shoving the symbol of his birth into his bag. He couldn't leave it behind.

Then his mind went to Bishi. As they left the temple and passed the garden the snake unobtrusively slithered up his boot, onto his back and then slipped into his bag. He made no motion to stop the reptile. Damn it! He was not going to leave his pet behind either.

They made their way to the edge of the city to the open spice market. Large billowing warehouse tents circled the area. The smell of cinnamon, cardamom, mint, ginger, turmeric, mustard seed, cloves and nutmeg, a pungent mixture of rich smells, invaded his nose.

Several caravans were loading bags of the rich smelling spices to trade in various parts of the DeLak Kingdom. Loriala went immediately to the obvious leader of one of the trading groups and a bag of coins was exchanged. She crossed back to him, "You're going to lead the back group of camels. Look like you know what you're doing. Think you can manage?"

He went to snap at her, but his guide abruptly turned and left her charge on his own. Larandar watched the small woman jump into the seat of one of the covered wagons and quickly flip the reins of the horses. His chaperon was posing as a driver. In her dark brown leathers and self-assured attitude, despite her small size, she looked the part of an ordinary caravan driver. Loriala never looked back at him; it was if he'd never existed to her. *Fine,* his mind angrily growled, *two could play at this game.* He confidently strode over to the camels waiting to leave.

"Hey boy, over here." One of the camel handlers yelled over to him. When he approached the smelly heavily loaded humped animals, the man offered him some advice, "Just remember to not let Taka bite you. She can be downright ornery and she also likes to step on her handlers, breaking their feet."

Larandar spent a miserable afternoon getting spit on and dodging the camel's snapping jaws, never mind the animal's large hoofs. When they stopped for supper, he was tired and irritable. He just stared at his lamb stew.

"Eat," Loriala had come up next to him, sitting, eating from her own mug bowl. "A soldier eats when he can, no exception. Never know when the next meal will be."

"Listen Loriala, I may not be a mage anymore, but I'm a good scout," he looked challengingly at her, "I don't need any soldiering lessons from you."

"Is that so, big boy," she sneered at him. "Call me Lori and you will be Lar son of Causia and remember that! You are of peasant parents. You are a Bombian sheepherder whose father is a desert nomad."

"You are kidding?" he sarcastically remarked. "Do I act like a sheepherder? Heavens knows I smell like one."

"I think we need a private talk. Follow me." The small woman headed toward the thick underbrush that now surrounded them.

Dragging their bags behind them, they left the camp. The sunset followed them into the thick scrub brush pines that were becoming more prevalent as they approached the southeastern Bombia border. They had not gone far into the cover when she turned around and slapped him hard across the head. "Come on big boy, let's see who is the soldier and who is the ignorant recruit."

Larandar stared at her. The woman was crazy! She hit him again. The drylander's anger rose. He charged her. The agile woman easily dodged him. His nimble desert body spun around grabbing her thin yet muscular arm. She flipped him over and then stomped on his stomach. Lar felt the air leave his lungs. "Humpf," was all he could manage.

The Bombian scout flipped up grabbing her leg this time, throwing her backwards. The tiny woman quickly flew at him - *flew* at him. A pair of wings had suddenly appeared out her cape and she rose into the air. With her legs, his guide shoved him hard. Her well placed kick made him roll backwards. She was on him in a second. Bringing her lips close to his, a light smell of lavender hit his nose and his body immediately couldn't move. Lori stood over him smiling. "Want a go at it again!"

He felt his limbs returning to normal. "You're a fairo!" he exclaimed. He'd never come across one of the Fairy people. They were literally myths, but he'd heard of them in stories told by his tutors. He'd never taken the stories seriously.

"Yes, I am of the Fairy Folk. Now get up. We're far enough away from the city. We are trekking inland." His guide threw his backpack at him. She had tied his bag tightly with a rope. "Be careful with that isso snake," she commented. "You're lucky I didn't kill it."

This time he obediently followed his guide as the two headed due south, stopping only when full darkness had fallen. They slept quietly under one of the big elm trees that marked the very edge of Bombia's southern region that lay between the Issla and Thera rivers. Bishi curled up under his arm. Lori kept silent as the snake emerged from his bag. She also did not try to stop the serpent in the morning when the black slithering pet returned to his bag. As the day wore on, Larandar could tell they were heading toward the lower Issla River.

When they reached the river, his guide threw what looked like a bar of strong lye smelling soap at him. "Get in the river and wash," she pointed to the Issla waters. "You smell like a walking spice bag." The fairo turned her back on him, giving him the privacy he'd demanded before.

He angrily yelled after her. "It is a good smell! It is the smell of my country. It is better than this sheep smell my clothes reek of."

"Yeah, it's also a dead giveaway that you're from Bombia." She turned and went back to the edge of the water, "I was going to wait until we got into town, but while you're at it, shave that sad excuse of a beard!" Lori threw a sharp razor knife at him, which he deftly caught.

When the drylander came out of the river, the ex-mage felt even more naked than he was. His hand went to his chin. The smell of the soap was disgusting to his nose. When the desert man put his peasant, sheep herding clothes back on, he was almost nauseated.

Lori, however, smiled, "Good job, now let's get going. We have a long way to go. The least you look like yourself the better off we'll be. We have to head east toward Zarin, at the border with Lakeland Barony. We have a ship to catch there at the Viamar Sea."

His angry words got caught in his mouth - *do as you are told. To be a Mothia mage you must sometimes be willing to sacrifice yourself.*

About midmorning four figures suddenly blocked their way. Bosular, Marlarar, Poklarar and Hasirirar walked right into their paths; his older brothers. "What are you doing here?" Larandar astoundingly asked.

"We are here looking for a colitatu when we got word of your banishment. We are here to bring you home, little brother," his oldest brother Bosular answered. "We need to confront father with this! He should not let Mothia dictate to him."

He could not believe his brothers would defy his father. "No, stop this madness," Lar told them. "I'm going willingly."

"We know better," Marlarar interjected, smiling at Larandar's guide. "Step back, young lady. There are four of us."

"Your brother is not going with you. Go home," Lori told them. "I do not wish to hurt anyone."

The brothers laughed at her. The fairo did not wait, but immediately attacked them. All four men were down before they knew what had hit them. Then she breathed quickly on each one, which totally immobilized her attackers.

"Please do not hurt them," Lar pleaded.

"Then let us hurry," she instructed him. "If I hit them with my breath again, it could make them quite ill."

They headed down the trail toward Bombia's southern border. "My father will punish them for disobeying him," the young nobleman lamented.

"They won't tell him," Lori dryly commented. "Would you tell your father that a small woman easily beat you? I think not."

They had not gone far when a *swishing* noise was heard ahead of them. Slithering down a huge elm tree came the largest snake Larandar had ever seen. The bright red eyes focused on them as the serpent coiled up. Slowly, the creature moved forward toward the two rattling its tail, swaying back and forth as if contemplating a strike.

"They don't bother humans," his dry throat managed to get out. "Stay completely still."

"It is not after you," the fairo took out her bow and arrow, not her long knife. "It smells me. I'm fair game to it. A delicacy if you must know. My breath will not have an effect on it."

Larandar's heart pounded, he felt bile come up as the immense creature homed in on them. His hand went for his staff, but it was not there. "Give me something. I can't fight it with my bare hands. For Theror sake fly away."

"I can't fly high nor fast enough to get away from its spitting venom," Lori told him.

The fairo threw her knife to him. "Run, get out of here," she instructed him. The weapon felt good, but without his magic the tiny blade was rather futile against the monster. Yet he crouched ready to strike the creature's face. The young drylander would fight alongside his guide; he would not leave her to the snake.

Lori, aiming for its head, missed as the snake swirled from side to side making it hard to hit. Several arrows stuck in its neck, which didn't seem to faze the colitatu. Larandar ran under the head and stabbed upwards, catching it slightly. Green blood oozed downward. The monster turned angrily toward its attacker. The serpent's tongue flicked in and out. Lar had to dodge the thick venom that would cause paralysis.

Suddenly Bishi was there, scrabbling up the large snake's body. The little black snake slithered down to the colitatu's eyes and spit into them. The large snake actually screeched and violently shook its head, sending the small reptile flying off.

The monster was now blind and in pain. Larandar struck again and again, stabbing the main body of the colitatu, but the snake did not seem to notice and instead headed toward Lori, its nostrils flaring, smelling her position. There was no way she could out run the snake. At the same time, with its tail, the body of the snake wrapped around Larandar, incapacitating him. The drylander struggled to get free but in vain. Lori was trying to dodge the snake's opened jawed mouth. Suddenly from the forest his four brothers came running, swords held high.

Circling the colitatu they struck it from all sides. As the large snake turned to strike one brother, the other would put a huge gash on the other side. Finally, in its confusion it lowered its jaws to strike. His oldest brother Marlarar deftly cut the head off.

Larandar was suddenly released. Everyone got out of the way as the monster convulsed, finally quieting and lay dead.

"My thanks," Lori said quietly.

Lar ran over the ground finding his pet snake Bishi quite unharmed. He held out his arm and Bishi slithered up to rest on his neck. Then he went and hugged his brothers. "Thank god you came after us, but you need to let me continue with my guide. If I've learned anything, it is that I need to learn a lot more. Perhaps I was depending too much on my magic. I will return a better scout."

"We will miss you, little brother," said Poklarar, who'd always been close to him. "Return, we will be waiting."

He followed his guide closely, both ran hurrying to the border into the barony of Lakeland, leaving the drylands behind and headed toward the coast.

Chapter Six
The Meeting

    Mar stretched his long legs out as the ex-mage sat on the enormous city's sturdy granite wall that separated the main thoroughfare from the docks. Smelly fisheries and enormous wooden and stone warehouses lined the wide street behind him. Huge heavy-laden barrels from those warehouses were scattered around him, ready to be loaded on the various ships that lined the dock area.

Scruffy looking boat crewmembers and stinking thick-aproned fishermen populated the wide wharf area. The coastal city of Osceta was the elfs' trading hub for the eastern DeLak Kingdom. The shops and inns began on the next street up. His attention though was directed at the sea. His black serious eyes watched the rolling somber grayish-blue waves of the Viamar Sea, named after the kingdom's water god, Viamarat. The massive body of water fascinated the young lord.

In his homeland of Arthinia there were an abundance of large lakes and wide rivers, but nothing as impressive as this large open body of water. He felt like a country bumpkin seeing the world for the first time. The young noble was beginning to realize how ignorant he was of the kingdom itself. Book learning helped, but it was not the real thing. The large coastal city of Osceta also captivated his imagination.

Mar actually felt a sense of euphoric freedom. Being the Arthinian baron's son had put restraints on his movements. In Arthinia there was no one who did not know who he was, who did not watch his every move. Even in Arient castle the servants scrutinized their master's son, waited hand and foot on him. In Osceta, no one knew him. The young lord had not realized how much his father had dominated every aspect of his life. It was like he was unfurling his wings and for the first time learning to fly.

The thought of his father focused in his head, *Baron Thard Arient had tried to kill me!* The unpleasant thought swam suddenly in his mind. *Why does he hate me so much, did he ever love my poor Kazian mother?* There were no answers so he let the thought dissipate with the sea breeze.

After settling into the Ram's Head Inn, Tilly, his dwarf guide, had dragged him all around the coastal city. For several days, they had combed the maze-like streets, investigated the many shops. To his inexperience senses, Osceta was like a complicated puzzle. He often just blindly followed behind his keeper.

His dwarf chaperon never told Mar what he was looking for - but looking for something Tilly was. Mostly they seemed to gravitate to the dock's area. *What was Tilly searching for? Who?* Marth was never allowed to go far from the guide, never out of his eyesight. His close watching of his charge, Tillman said, was because the city had "dangerous people". Mar looked down at his wolfdog Gorg, the hillman knew better. None dared even come close to them, taking a wide berth. The fierce looking dog was the perfect guardian.

Compared to his hometown of Arianta, this city was a complicated wonder. Despite being Elf controlled, all the kingdom's races seemed to congregate here on the coast and in the shops especially those near the immense unloading cargo trading area. The sights and smells of the various Highlanders, Hillpeople, Dwarfs, Elfs, Drylanders, and a few mixed races were almost overwhelming. He'd never seen such a mixture before. Arthinia consisted mostly of sheepherders and cattle ranchers. It was a very isolated barony and Baron Arient preferred it that way. Travelers and traders mostly stayed by the coast. The sailors were not only a mixture of the various DeLak races, but seemed like rough and dangerous people.

Most of the sailors were dressed in black leather clothing with several nasty looking weapons hanging from their belts. All carried sharp spears festooned with decorative feathers representing their ships, their only flair of color. The inhabitants that lived on the Viamar Sea docks may be dangerous scum, but they were able talented seamen. Their ships were fast, sleek and could carry large loads. The crewmembers did not mingle with anyone but themselves. But then, none wanted to mingle with the unscrupulous sea traders either.

His gaze fell to Tilly who was standing at the bottom of a rather decrepit looking freighter's unloading ramp. The words "The Fire Goddess", were boldly written on its red rusted side.

Down the ramp came a tall slender woman. Even from this distance the Arthinian could tell she was exotically beautiful. On her head was a turban and a flowing colorful scarf was draped around her neck. Tilly greeted her warmly, giving her a soft friendly arm clasp. His guide pointed in Mar's direction. Behind the beautiful woman was a slightly built boy who seemed to protectively cling to her. Even at this distance the child looked pale. All three headed in his direction.

As they drew closer the woman's oversized slanted, heavily decorated sandy gray eyes caught his attention. Just from studying the different baronies, given the turban, he knew she was Bombian. The tall figure was a typical female desert drylander except she wore no veil. Bombia was a new

DeLak barony. He'd heard their newly created baron was trying to assimilate into the rest of the kingdom.

The desert people occasionally traded in Arthinia for sheep products. His eyes drifted to her long rapier that hung on her ornate, gem-inlaid wide belt. He also noticed a knife protruding from one of her tall boots. Strapped to her pants' side was a third scimitar knife. Not someone to take lightly. Despite the admiring glances of the sailors, none bothered her.

Gorg stood up; a low grumble came from the wolfhound. Mar saw the woman draw back, grabbing her rapier. "Easy boy," Marth touched his dog's ear. "He'll not hurt you," Mar forcefully got out as he tried to stand in front of his pet, protecting the animal. The Bombian's hand left her weapon and she took on an amused smile.

A small frightened gasp came out of the small figure that actually bumped into the Bombian having been following so close. He turned his attention to the boy and suddenly realized it wasn't a boy at all. The small figure was a slender shorter woman. She was young and her big emerald wide eyes had a frightened stare. "He won't hurt you," he repeated to the small figure, but the girl seemed to slide defensively behind the Bombian.

"This here is Mar, son of Roth. This sorry excuse for a human is one of the new recruits," Tilly pronounced, laughing lightly. Marth felt his face redden, but bit back the sarcastic remark that hung on his tongue.

The woman actually held out her hand, "I'm Sari." She pointed to her companion, "This is Dani, another recruit. And who is that?" the Bombian nodded to the wolf.

"That is Gorg, he's my wolfhound." Mar put his hand affectionately on his massive dog that stood almost up to his waist.

"Impressive," was the all the woman said and then turned to Tilly, "is everyone here?"

"No, you're the first. They should all be here by tonight if nothing has gone wrong." The dwarf pointed to the city, "He got us rooms at the Ram's Head. It ain't the fanciest, but it'll do."

"After that ship," her beautiful head nodded toward the red painted freighter, "anything will seem great. Dani has been seasick the entire time." *The girl does look white as a ghost,*

Mar thought, taking in the almost pale green complexion of the small woman.

Sari and Tilly took the lead with their two charges following behind. The young woman refused to even look at him, keeping as far away from Gorg has she could while staying close to Sari. That was fine with him; the Arthinian was not one for conversations yet he couldn't help but sneak glances at the small figure. Auburn curls had escaped from her overly large cap, her hands were soft and delicate, certainly not those of a peasant. Yet despite her obviously being scared and her clothes hanging loosely on her small frame, the woman held herself in a self-assured manner. She verged on arrogance toward her surroundings as if she found them wholly inadequate.

His instincts told him the small girl was also from one of the noble houses, but which one? He shrugged - did it matter? He had to concentrate on getting through this and back to his studies. *Each to his own life,* his mind warned him, *stay out of complications.*

As they neared the Ram's Head Inn, someone called out to Tilly. Behind them came a small two-wheeled cart. Driving the small wagon was a pair of dwarfs, male and female. The woman waved and jumped down. "Glad to see ya Sergeant Tillman," giving the short man a big hug.

So, he actually is in the army, Mar surprisingly thought.

"I see youse brought ya rift raft with ya, Maggie," Tilly yelled up towards the cart's driver.

"Don't call me rift raft, you rift raft," the stocky driver yelled as he also jumped down going over and shaking Tilly by the shoulders. "Glad to see ya made it okay."

"You go and steal that cart, Mathie?" Tilly snidely remarked. "Ya late ya know, youse were supposed to be here two days ago." He turned to the female dwarf, "What happened Maggie?"

"Ran into some problems in the Elmwood," the female answered him. "Some wildones attacked us. Had to take the long way around, keeping away from the regular roads. Put us behind. We had to trade one of our swords to this farmer who willing gave his wagon up with the promise we'd send it back. Guess with all the wildones' attacks, he could use the weapon."

"Laren ain't gonna like that news," Tillman nervously told them.

From the back of the wagon two elfs appeared. They were dressed in peasant sheepherder clothes, but from their stance they weren't sheep farmers. Typical proud elfs, the two stood straight and towered over the two cart dwarfs. The woman was a silvery blonde pale beauty. Her purple eyes were intelligent. She disdainly gave each of them the once over. The good-looking roguish male stood behind her, just as tall but not as self-assured. He had her intelligent violet eyes, but not her haughtiness and looked at them inquisitively. His stare, unlike hers, was not condescending, but more curious. To everyone's surprise two woodland gray owls came floating down, each one settling on the elfs' shoulders. Somehow the two prideful birds matched the pair.

"We could have used that wolf over there," Maggie's eyes went to Gorg, who stood stoically next to Mar.

"He's a wolfhound," Marth corrected her, "he's a tamed dog."

"Sure, he is!" Mathie skeptically answered. "Wait until Laren sees him."

As if hearing his name, a man stepped out of the Ram's Head Inn. He was almost as tall as Marth. His dark grayish lilac serious eyes matched his curly mop of russet hair. Besides the color of his eyes, his somewhat pointed ears lent to some elfen ancestry. Although he wore bland tan colored country clothes that accented his muscular yet lean build, he could have been wearing a soldier's uniform. His bearing was one of a capable warrior, someone not to trifle with. He not only commanded attention, he commanded steadfast accepted loyalty - a natural leader. *A powerful man,* came roaring across to Marth.

The four guides seemed to "fall in" around him. They all appeared inclined to salute him. They stood as if waiting for orders. Laren's glance went to Gorg then to the two owls, but although a serious frown dressed his face, he said nothing about the dog nor the two birds. Instead he stepped authoritatively forward.

"I want to welcome you to the king's service. My name is General Laren. I'm glad you all made it safely," he nodded first to the small frightened looking woman, then to the proud elfs and lastly to Marth. "Supper is just being served so you may join the others and then it's an early retirement. The Errtie dwarfs just arrived and are already inside the inn. We have to be up before dawn and on our way." Despite his authoritative soldier demeanor, his king's language was refined and precise.

"Dwarfs - as in more than one?" Tilly nervously interjected. "Is everyone here?"

Laren answered, "The dwarfs have just arrived with Schaller and yes, we have an extra dwarf recruit we had not counted on. There seems to be several extras I had not counted on." The serious leader's cold stare drifted from the white owls to Gorg then continued, "Loriala has not arrived yet with her charge. We cannot wait for her. If she doesn't come today, she'll have to catch up with us. I have to get back to camp"

As they followed their new leader into the busy rustic inn, Mar seemed to feel a sense of displacement. *What was he doing here?* The ex-mage sorely missed his shared thoughts with his pet, Gorg. His only consolation was that the rest of the recruits also seemed to "not belong".

Smells assaulted his noble aristocratic nose; acid reeking smoke from the large blazing fireplace, roasting dinner meats drifted in from the kitchen, the slop ale that soaked the floors stunk. The whole smoky dark room was a buzz with the local customers' interaction. Several large bosomed women hurried between all the rustic wooden tables bringing out food and drink. Their friendly flirting banter drifted across the crowded tavern.

The recruits were all placed at one long makeshift wooden board with benches on either side. Their guides were seated close with similar accommodations. Laren sat on a chair at the head of the recruits' table. Mar had grabbed the other end chair facing their leader. The general introduced everyone seated; Ash, Lura, Natalia, Dani, Huff and Mar. Gorg sat near Marth under the table. The dog was contentedly chewing on a lamb bone the barmaid had slipped to him. The two owls sat serenely in the tavern's high rafters, their bright eyes peering down at the table through the hazy bar's smoke.

Marth scrutinized each of the recruits. To his immediate left were the two elfs Lura and Ash. He'd bet they were related. The two looked so much alike; same eyes, hair, long tapered fingers and curt mannerisms. The male was picking through the carrots, turnips, and potatoes in his bowl. The female elf was just dipping the bread in the stew's gravy and eating it with a frown. He heard the male tell the female that she should eat more. *Ah,* he'd bet sister and brother. His own sister Lilith came flooding into his memory causing him to cringe at realizing how much he missed the small child.

Next was the female dwarf, Natalia. She was rather pretty for a dwarf. Her nose was not the usual large feature, but was small and straight. Her lips were full and matched her high rosy cheekbones. Her hair was tightly woven in an attractively plaited blonde bun and there was cleverness in her bright blue eyes. From his studies of the kingdom, he'd bet she was from the western High Mountains far from the dwarf's Erry capital. She kept glancing at the male dwarf as her fork picked at her food. *I wonder what their relationship is?* poked into his mind.

Mar looked down at the end of the table. Laren was watching them all, his sharp almost rose-colored eyes taking in everyone's movements. When his gaze met with Marth's, the commander seemed to be peering into his thoughts. Mar quickly looked away and settled his observation on the male dwarf.

Huff, he was called, a classic mountain squat dwarf. Unlike Natalia, who was taller, he was a typical Errtie mountain dweller that was of stocky build verging almost on fat but not quite. He certainly was digging whole-heartedly into his stew. His nose was typically the largest feature on his ruddy rugged looking face but like Mar's guide, Tilly, he had a contained fierceness about him. The young lord would not underestimate him as he had done his guide. Marth noticed the dwarf's sizeable calloused hands. The short man worked with either wood or metal, he'd bet. Mar had seen the hands and arm muscles of his father's blacksmith; Huff's were the same.

Lastly, he focused on the small woman. She'd taken off her cap and her best feature was her curly long auburn hair. The girl was probably quite pretty, but her face had a constant pouting look. Her lips were drawn tightly in a thin disagreeing smirk. She looked at no one and just sat staring at her food. She hadn't even picked up her mug. The tasty refreshing apple cider was untouched. *A spoiled child,* entered his head. *Who is*

*she and where did she come from? Maybe she was from Ka-
zia, like my mother, or from Lakeland itself. Was she a cousin
to the king perhaps?*

Behind him he suddenly felt the presence of magic. He
almost choked on his stew. He hadn't felt a smidgeon of magic since Yanith had taken his staff. The ex-mage quickly
turned around. Although the feeling had been fleeting, it stuck
with him. His eyes rested on a petite refined lady. Marth knew
immediately she was of the fairy folk. He had fleetingly met a
few when he visited the drifters in the northern most hills of
Arthinia. The fairy folk also lived there, but were reclusive,
secretive and highly magical. They had been fascinated by
Gorg and had come into the drifter camp to see the strange
intelligent wolfhound. It was rumored that they were friendly
with the wild wolves that lived among their kind.

Mar felt Gorg had also sensed the fairo, as the dog was
curiously looking straight at the woman. Her bright pink eyes
smiled down at the wolfhound. Whatever passed between dog
and fairy he no longer could tell, but Gorg seemed to nod to
the small figure then turned and settled down once again
chewing his lamb bone.

Marth's eyes went to the tall man standing behind her.
He was dark skinned and muscular in a lean hardened way.
His light gray eyes pronounced him Bombian, but he did not
wear a turban and was clean-shaven. Not a typical drylander.
He was dressed like a Highland hill sheepherder. *He's not a
sheepherder,* Mar thought. As an Arthinian, he'd been around
sheep ranchers all his life, spent his childhood among the
Arthinian hills. The man had an overall intensity about him.
Of all the recruits, he was the closest to a real soldier, a fighter. His slender long fingered hands were used to holding a
weapon and of using it. The desert seemed to cling to him
despite the attempt to hide it. The dark man exuded anger, a
dangerous anger. Marth cringed despite trying not to show any
emotion.

"Loriala, glad to see you," the general had come to stand
next to the fairo. He turned to her tall companion, "I presume
you are Lar, son of Causia. Welcome. Have some supper."
Laren introduced everyone and then pointed at the empty seat
next to Mar. The towering slender man slipped quietly into his
place with only a nod to the others. After taking a big draw of

cider from his mug, the man dug right into the stew that the barmaid put in front of him.

Laren returned to the head of the table. "We will be leaving before the sun rises. You'll be in total wilderness for the next several days, so eat well now. You will need all your strength and sharpness for the journey ahead to the camp."

Marth's eyes slipped to the table next to them. *So, these were the guides that had been sent to get the recruits.* He noticed among them an extremely large man, almost a giant. He sat at the end of their table and had been given a sturdy bench instead of a chair. Several mugs and bowls had been put in front of him. Mar searched his brain, but did not come up with anything that could explain the man's origins. The male elf, noticing his interest, leaned over. "That's an Okian from the far northern ridge wilderness." He leaned even closer, "They are said to be wild. I'd stay clear of him. They are not allowed in the Hartland."

Despite it being softly said, Laren responded from the end of the table, "Do not believe everything you hear, Ash. The Okians are intelligent. They owe their allegiance to no one. Be glad Okste has decided to join us. Where we travel is dangerous and his battle expertise will be sorely needed."

The male elf just nodded, but the female elf glared at Laren, "They are barbarians, everyone knows that!" as if her brother needed defending. Her typical elf prejudices came ringing loudly in her words.

Laren half smiled, "Remember your own problems with others judging *you*, Lura. Think twice before passing judgment on others."

The pale skinned elf woman blushed profusely. *Laren has touched a raw nerve,* Marth guessed. What was the general referencing? What had the two elfs been misjudged on? He stored the thought away for further notice.

Mar turned to the towering man sitting next to him, "Where you from?"

He noticed Laren's head turn in their direction, concern in his eyes. Were they not even allowed this question?

"From Drazio, on the border of Bombia and Kazia. My father has a farm there. We mostly raise sheep." The misty gray eyes didn't even look up and the drylander went right back to eating his meal. Laren seemed to nod with relief, turn-

ing his attention back to his own meal, but not before glaring
at Marth - no more questions he seemed to be saying. The
table went quiet, each looking only at their food.

The man called Lar is lying, Mar immediately realized.
The desert man was not used to lying and did not do it well.
He did notice the man kept glancing over at Sari, the woman
drylander guide. Did he know her? The exotically beautiful
woman never once looked at him.

It was Huff that broke the silence. "Hey, Lass," he lightly
touched the arm of the woman called Dani, "if you ain't gonna
eat that, I'll take it."

For the first time, the woman looked up. Her face was furious. "How dare you talk to me? Don't ever touch me, you
imbecile!" she screeched at him. Then she literally threw her
food at him. The mutton stew flew all over the dwarf, landing
in his bristly beard, in his thick curly orange hair and all over
his peasant shirt. He looked completely startled. It would have
been comical if not for the furious look on Laren's face. For a
few moments, everyone seemed stunned into total inaction,
then the room seemed to erupt in confused chaos. The other
full tavern tables strained to see what the commotion was all
about.

Laren instantly jumped up and went over grabbing the
woman by the collar, easily lifting her right off her seat. Her
small frame flailed in defiance, but he effortlessly dragged her
over to the stairs leading to the inn's upper floor. With little
fanfare, he hauled her up the steps. Drifting down from the
higher bedrooms an angry voice said, "Stay in there until I
come get you. That was inexcusable bad manners. Think about
apologizing or you'll get nothing more to eat. I don't care if
you starve to death." Then a door loudly slammed shut.

Meanwhile Tilly had jumped up from the guide table.
"Go into the kitchen and wash up," he ordered Huff. Then the
mountain dwarf turned to the group, "Eat your meals and no
more talking! Understood?" As Natalia got up to help Huff,
their short guide quickly and loudly snapped at her, "Stay
put." The female dwarf immediately did so.

Everyone nodded as Laren returned and took his seat.
The room went back to a quiet confused mumbling. Huff returned from the scullery, the stew gone from his hair, beard
and clothes. "You heard Tilly!" their leader barked going back

to his own meal. He was like a dangerous thunderstorm, his anger easily encompassing them all. The table stayed silent with the recruits all quickly finishing their meals.

When Laren got up so did all the rest of them. The commander, snapping out orders, pointed to the stairs, "Follow Sergeant Tillman, he'll show you your rooms. All lanterns out. No talking. You will be up early, have your bags ready!" With that announcement, he left the tavern, angrily walking out the swinging doors. Tilly took charge, leading them up the stairs that Dani had so unceremoniously been yanked up.

Marth was to have the same room he'd been sleeping in for several days, but now he would share it with Ash, Huff and Lar. Marth noticed Lura and Natalia were shown to the room next to theirs. He'd bet the bedroom contained the unruly girl. He didn't envy the female elf and dwarf. Lura's brother Ash half smiled at his sister in sympathy before she disappeared into the next bedroom.

Extras straw beds had been brought in. "I suggest you don't sleep on those beds," Mar told the other three. "The straw is full of bed bugs. I made the mistake of sleeping on mine the first night. I awoke to a bunch of bug bites. Not pleasant. Tilly had to take me to an apothecary and I got some salve. Best to avoid the beds, sleep on the floor."

It was Ash who replied, "Whenever we spent a night in the country with my father we'd have to protect ourselves when the beds were packed straw. It is a simple spell..." The elf caught himself, ending his words abruptly. He almost choked trying to finish his sentence that seemed to get caught in his throat. The male elf just quickly ended his thoughts with "Yes, you're right, sleep on the floor."

He's got the same Yanith's enchantment, Marth realized. *I'd bet he was a mage too.* Things were beginning to take shape in the Arthinian's mind. *Was that what every one of them had in common? Surely not the young spoiled girl. Yet...*

Mar spread out his bedroll. A bucket of water by the window was used to wash up. He didn't undress. None of them did except Huff who got a new set of clothes out of his bag, replacing the old "stew" clothes. "Laren told me to leave me clothes outside the door. They'd wash them," the dwarf told them.

The group would be up early. Better to be ready when the general woke everyone. The displaced Arthinian lay in the dark. Despite the cold fireplace, the night was too warm for a fire. Still, the smell of old burnt wood filled the room. The room was small. He could hear the breathing of each of its occupants. Soon the dwarf was snoring loudly.

Despite the snoring noise, the downstairs clamors of the tavern drifted up to his ears. It was a low rumble of voices and clanging of tankards being filled with ale. He was just about to drift off to sleep when he heard the guides heading up the stairs. Had Laren returned, he wondered? He didn't hear the man's voice among the group.

To his surprise, he noticed Lar was standing by the door. The entry was just barely ajar. He hadn't even heard the desert man get up. The drylander silently slipped out into the hall-way. Mar crawled over to the door, being careful not to awake the other two. Standing, he carefully eased the door open. He felt Gorg's furry body rub against him. The dog had followed him.

Lar was standing in front of Sari. There was only the two of them barely visible in the dim hallway light. "Does my father know you are here?" the male drylander was whispering to the strikingly beautiful woman.

"He knows I'm in the service of the king," she quietly answered. "You should not be talking to me Larandar. You put our barony at great risk. Yanith does not want our enemies to know Bombia is involved in any way."

"You must help me get out of this, cousin," he was pleading with the woman. "I need to be in Bombia. Enemies are within our country."

"Do not jeopardize this mission," she was shaking her finger at him. "You are sorely needed here. Do not talk to me again. Do as you are told!"

Ah, the Yanith pronouncement - do as you are told. Marth cringed at the words that flooded his thoughts.

"I am leaving for an assignment," Sari told him. "I will see you again. Make Bombia proud Larandar, do not disgrace your father."

He saw the tall man bow. The female drylander reached up touching the white hawk feather stuck in her turban. The desert woman then embraced him. "May Theror and Osiana be with you. You must trust them Sahib, please." With that she turned leaving, but Marth saw tears falling down her lovely shaped face.

Mar suddenly realized Ash was behind him. The male elf had seen it too. For a moment, the elf's violet eyes seemed to brighten, but he was quicker than Marth and was back in his bedroll when Lar returned. Unfortunately, Mar was caught at the door having bumped into his wolfhound as he turned to go.

The tall desert man grabbed him by his shirt. "How dare you eavesdrop on me!" he softly sneered. The man's eyes glowered; his white teeth seemed to curl into a snarl.

The Arthinian's lord's words got stuck in his mouth as a snake that was curled around the drylander's neck reared up, tongue pulsing out, threatening Mar. Gorg immediately let out a low threatening growl.

"Stop, Bishi," Lar ordered the snake. It drew back, so did Gorg who sat quietly next to his master. "Do not mention this to anyone!" the desert man warned. It was a threat delivered with the backup of venom and personal violence. Mar just nodded. The man's anger flooded over him.

Marth crawled back to his bedroll. Gorg curled up next to him. He lay awake a long while, trying to calm his nerves. *What had he gotten himself caught up in?* Marth drifted off to sleep, but it seemed only moments later that the pounding on their door announced it was time to go!

Chapter Seven
The Journey

Sobs wracked the slender, delicately framed woman's body as she lay in the darkened room. Danella had been crying ever since Laren had thrown her unceremoniously into the Inn's rented bedroom. *What has happened to me,* she moaned as her body lay in a fetal position on the straw bed. She hadn't even bothered to use the bedroll that lay still strapped to the

sheepskin knapsack that lay nearby. Her head rested on the
cot's feathered pillow, but unlike the goose down pillows in
the castle, these were filled with chicken feathers. The smell
assaulted Dani's nose causing her to sit up abruptly. "Ugh,"
her pampered stomach turned upside down wanting to throw
up as nausea overcame her mollycoddled senses.

I hate them, her mind reeled in misery. 'Them' seemed
to encompass everyone in the general vicinity. *Those peasants
are disgusting. That dwarf is revolting. How dare he talk to
me, never mind touch me.* Danella's anger bloomed into total
disgust. Every part of her body hurt from red sore crying eyes,
to her tired overtaxed back muscles that hurt from carrying the
dreaded bag. The tender and soft, once beautifully manicured
hands sent pains up to her slender fingers. They were not used
to doing even little chores like carrying a water bucket or
scrubbing her own eating utensils. The Bombian guide, Sari,
had shown Danella little deference on the ship despite being
seasick.

The sea voyage had been a miserable journey. The grubby sleazy deckhands, despite her trying to appear to be a boy,
had easily seen through the disguise. Leering and snide remarks came her way, especially when Sari left her alone. The
dirty lowlife men would "accidentally" bump into her; unwanted hands grabbing her. Danella's mind puked in revul-
sion.

The guide had given her a knife for protection, but the
new recruit could only awkwardly hold it. Dani had spent
most of the voyage awake, fearful of the crew, clutching the
useless weapon. Consequently, the former mage apprentice
was totally exhausted. Dark circles lay around the princess's
once striking green eyes. Now they sluggishly followed Sari's
movements as close as possible, keeping near to the Bombian
for security.

The ship had docked at several ports along the coast.
Every one of the busy harbors terrified her, but at Fasa, which
lay on the border between Lakeland and Hartland, the city
seemed somewhat friendly. The industrious well-organized
merchant city was known for its prosperous elf businesses and
for its many timber-producing mills. Dani had considered re-
belling. The thought of getting back on the ship and of the
relentless bouts of seasickness gave her the courage to attempt

to flee. Her thoughts never got beyond how she'd manage to survive, just the thought of freedom made her run.

When Sari had gone into a shop to buy supplies, Danella ran quickly down the town's wide merchant street. It was not long before she entered a flamboyant booth-laden bazaar. Farmers' wagons with their stinky horses were everywhere selling their produce, hawking loudly for customers. The whole area was crowded with shoppers, all bargaining with deafening shouts aimed at the various vendors. The confusion of the yelling crowd, the bright colorful sights and unusual smells brought her fears to new heights. Panic taking over, Danella hurriedly scuttled down a small tight alleyway trying to escape the chaos.

It wasn't long before the confused princess knew she'd made a mistake. The alley was dirty and garbage littered the ground. Rats and other small rodents were scampering between the rubbish mounds, squealing loudly as they fought over the scraps. She immediately turned around to head back to the bazaar.

To her horror, two bulky shadows blocked the way back. As two men stepped closer, they both wickedly smiled, showing rotten blackened teeth. Dani could smell their rancid body odors even above the garbage stink as they approached her. "What ya doin here girlie?" one of them eyed her leeringly. Both held long nasty blades that they waved in her direction. "Youse will bring a pretty sum," one of them laughed.

"Not before we have some fun," the other sniggered.

She backed up, her eyes on the approaching riffraff. "Leave me alone," the frightened woman yelled. "Help," desperation now taking over. She didn't even recognize her own voice. It sounded strangely distant as the sound echoed off the sides of the alleyway. The few second-floor windows that surrounded the alley suddenly were all quickly closed as the buildings' inhabitants shut themselves away.

"No one gonna help ya, youse little tart," the bigger man laughed.

Dani turned to run, but slipped on the slimy rubbish and went down hard. She lost her breath. The two men stood above, evil wicked thoughts reigning all over their pocked ugly swollen faces.

As one of the men went to grab her, he suddenly stopped and fell backwards. Sari stood behind them, the Bombian's hand tightly clasped on the man's shirt. "Gentlemen, although I use that term lightly, I don't wish to kill you, so leave while you can," her deep desert accent seemed to emphasize her ruthlessness. Her fierce gray eyes took in the surroundings as the pupils darkened to almost black.

"What?" the man that had fallen after Sari had yanked him back, looked confused, but the other roared with laughter.

"Now what ya got here?" his gruff voice roared in amusement. "Another tart? Well ain't this our lucky day. And a foreign tart to boot!"

Both men now faced the Bombian. Sari drew her sabre from her side and waved it in front of both their faces. Then the knife neatly put a nick in each of their arms.

"Think ya know how to use that, lady?" the large man advanced on her. "Youse is gonna pay for that," the ruffian robber said as blood dripped down from the knife wound.

The two thugs tried to surround the female drylander, circling her slowly. As they cautiously approached, Sari deftly tripped one of them, sending him flying into one of the trash heaps, the other she bonked on the head with her weapon's handle. The ruffian fell like a stone, lying unconscious in another rodent infested litter heap.

The first man tried to get up swearing as the drunken lout regained his footing. The Bombian woman, however, jumping upwards, kicked him right in his chest. The scum fell hard against the alley's wall and then joined his companion slipping down to the garbage ridden ground.

Dani was still sitting on the dirt when Sari unceremoniously grabbed her and brushed the princess' clothes off. "You're a foolish girl," the Bombian snapped at her. "I should just leave you. You'd end up on the slave block before the day is over. Laren has no idea what he's getting into!" The drylander shook her head in disgust. "Laren owes me for this. Let's get out of here before someone gets the city guard. I haven't the time to spare on these two vermin."

The princess, her heart still pounding, obediently had followed her guide, now actually clinging to the Bombian for protection. Dani had given Sari no problems after that, sticking as close to her guide as she could. Now the ex-mage princess knew who Laren was and she hated him. *When I return home, I will have him disciplined,* she consoled herself.

Danella's attention became focused on the only dim light in the bedroom; the half opened shuttered window at the far wall. She stood up going over, opening the shutters letting the Viamar Sea winds filter in, giving the room a less stuffy feeling.

Evening was almost full on; the street lanterns were being lit. She leaned out breathing deeply. Her eyes wandered downward to the Inn's entrance. The man called Laren was there talking to an extremely well-dressed elf. Despite the general being rather tall, the elf towered over him as most Hartlanders did. To her experienced noble senses, she knew the elf was someone of importance in the way he handled himself and of the several attendants that surrounded him. It piqued her interest; Danella leaned further out so that she could catch their conversation.

"You must keep your eyes open around the city, Arundenwel." Laren stood stoically in a serious stance before the elegantly clothed Hartland male. "If you see anything unusual, especially in the sea traders, send word to both the King and Baron Falsteff. Let the city's mages know so they may take action. If war comes, Mayor, it will begin here on the coast. Be diligent."

Ah, I was right. It is the ruler of the city, the Mayor. Dani tried to lean even further out the window. Her woes were forgotten as her curiosity got the better of her. She was an expert at gathering castle gossip. To her surprise the head of the city bowed to the general.

"It will be done. Good luck my friend," the refined elf then turned and left. Laren started to look up, so she quickly backed into the shadows of the room. When Dani chanced a glance out again, the overbearing man was gone.

War! Her fingers grabbed onto the windowsill steadying her nerves. *War, the kingdom is at peace, has been at peace for a long time. Why had not her father mentioned this to her?* The minute she thought it, the answer came unwillingly flooding in. Her father would not bother his daughter with such important matters. The king thought her frivolous, someone to be used as a pawn in a good marriage. He'd already indulged his only daughter, letting her study with a Mothia mage.

Her mind reeled at the thought. Tears, once more, flowed down her cheeks. *How could she have been so blinded? I'm a fool,* Dani reluctantly admitted. *A stupid fool! She should have taken the first opportunity at marriage that her father had offered. Now look where she was - a peasant, a lowly soldier recruit!*

Her eyes went to the distant sea. Oaris and Porlis, their two moons, emphasized the water's whitecaps. They were in their full orbs of the light cycle, shining brightly down on the Viamar Sea. One moon followed closely by the other. Porlis followed his wife, never leaving her side. The legends had them as the gods of love and marriage, forever together.

"Help me," the princess pleaded to them. They did not answer her, but then she'd never been a good worshiper despite her once magical abilities. Castle life had been wrapped up in her own concerns not those of the gods. What need did a king's daughter have with the gods? No, she'd get no help from the moon gods. Danella was on her own.

The door opened. The she-elf came into the room followed by the squat female dwarf. Dani just stared briefly at the tall statuesque woman then turned back to window ignoring her roommates. The women held no interest for her. Abruptly two gray owls landed on the windowsill. Dani, startled, drew back almost falling over her cot. The young royal let out a frightened gasp.

The elf let out a laugh. "My, aren't you skittish, afraid of your own shadow. How do they expect to make a soldier out of you?" Again, the woman snickered, "They are only our pet birds, Boris and Hilda. They won't hurt you."

"Keep them away from me," Dani ordered.

The elf called Lura went over to the window. "I have brought you some food." The Hartlander petted the two birds and brought out two chunks of mutton. "They prefer worms," the elf commented, fondly smiling at the pets. Both birds snapped up the offered meat.

The owls seemed to shine, their silvery gray feathers reflecting the moon's rays just as the Viamar Sea had done. Dani had to admit they were quite beautiful, much prettier than her father's hunting falcons. She did notice, however, that they had long sharp claws that clung easily to the windowsill.

"I even brought you something," Lura turned to Dani. In her hand was a brown apple taken from the bowl on their dining table. The princess looked with total disgust at the piece of fruit. It was probably half rotten. Her stomach however, betrayed her as it rumbled in its emptiness.

"Well, if you don't want it." The she elf went to throw it out the window.

"No, wait," Danella loudly said. The hungry woman took the apple. The smell was sharply pungent. It obviously was over ripe. Still, hunger overcomes pickiness and it actually ended up tasting refreshingly good. To her surprise, she ate every last bit of it, just leaving the core stripped clean.

The female elf Hartlander ignored her, rolling out her bedroll on the floor. As the haughty elf washed up by the bucket of water, she turned to Dani. "I wouldn't sleep on that cot, it's made of stale straw. It's probably full of bed bugs. I cannot stop them. Our teacher taught us the …" Lura never finished the sentence yet the sadness in the woman's voice was obvious. "Well, never mind, keep off the straw."

What is she gabbing about, Danella wondered? The princess was missing something, but she had no idea what it was. *Who is this elf?* As princess, she'd met several elfs at court. The king's daughter never liked them. They seemed to think themselves superior - even to her father! *Creatures to be ignored,* her thoughts immediately dismissed the woman.

Dani, however, was also not going to sleep on a hard floor. She'd had enough of hard decks on the ship. Elfs and dwarfs were probably quite used to sleeping on floors. Princesses were not! Danella spread her bedroll on the roughly made straw bed and lay down, this time trying to ignore the smelly chicken feather filled pillow. Sleep came rapidly as her exhausted body surrendered to the peace of past dreams.

It seemed her head had just hit the pillow when loud knocking woke them up. "Get up, meet in the kitchen!" Laren's words were not a suggestion but a command. Lura was immediately up; the elf had not undressed, but had slept in her clothes. Grabbing her bag, the elf quickly left. Natalia followed her out, slinging her backpack on her shoulders. The female dwarf had said very little, seemingly wanting to be ignored.

Dani slowly put on long pants and laced up the deerskin boots over them. Sleep cobwebs clouded her mind. Her body now not only ached, but she itched everywhere. When the new royal recruit descended down into the kitchen, everyone was already eating breakfast. The only people present were the guides and the recruits. Unlike the main dining area, this room had one long table with the scullery surrounding it. Candles dressed the table, as it was still dark out! Danella took the only seat left at the end of trestle. The smell of apple-sweetened porridge assaulted her nose, as did the aroma of fresh baked bread. Maggie, with Tilly helping, was handing out bowls and filling them. When he got to her, the sergeant left her place empty.

Her hunger made her reach out to his arm, stopping him. The stupid dwarf had missed her. "Sorry Lass, no food for you. General's order," came floating out of his thick puffy lips.

Dani's angry eyes focused on Laren, who sat observing them at the end of the long wooden table. The general seemed to ignore her as the princess tried to get his attention. *How dare he. He's punishing me like a child,* her thoughts reeled. *How dare he!* Everyone was snubbing her, all busy eating their breakfasts. Dani had forgotten how she'd ignored them all the night before. *Do as you are told,* flooded into her mind; Yanith's voice seemed to be yelling into her thoughts.

Dani's stomach ached. The remembrance of the apple made it rumble even more. Furthermore, she was itching. Looking down at her arms she noticed several red marks. Lura noticed her predicament. "I tried to warn you." Dani just glared at the elf while scratching her neck. "Don't itch them, rubbing makes it worse," the female Hartlander commented.

"Let's hurry up," Laren was telling them. "We have a long day ahead of us. We will be traveling along the Elmwood coast heading north. Despite Baron Falsteff's best efforts, he cannot keep the wildones or their masters from causing havoc. They raid from the sea. So be sharp!"

"That's not true!" Lura spoke up; once again the proud elf seemed to contradict Laren. "We keep the wildones in check. Our woods are safe!" Dani noticed the other male elf touch her arm trying to calm her.

It was the female mountain dwarf, Maggie that spoke up. "No doubt he's trying, dear, but ya know wese were attacked by the wildones. Evil pirates are coming in off the Viamar. Falsteff hasn't the troops to patrol the entire coast."

"You will find out soon enough," Laren interjected. "Now everyone *eat up!* Tilly will give you the supplies you need, so see him when you are done. Everyone helps carry what we are going to eat."

Supplies, Dani's mind raced, *would they give her no food!* Her stomach rumbled again. Reluctantly, she knew there was no choice. Getting up, the princess walked down to where the dwarf called Huff sat. The portly dwarf was gobbling down his meal.

She stood behind him, but he didn't look up at her. Everyone else did though. The whole table was looking at her! Her hand tentatively reached out to him, touching him lightly on the arm. Still, he ignored the poke. *Damn!* She again tapped him with her hand. The portly dwarf turned around and seemed startled, drawing back from her. What did he think? Was she was going to throw something at him? *For a moment Dani wished she had something to heave at the damn peasant.* But the little common sense the spoiled king's daughter had took over.

"I am ...." she almost choked on the word, "sorry." She looked over at Laren who seemed to say he wanted more. Taking a deep breath, she continued, "I should not have done what I did." Again, Laren seemed not satisfied. "I AM REALLY SORRY!" Dani looked more at the general than the dwarf, spitting the words out forcefully.

"It's alright, lass," Huff responded after he'd looked over at the other female dwarf as if asking what he should do. It was the nod from Laren, however, that Danella noticed.

The princess returned to her seat. Tilly placed a bowl of gruel in front of her and a large piece of bread. Dani took no notice of the brown pieces of apple floating in the oatmeal. She ate every bit of her peasant food, her thankful stomach sighing in relief.

"Let's move, recruits," Laren urgently yelled down the table. Everyone was led out a back door. All candles were extinguished. It was still dark, but the moons were gone and dawn seemed nearby. The birds were waking up; the night's chill was still in the air. Everyone put on their sheepskin vests. Tilly went to each of them. Their backpacks got a couple of bags of beans, a good size chunk of cheese and some wrapped bread. They all filled their water sacks from the community water well.

Dani looked for Sari, but the woman was not with them. Panic almost took over as she realized her protective guide was no longer there to watch over her. All the other guides were. Her hand pulled on Laren's sleeve, "Where is Sari?" she blurted out.

"It's none of your concern," he barked. Danella drew back, not used to being snapped at with such disregard to her station. Her eyes went wide as her hands dropped; her mouth gaped open in astonishment. It was in that moment that the pampered spoiled woman realized she was no longer "the princess" but just a plain recruit. Her whole body seemed to shrink in the realization. Then the general's eyes lost their anger, he seemed to soften slightly, "You'll have plenty of protection, Dani. If it makes you feel better, keep close to Ok-ste. If I may take this opportunity to point out that the faster you learn to protect yourself the better off you'll be."

She glared at him. The frightened woman had no intention of getting anywhere near the barbarian. The Okian mountain men's reputation of savagery was well known. Her father had tried to recruit some of them for his army. He had given up the thought as their allegiance was only to themselves and not to the DeLak Kingdom, never mind the king thought them not trainable. Dani was not getting anywhere near the giant uncouth man.

The royal instead followed closely behind the man they called Lar. Despite him smelling of sheep, there was a refinement about him. Yet, he had the same ruthless aura as did Sari. He reminded her of the absent Bombian guide.

Laren and Schaller took the lead with the dwarfs, Tilly, Maggie and Mathie taking the rear. The group of fourteen quietly left the city and headed north following the Viamar coast. Schaller was their scout, often forging ahead with the Okian barbarian close behind. The two men would return giving Laren updates on what lay ahead. Often, the Kazian scout trekker would have a black good-sized raven or a large white-headed eagle on his shoulder. To Dani's amazement, the man seemed to be conversing with the birds!

The pace was fast and she found herself almost running to keep up with the long-legged man in front of her. The two elfs were right behind and kept almost bumping into her, making Dani hasten even more. At one point, all three collided together. Lar had helped her up while the elfs sputtered at her physical ineptitude. His sandy gray slanted eyes seemed to bore right through her. Yet unlike the elfs, he did not seem to berate her slowness. His hands were strong, easily lifting her back on her feet.

Her own legs ached when they stopped as the sun was mid-point. Stopping made her once more focus on her bug bites. "Lura is right, do not scratch them," a voice floated down to her as she miserably sat on one of the protruding rocks that seemed to dot the area.

Dani looked up into the blackest eyes she'd ever seen. His whole being was dark including his onyx colored curls. The man named Mar was standing over her. He was solidly built with large hands and broad shoulders. Despite his ominous serious looks, he had a scholarly manner to him. His monstrous wolf sat next to him. The dog's eyes matched its master's, foreboding and dangerous. Frightened, she scrambled to her feet, desperately looking for assistance. "I have some ointment," he continued and held out a vial. "I made the same mistake my first night in Osceta." Dani looked at him, not moving to take the much-needed medicine.

"Oh, for Theror's sake!" came from behind her as Lura stepped forward. She looked at Mar and grabbed the vial. "Take the medicine, you idiot!" The tall female elf forced the bottle into Dani's hand. The king's daughter looked puzzling at the medicine. She had ladies-in-waiting that fawned over her. The pampered royal hadn't the slightest sense of how to take care of herself.

Lura grabbed the vial, "Turn around you dunce. I'll help you put the ointment on." When Dani just stood there the female elf forcibly whirled her around. Lauranna began to apply the cream on her back. Immediate relief! The princess couldn't help but emit a sigh. "Now put this everywhere else! Go behind that bush there!" The disgust in Lura's voice pierced Dani's pride, but the relief the cream gave to the itchy sores made her head for the bush.

Dani felt like a scolded child and blushed profusely, but did as Lura had said. When she entered back into the clearing, everyone was eating. Her body felt so much better. Relief! As the royal emerged from behind the bush, she noticed the smile on the dark man's normal serious look. Danella wanted to slap the smirk off him even though he'd given her the medicine. *He's mocking me!* She frowned deeply. Tears came to her eyes as she realized they were all half smiling. *They are all mocking me!*

Each ate some cheese and a little of their bread that was already getting hard. Dani, despite having no appetite, forced herself to eat, as she felt light headed. The small woman called Lori had encouraged everyone to take enough water. "We will be coming on to a large lake later this evening," the slight almost childlike figure had explained in her lyrical high voice. "You'll be able to refill your water pouches then. So, it's alright to drink as much as you want." Despite her small slight stature, the woman was full of energy. The fast-paced trek did not seem to bother her at all. Dani envied her self-assurance despite the woman's physical disadvantage.

Close to sunset, the group had stopped in a clearing that was surrounded by thick scrub brush. Nearby was a good-sized lake of fresh water. Maggie took charge of setting up the camp. A small fire was soon blazing onto which the pudgy female dwarf had put a large clay pot. A sizeable bag of beans and a handful of dried salted venison was emptied into the cooking crock that set everyone stomach growling as the smell of the stew reached their noses.

"Youse got a little time. Head to the pond and wash up. Women first," Maggie yelled out. "I'll have the grub ready when youse get back."

Lura, Dani, Natalia and Lori all headed toward the refreshing water. "Wait," Laren ordered. "Mar, have Gorg go along. He'll be a good guard." With a wave of his hand, Marth sent his wolfhound with them.

As the huge guard dog trotted up to the fairo, she put up her hand. "It's not that far, let the wolf have his dinner," Lori commented, but the fierce dog had already moved to take the lead without Mar saying a word. Her pink eyes floated down to the wolf, something passed between her and the animal. The fairo's small hand scratched his ear. "Okay, boy, let's go." The pain in Marth's eyes was so evident as he watched his pet follow the small woman. Dani wondered why Marth seemed so bothered by his wolf's closeness to Lori.

"Don't be too long," Mathie yelled after them. "We'd like a dip too!"

Dani marveled at the huge oak trees that lined the outer rim of the clearing. She noticed Lura touch each one - then frown. The same pain that had been in Mar's eyes seemed to enter the she-elf. "I miss you, damn that mage," she heard the lanky silvery woman say after leaving an exceptionally large oak. They followed a good-sized stream which led them down to a crystal-clear lake that seemed to invite a much-needed cool swim.

"The trees will return to you," Lori commented as they came upon the large pond. "Be patient, Lura. Find it in yourself to enjoy life without magic."

Dani's ears picked up as the word "magic" entered her thoughts. "What do you mean?" She followed the woman down to the fresh water, her interest perked at the thought of *magic*. Lura was already out of her clothes and into the water. Natalia had quickly followed. "What do you mean?" Danella shouted as she followed the small guide down to the edge of the lake.

"I give the same advice to you Dani," Lori's pink eyes glowed. The princess did not reply as two wings appeared behind the small woman as she disrobed. Danella stared, not believing her eyes as the fairo dove into the water.

"What?" Dani stood there totally unable to think of anything else to say.

"She's from the Fairy Folk, you dunce," Lura yelled at her. "Now hurry up and wash up."

Danella had never disrobed in front of anyone. She hesitatingly removed her clothes, blushing profusely and hurriedly ran into the water, covering herself as quickly as possible.

"Good grief, you really are covered in bug bites," Natalia swam up to her. "When we get out, let me help you. I'm a healer."

"A healer?" Lura had come up next to them. "Really? You still can heal? Did Yanith not take away your powers?"

"No, I'm not supposed to be here," the perky cute dwarf answered. "But then, I'm untrained. However, I can help a little, I have no staff."

"Ah, so you're a natural, a raw one," Lori had swum over to them with Gorg treading water next to her. The four women stood in a circle as the cool water splashed teasingly around their bare shoulders.

"I know not what you speak of," Natalia admitted. "My family is quite ashamed of it."

"Such ignorance. My folk wonder at the stupidity of the kingdom's races." Lori angrily sputtered out and swam away. Anger seemed to radiate off the fairo.

They finished washing in silence and once again returned to the beach. Lura, Lori and Natalia took their time, letting themselves dry, taking spare clothes out of their packs, washing their old clothes out in the pond. Dani, however, embarrassed at her nakedness quickly dressed, getting her newly gotten clothes damp. She watched the others wash their old clothes and did the best she could to mimic their actions. The princess had never washed clothes in her entire life. Yet she did it, a new recognition had come.

Natalia had walked up, "Let me have your hand."

Dani stared at her. *No one touches me!*

It was Lura who once again spoke up, "Don't be a silly goose. What harm can she do you?" She grabbed the king's daughter's arm and held it out to the small woman dwarf.

Natalia took the hand. A sweat appeared on the perky woman's cute face as the dwarf seemed to deeply concentrate. Dani suddenly felt such total relief as the bug bites healed and then disappeared. She looked at the dwarf in amazement.

"Say *thank you*," Lura smacked her on the back. "Stop being such a stupid dunce."

"Thank, thank you," Dani managed to get out. Natalia smiled and then sat down catching her breath.

Gorg had shaken himself dry and waited patiently as the women gathered their packs. As they turned to leave, the dog let out a deep growl. His haunches went up as he stared intently into the surrounding wood.

"Something is coming!" Lori yelled. "The wolf says it's dangerous. Get behind me!"

From the woods came a troll. A large wrinkled greenish skinned monster. It stomped his way into the pathway leading back to the camp. The troll was immense, towering over them. The brute's arms dangled down to the ground, dragging in the sand as it slogged toward them. Drool flowed freely from its wide grin. Large pointed brackish yellow teeth showed as it drew back it's black lips.

Dani lost her breath. It was a terrifying sight. The wolf-hound attacked immediately biting one of the ugly giant's legs. A piercing howl came from the troll as it tried to grab onto the animal. Gorg, however, had already backed off, easily missing the swinging arms and attacked the troll from behind, jumping high onto its back as the troll swung down to turn.

Lori had also immediately taken to the air, flying high enough to stab the troll's neck with her knife. Again, another loud howl, as the monster started to swat at her. Despite trying to get out of its way, he slightly brushed the fairo sending her flying back into one of the big oak trees. She had grabbed on to one of the large branches trying to catch her breath.

Lura drew her bow and sent arrows were flying. Despite several hits, the troll turned back to them with Gorg on its back, the monster advanced toward the women. Natalia had retrieved a knife from her bag and bravely ran forward stabbing the troll's feet.

The mammoth grabbed her, lifting the small dwarf in his grasp. Lura let an arrow fly and hit monster's hand that was squeezing Natalia. He howled, flinging the dwarf and glared at the she-elf. He stomped forward, now intent on Dani and Lura. Natalia lay unconscious where he had thrown her.

Gorg was still hanging onto his back. The wolf had crawled itself up towards the troll's head. The hound's large jaws clamped down on the beast's neck. Green blood spurted from the large gap in the wound. Howling, the troll reached up and grabbed the dog with Lura's arrow still protruding from its long-fingered hand.

It violently shook Gorg, but the dog bit down on the monster's thumb. It made the troll drop the hound, but it tried to stomp on the animal with one of its two enormous cloven feet. Two gray owls attacked, using their clawed feet to tear at the troll's head. One of the long arms of the monster hit one of the birds, sending it flying into the trees.

From the woods Laren, Huff, Lar and Tilly leading the group ran out. First the men hacked at the troll's legs with their swords, while Huff swung his axe. Maggie ran over to the two women placing herself protectively in front of them. Schaller and Mar attacked from the front, aiming at the swinging arms. It was the giant Okste that jumped on the troll's back, bringing the monster down and then rolling on top of him. Ash and Lar, running up, pierced the trolls head with their knives. Lar kept hacking forcefully as if he'd done it before. The monster finally lay dead.

It was over, but not without consequences. Lori climbed down from the tree; one of her wings had been slightly ripped. Ash was bleeding from a cut on his forehead. Marth had run over to Gorg. The dog whimpered with a hurt leg. Huff's arm was bleeding. Natalia was stunned, slowly getting up, holding her head. They all stood dazed and speechless as green slime covered their clothing.

Dani stood silent being able to have done little to help. She ran over to Lar, who was favoring his leg. The desert man's eyes were blazing as he clutched his sword. She drew back as a black snake slithered around the desert man's neck and hissed as Dani came close. Frightened, the royal daughter quickly drew back.

Dani sat on the ground, drew her legs up to her chest and cried. She felt disoriented, scared and completely useless. Her eyes scanned the group, taking them all in. They had all helped; all had taken part to defeat that horrible creature. The feeling of being left out overwhelmed her. *I will change. I WILL BELONG.*

Chapter Eight
The Trek

Marth quickly washed off the green slime that covered most of his outfit at the edge of the lake, as did the others. Even Lori, after climbing down from the tree, had hobbled down to rid herself of the troll's blood. Huff was assisting the still disoriented Natalia who was holding her sore head. Still,

Laren, shouting orders, was hurrying them back to camp. The general was worried about another attack.

"Trolls can be loners, but it's not more trolls I'm worried about. Their controllers cannot be far behind. This troll's masters are probably Bracaard raiders coming off the coast to cause havoc in the elfs' Hartland. They come through the Elmwood Forest attacking the outlying elf villages then retreat again to the sea before Baron Falsteff can send his guards."

Mar noticed the look of alarm on Lura and Ash's faces. The she-elf went to reply, but the male elf touched her arm as if to warn her not to say anything. She shook her head disgustingly at her brother. Marth noticed and thought, *I'm sure now that the two are indeed sister and brother and I'd bet twins too!* His own sister Lilith came to mind, he'd done the same thing when the young girl disagreed with their over demanding father. His young sibling had entered his head often on the journey up the coast of Hartland's Barony, especially with the young small woman that had come off the ship with Sari. He worried how Lilith was handling his father without him being there to intercede.

He glanced over at the pale woman who was sobbing slightly as she sat on the ground hugging her legs. The friable figure kept reminding him of his sister, fragile and innocent in a weird way as if the world was totally new to her. Dani, they called her, but the name didn't fit. It was not flimsy enough, perhaps Miral would be better, the name of their wind god - flighty and frail. Yet, the goddess hid her breeze's hearty strength until it roared forward.

He had tried to help the woman; she was suffering so much from the bug bites. Dani shunned him, however. He'd even tried to befriend her, but the bitter look she'd given his assistance kept him at bay. Her fear of Gorg was evident. For Theror sake, the girl was afraid of her own shadow. *What kind of sheltered life had the woman led? Where did she come from? One of the spoiled royalties?* Marth bet he was correct, remembering that he, himself came from privilege.

Marth noticed Lar had gone over to the dead monster, scrutinizing it closely. "This one came from beyond the Western Ridge. They are bigger than the southern region's trolls," the drylander had explained. Mar was sure now that the man was totally Bombian. Mar recognized the deep foreign desert accent. The king's language was new to the drylands' barony. Lar's words seemed strange and forced as if the words did not come naturally.

Lar continued as he jumped down from the troll's body, "How did this monstrosity get here? They aren't the smartest creatures in the world. They've been attacking Bombian spice caravans all summerseason." Lar's words made Marth know he'd been right about the man. The Arthinian had seen the desert man wield his sword effectively and powerfully against the troll. The man was a good experienced fighter despite his young age! Had he come from the Bombian army forces?

General Laren had just shaken his head at the desert recruit, "The Bracaard pirates have bribed them with promises of gold. The trolls love gold. Although dumb, the monsters are fierce obedient mercenaries."

Marth, after helping kill the troll, had immediately gone over to Gorg. The wolf's leg seemed broken. When he tried to get his pet to stand, his back leg just hung there. To his relief, the giant Okian had come over and had carried the animal back to camp. The huge barbarian had no trouble lifting the massive hound. Gorg whimpered lightly in pain as the two headed for the encampment.

Marth watched Lar go over to Dani. The woman drew back as if the desert man scared her to death. The Arthinian went over, "You can't stay here. Come with us!" The young lord held out his hand. Her eyes were dull and seemed uncomprehending. Mar took one of her shoulders and Lar took the other, lifting the slight woman onto her feet.

"Don't touch me!" the small woman screamed. "Keep that snake away from me!"

For the first time, Mar saw the desert man smile. "Bishi, come out and meet Dani." A black slithering snake came out of the drylander's vest pocket and went up his arm to his neck, curling around his master's ears affectionately. "He is my pet, he will not harm you." The words rang out with truth and conviction.

Still Dani backed up bumping into Mar as the snake picked up its head and its bright yellow rimmed eyes actually looked straight at her. Instead of scaring him, the reptile fascinated the Arthinian lord. Mar trusted the drylander. It settled in his mind that the man was honorable. He held out his hand.

The snake curled up the Arthinian's arm. "What type is it? Arthinia has lots of snakes in the hill land but none like this." He held onto the squirreling Dani with his other arm, as she pulled hard to get away, but Mar easily could keep the scrawny woman in tow.

"It's an Isso, a desert dweller. My pet is poisonous, but it is also well trained. This snake will not hurt anyone unless I tell it to. My pet would die before it harmed the woman," Lar nodded toward Dani.

The words seemed to settle the girl down. She now just stared wide-eyed at the snake in Mar's hand. Marth handed the snake back and watched, fascinated as it returned to Lar's pocket. Dani unfortunately had to be dragged to camp between the two men. They were the last of the group to return. She withdrew to the farthest corner of their campsite as far away from the others as possible.

Mar went immediately to Gorg. Lori, her bent wing limply hanging by her side, was over the animal petting it. "He's hurt his leg badly," the fairo informed Marth. The fairy could not keep her own pain out of her voice. "Natalia will help as soon as she's done with Lar's leg."

"Natalia?" the Arthinian looked over at the quiet female dwarf who was wrapping the desert man's leg. Laren was helping her, providing the bandages from his pack. Marth had not paid much attention to the "extra" dwarf as she had kept to the shadows, seemingly not wanting to be noticed. Her strong bond to the other dwarf recruit was evident.

"She's a healer, an untrained healer, but she's strong," Lori added. "We are lucky she followed Huff. The gods have sent her," the fairo gratefully acknowledged.

"And have they sent you too? Why are you not with your tribe?" The reclusive fairy folk he'd met in the Arthinian backland remote hills came to his mind. The Fairy Folk did not like to mingle with the other races, even preferring the wild wolves to anyone else. In some ways, they were more prideful than the elfs.

"Perhaps Osiana gives me my path," her light rosy eyes seemed to wander back to her home. "I feel my kin are wrong. We cannot hide from this growing evil that is coming from beyond the western ridge and from beyond the Viamar Sea. The foul stench will also eventually come for us too. We cannot fight against demons. The Fairy Folk think themselves safe within their magic, but it will fail them. Yanith knows it, so I follow him."

She said nothing further as Natalia cautiously approached Gorg. The female dwarf reached out her stubby hand to touch the dog, but the wolf let out a deep growl. "Stop, Gorg, stop," Marth sternly told his pet. It was Lori, however, that seemed to quiet the animal. The fairo bent down looking deeply into the hound's eyes and then breathed upon him. The smell of lavender came wafting up. Gorg fell sound asleep.

Natalia looked at the fairo in wonder, "You put him to sleep!"

Lori smiled, "Yes, hurry though. The spell will not last for long."

The female dwarf took Gorg's leg in her hands. She seemed to stretch it out then rubbed it. Sweat poured from the woman's brow as she intensely concentrated. "Get me a stick, about as long as my arm," she told Marth. When he'd found one, the inexperienced healer took a piece of wide bandage cloth and rope, tying it securely to the dog's lower leg. "I think this will work, although I've never worked on a wolf before. I have set the broken bone in place." The dwarf looked up, "The procedure works on our rams though."

Ah, Marth reflected upon her words, *so she's not from Erry but from the western part of the Great Northern sheep filled mountains.*

The healing did work as Gorg awoke shaking his head then slowly got up and with some hesitancy stood. The dog slightly limped, but he could walk.

When Natalia tried to help Lori, the fairo shook her head. "You're magic cannot be used on me. I'll heal, but it will take time." With a look of great pain the tiny woman folded her wings. Marth was amazed at how well the wings fit to her back. Once Lori put on her cape the thin membranes became imperceptible.

"Everyone grab something to eat and fill your water pouches in the nearby stream. Then we need to move on, we can't stay here," Laren informed them as he already was storing everything in his bag. "Maggie, pack everything up and make sure we cover that fire. Leave no trace we've been here." The pudgy female dwarf just nodded and started placing her cooking utensils away.

"Mathie, get me some leaves to cover all this up," she ordered her husband. The dwarf immediately set off gathering enough leaf coverage to hide their presence.

"You must be kidding," Huff loudly spouted out, nervously stroking his briskly red beard and touching the bandage on his forehead. "We need to rest. Nightfall will be coming soon and we haven't even eaten yet. We can't trek through these woods in the dark. Look at us, half are hurt."

"We can and you will!" Laren snapped. "Unless you'd like to fight the invaders. Make no mistake, they will find that troll and will be tracking us. None of us are in any shape to fight a band of Bracaards, never mind what abominations they have with them."

They paired off, keeping close together and set off into the darkening woods. Laren no longer kept to the coast but headed inland. The trees became congested, blocking even the fading light high above them. The two owls clung to the two elfs' shoulders, disagreeing by chirping loudly before they flew off. Gorg hobbled next to Marth, but kept up. Looking at his limping hound, the Arthinian silently thanked the gods for the female dwarf healer.

Lar and Mar also kept Dani between them. To his surprise she gave no objection. The Arthinian did notice the small woman took two steps to each of the men's, but she silently kept up. Not once did she complain or ask them to slow down. *She's so frightened,* Mar conjectured. *She's afraid to lose us and be left behind.* One look at the delicate pale face showed that the woman was exhausted. *Fear is keeping her going,* he thought. The entire group was living on fear to keep going. The thought of the Bracaards catching up with them kept the march at a fast pace.

The group silently continued through the night - most of the time groping along and stumbling over branches. They finally stopped near dawn. Every last person was bushed. Laren and Schaller took the first watch as each of the company just lay close together not even pitching out their bedrolls but sleeping where their bodies had dropped.

The sun was high up when Mar awoke. His eyes opened to Dani's wide eyes watching him from where she lay close by. He wondered how long the woman had been awake. Her soft emerald eyes were more alert and had less fear in them. *Maybe she's come to terms with this,* the Arthinian hoped.

Lar was on the other side of her, sitting up. In his long-fingered hands was a steaming mug. As Mar rose Maggie came over with a pot full of hot vegetable and bean broth. To his surprise, the soup was amazingly filling. He noticed Dani ate every last drop, dipping a small piece of her bread and gobbling the potage down. Her eyes were intensely watching the camp as she took in the rest of the group.

Ash was handing Lura her cup. The she-elf kept glancing over to where Laren was talking to their guide. The owls were nowhere to be seen.

The general was talking animatedly with Schaller. To his surprise, a good-sized white headed bald eagle was on the arm of their scout. That explained the absence of the owls. The two bird species were rivals. The man, Schaller, puzzled him. The scout obviously was an avian raconteur, yet unlike the fairo, Marth felt no magic associated with him.

The lank tall fellow had a mysterious dark presence that hung protectively around his very being. He projected the same warrior acuteness that Lar did. The man was a keen skilled soldier. Laren obviously thought highly of him, often consulting the man before setting their course. Now it seemed the man was once again conversing with the large predatory bird. Their guide was then talking to Laren, explaining what the eagle was telling him. The Okian barbarian stood close by seeming to also be intensely listening.

"Our best course is to head due north. The eagle says there are bands of pirates roaming along the coast, probably trying to cut us off. We need to reach the eastern frontier as fast as we can," Schaller was urgently explaining. "The invaders are scared of the Wildmen. Safety lies in The Wild borders."

Ash interrupted the two men. "We are safer in the Hartland, no one goes near The Wild, no one. These people are the enemies of our barony. They are enemies of the DeLak Kingdom, like the Bracaards. Let's return to Elvasor. We can get Baron Falsteff to help us."

"No Ash, there is no safety in the Hartland for us. The elfs will soon have enough problems just to take care of themselves," Laren patiently explained. "It is to The Wild we must run. Prepare to leave, keep your wits about you!"

With Schaller and Okste forging ahead, their leader drove them due north. The farther they went north the smaller the trees became. They left the ash and oak trees of Hartland behind as pine scrub took over. The terrain became rugged and uneven. The cooler winds picked up, reminding them that the ocean breezes were drifting in.

When the group finally stopped for the night, they lay among large boulders that marked the boundary of the elf's land. They were approaching the far eastern border of the Elmwood forest, the very edge of the elf's Hartland Barony.

"We should not be here," Lura said as they ate their thick bean meal around a small campfire, giving the chunks of salted mutton to their owls. The night was chilly, all got as close as they could to the little warmth the fire provided. "The elfs are forbidden in this part of the Elmwood," Lura urgently pressed. "Man-hating massive white wolves, huge boars and the Wildmen are just across the border. People say even the deer and elk are unfriendly."

"The Wildmen ain't crazy about us dwarfs either," Maggie interjected as she stirred the beans. "But as long as wese are with Laren, wese be fine. So, don't be worryin ya pretty head off, my dear."

Neither Lura nor Ash looked convinced, even their returned owls looked skeptical as they nervously fluttered their wings. The birds' wide eyes seemed worried, taking the entire group in. They were the perfect pets for the elf twins - proud and haughty.

Mar had to admit he was nervous. Even in Arthinia they'd heard of "The Wild". It was an untamed wilderness, which included the mysterious Gray Islands that lay just beyond their coasts. Because of the unpredictable whirlwinds and sudden storms, no one ventured near the small shrouded misty clouded isles. The Wild's coastline was un-navigable. Plain and simple, no one went there.

When the company awoke in the morning, the area was covered in fog. Everyone felt damp and disheveled as the group trekked more easterly toward The Wild border. Mar's joints ached from lying on the cold ground. Gorg stiffly stretched, his leg seemed better. Midday, the group came upon the wide turbulent Mad River that marked the end of the Elf's territory and the beginning of the territory known as "The Wild".

The Great Mountain tributary was aptly named, as the expanse was turbulent with huge boulders sticking out of the river bed creating numerous nasty rapids. The waterway cascaded over the rocks spraying them all with a cold mist. The river looked un-crossable and dangerous.

Single file they followed the rocky shoreline. The inside of their boots were soaked and big droplets fell from their eyelids as the dampness clung to each traveler. Only Lar seemed to enjoy the wetness. The desert man seemed to marvel at the presence of water everywhere. Perhaps the stark difference with his own dry barony stuck in the drylander's mind.

Schaller stopped them near what appeared to be a narrowing that preceded the top of a gushing waterfall. Hefty boulders stuck prominently across the opening making a precarious pathway across the water.

"We cross here," Laren shouted above the roar of the water. "Make sure your packs are well secured."

"You have ta be kiddin," Mar heard Huff sputter. The portly dwarf was defiantly standing right next to the Arthinian, his fist closed as if angrily disagreeing with the decision to cross. The Erryian's arm was protectively around a frightened looking Natalia. "We can't cross, we'll all drown or even worse plunge over the falls. I don't swim!"

Marth agreed. One slip and they would go over into the dangerous rapids below. It was the Okian that first defy skipped across the opening using the rocks as stepping-stones. The big man carried a thick rope that was held at the other end by Schaller. The giant stood at the far shore tightening the rope around a large fir tree until it was taut. Schaller pulled tight, testing it. "Okay, ready," their guide waved them on. The tall scout was holding on to the safety line, as there was no place on this side to anchor the rope.

"Watch me, do the same as I do when you cross," Laren explained as the man entered the river holding onto the rope. The general quickly crossed clinging to the security line.

Next Lura, followed by Ash, stepped forward. Both owls had flown across on their own and waited in an overhanging tree branch. The agile elfs easily went to the other side hardly using the line. Huff and Natalia went next. Huff fell, but the female dwarf grabbed him, forcing his hand back on the rope. Laren helped them get up the last few steps.

Marth looked down at Gorg. How was he going to get the wounded animal across the water overpass? The wolf was too heavy for him to carry. To his surprise, Okste came skipping back and grabbed Gorg. He put one of his massive arms around the dog and then once again deftly crossed.

Mar started to head over, but his eyes went back to Dani who stood frozen to the ground. Lar was trying to take her arm, but she'd shake her head furiously. Marth returned. "I'll carry you across," he told her. "Get on my back, hold tight."

She shook her head vigorously no. It was Tilly that settled it, "You either go with Mar or I'll have Okste come get you." Terror filled her eyes as she realized the barbarian would take her across like the giant had taken the dog. The alarming thought made up her mind. She climbed onto Mar's back.

The woman was amazingly light. He hadn't realized just how little there was of her. The rocks felt slippery with slimy moss keeping him off balance, but the rope helped. Marth cautiously stepped from one rock to the other. The roar of the waterfall was deafening yet he could hear the terrified girl's breathing heavily in his ear. They were almost across when he felt her arms slip; her hands tightly gripped his throat, choking off his air. The Arthinian almost lost his balance.

Suddenly, he felt her lifted higher. Her arms once again went around his shoulders giving him back his breath. Lar had followed right behind the two and had pushed Dani upwards. Marth quickly took the last few steps grabbing onto the general's outstretched arm.

He fell forward onto his knees, gasping for breath. The slight woman rolled off him. By the time he'd gotten enough strength to stand Lori, Maggie and Mathie had also made it over. Tilly came last, transpiring the stone walkway easily as if he'd done it many times.

Laren led them up a well-used pathway to an overhanging cliff. It was dryer and offered relief from the cold wind. He gave them all a much-needed rest. Everyone took some bread and cheese. Maggie, after setting a small fire, passed out a hot clear broth that helped chase away the bone chill that had taken over their wet bodies.

To Marth's surprise, Dani had come up and sat next to him. "Thank you," she managed to get out between chattering teeth. He felt bad for her; her body was violently shivering. *She's going to catch a bad chill,* he thought. The Arthinian lord reached into his bag, taking out his extra dry shirt. "Put this on," he handed it to her.

She started to shake her head, but Lura who was sitting on the other side of him, yelled at her, "Don't be stupid, put it on. You'll get sick and then where will we all be! Of course, if you want the barbarian to carry you…"

He marveled at the elf who, once again, had taken charge of the small woman. It was not like an elf to bother with anyone other than their own kind. Yet, the elf seemed to have taken Dani under her wing talking to the small woman like she was a child. The barbarian threat worked since the small woman had taken his shirt and put it on. It was way too big, but he could tell it helped to warm her body. The shivers subsided.

When they continued, the sun had burnt off the fog. The summercycle warmth was much needed and welcomed as they headed into the land known as "The Wild". The area flattened the further they went from the river. Huge boulders became smaller rocks that led down into a thick forest of fir trees. Marth was surprised when the forest opened up into a wide plain. The meadow was expansive, the wind blowing across the tops of the high grasses. The return of ash and willow trees was a welcomed sight. The warm breeze helped dry out his damp clothes. Marth kept catching movement on either side of the group. Gorg was growling, barring his teeth at the surrounding field. Once more the Arthinian lord missed the mental bond with his pet. What was the dog seeing?

Schaller led them into the field keeping a brisk pace. The Okian followed close by, his huge body parting the grassland easily. The rest had to plow their way through. The smell of the rich pastureland vegetation filled Mar's nose. He felt disoriented, as it was impossible to see over the tall plants. Thus, he was totally surprised when the young lord realized a large band of Wildmen had surrounded the group.

Toweringly tall, skeleton-thin men and women, all pointing long sharp spears in their direction, completely encircled
them. Marth had never seen anything like these fierce looking
fighters. Each was covered from head to toe in animal furs.
Their long black bear capes dragged on the ground. In their
other hand was held a crude shield that they protectively held
in front of them. Each face, male or female, was decorated in
white paste. Their pure yellow diamond shaped eyes were
ringed in white. Their furry ears were canine like, prominently
pointed upwards. The most disturbing feature, however, was
their long jagged teeth that protruded beyond their lips. To
make matters worse, several large white wolves roamed
among them, snarling at the intruders.

The group all surged together forming an informal protective circle. The recruits had their weapons in their hands,
even Dani had her knife pointed in front of her. Laren held up
his hands. "All of you, put down your weapons. They mean us
no harm." Everyone did, but the two elfs, who continued to
point their armed bows at the Wildmen. "Lura, Ash, I said to
put your weapons down!" It was the sharp command from the
general that finally made the elfs reluctantly lower their weapons.

Deep guttural words flowed from the Wild group as they
also lowered their spears. An extra tall woman stepped forward. The Wildwoman spoke excellent king's language, "Lar-
en, first dwarfs and now more elfs!" A massive white she-wolf
stood close by her, baring its teeth at Lura and Ash.

"They mean The Wild no harm," the general waved his
arms toward his soldiers. "We have discussed this before
Sarura, you and the elfs will one day stand together, or die
together. The Bracaards will not distinguish between you."

Lori stepped forward. When the tiny woman came front
and center, every Wildperson knelt and bowed their head. The
fairo rubbed the huge white she-wolf's ears and the animal
amazingly licked her hand.

"Welcome, great mother," Sarura bowed even lower.
"We are once more honored by your presence."

"We look forward to your father's hospitality," Lori
touched the woman's forehead. "Osiana be with you my
daughter," giving her the god's formal blessing. "We are tired,
it has been a long hard trip to come to your great land."

"Then come. My father will be glad to see you. The Chieftain hungers for news of the outside world. You know the way." The Wildwoman turned and disappeared into the high grass, as did the entire warrior group.

Schaller did indeed know the way as the scout forged forward. It was not long before the trekkers came upon a well-traveled pathway that became a rugged dirt roadway. The thoroughfare was full of Wildpeople, all carrying different types of crops such as squash, grain and even ears of corn. One tall skinny woman pushed a small cart full of poultry eggs. The Wildpeople took a wide berth of the group, yet Marth noticed none seemed surprised at seeing them.

When the company entered the settlement, both sides of the main village square were packed with spectators. He was surprised to see so many happy healthy-looking children running among the adults. White wolves, along with their cubs, also mingled easily among the villagers. Some of the cubs were playing freely with their human toddlers, rolling good-naturedly on the ground. The she-wolves were keeping them all under their watchful eyes. *By Theror, the wolves are acting like nannies,* Marth thought.

Along with their elders, all the youngsters had white painted faces. Every villager wore animal bones as necklaces, bracelets and earrings. Unlike the warriors, many of the adult villagers did not wear long bear capes but were decked out in lighter animal skin layers. The tall thinness of the Wildpeople became very evident. Without the heavy coverings, one could see how bony and long limbed they were. The resemblance to their wolves became very apparent as the wolf-like ears, pointed teeth and paw-like furry hands showed the unmistakable canine bond.

The group of fourteen stood in the middle of the square, surrounded completely by the village's inhabitants. Part of the group parted as an extremely tall slender man stepped forward. The chieftain was dressed from head to toe in a black bruin cape, including wearing the head of a snarling bear on top, making the man seem even taller.

The Wildman stood intensely staring at each one. Then he smiled; his long tooth grinned seemed more like a sneer, his furry paw-like hand thoughtfully went to his chin. His hearty amusing laughter, however, rang loud relieving the built-up tension. Like his daughter, a huge white wolf sat at his side baring it sharp teeth. "Welcome to Westwood," his long tooth smile seemed thoughtful as his yellow diamond shape eyes took them all in. "Well, my friend Laren, what have you brought this time?"

"My greetings, Chief Thira. Once again, I bring warriors to train. I bring more to help you fight the evil that is coming from across the great sea. The king sends his greetings and hopes to visit you soon." Laren widely smiled, bowing his head as he did so.

The king, Marth was shocked. *The king has an alliance with The Wild? Like the Bracaards, aren't they the kingdom's enemies - weren't they?*

"Ah yes, my new friend, the king," the words were mockingly said. "I see you have brought elfs with you. Welcome my neighbors." He looked directly at Lura and Ash who stood glaring at the Chief. "My daughter tells me that you need rest. Please use our village as your own. My people are preparing for a feast tonight, relax until then." The chieftain raised his face to the sky and let out a loud piercing wolf howl. Immediately the crowd dispersed. "Come Laren and Lady Loriala, we need to talk," he turned and left with the general and the fairo following closely at his heels, all three conversing in the deep guttural language Mar had heard earlier.

"Ok, all of youse follow me," Tilly sternly instructed the new recruits. The Arthinian noticed the guides of their group had seemingly disappeared into the crowd. Marth observed the Okian barbarian talking with several of the villagers. The giant once again amazed the young lord. He certainly did not appear the dumb brute that most thought. Schaller was of course close by. Mar didn't see the married dwarf couple, Maggie and Mathie. Being short, they got lost among the tall Wildpeople. He was sure now that they'd all been here before and he guessed many times.

The village was built around a center area. Huge straw huts that were reinforced with a type of mud clay were arranged in layers around the town square. Marth marveled at the symmetrical layout of the Wildmen's community. The mud huts that would have been dreary and drab were instead painted in bright colorful murals, each depicting the wildlife that obviously dwelt close by.

Some of the buildings depicted their function. One had sides that were mostly opened. It was set up for a communal eating area with an attached scullery area next door. Large opened pits had delicious smelling dishes cooking. The buildings' artists had painted scenes of people eating which adorned each of the structures' walls. Even the wolves were included in the picture contently gnawing on good-sized bones.

Another great sized construction seemed to be the central meetinghouse, which depicted different types of ceremonial gatherings. Marth could see that there were benches and platforms inside, probably built for speakers.

Tilly led the seven recruits to a large round shelter. The outside was ringed with murals depicting a circle of wolves intensely gazing outward, protecting the structure. The intricate artist's details of the animals' stances and intense facial expressions were amazingly realistic. The building, like those surrounding it, was twice Marth's height with a plume of smoke puffing from the roof's center chimney.

Coming from the bright sunshine to a darkened interior at first disoriented the Arthinian. He felt Dani bump against him when she too was half blinded. Marth caught her as she started to fall. She quickly brushed him off - his touch was unwelcomed. Lar stood on Mar's other side, the desert's man's sandy gray eyes were wide with wonder at the layout of the immense room. Huff and Natalia were already warming their small bodies by the center fireplace while Lura and Ash nervously paced the room still holding on to their bows.

When Mar's eyes adjusted, the immensity of the room dawned on him. In the center was a large fire pit that glowed warmly. A soft clay, carefully laid tiled floor covered the entire area. Several good-sized feather-filled pillows were spread around the area big enough to relax on. Four large shuttered windows were being opened to allow a nice flow of fresh air. The Arthinian went over to one of the openings. Buildings like their guesthouse seemed to be ringed all around them.

"They do not seem to be so 'wild'. They are civilized in their own way," Lar commented while he stood behind Mar, also looking out. "Of course, nothing on this trip is what it should be." The desert man continued, "It is good to see the world. My father was right, my people need to mingle more with the outside."

"Your father?" Marth looked back, seeing the drylander catch himself and quickly covering for what he had said.

"My father is wise for a farmer," he quickly explained and quickly left.

Dani was on the other side of the Arthinian, "He calls them civilized! Did you see their claws?"

"Claws?" thinking the woman was talking about the wolves that seemed to be everywhere.

"Their hands!" she shuddered. "They have claws that come out! The Wildmen have claws!"

Marth felt himself tense, *no, he had not noticed!* What next!

Chapter Nine
The Islands

Larandar was feeling almost overwhelmed on the journey, especially after they had crossed the raging Mad River. Once the group had forged the mountain river, thick woods and lavish prairies abounded. The land was so very different from his dry homeland. Earlier, when they were at the coastal city of Osceta, the Viamar Sea had overloaded the drylander's senses. The seemingly endless body of water had been beyond his imaging.

It amazed him even more that none of the others even flicked an eye. The abundance of water was normal to them. Their indifference made him realize just how different Bombia was from the rest of the DeLak Kingdom. *Well,* he thought, *they don't call their land the "Kingdom of Lakes and Rivers" for nothing. How well do my people belong in this land of plenty? Are we foolish to even try to fit in?*

Despite the lush fertility of the land, he still missed his barony. He yearned for the solitude the desert allowed. He missed the thirsty wind that played with their tents reminding them of the riches of being Bombian, of taking nothing for granted as they did here. Despite the varied wildlife he'd recently seen, the drylander's home teemed with a very different type of life. The western DeLak barony was full of a host of self-reliant and tough creatures, including the Bombian's themselves.

Yet, he knew his father had been right. Hiding in their own little world would not serve the new Bombia Barony well. Before joining the king's alliance, Mothia and its magic had been the only outside contact as both shared the same gods. Life was better now that they had become part of the kingdom, assimilating and learning with the rest of DeLak to defend themselves against the surging evil. Bombia could not fight the Bracaards and their wicked allies alone. Lar hadn't realized how isolated his barony had been, how ignorant he'd been of the rest of the world. Once again, his father's wisdom amazed him.

At first, the Wildpeople had alarmed him. Their fierce appearance had seemed to confirm everyone's warnings. Yet, he'd been pleasantly surprised as the inhabitants of The Wild had opened their arms and welcomed the entire group, including their neighboring rivals, the elfs.

The elfs, his mind wandered to the two proud twins, *the woman is strong, but thinks too highly of herself. She'll have a rude self-awakening. The male perhaps to counter her, seems to not take life as seriously. He at least listens to others.* Lar, however, was drawn to the she-elf. Like Bombian women, she was resilient and easily gave her opinion. *She'd be good at watching your back,* he half smiled as the drylander remembered her fighting the troll. She shot one arrow after another despite the monster advancing toward her. The woman had stood her ground. The male elf, he just plain liked. Larandar imagined Ash would do well in the desert, taking it in his stride. Lura, however, would hate the dry surroundings, finding no beauty but only barren land.

Lar's eyes scanned the room. Many were asleep on the big pillows that lay around the central fire pit, catching some much-needed rest before the evening's feast. The recruits all relaxed after Tilly had come in bringing goat cheese and several types of fruit. "Eat just a little because there will be lots of food tonight," the sergeant dwarf had sternly told them as the Wildwomen had passed around the platters and poured a sweet fruity refreshingly simple drink.

He noticed the small woman, Dani, just lay on her pillow with eyes open. She was probably too frightened to sleep. The woman was a mystery to him. Lar couldn't help but think of her as a child. He had tried to protect her, but she was so frightened of Bishi that the woman kept far away from him.

The two dwarfs were snoring loudly. The female dwarf, Natalia, had tended to his leg. Larandar had felt her magic start to heal his deep wound caused by the damn troll. Unlike Dani, the female dwarf controlled her fear. Her deep green eyes showed her fright, but her manner did not. She had courageously fought the troll. The male dwarf, he had no doubt, would defend her to his death. Lar admired that. Huff was deceiving strong. Despite his stocky short body, his arms were muscle bound, his hands rough and callused. The male dwarf could easily swing an axe or even a short sword. Those that underestimated Huff did so at their peril.

The man Mar was sleeping close by the frightened Dani. She had turned to the Arthinian when Lar's snake had scared her. He respected the hillman. The man was a natural leader. A serious person, probably a scholar, yet he'd had helped in the killing of the troll. He had taken upon himself to carry Dani across the rapids, had even given her his spare shirt to keep warm. Mar had helped around camp, doing whatever was needed without complaint unlike some of the others. His protective massive hound dog lay quietly next to him. Like Dani, the wolf was awake watching them all, guarding his master. When Lar looked into the dog's intense black eyes, he saw a strange type of intelligence similar to his own snake's cleverness.

Evening was approaching when several Wildwomen entered their room with Tilly following them in. "These folks are gonna get ya all set up for the festivities tonight. No arguing, just let them get ya ready." The sergeant looked directly at Dani, "No food without lettin em decorate yar face!"

Lar noticed the small woman cringe when one of the servers approached her with a bowl full of white chalk. Lura, who had sat next to her, had gone first getting white goo spread all over her nose and cheeks. "It doesn't hurt, just do it!" the Hartlander instructed Dani. Once again, the frightened woman listened to the she-elf. She let the Wildwoman spread white cream on her face, but her expression was one of disgust. The fragile woman, however, seemed to enjoy it when the villagers did up her hair, adding flowers to her long auburn tresses that they intricately braided.

Tilly had then led them out to the village center. A huge bonfire was roaring in the middle of the town circle. A sweet smell permeated the air, tickling their noses. It reminded Lar of the many spice scents he was so used to in Bombia. The desert man was guessing that they were burning incense probably made from local plants. The drylander proved himself right as he noticed The Wild adding several full leaved branches to the fire. Billows of scented smoke reached high into the air.

Wildpeople, men and women, densely filled the town center. Besides having white painted faces, they were no longer dressed in animal furs but in straw skirts and tops, all dyed in blues, reds and yellows. Even their feet had woven straw boots held together by rope, decorated in hanging beads that loudly clapped when they walked.

Besides the smell of incense, the aroma of rich spiced food floated over the group. It reminded him of home where they seasoned all their dishes with all sorts of intense flavors. His stomach growled in anticipation. Lar had found the cooking so bland so far. The meals the group had been fed may have been nourishing, but the food tasted like sand.

He noticed the guides had joined the group, including Laren and Lori who sat next to the chief. Okste seemed to especially be enjoying the festivities. The big giant was with the villagers who were dancing to the rhythm of musicians pounding several crude drums and hollow sticks. Several of The Wild were playing what looked like a type of bamboo flute. Melodic sweet toned notes floated in the air. The barbarian was surprisingly agile as his feet kept the beat, his arms waving in unison with the others. The dancers were circling him; their bodies swaying rhythmically with the firelight. The beads on their feet added to the drums' loud thumping. Lar found his hands unconsciously keeping the beat.

Maggie and her husband, Mathie, were also enjoying themselves standing just outside the dancing circle, watching the barbarian. Their hands were clapping in rhythm as the two dwarfs also yelled encouragement to the giant. Schaller sat close by on the ground, smoking a long pipe that was being passed around. His golden bright eyes were intently watching the group. On his shoulder was the big white-headed eagle. The bird seemed to also be intently watching the festivities. The bird's beady black eyes kept sweeping the crowd.

The food arrived by several brightly dressed women carrying huge platters heaped with a variety of fare. Their group, after the Chieftain was served, got bowls of fruit, cheeses and meats. Larandar had been right, everything was highly spiced. It tasted heavenly, burning his tongue. Yet he noticed many of the recruits had trouble eating it. When the rich fruit drink arrived everyone gladly gulped the liquid down. Tilly, who had sat with his recruits, took large sips, smacking his lips. Their sergeant dwarf was actually laughing and seemed to be totally enjoying himself.

Larandar, before drinking, smelled the juice. There was a strange smell he did not like. The drylander realized a drug had been added. It was prevalent in Bombia also, added to entice and enhance the senses. The desert man didn't drink it. Lar put his hand on Mar's arm as the Arthinian went to drink. The hillman looked quizzingly at him.

"There is riceal berry in the drink. The juice will not harm you, but it will make you a little drunk," he told the Arthinian. Mar took his mug and emptied it behind him as did Lar.

The music intensified. Almost all the villagers seemed to be dancing, including the children. Large wolves seemed to mingle among the inhabitants. Like the Wildpeople, the animals' amber bright eyes gleamed in the light of the fire. In the smoke of the blazing logs, the whole scene seemed to pulsate. Lar had to keep focusing his mind. The combination was all too mesmerizing. The mixture of the smoke, the heat and the berry drink had everyone in a merry stupor. Even though he'd not taken a sip of the drink, it was hard not to be drawn into the hazy hypnotic atmosphere.

Lar noticed Mar kept his arm around his dog as if protecting him. Yet the hound did not seem to be disturbed by the number of wolves. At one point, the hill man's pet got up and left his master. The animal joined in with the Wild wolves, circling around the fire, rubbing against the white she-wolves. Mar went to get up to get his pet, but Larandar put his arm on the man, pulling him back down.

"Let your wolf have some fun too," he said.

"Yes, you're right," he answered the desert man. "Gorg spends time with the untamed wolves in my barony. My pet seems to be right at home here."

The music intensified. The entire group seemed now to be enjoying themselves immensely, including Dani. *She's intoxicated; the woman had some of the drink,* Lar realized. *Even the elfs are benevolently smiling.*

It was Laren that caught his attention. The general had stood up. It was then that the Chieftain again let out a loud piercing howl that made everyone quiet down, letting the DeLak leader talk.

"I would like to thank you all for the feast," Laren shouted above the crowd. "We stand with our friends. The Kingdom of DeLak stands with The Wild!"

A roar went up from the villagers as even the wolves howled in agreement. Lori then stood up. Despite her small stature, all quieted and bowed. To Lar's astonishment the tiny woman unfolded her wings and took to the air. She floated just above Laren. He could tell she was making an effort due to her torn wing, yet she spoke strongly.

"May Theror and his daughter, Osiana, bless you." The fairo raised her hands over the crowd, "May your land thrive and your people multiply. Let us all give thanks to the generosity and goodness of our gods."

The entire village howled. Men, women, children and wolves filled the night with a cacophony of voices that swelled to a high pitch. Lori once again sat down next to the Chieftain and Laren. The music began once more, the dancing even more intense. The clapping of hands and their beaded boots seemed to make the very air pulsate. Black silhouettes swayed to and fro in crazy firelight frenzy. Larandar felt light headed as the night deepened.

Maggie and Mathie joined in the stomping of feet. Even Schaller stood and went with his barbarian friend in the circle of dancing. Dani, Lura and Ash were standing swaying to the beat, clapping their hands as the light played on their faces. Huff pulled Natalia into the dancing circle next to Maggie and her husband.

Lar and Mar joined the wolfhound circling around the fire as the burning wood crackled sending sparks up into the dark starry sky. The incense was strong around the bonfire and Lar breathed in deep thinking of his Bombia. *Despite our differences, we are in many ways all alike,* the drylander couldn't help the thought from entering his mind. *We share a common bond of being people.* The two moons had disappeared and dawn was not far off when the recruits staggered into their beds exhausted.

Early morning brought Tilly yelling for them to all get up. Dani, Lura, Ash, Natalia and Huff all staggered outside holding their heads. Only Lar and Marth seemed to be alert. The two didn't have hangovers from the drink like the others. Except for the two men, none ate any breakfast, but managed to get the herbal hot drink Maggie had passed out. It seemed to help as at least some of them had picked at the porridge and had kept it down.

"Thank you for warning me," Mar sat next to the desert man with his hound dog at his feet. "I think it did Dani some good to relax, although she doesn't look too good right at the moment."

Lar looked over at the small delicate woman. She did look pale, but her eyes did not hold her usual frightened stare. The elfs didn't look so haughty in the morning light, so perhaps it did them some good too. Their owls had returned, settling on the tall elfs' shoulders. Huff seemed to recover the quickest as he ended up eating all his breakfast. The dwarf tried to encourage Natalia to put something in her stomach, but the female dwarf was having none of it.

"We're heading out," Tilly firmly ordered them to get their gear in order. By mid-morning the entire group, recruits and guides, headed out of the village. Sarura and several other Wildmen led them out into a scantily treed forest. Willow and ash saplings dotted the area with sweet grass growing in-between. Several packs of healthy fat buffas appeared grazing lazily on the thick foliage. Local herdsmen supervised the cows moving them from one field to another with the help of their wolves. Several flocks of ewes and their small baby lambs could be seen foraging in the distant rich pastures. Again, a group of wolves could be seen carefully watching, guarding the entire cluster of white dots.

They kept to a well-traveled road that swerved between the groves of trees and the rich fields. Sarura led them through several villages, all much smaller than their main settlement. Once again Larandar noticed that no one seemed surprised to see Laren and his group of soldiers. *He's done this before,* the desert man speculated.

Flocks of seagulls appeared overhead, a warm continuous breeze and the land was becoming sandier, all signs that they were again approaching the coastline. The two owls, Boris and Hilda, flew high above catching the constant sea winds.

The group stopped at a village that lay on the side of a river, an estuary that led to the sea. The villagers fed them several types of fish dishes served with tasty corn meal bread.

Large dugout boats lined the inlet beach area. Many of the inhabitants wore loose fitting clothes more suited for fishing and the warmer climate that the Viamar Sea promoted. Lar took off his vest as the intense sun made it unnecessary, as did the warm breeze. The desert man enjoyed the brisk sea air. The winds reminded him of home.

It was here that Sarura left them, as did Lori, yet the eight Wildmen stayed. Laren bowed to the tall chieftain's daughter, "Thank your father for the extra recruits."

The general turned to the fairo, "I will see you later. Be careful Lori, nowhere is safe any longer. Despite the Wildpeople's vigilance, our enemies are determined and cunning."

"I am always careful, Laren, always. I'm needed in the west farmland. I promised Thira that I'd bless the crops at the midsummer festival. I'll join you as soon as I can." She grasped the general's arm, "May Theror guide you on your pathway."

Schaller now took the lead. Instead of continuing along the well-traveled road that headed out of the village, they followed the inlet waterway most of the day until it opened onto the sea. Then the scout led them along the shore heading northward. After their mid-day meal, an island could be seen in the far distance. Everyone shaded their eyes trying to get a better view of the horizon, but clouds kept shrouding their sight.

The sea was becoming choppy. Large waves struck the sandy beach. They moved inland slightly to keep dry as the water sprayed upwards causing a layer of fog to drift in and out. "This part of the Viamar is not navigable," Tilly, who once again took charge of the recruits, explained to them yelling over the pounding of the waves.

When night was falling, they built a small fire from the little scrub brush they could find. Maggie with Mathie's help cooked them a fish stew using the supplies the last village had given them. Besides the village's fresh fish, the soup was full of potatoes, carrots and a type of green pea bean. Everyone gladly ate the rich spicy mixture; even the elfs ate every bit of their meal, not sharing any of it with the owls.

Dani, who had sat between the Arthinian and the desert man, surprised both of them by saying her first conversational words. "The sea does not seem safe here. I don't see any ships." Her bright green eyes drifted out to the horizon. Even in the dying sunset the ocean seemed turbulent and loud.

Lura, who had been close by answered, "I don't think any ships would survive out there. The air seems like constant torrent squalls brewing."

"Good observation," Laren commented. "This part of the northern Viamar is full of whirlwinds and storms. That is why the Wildpeople do not need to patrol this part of their shore. No ships can make it this far. We need not fear pirates here."

"Are those the gray islands we have been getting glimpses of all day?" Marth asked the general calling upon his geography books that he'd so scrutinized when he was studying for the Mothia tests.

"Yes," it was Schaller that answered. "We will get a better view of them tomorrow. There are several islands, all clustered together. Most of them are uninhabitable."

"Most of them?" Huff spoke up. The dwarf repeated, "Most of them?"

"Yes, most," Laren frowned, "now all settle down, we have a long day tomorrow." His gruff tone left no doubt that all conversation was at an end.

Morning brought coolness in the air. The hot thick bean mush in their rustic bowls that Maggie had made and their mugs filled with a steaming dark broth drink was welcomed by them all to stem off the chill. Vests and their pull-down caps came out of their bags. A thick fog drifted off the sea, making them all damp with its heavy dew.

Schaller had been right; the islands came more into focus by mid-morning. The mystical isles dotted the horizon, seeming to drift in and out with the misty clouds that hung over the sea. By noon the sun started peeking through the clouds bringing warmth and drying their clothes somewhat.

They followed the Kazian scout and the Okian giant on paths that led them inland once more. They scrambled over large sand dunes sliding down the shifting mounds to grassy marshlands that smelled of brine. They came upon a road that was set on higher ground. To their relief, the fog and dampness was left behind. Tall reeds lay on either side, gently swaying in the sea breezes.

Lar noticed that Mar's wolfhound seemed nervous, often looking to the marshlands and growling. The desert man's sharp eyes caught movement. When the grassland thinned out huge bears became obvious. Several large bruins were stalking the group.

Marth took hold of his dog. "Easy boy," his voice sounding nervous. He looked at Lar, "We have bears, but I've never seen them like this. At home, they are usually loners. I've counted at least five circling us." The hillman held his blade firmly in his hand.

"I've never seen such massive animals all so close," Lar agreed grabbing his sword. The ex-mage missed his large sharp curved scimitar but even more the magic that the weapon had carried. He noticed Dani had her knife out, holding the blade in front of her. Her hands were shaking, but her stance was firm. The elfs had notched their arrows, while Huff had taken his axe from his belt while shoving Natalia behind him. The female dwarf was having none of it as she pushed her way forward holding her own sword.

"Put your weapons down," Tilly ordered them. The other guides circled the recruits; none of them had their weapons out. "The bears are not threatening us. Everyone calm down," the sergeant dwarf barked. "We wait here."

"What the hell are we waiting for, for the bears to eat us!" Huff angrily yelled out. The Erry dwarf got a scowl from Tilly.

They did not have to wait long. A tall bulky figure came walking down the road. A male child was skipping alongside of him. The man held his hand up in greeting. Laren waved back and went to meet him. What was more astounding was that several white wolves were also traveling with him.

"Dohar, I'm glad to see you," Laren grabbed the man's arm. "Well, hello Bick," he knelt down addressing the young lad.

The smiling boy answered in the strange guttural language of the Wildpeople.

"You've sent the bears?" Schaller directed the question to the man as he approached them.

"Strange sightings have been reported in the woods," he answered in perfect king's language. "Weaselworts and border trolls have been killing our farmers' sheep." The man's wolves circled their group then had sat on their haunches quietly watching. Marth's hound growled deeply but made no threatening moves. The owls circled overhead watching intently, their claws extended as if ready to attack.

Dohar grimaced, "We have reports of monsters coming up the coastline. I have sent word to Chief Thira that he needs to patrol the northern shores."

Laren had said the coast was safe, Lar remembered. *This is not good news!*

Larandar focused on the man that now stood scrutinizing the group. He was not a typical Wildperson. Although he had snowy white hair, pointed teeth and yellow eyes and he was tall, he had a bulky build. Like the Wild, he was extremely tall but unlike the local inhabitants, he had strong wide shoulders, big muscled arms, thick well proportion legs. His well-shaped slender ears were quite large and pointed like an elf's. He wore regular jerkin clothes, workmen clothes that although clean, looked frayed with several patched areas. His large feet had heavy buffas skinned boots that also looked well worn.

Their group, with the guides leading the way, headed down the road. The bears followed on either side with the wolves in-between them and the travelers. Farms came into view, their fields full of crops ready to be harvested. Many of the pickers waved at Dohar and a few even yelled out Laren's name. As they approached the town, the bears disappeared, melting back into the nearby woods, but the wolves still surrounded them.

The village named Forge Haven was a compact well-built township. The buildings were made of a mixture of wood and stone. The strong structures were obviously made to withstand whatever the Viamar Sea threw at them. A variety of shops lined either side of the one main road that led down to the sea. The town seemed more like it belonged to the DeLak Kingdom than the complex huts of The Wild.

A wooden walkway, that was well kept, lay before the town's businesses. They passed a general store with an attached clothing shop. On the other side was a store that seemed to sell furniture and tools and a large bakery with the smell of fresh bread wafting out. Each shop had their shopkeepers curiously peering out at the group marching down the main street. Further down the street was a combination Inn and tavern that took up a good portion of the area. Again, the town's inhabitants came out to stare at Laren's newest recruits.

What struck Larandar was the mixture of people that seemed to inhabit the township. All seemed to have the Wildpeople's dominant white hair and slanted eyes, but there were short dwarf type people, tall human types like Dohar and even dark skinned Bombian types. Some of the town folks were fat, some were thin. The mixture was astounding.

Next to the tavern was an extensive mill that at one end ground grain while the other side of the same factory was a lumber business. The last building on the opposite side was a blacksmith shop.

Main Street ended at the town's harbor. It was here that two of the Gray Islands could be seen on the horizon; one next to the other. A sturdy dock that held a raft-like boat was a prominent feature of the beach. There was room for another one in a close by dock area. It was here that Dohar led the group. He and Laren conversed with the people who seemed in charge of the ferries.

To everyone's surprise, a large clanging bell suddenly came rolling over the soldiers. The chiming echoed loudly, reverberating off the waters of the Viamar Sea.

"They've called for the other ferry. It will probably be awhile before the boat comes. Tilly, take them to get something to eat." The general then addressed the entire group. "After you eat, go where you like, but when you hear the bell, come down here!"

Tilly led the recruits back to the tavern, "Did everyone understand?" They all nodded as each took a seat on the benches provided for them. The long table was already full of great smelling food. Chunks of roasted peppery buffas, soft goat cheeses, steaming bowls of squash-like vegetables and refreshing apple cider were provided. Several barmaids brought fresh baked bread. Everyone ate their full. The guides were scattered at the other tables, all in lively conversations with the locals. They had obviously been here before as they easily mixed with the town's inhabitants.

"This is not a typical Wild village," Marth leaned over to Lar. "Who are these people?"

It was Maggie that answered him as she was walking by, "They'se is outcasts, me dear."

"Outcasts?" Huff blurted out in his usual blunt loud outburst way, causing everyone to look over at the recruits. Natalia grabbed his arm, shushing him.

"Yes, they is all part Wild, but they be a mix." The lower mountain female dwarf laughed, "Like me and Mathie. We are neither dwarf nor mountain people, but a combination of the both. Although we ain't discriminated like these folks are. Ya know borders can be crossed and children born that are cross breeds. They's come here cause they's ain't welcomed in The Wild villages. The Wild tolerate them here."

That explains a lot, Larandar thought as he looked around. The tavern's local customers were a mix of all the breeds. The inhabitants ran the gamut with characteristics of the Elfs, Dwarfs, Humans and The Wild.

"Are you saying that they have some elf ancestry here? The elfs do not interbreed with The Wild!" Lura almost exploded with indignation. Now, once again, Ash put his hand on his sister's arm trying to quiet her. The she-elf glared at her brother.

"Think of what you are saying," the male elf softly told her. Lura did not say another word, but with a flushed face turned away from her brother.

What is the brother reminding her of? Lar wondered. The she-elf actually seemed embarrassed. *Did they have some mix in their own family?*

Lar and Marth left together. To their surprise, Dani followed them out. She was wide eyed as the small woman glanced at each of the town's residents. Yet, she had lost the fear in those big emerald eyes that had been prevalent throughout their trip. Curiosity seemed to overcome the anxiety she normally held.

They went into several of the shops. The three of them found the shopkeepers friendly and curious, asking a lot of questions about their travels. The elf half-breed that ran the bakery had even given them a just baked pumpkin tart. The pastry was delicious.

When they passed the granary, the factory was noisy. Entering, the three found a large water wheel that was situated between the grain shop and the lumber shop. A small forceful stream headed down the middle of the room. The water most likely finished by dumping into the close by sea. Both sides shared the power of the wheel to grind the grain and to cut the wood.

The owner was an industrious dwarf mix that reminded them of Mathie's build. Although the shopkeeper was undersized, he had long arms and bright red fuzzy hair. Yet his eyes were white and his pointed teeth were obviously from The Wild. The owner had several hill type people working for him and even one enormous man. Although not as big as Okste, the mill giant was close. Still, the large half-breed Okian had bushy white hair and a scary long toothed smile.

They headed down toward the end of Main Street toward the beach area. Huff and Natalia had joined them. Two sizeable opened wooden doors led into the blacksmith shop. The warmth coming from the forge immediately hit Lar. The smithy shop was much bigger than it had appeared from the front entrance, with a large stable in the back.

A mixture of smells assaulted his nose. The odor of horses, melting ore and the steam from the hissing smelting all combined to add to the busy nature of the shop. Several blacksmiths were pounding away, shaping the hot metal into various agricultural tools, horse equipment and even pots and pans.

What surprised the desert man the most was the sight of Dohar yelling orders above the loud din. The bulky muscular man was obviously the owner of the smithy. The man now wore a stained canvas apron and held a sizable sledge hammer in his big callused hands. When the blacksmith saw them, he nodded.

Huff was so excited. The dwarf went from one black-smith to the other inspecting each one's work. "Where's ya get yar ore?" he asked Dohar. "This looks to be metal from the Great Mountains."

"Yes, I visit Osceta twice a cycle to buy ore that comes from up North," the smith owner told him as he pointed to a big heap of uncured ore at the back of the shop. "Do you know blacksmithing?"

"Aye, I did some," Huff admitted but said no more. The dwarf pointed to one of the leather workers, "What is he making? Is it a type of harness?"

Dohar seemed to grow uneasy, "It is something for the general." But the blacksmith would say no more. There was no further time for any discussion as the town's loud bell clanged.

"The ferry is here. You'd best go before you miss the boat," Dohar pointed to the door. "Ain't good to get the general mad."

They all heartily agreed and hurriedly headed down to the harbor. A large wooden flat boat was docking. The ship was quite bulky with a huge mast placed right dead center that held a small canvas sail. The boat was obviously made heavy to keep it steady. There was a secure crudely made wooden railing that ringed the outer edge. A small wooden cabin was right behind the mast. Four massive oars were attached to the sides with seats in front of the holes to anchor the rowers. The oars would slide in, but at the moment lay on the boat's deck. A good-sized ash wooden tiller was attached in the back. It looked elf made. The tormenting rough sea was rocking the vessel back and forth, tossing it easily against the dock. The rhythmic banging grated on their ears.

Several strong boatmen were tying up the ferry to the biggest dock. A good-sized female came strolling off. She had bright orange hair whose curls peeked from under a cap. The woman was as tall as Okste, but not as heavy. One word seemed to describe her - tough. Even her black leather clothes looked threatening; a long curled up whip was tied to her belt. Her face was rugged; her nose large and long pointed teeth lay on either side of her big full mouth. In her strong four-fingered hand was an immense axe, in the other hand was a long rapier. The flatboat's captain was not someone to question.

"So ya have more to take over?" the woman had confidently strolled up to Laren. "These look a ragged worthless batch. Youse getting desperate?"

The general laughed, "Bessie, I take what I can get. We'll whip them in shape."

"Well, good luck to ya with this lot," she smiled, her sharp pointed teeth gleaming large, white and dangerous. What made her even more fierce were the large claws that appeared from her hands. They extended to long dangerous talons.

Lar heard Dani gasp from behind him. The desert man looked back at her. The woman once again had eyes full of terror as she took in the boat. Large waves were rocking the ship, splashing over the railings. He noticed Dani's hand went to Marth's arm, "I'm not getting on to that!" she emphatically announced.

This is not good, Larandar speculated as he watched the Viamar Sea challenge the ferry. *Are we really going to cross with that?*

Chapter Ten
The Camp

Marth felt the urgency of Dani's panicking grasp on his arm. The young lord was trying his best not to panic himself. The thought of crossing the turbulent sea's channel to the islands in the unstable flat boat made his heart rapidly beat. He'd often been on his father's Arthinian ships, but on lakes and rivers, not on this huge rolling unstable body of water. Still, what choice did they have? Laren was already aboard directing the boatmen on loading various supplies. Wooden boxes and heavy barrels were on-loaded and tied down in the boat taking up half of the ship's deck.

Bessie was hustling them all on, "Get a move on it, we ain't got all day." The woman giant had her whip out crackling at two substantial grayish brown oxen. The animals were just as scared as the recruits. Their loud complaining brays echoed Marth's concerns. It took her quite a while to get them tied securely to the main mast. Maggie, Mathie, Schaller and Okste all took seats on the various boxes being loaded. They did not seem to be concerned. *They have done this before,* Mar once again thought, but it didn't calm his nerves. *I can't imagine ever being at ease on this endless rolling sea.*

The two Hartland elfs jumped on, casually taking a seat on one of the boxes going to the island, but Marth thought the she-elf rather pale; her mouth formed a tight grimace. Even easy-going Ash had his long well shaped fingers tightly wrapped around the outside railing. His knuckles were white as the elf took a good hold. Their pride would not let them admit fear so they stoically sat with dread in their violet eyes as the only indication of their uneasiness. Their owls held firmly to their shoulders and snuggled as closely to their elf masters' necks as possible. Still, the birds let out several loud hoots as the wind played havoc with their wings.

It was Natalia who pulled a sputtering Huff on board. The Erry dwarf loudly complained, "I can't swim, wese all gonna drown. Look at it out there. Is everyone crazy!" His cap had been pulled off by the wind. His bright red hair was in flight every which way making him look even madder. His long bristly beard was flying up in his face, his bright green eyes flared above his big flushed rubicund nose and cheeks.

Bessie growled at the pair, "Youse dwarfs are such babies!"

"That ain't fair Bessie," Mathie yelled from the back of the boat with Maggie shaking her head in agreement.

"Youse half dwarfs," the large woman yelled in return. "The Great Mountain Erry Dwarfs have no spine. Everyone knows they's a pampered selfish breed."

"How dare ya!" Hoffler stood up. The dwarf was perhaps a third of the height of the boatwoman and had even less of her weight. His hand went to his belt where his ax lay. An anxious Natalia was trying unsuccessfully to pull him down. It was Laren that shoved him back and scowled at him.

"Shut up Huff, Bessie has been known to throw trouble-makers overboard. Unless you learn how to swim real quick, I'd keep quiet." The general's voice was hardened with a sharp *don't argue* edge to it.

Huff scowling sat down, his hand defiantly still on his ax, but the undersized man said not another word. As Marth was getting ready to board, he heard Dani behind him clearly state she was not going on board. "You are NOT getting me on that pierce of junk!"

Mar nodded to Lar and the two grabbed each of her arms to drag her onto the boat. The woman, however, was not going. Her slim small body dug in her heels and violently fought them. "NO, I'm not getting on that!" she piercingly screamed at them.

The Okian jumped off the boat. He grabbed Dani around the waist. With the woman kicking and screaming, he carried her to the center to the ship. "How dare you!" Danella screeched at the giant. The barbarian just plain ignored her. He kept one of his large arms around her slim waist and the other around the mast of the boat. Despite her legs kicking him and her fists pounding against his massive chest, Okste held on tight. He just ignored her struggles as if they didn't even exist. She looked like a small rag doll, her clothes flapping in the wind.

Marth and Lar leaped on, taking seats near the railings. Gorg reluctantly followed. Mar noticed the dog's leg was al-most healed. Natalia had taken off the splint and his pet hardly limped anymore. The hound sat between his legs looking un-easily at the surrounding sea.

"Youse got some good ones this time," Bessie laughed at Laren. "Desperate are ya?"

"You might say that," the general answered her as he took a box seat wrapping his arm around the wooden railing. The boat captain roared with laughter. Bessie went back to operate the tiller.

Four of the boatmen fitted the oars into the sides and immediately started rowing away from the dock. They hadn't got that far out into the sea when one of the boat's men unfurled a large sail that flapped above the barbarian's head. It immediately caught the wind. At first, the flatboat tipped sharply to the right, but it quickly remedied itself and was expertly turned to head towards the island.

The tremendous accelerating swiftness of the boat caught Marth's attention. The flatboat seemed to race forward with waves lapping precariously over the sides of the deck. The salt water sprayed them all with its cold fine mist shower. The Arthinian looked back at their boatwoman. She stood stoically moving the tiller while another sailor matched her movements with a rope tied to the flapping sail. Bessie seemed to be in her element, a look of total contentment crossed the rugged wind burnt woman's face. *She is totally enjoying herself,* Mar thought. *What is she? Half Okian, half Wild?*

He noticed Lar was also enjoying himself. The desert man had stood up by the barbarian holding tight to the center mast. The drylander seemed to lean into the wind enjoying the turbulence of the sea. His gray eyes sparkled with wonderment as the mist soaked him. His pet snake had stuck its head out of his shirt pocket, seemingly to catch the wind. *Another strange pair,* Marth thought. *Bessie is right. We are quite the weird group!*

Dani had gone limp, just hanging loosely in the Okian's grasp. Even the oxen seemed to accept their fate and raised their heads catching the strong wind in their flat snouts, no longer braying. Marth looked back at the receding shoreline. The town already looked far away and inconsequential compared to the massive sea.

The island suddenly loomed ahead of them. A long sandy beach with a wide dock jutted out into the Viamar. The boat came upon the berth quickly. The Arthinian held his breath, as it seemed the boat was going to crash right into the landing area. All four oarsmen rowed strongly in the opposite direction slowing the speed of the ferry. Once again, the boat woman steered the ship around. The sail was brought down and securely tied as they approached the docking area.

Just as they had easily tied up at the town of Forge Haven's dock, so they easily tied the ferry to the new moorings.

No one hesitated this time. The recruits all hurried off the boat, heading down the long wharf that jutted out from the wide sandy beach. Dani quickly staggered off ahead of everyone else and fell gratefully on the soft beach crying quietly.

The whole area was busy with men and women tending to what seemed to be a bustling storage wharf. Several makeshift small lean-to buildings dotted the area. Boxes were being loaded onto ox-driven wagons. Several types of boats were tied up with what seemed to be fishermen dragging nets and baskets full of fish. Teams of oxen were dragging cut logs behind them from a nearby wooded area.

What really struck Mar was the army atmosphere that permeated throughout. Even though there were Dwarfs, Humans, Wild and a few Elfs, all were dressed in the same type of green uniforms. It was a simple dress; woolen shade caps, loosely fitted gingham pants and shirts with a thick hemp rope belt. Small knives hung from waist straps. They had buffas leather boots with woven wool leggings that went up to their knees. They got a few nodded heads, but mostly the group was ignored as the soldiers hurried on their tasks.

It was Tilly that gathered all the recruits. "Everyone line up over here," the sergeant loudly ordered. Mar and Lar grabbed onto the motionless Dani, dragging her with them. This time the limp frightened woman didn't fight the two men, but took her place between them. Her small body was slightly shaking; her eyes were focused on the ground as if trying to ignore the whole situation.

She isn't going to last, Marth conjectured. *What will Laren do with her?*

Tilly marched up and down in front of them. "Ya are at Camp Hope," the hill dwarf waved his arms seemingly pointing all around. "It is here that ya will get ya trainin to be soldiers. No more coddlin! Youse will *ALL* do as ya are told, when ya is told and there will be no arguin! Remember Yanith's words, *Do As You Are Told* and ya'll be fine. Leave behind any notion of what ya think youse were." The lower mountain dwarf flapped his hands as if to emphasize his arguments, "Everyone is equal here, no one is pampered."

We are in the army now, Marth realized. *There's no getting away from it - there's no escape, we're on a frigging island!*

"All of ya help load the supplies onto the wagon." The sergeant pointed to the boxes and barrels that filled up one area of the beach. Bessie and her sailors were still unloading the rest of the supplies. Laren was nowhere to be seen.

A long wooden wagon hitched to two oxen was waiting close by. Bessie was leading the two new oxen carefully down the wharf. Okste grabbed onto them leading them away. Maggie, Mathie, and Schaller were already lifting boxes into the back of one of the farm carts. The seven recruits pitched in with even Dani managing to load the small boxes.

When everything from the ship was unpacked and on the cart, Tilly lined them up and marched them behind the oxen down a wide dirt road. Just past the beach the land flattened out. A rustic camp had been parceled from of the surrounding forest. The encampment was obviously still being constructed, as several buildings were half finished with people working on them. Loud bangs from hammering and orders being shouted filled the air.

In the center of a circle ringed with buildings, Laren reappeared. The general had changed into one of the green uniforms; his only distinction was five red colored cloth strips sewed on to his shoulders. Tilly smartly saluted and glared at the seven recruits until they followed suit, even Dani limply raised her hand.

"Welcome to Camp Hope," their head leader began. "As you can see, we are still in the process of building the encampment. You will be expected to pitch in. Tilly will be your sergeant. He will instruct you in what you need to do and know. We do not have your barracks finished yet, so you will sleep outdoors until the building is done. It will serve as an incentive to get those sleeping quarters done quickly."

Tilly stood at attention nervously in front of them. Their sergeant seemed anxious to get them going.

Laren's sharp grayish violet eyes scrutinized each one of them, "I will now let you all go with Tilly, who will get you ready to be an important part of Camp Hope. Sergeant Tillman will explain your schedule to you. Then he looked over at Natalia, "You will come with me."

"What!" Huff yelled. "What ya gonna do with her?" as he watched his fiancée follow behind Laren.

"Did someone give you permission to speak, private?" Tilly screamed at the pudgy recruit. The Erry Dwarf was taken aback at the vehemence of the sergeant's voice. "Keep your mouth shut unless asked to speak!"

"Ya can't just take her away," Hoffler screamed back at him, "I won't allow it."

"Shut up!" Tilly once again yelled at him. "Wese will see if no food tonight will keep that mouth closed!"

"Ya can't do this!" Huff still persisted.

"Well, now ya made it so yar whole group won't be fed. Keep that mouth going and Natalia won't be fed either."

"For Theror sake shut up," Lura growled at the belligerent dwarf.

The Erry Dwarf did indeed shut up, but his angry eyes glared at Tilly with silent threats.

Tilly marched them across the large opened space in which the buildings seemed to be built around. On the far side, in a newly cleared area, he stopped at a semi-constructed building. They were far enough away from the main camp that they seemed to be all to themselves. A good-sized brook ringed the back of the area. The noise of the busy encampment was softer, the banging and yelling muted among the trees. Large piles of wood lay scattered about. "This will be yar home," their sergeant laughed pointing at the unfinished building. "The faster youse get it built, the sooner ya will be under a roof. It ain't pleasant here when it rains." He chuckled, amused by the thought of them all getting wet.

No one said a word, Tilly's threats were still ringing in their ears and their rumbling stomachs reminded them of no supper. He led them to partially cleared area behind the construction site. Large elm trees loomed overhead. A good-sized babbling brook ran close by. "Wese will set youse camp here. Since there will be no supper, ya might as well hit the sack early. Ya will be up with the dawn. Wese will spend the first part of each day building the camp. In the afternoon ya will meet with combat instructors."

Their squadron leader stood looking over the six of them, glancing from one to the other. "Now, ayes give you permission to speak, any questions?"

"Will we be getting those god-awful uniforms?" Lura quickly spoke up.

"Youse'll get them tomorrow," Tilly answered. "Be glad…"

"What did they do with Natalia?" Huff loudly blurted out before Tilly could finish his answer.

"Oh, for Theror's sake!" Lura shouted at the dwarf. "Will you shut up! I'd like to eat some time!"

"Ya best listen to the she-elf," Tilly told Hoffler. "Youse either gonna get along, or youse be gone! Then where ya Natalia be? Understand?"

Huff shut up, but again the glare he gave the sergeant was of pure hatred.

The recruits set up their camp, spreading out their bedrolls. They used the nearby brook to clean up and change into their extra clothes and rinse out their dirty garments. Huff started a small fire with some wood that Ash and Mar had gathered. Lura set up a line close to the warmth of the woodburning blaze so their clothes would dry. The makeshift camp seemed so strange, no Maggie starting their supper. The hooting of the elfs' owls could be heard in a close by tree. Tilly had brought Gorg a bone with lots of meat on it. The dog lay nearby chewing on his meal occasionally guiltily looking up at his master, but ravishing the food anyway.

"Pretty sad, the dog gets more than wese do!" Huff moaned. They all looked accusingly at the dwarf. "Okay, I'm sorry," he finally told them.

"We'll all make mistakes, Huff," Marth spoke up. "I'm sure we will all be saying *I'm sorry,* soon enough."

The Erry Dwarf looked up, his green eyes dull with worry, "It's just I'm worried about Natalia."

"Oh, for Theror sake, she's probably getting the supper we didn't!" Lura snapped at him. "Do all dwarfs get such baby love?"

"Leave him alone," her brother softly said to his sister. "On hunting trips, we've gone without supper a time or two. It didn't kill us then, won't now."

"We'd best get some sleep," Mar told them. "I have a feeling morning's coming real soon."

The Arthinian had just slipped off to sleep when Tilly woke him up. "Get up private, ya got the first watch. The sergeant then went over to Lar and poked him too. "Both of ya keep watch until I relieve ya with someone else. Keep awake. Watch yar area."

Marth stretched his stiff limbs and shook the cobwebs out of his brain. The boat ride had taken more out of him than the young lord had realized. His muscles were sore from the trip's tension. The Arthinian hated to admit that he had been flung around despite holding onto the railings tightly.

With Gorg by his side, Mar walked the perimeter of their small camp. The fire was just about out, just the glowing embers. His ears picked up the night crickets, the sound of their clothes flapping in the constant sea breeze and the occasional hooting of Boris and Hilda. The owls were probably out hunting.

The young man could hear the dwarf snoring. The rest seemed quietly sleeping, including Dani. In the firelight's last glow, her face seemed almost childlike. His thoughts once again went to his sister Lilith. *How was she managing alone without me to protect her?* He once again cursed his father. *Someday when I return,* his mind reeled, *I will settle the score with him. IF you return,* his thoughts sorrowfully reminded him.

The stars were bright tonight because of no moons. The constant sea breeze filtered in-between the trees making him shiver. Marth wished now he'd taken his vest from his bag. Lar joined him, leaning against the tree and staring upward. Bishi, his snake, lay curled around his neck; the reptile's big eyes seemingly watching everything.

"I wonder what we are keeping watch for," the desert man cocked his head, looking straight up as if searching for answers.

"Can't imagine, considering we're on an island, but then I guess it's part of being a soldier," Mar half laughed. "I have a feeling there's going to be a lot of stuff that doesn't make sense."

He saw the drylander nod in agreement. "I miss my homeland," the gray-eyed man confessed to the Arthinian lord. "I often dreamed of having enough rain and water, but now I actually miss the dryness of the desert and I miss my people."

"I always dreamed of leaving my barony, of being free, but I too miss the rolling hills and I miss my sister. I worry about her." It was the first time Marth had talked to anyone about himself since they had left. The Arthinian wished he could share more with Lar. They held a bond the two could not discuss - the men both missed the power of magic. Mar felt that he could not talk about it. Yanith had somehow placed a spell on them all. The ex-mage felt the lack of magic, but there was nothing the recruit could do about it. Mar had an inkling about the recruits in their group, were they all ex-mages?

"Ah, I have no sister, though my mother would surely like a daughter," the Bombian confessed, but said no more as the desert man went back to his patrolling. The tall lean man slipped silently into the surrounding woods. It amazed Mar how stealthily the drylander moved, he became only a vague shadow silently moving between the trees.

Gorg, once more, followed his master around the perimeter of the camp. It was toward the middle of the night that he was relieved by Huff and Ash. He slipped back into his bedroll. The young lord was surprised to see two large emerald eyes watching him; Dani was awake. "Go to sleep," Marth ordered her as he would have his sister. To his relief, the woman did just that. The Arthinian then followed suit.

The sun was just filtering down from the misty clouds when Tilly had them all up. The air was damp with heavy fog dew. Marth had a feeling this was the normal island morning. Tilly quickly let them wash up in the brook and then led them into the main camp. "Look lively, keep in line. Bring ya eating implements," the sergeant sharply ordered the squad. He headed them to a large pavilion building. The sides were opened to the elements, but the structure had a good sturdy shingled roof above.

Large groups of soldiers were already at the long crudely made wooden tables with long matching benches. The din of animated conversation filled the room. Some of the soldiers nodded in their direction, but most were busy eating their breakfasts. Huff looked frantically around for Natalia, but the female dwarf was nowhere to be seen.

The smell of cooking eggs, cured hog bacon and browning root taters made the recruits quickly take their seats. They took up half a table while the other half had soldiers already eating. They were mostly made up of human and dwarf soldiers, male and female.

Heaping plates of food were put in front of them. Bowls of melon fruit and berries also dressed the table. Long loaves of just baked bread with lard butter filled the center. The meal was quickly passed around as each took their fill. Hot carafes of thick rich brewing tea was poured into each mug. Goat milk and honey lay close by and each of them helped themselves, except the drylander who took his tea black. Tilly, who seemed to have taken a shine to Mar's pet, brought Gorg a bowl full of raw mutton, which the hound quickly gobbled down.

"Eggs!" Hoff excitedly grabbed the bowl of peeled hard-boiled eggs.

"You won't say that when you get filthy chicken duty! Cleaning the poultry pens ain't no fun," one of the other soldiers jokingly said. His fellow privates softly laughed. "From what I hear, your dwarf mouth gonna get you doing that duty a lot!"

The Erry dwarf went bright red. Marth actually felt sorry for the small man. "I imagine you have the same problem," Lura shouted down to the man as the elf now surprisingly defended Huff. Her brother rolled his eyes and once again put his hand on her arm.

"Yeah, you got that right! Gerpe gets that job a lot!" the soldier at the very end of the table agreed making the entire table laugh loudly. It was Gerpe's turn to blush profusely and scowl at the she-elf.

"Aren't we a lively bunch this morning," Tilly had come up next to the table. He was wearing a regular uniform with two stripes on his shoulder. The lower part of the benches all quickly saluted. Marth taking the cue also saluted, as did the rest. "If ya is all so happy perhaps ya need to work it off. Hurry up and eat. Ya got some building to do."

A silent moan could be felt all around as the recruits dug into the food that each had missed so much the night before. Tilly wasn't done yet, "This here is Quinn." Standing next to the lower mountain dwarf was a burly thickset man. "He is in charge of the building projects. The sergeant's gonna teach ya the right way to do construction. So, as soon as yar done, youse all get back to where ya started!" The dwarf turned to go, but yelled at them one more time, "And don't take too long! Time's a wastin."

As they were leaving, a large bulky female half-elf with two stripes on her shoulder stopped them. The half-breed had a typical elf disposition as she looked scathingly down on them. The woman led them to a table with four stacks of green uniforms. "My name is Sergeant Pisala, I'm in charge of supplies." Her hand waved at the stacks of clothes, "Small, medium, large and dwarf size. Take your pick! Take two sets and only two sets!" Her harsh tone gave little doubt that the sergeant would be watching them.

"Ladies, a word of advice, take small pants, but medium shirts." Pisala looked at Huff, "dwarf, do the best you can. Nothing is gonna fit you right and you're fat to boot. I understand you don't have quarters yet so there are public bathrooms over there!" She half pointed as if easily dismissing them to find the facilities on their own.

It doesn't seem to be Huff's day, Mar thought. At least this time the dwarf stood up for himself. "I ain't fat and look at yarself first!" he snapped at the woman soldier who did indeed look heavy for an elf.

"Tilly!" the half-breed female sharply yelled. The sergeant came walking over, a look of *Oh no, now what!* on his face. "This private needs a lesson in manners! Take care it!" the supply officer demanded, pointing to Huff.

He nodded, "Aye, Sergeant Pisala, I'se will." He eyed his dwarf recruit, "Ya ain't gonna learn are ya? Tonight, before ya eat, give the cooks a hand. I'm sure they'se got something for ya to do!"

Huff didn't argue just shook his head. The six all headed toward what looked like communal bathrooms. Each dressed quickly and headed toward their campsite. Marth's uniform fit fine. It was a little big around the waist, but his rope belt was put to good use. The pants were slightly too long. He noticed Lar had the opposite problem as his fit snuggly around the hips but was a little short. Once they had tucked their pants in their boots it didn't matter as the high boots hid the bottoms.

Huff's pants were indeed tight, but he had managed to snuggle into them. He had grabbed a medium regular sized shirt so it hung over the tight pants but also drooped down to his knees. His cap was also rather wide, covering all of his briskly hair and thick hairy ears. The Erry dwarf did not look happy.

Both elfs actually looked great, especially once they had tucked the too short pants in their boots. Their caps, however, were uncomfortable as their big delicate pointed ears got in the way and ended up tucked under their brims.

Dani looked lost. Even the small pants were rolled up and tied tightly with her belt, the small shirt hung loosely on her. The cap was way too big. She looked like a poorly dressed puppet. Lura had gone over and tucked everything in, "Don't you know how to dress yourself?" The Hartlander chastised the small woman, once again taking charge.

When they all tromped over to the half-constructed building, Quinn was already there with several other soldiers. "Listen carefully when I tell you something," the one stripe uniform told them, "pay attention. I don't want to repeat myself!"

The builder waited, expectantly taping his foot until all of them yelled, "Yes, Sir."

Marth and Larandar were put to nailing one board over the other, using the existing beams to make the outside walls. The sure-footed elfs were placed on the roof putting up sheaves of large wooden shingles onto the upper planks. The heights seemed not to bother them at all. The two siblings appeared to be in competition on who could out shingle the other with Lura winning slightly. Huff was busy dragging over the lumber, piece by piece and once the boards were up he tar-pitched the seams. Dani carried everyone's supplies. Pails of iron spikes went to Marth and for the smaller tack nails, she had to climb a ladder to hand them to Ash. Mar's arms were aching by mid-afternoon when Quinn called the midday meal break. Despite depleting their water skins, they all were parched and tired.

No one seemed to want to eat at lunchtime. They were all having trouble putting their tired arms to work lifting their cutlery. Dani had her head down on the table, her arms hung limply at her side. Tilly snorted when he saw them. "Where's the laughin now?" the sergeant snickered. "Everyone eat, ya are going to need strength for this afternoon. It's combat training until supper. So, *eat!* That's an order."

The noon meal was a thick hearty vegetable root soup served with dry grain biscuits that were excellent for sopping the mixture up. The ample potage seemed to revive Mar's energy. Dani, who was sitting between him and Lura, still sat with her head down. The Arthinian reached over pushing her up. "EAT," he sternly ordered. Dani was staring off into space; her glazed-over green eyes unseeing. The small woman glared at him, but her hand went to her spoon and she managed to take a few sips of the soup's broth. The food seemed to help as she ended up slowly eating everything in her bowl.

It was near the end of the meal when Natalia appeared at a far table. The dwarf was dressed in a uniform very similar to their own but of a tan color. She was at a bench where the entire group were all dressed similarly. Huff started to stand up, but Lar pulled him back down. "We like eating, you'll only make the situation worse!" The drylander voice was stern and his harsh words made the dwarf sit back down.

Marth leaned over to one of the human soldiers, "Who are they?" he softly asked.

"They're medical," the soldier answered. "That group is in the med building. First structure built, right next to the barn."

Huff had heard what the soldier had said. The dwarf's eyes never left the table that his fiancée was sitting at, but the female Azirran didn't once look up. Mar noted the healer was hardly eating. *She has more sense than Huff,* the Arthinian pondered, *she's afraid it will set him off if she looks at him. Huff could use some of that common sense.*

After Natalia left the common eating room, Huff finished his soup, but the dwarf was not his gregarious self, not even looking at the other recruits. The Erryian said not a word when Tilly assembled them in the courtyard. "Wese first goin on a march," their sergeant informed them. "Try and keep up. Wese will do this every day until wese can jog the entire time. Do ya understand?"

"Yes Sir," the entire group now automatically answered.

They left single file, slowly walking past the courtyard and into the outer area of the camp. Marth ordered Gorg to stay put and the big hound laid quietly by the edge of the camp. He noticed Lar's snake just peeked out of his pocket and then disappeared once more. The owls were nowhere to be seen.

The marching exercise was the new recruits' first time actually seeing the entire army community. They passed a large post and beam barn with the medical building right next to it. The large wooden structure was a sturdy edifice covered with a gray paint. Extensive paddocks adjoined the back of the barn. The corrals held only a few oxen. Several large wagons were scattered about. One large opened enclosure held a size-able flock of fat sheep guarded by several large wolves. Still in another, there were herds of buffas and elk all mixed to-gether. Each seemed to be ignoring the other while they munched on bales of hay that dotted the area. In the middle of all the animals, the herds strategically shared a good-sized pond.

There were other corrals that were empty as if waiting for more livestock. They also passed a nearby hen house. Red-feathered chickens were pecking contentedly on the ground while several soldiers spread seed for them. Numerous pens of hogs were the last part of the farm.

"There ain't no horses," Huff spouted out

"They'se don't survive here on the island," Tilly told them. "It's probably the weather or somethin. The oxen do just fine. Now shut up, no more questions."

Mar's nose was relieved when they passed into the nearby forest. Here a well-worn road led deep into the wood-land proper.

Tilly picked up the pace, jogging slightly. Their basic training leader kept it up until Huff and Dani were quite a dis-tance behind. The sergeant stopped and patiently waited for the two to catch up. Then the hill dwarf walked again for a while then he paced them faster. Each time he'd wait until the same two stragglers caught up.

There were quite a few pathways to take. Often other soldiers jogged by going back the way they had come. The recruits came upon a wooden bridge passing over a bubbling brook. *It's most likely the same one that runs behind our camp,* Marth thought. *It probably circles the middle of the island. I wonder what its source is?*

The Arthinian didn't have to wonder long as they fol-lowed the brook until it opened into a large beautiful pool fed from a cascading waterfall. "Wese will take a short rest here, if ya want to take a dip, make yar swim quick!"

Several other soldiers were already enjoying the crystal clear water. Both men and women swam naked seemingly unbothered by their lack of clothes. Mar and Lar didn't hesitate, the two men stripped and jumped right in. Their bodies gratefully soaked up the coolness that revived their tired muscles. The two were joined by the twin elfs. Lura and Ash unabashedly swam out to the waterfall sitting on one of the rocks that let the waterfall's spray fall on top of them.

Huff, who couldn't swim, only went up to his waist. The look of total contentment on the dwarf's face said it all. Dani just sat on the shore, watching. The small woman could not bring herself to disrobe. She ignored Lura trying to coax her to join them.

The rest time was over too soon as Tilly set them on the return march in short order. Yet, all except Dani felt revived. Mar would not forget this place for the quiet pool reminded him of his homeland. Nor, the Arthinian guessed, would Lar for the exact opposite reason. It must seem strange to the drylander, so much water.

They did not retrace their steps, but went further into the woods, coming up on the Viamar shore. The sea raged, large boulders overlooked the massive pounding waves. In the distant horizon, another island poked out of the water. Like this island, it was shrouded in intermittent clouds keeping the land's topography a mystery.

Suddenly, the sky was filled with birds; huge birds that flew in and out of the gathering clouds. The flock seemed white feathered, although it was hard to tell since the birds were high up above the clouds. The recruits got a better view of the creatures when some dove down into the sea scooping up large fish with their immense clawed feet. Yet they were so quick, it was hard to get any details. Then the birds quickly soared above the clouds disappearing from sight.

"What are those?" Huff blurted out. "I's never seen the likes of them before!"

Tilly just shrugged, "Just some common birds." Yet, Mar noticed the sergeant was intensely watching the flock as they flew overhead with feigned indifference.

Even the elfs exclaimed surprise. Dani's emerald eyes were wide with wonder as she followed the birds' path. Marth just excitedly stared. Arthinia had plenty of large birds, but nothing like those that soared above this sea. It was Lar that voiced what everyone was thinking, "What else is on this island?"

We'll find out, Marth had no doubt that they would find out.

Chapter Eleven
Training

Dani watched the white winged creatures disappear. *They are from the other islands,* her straining eyes watched the enormous retreating birds through the hazy clouds. She wondered if the flocks used to live on Hope Island? Had Laren chased them away? *I want to go with them, sprout wings and fly away,* the princess sorrowfully wished. *Anything to be away from this nightmare!*

Her gaze went to the turbulent sea. *The view from my castle window was so different of the Viamar Sea,* her wishful thoughts drifted back to her former life. *It had been so calm, so beautiful.* She had not appreciated the serenity enough, the security that the calm waters had represented. *What do I have now?* the king's daughter questioned. *I do not belong here.*

Looking down from the cliff, the sea was violent and in such turmoil, the waves crashing brutally against these rocky bluffs. *The sea is just like my life, no longer peaceful but full of confusion and uncertainty.* Tears filled Dani's eyes as self-pity seethed through her. The princess caught herself, *I'll not let them see me cry! They all think me a weak bumbling idiotic fool.*

Tilly had headed the squadron back to camp. The royal woman tried hard to keep up, but her legs would not move fast enough, repeatedly cramping. The group would often have to wait for her and the fat dwarf. Yet, Danella was grateful to Huff. She had a feeling the small man was purposely keeping back for her sake. *Maybe he's not so fat,* she chastised herself for thinking badly of the dwarf.

Every bone in her body ached when they finally reached the outer rim of the army base. Dani had hoped Tilly would let them rest, but the sergeant only gave the recruits a short respite. "Ya gonna get some combat trainin. If ya do good, wese go to supper at the first serving. Otherwise, wese will keep trainin until the last serving, all except Huff who has to help in the kitchen. He will eat with the cooks that make our supper."

Dani heard the dwarf moan, everyone else just gave a big sigh. Their squad leader led them to a large grassy clearing behind the barn on the other side of the pond. Here were several groups of soldiers practicing their combat techniques under various instructors. To their surprise, all the trainees were dressed in short pants, short shirts that were sleeveless and all were barefoot. Various types of weapons were in play, but it was to a non-weapon instructor that the group was first taken.

"This is Sergeant Motos, she is gonna teach ya hand-to-hand fighting. Listen good!" Tilly then stalked away, leaving his squad alone with the slender but well built busty half human female instructor. The combat teacher sported yellow no nonsense eyes that were Kazian, but her thick pointed hairy ears and large nose heralded some dwarf ancestry as did her thick pudgy fingers. She was of medium height with blonde hair pulled back in a tight bun. Her outfit was like everyone else, skimpy and tight. The lack of clothes showed off her muscular build.

Is everyone a half-breed here? Is that what Laren mostly recruited for his army? Dani sarcastically thought. Few mixed breeds came within the scope of her castle life. The princess had always thought them inferior to pure breeds. *Although those damn superior proud elfs could use a few better traits,* the royal mockingly rethought, her eyes focusing on Ash and Lura.

"First, you see that building over there?" Motos waited until they had all nodded. "Go over there and change into training clothing. You will do that every day before coming onto the training fields. You will leave them for washing every day. Do you understand? They had better be dirty after training or you have not worked hard enough!"

Again, Motos waited until the group had all nodded. "Okay, I expect you to hurry!"

Hastening up a hill, they found a post and beam building. The inner two rooms were quite large with several curtained off sections. Dani and Lura went behind the female curtain section while the men had their own area. Danella embarrassingly turned her back on the female elf, quickly slipping off her green uniform and getting into the training outfit. When she turned around, the king's daughter blushed profusely as the she-elf's long limbs looked scantily exposed, her amble breasts and bared mid-section were quite noticeable. The princess realized she too must look the same. Still, there was a certain freedom in the outfit, movement was easily done, but Dani still reddened under Lura's amused scrutiny.

They left their standard uniforms folded on the benches and joined the men who were already on the field. Dani, reddening, felt the intense gaze of the males as they approached. The feeling, however, did not last for long as the female instructor got their attention by smacking each of the recruits smartly with a thick bamboo stick. Each one flinched, some yelled "ouch" but all quickly gave Motos their full attention. Dani rubbed her arm where the stick had stung.

"Pain is not pleasant," the instructor glared at each one of them. "That pain is nothing compared to a knife or sword wound. Keep that in mind as I teach you to not only defend yourself, but that the best possible outcome is overcoming an enemy physically. Depending only on your weapon or body armor can get you killed. So, pay attention!"

She pointed at Ash, "Stand here private." The tall good-looking elf stood where the instructor indicated. "Now there are several easy targets on the body." Motos pointed to the elf's eyes, his knees, his throat and to just below his waist. "Men are particularly vulnerable in the lower area." Dani, despite herself, found the instructor's lesson fascinating as the hand-to-hand combat teacher pointed to several attack techniques on the elf's torso. Ash looked haughtily amused, as he was much taller and leaner than the instructor. Dani could tell that Ash did not think that Motos posed any type of threat to him.

"Your first problem is to assess your attacker. Tall, short, stocky, all makes a difference. The taller an opponent the lower the kick for throwing them off balance." A stunned Ash quickly found his legs out from under him. Then she took Huff and easily toppled him. Motos did the same to Marth. Lura easily landed on her fanny with a loud *oomph*. The female Hartlander looked embarrassed and defiant when she got back up. Dani tried to sidestep out of the way, but Motos easily flipped her legs from under her, effortlessly sprawling the small woman to the ground. Only Lar kept his balance the longest, but still eventually landed in a sitting position.

The training sergeant paired them off. Dani found herself opposite Mar. They practiced kicks, learning to bring back their legs before bringing their feet forward for the best results. Motos showed them how to grab someone's neck, putting your hands on their collar and pressing the larynx in the middle. Next came how to gouge eyes and how to bite in sensitive areas such as the thumb. "Don't hesitate, bite hard!" the instructor exclaimed, bringing her sizeable square jaw tightly together to make the point.

Lar was the quickest learner; he obviously had more experience in fighting. Lura tried the hardest. Dani was aware that Mar was careful with her. Although the small woman was somewhat grateful, the defiant woman in her also resented it. Dani, however, noticed the Arthinian went full out with Lura, the two ending up wrestling on the ground. Motos had to separate the two, as Lura wouldn't let up. Even Huff, caught in an over passionate moment, lowered his head and full out butted directly into Ash, who went down hard losing his breath.

Tilly came back late afternoon. All six of them were exhausted and sore. Dani could hardly walk, limping from a kick that had hit Marth and done more damage to herself than to the man. Sergeant Motos told Tilly they had done well and released them. The recruits stumbled up the hill to the changing rooms and gratefully got back into their clean green uniforms leaving their sweaty dirt covered clothes behind. Their sergeant marched the group off to eat at the mess hall, except poor Huff who had to go and help the cooks before the dwarf could eat.

Dani, to her surprise, was starving. The smell of the food made her stomach growl. "I don't know why you're so hungry," Lura had leaned over and chastised her. "Everyone knows Mar went easy on you."

Mar, who sat next to her, touched Dani on the arm as if she was a child, "Don't listen to her."

Her temper flared, the elf's words had hurt her pride. Forgetting that she'd been grateful to the much larger man for going easy, Danella snapped at the him. "She's right! I don't need your pity. Don't ever do that again!"

Mar's black eyes had a moment of hurt, but Dani ignored him, tending to her meal. *He looks so familiar,* her mind returned to her DeLak father's court. *Where have I seen those eyes before?* It hit her, the ugly Baron Arient from Arthinia. *Mar is Arthinian. Do they all have black eyes?* Danella had not liked the baron. His scarred face frightened her; the disfigurements gave him a cruel look. She had not stayed long at the reception her father had given the visiting royal. *Yes, that was where she'd seen those eyes.* She involuntarily shuddered, remembering her parents had also seemed leery of the dark powerful Arthinia baron.

Forgetting her court manners, Dani dug into her mutton stew, using her chunk of bread to sop every last part of the hearty broth. Then she ate some cheese and apples until her belly felt full. The small woman sighed contentedly and to her horror let out a large burp. To her relief, no one seemed to notice.

Tilly joined them near the end of the meal. "Youse is free to do as ya like, but I expect ya to hit the sack early. They'se a troop rec building over there," his hand pointed to the outer camp. "Youse welcomed there. Follow the crowd, youse'll find it." The hill dwarf then left them to their own devices.

Dani followed Lura as they headed toward a large semi-opened building that seemed to be attracting just about everyone. As they approached it was loud and boisterous. Inside was crowded. There was a long crudely put together bar serving apple cider or some type of red berry drink. Bowls of various types of fruit lay on the small tables that surrounded the bar. In the far corner were shelves of books. Mar, with his dog, headed in that direction with Lar close behind.

The elf twins found a group of half elfs that they were animatedly talking with. Dani noticed Schaller and Okste playing a card game in the corner. It was the first time that she'd see any of the guides. The king's daughter looked for Maggie and Mathie, but they weren't in sight. There were very few dwarfs in the boisterous room, being mostly filled with half-breed Humans/Wild.

Where do I belong? the princess wondered. She wandered around the room. Lively conversation and laughter filled every corner. Unlike the castle no one paid her much mind, no one fawned over her. Danella was just another soldier. Bored, Dani slipped out a back door. Outside, along the back yard, there were several lively games being played. Some of the soldiers, this time both dwarf and human types, were kicking a pig skinned sphere around chasing each other, yelling loudly.

One game seemed to involve horseshoes. It was mostly dwarfs throwing the metal shoes at sticks stuck in the ground. Huff was taking a turn while Maggie and her husband cheered him on. The Erryian was playing against Tilly, who was waiting patiently for his turn to throw at the stick. *So, this is where the dwarfs hung out.*

Feeling out of place, the noble woman walked past the games to the wide courtyard. It was mostly deserted with everyone at the rec area. *I don't belong here,* she once again sorely mused. *Well, you're stuck here, so make the best of it,* reluctantly flooded her thoughts, *like it or not!*

On the far side of the main camp area, she headed down towards the woods. The barn was larger than Dani at first thought. The post and beam structure was probably the biggest building in the army complex with its various attached corrals. Several soldiers were coming in and out of the barn bringing feed and hay to the animals. Her nose wrinkled at the smell of the different livestock causing her to head in the opposite direction. The smells were so unfamiliar; as princess, she never had to contend with dirty smelly animals at the castle. The odors were mildly nauseating her stomach.

She passed the gray painted medical building. Several tan uniformed soldiers came in and out, but Natalia was nowhere to be seen. Dani noticed several of the medical personnel headed toward the barn. *Do they have to take care of the animals too?* Danella shuddered at the thought of having to touch the livestock. Where was Huff's female dwarf? Did she have to tend to the livestock? *UGG!* screamed into her brain.

Her mind went to Huff. Danella could not imagine the closeness Huff felt for his fellow dwarf partner. It was an alien feeling for the king's daughter, who only concerned herself with her own needs. Love was not something to contemplate. She'd have an arranged marriage, the less emotional entanglement the better. Her own mother had come from upper Kazia, a sister to the country's baron. The Kazian female royal had not even seen her father until a few days before the wedding. It was the way it was; a perfectly designed royal matching.

She approached a good-sized building on the opposite side of the courtyard. Her head felt several raindrops. Dark clouds were overhead. Suddenly the whole sky burst open. Heavy drops came pouring down. Danella quickly went in a side door, leaving the rain behind.

One side of the building was opened looking down on the distant pond and the combat instruction area. The torrential rain could be seen. An open wooden floor lay before it with several soldiers practicing under the intense scrutiny of a tall slim but muscle bound dark skinned human female. Her body gleamed in sweat. "Kick, kick harder!" the instructor screamed at her students. Grunts abounded as each soldier did just that. "I said kick harder! Get those legs up!"

Dani, fascinated, hung back in the shadows watching. "Punch, punch! Use your arms with your legs. Let me see some effort!" the instructor shouted even louder. Each soldier, dressed in one of the practice outfits, was covered in sweat. Each had a face that focused passionately on the trainer. The teacher had them run in place, making them lift their knees high.

"Drop, give me twenty sit-ups!" she ordered the group who immediately dropped and with loud groans puffing out as they touched their toes. "Okay, rest for a few moments then pair off for our combat exercises."

Every soldier reached for his or her water bags, drinking deeply, including the instructor. It was then that the woman noticed Dani. "Come here, private," the teacher ordered.

Danella thought of running back out the door, but instead took a few steps toward the woman.

"Come on! Who sent you?" she demanded.

Dani's mind raced, instinctively the small woman said, "Tilly."

"Tilly? Now that's a first," the sarcasm in the woman's voice was unmistakable. "He rarely sends me anyone, especially females. I think he doesn't believe women are worthy enough for extra training. It is a typical lower mountain dwarf feeling. They resent the Erry female baron."

Dani said nothing. Her mind raced and came up with nothing to say. The practicing soldiers were a mix of dwarfs, a few elfs, humans and half-breeds.

"You realize it means giving up your free time? There is not much to you," the instructor picked up Danella's arm emphasizing her point. "How long have you been here!"

"A few mooncycles," the princess lied, not wanting the scorn of this powerful woman think her a new recruit.

"It doesn't show, again there is nothing to you." The woman disgustingly shook her head. "What does Tilly expect me to do with a scrawny soldier?"

It rankled Dani to be so easily dismissed. How dare this woman judge her! "I want to join. I'll work hard, honestly." The words flowed forcefully out, surprising the princess. It was not the words she had intended to say, but nevertheless, the small woman meant it.

"You think you can handle being in this class?" skepticism dripped from the dark woman's voice. "See if you can even give me twenty sit ups."

Dani groaned but did as the woman had instructed, dropping to the floor, copying what she'd just see the trainees do. The first five she managed, but after that it got harder and harder. When she got to twelve, her chest started to ache, she couldn't catch her breath. She heard the snickers coming from the watching soldiers. Gritting her teeth Danella managed the last eight grueling sit ups as her stomach even rebelled. She had to fight from losing her supper.

"You will have to show up everyday. I allow no excuses so don't go getting into any trouble and getting extra duties." The instructor's large brown colored eyes looked dubiously at Dani, "That is hard to do with Tilly."

"I won't get into any trouble," the princess promised. "I will show up."

"All right," the woman looked highly unconvinced. "I'll take a chance on you - what's your name?"

"Dani daughter of Yorith," she quickly answered remembering her recruit name - still it sounded strange and alien.

"My name is Corporal Ransa," the instructor informed her. "Be here promptly after your evening meal dressed in a practice outfit. Ask Sergeant Tilly for an extra one." She then turned back to her trainees ignoring Dani.

One of the women soldiers softly said, "Think she'll show up?" getting a shrug in reply from Ransa. Dani watched for a while as the group paired off and began mimicking their instructor as the corporal showed them how to fight. Unlike Dani's earlier lesson, this was even more intense, rolling around on the hard floor. Actual punches and head holds were normal. The group was deadly serious. Loud grunts and yells filled the room. Dani shuddered, *what have I gotten myself into.*

When Dani left, the rain had stopped, but everything was soaked. Corporal Ransa had insisted that students show up in practice outfits. Asking Tilly for one was out of the question. The sergeant would stop her for sure. Danella headed down to the practice fields going straight for the changing building. No one seemed to be around. She silently slipped in the doorway. The practice outfits were against the wall, all neatly lined up by sizes. Her hands grabbed two tops and two bottoms.

"What are you doing?" came from behind her. A heavyset female dwarf stood glaring at her. "You aren't allowed to take them clothes," the high-pitched voice harshly demanded. "Whose you're commandin officer?"

"I need to have some for my combat classes. Sergeant Motos sent me," she told the woman who seemed to be gathering the day's used dirty clothes for washing. Her arms were full of the skimpy outfits. As princess, Danella had dealt with a lot of servants. The noble put as much authority as possible in her voice, hoping the woman was used to taking orders. It worked.

"Oh," came from the surprised woman. "All right, but you tell Sergeant Motos to come get them herself, next time."

Dani just nodded as she shot out the door. The extra clothes got stuffed into her bag, putting them at the very bottom. Her heart was pounding, her emerald eyes looked sharply around. No one was nearby. She hurried up the hill again returning to the courtyard.

The sun was setting so she hurried back to their campsite. Dani was the last one back. Lura looked up from feeding her owl a worm, "Where have you been? Didn't see you at the rec hall."

"I was just walking," Danella quickly answered and was relieved to see the she-elf did not ask any further questions. She unrolled her bed blankets. The rough cloth layers were damp from the rain. The king's daughter got as close as she could to the bonfire that Huff was heaving large branches on, trying to get the wet wood to burn. Smoke filled the air as the branches tried to catch. Dani sat next to Mar who was deep in a book. He'd obvious brought the roughly made volume from the rec room. The dark scholarly man was leaning the document towards the light of the fire to see. Lar was doing the same on the other side of the Arthinian with his own loosely bound manuscript.

Curiosity got the best of the princess, as she tried to look at what the Arthinian was reading. "Do you know how to read, Dani?" the man's black eyes gleamed in the growing fire's light.

"Of course," Dani indignantly answered. She grabbed the ragged bound book from his strong big hands. Leaning toward the light, she read the title out loud, "*Herbs And Their Medicinal Uses*". Her mind wandered back to her last day at the castle when her tutor, Master Tobus, had wanted her to study herbs for the coming Mothia testing. It seemed so long ago, so far away. The princess forgot to inhale, as the almost forgotten memories seemed to flood in. The sweet smell of the flowers in her bedroom, the touch of soft silk fabrics…

"Dani," Marth prodded her, "where are you?"

She suddenly returned, shuddering at having been caught deep in thought. *Why was this man reading about herbs?* His dark eyes seemed to bore into her thoughts. Catching herself, her bright eyes looked wildly around, taking in the circle of those around the fire. The elfs were busy with their pet owls. Huff was fanning the fire with little success. Her eyes found

Lar and she quickly changed the subject, "What are *you* reading?"

He handed her his rather beat up loosely bound leather book. It had obviously been read often before. She again read the title out loud, *The History of the DeLak Kingdom.* "This is a popular book," Dani fondly fingered the volume. It was one of the first books in her library that Master Tobus had made her read. Of course, the castle's volume had been splendidly soft leather bound with fancy lettering unlike this crude edition. Her mind regretfully went to all the books she had not read. The princess had not bothered with them, despite her tutor's encouraging her to do so. *What a fool I was,* Dani chastised herself. *I'd give anything to be curled up reading in my library.* She fought back the tears that welled up.

Dani regretfully handed back the history book to the drylander who looked rather inquisitively at her. "I wouldn't know, we have a limited supply of books in Bombia," the gray-eyed desert man dryly announced but said no more, once again returning his eyes to the worn pages.

Did not Bombia have books? At least he knows how to read, she wondered. *Ah, Bombia had just become a barony of the DeLak Kingdom.* The king's daughter embarrassingly knew very little of the desert people. As princess, her attitude had always thought of Bombia as a backwards wilderness. Perhaps she'd been right, but perhaps she'd been wrong, as the drylander and her guide Sari seemed unusually smart. The king's daughter wondered where Sari had gone off to. Dani had liked her guide who had protected her on the first leg of her journey.

Danella was tired. The fire's warmth made her sleepy. The exhausting day was catching up with her mind and body. Yet, the woman didn't want to sleep. Her brain was racing, her thoughts rushed back to Ransa's classes. *Could she do it?* Trying to keep her attention off the topic, the noble woman leaned towards Mar trying to see the drawings on his book's pages.

"That's lavender," the Arthinian told her, pointing to the illustration. "The plant is used to soothe burns or blisters."

"It's also used for perfumes," she leaned closer to the handsome hillman. "What's that next to it, it doesn't look familiar."

"Ah, that is costiac, mostly used to help in child birth. The herb aids to cut the pain of contractions," Mar lectured like a scholar, tracing the outline of the picture. "It says you can find the white flowered bush at the edge of fields near springs and such. It can easily be confused with the shorter stemmed Tatica which is a totally useless flower."

The princess could smell the closeness of the Arthinian, could feel his body's warmth. Drowsily, she enjoyed both. His long curly black hair touched her face. His hair felt soft yet his face's skin was rugged and manly. His big strong hands were grasping the book as if it was a precious jewel. *He is really quite good looking,* entered into her confused tired thoughts as drowsiness took over.

"Dani, are you falling asleep?" he softly whispered in her ear.

Dani shot up, sitting straight, "Of course not, please continue, it is fascinating." Her face felt flushed. Mar continued reading about the different herbs. The tuckered-out woman didn't even remember falling asleep. When Danella awoke, the sun was peeking through the trees and her bedroll was over her body.

The day followed as the day before. The new recruits worked until midday building their sleeping quarters. "The faster we get this done, the quicker we'll not get wet anymore," Lar's deeply accented voice had matter-of-factly reminded them.

They all agreed and put their backs into it. The elfs had finished the roof and then helped finish the outside walls. Even Dani helped tar the timbers when she wasn't carrying the supplies. When Quinn called it a day, they had only the floor and the inner walls to finish. It was crude, but the structure would protect them from the outside elements.

At noon, they all ate and then started once again on their hike through the surrounding forest. Tilly marched the squadron through a different route, although they again ended up at the cool refreshing pool. This time Dani went in for a swim, but kept her undergarments on. She trudged the rest of their hike damp but at least refreshed. Of course, Lura teased her, calling her *an overly modest stupid dote.* Her and Huff once again brought up the rear, catching up when the group rested.

The day's first afternoon combat class used long thick solid wooden bamboo rods. Each recruit picked a shaft and followed the instructor as the Wildman expertly wielded the staff back and forth in front of his lean skeleton torso. "I am Corporal Bunara. With your height in mind, pick a bamboo that will be the right size." The white-eyed tall bony instructor had a deep guttural accent. Long sharp pointed teeth protruded prominently from his thin lips as he pointed to the deceivingly innocent looking weapon sticks.

Dani didn't mind it too much as her sparring partner, Ash, just got in a few whacks, especially in her upper thigh. Her small frame wasn't as burdensome as hand-to-hand, making her more equal in the pair offs. The second time she was paired with Huff. The stocky dwarf had trouble because he was so short and stubby compared to the even the shortest stick. His rotund belly kept getting in the way. Dani had to suppress her laughter at the comical struggling figure. The dwarf was more frustrated then she was. Danella hadn't realized how deadly the rods could be as the instructor showed how to poke eyes, break ribs and cripple legs. Once again, to her surprise, the princess found it fascinating.

Then the rest of the afternoon they spent with a sword instructor, Corporal Mantile. The large human had bulging arm muscles, huge beefy thighs and callused extra-large hands. Not someone to challenge. The fighter stood before them wielding a massive sword that actually seemed to sing as the blade swished through the air.

The weapon, despite Dani having the lightest version, still felt heavy and burdensome. The sword class had several other squads. The blades were made of light flexible wood, so as to prevent serious injury. The Princess's arms ached from raising and thrusting. The woman's thighs, arms and legs got pounded as her partners easily outmaneuvered any move.

After one exhausting sparring, the instructor gave the class a rest. As Dani turned her back on her sparring partner, the much larger woman smacked her backside - hard! Anger swelled up as the pain filtered into her already sore muscles. Danella turned back, her eyes large and blaring. Without thinking, rage taking over, she charged at the woman. Raising her wooden sword, the king's daughter smacked the half Human/Wild female soldier hard and kept charging, hitting her sparring partner several times. Yelling obscenities at the cheating soldier, she furiously kept fighting.

The soldier tried to defend herself, but Dani's uncontrolled onslaught didn't let up. Fury controlled every one of her actions. Finally, the instructor came over grabbing the sword from the slighter woman's tight grasp, wrestling it free.

"Enough private, let go!" the large man yelled at her. His voice finally got through to the furious princess as Dani relinquished the weapon.

"She cheated," Danella indignantly yelled. "That idiot struck me in the back."

"Let this be a lesson," the sword teacher looked at them all, "never turn your back on an opponent. That mistake will get you killed." His blue eyes flashed at each one, his large arm pointing accusingly at them in an ominous warning.

Tilly, who had been watching Dani's onslaught, actually laughed. "Well ya are full of surprises ain't ya. Maybe there is hope for youse after all." Dani frowned at the lower mountain dwarf, but secretly was pleased with the praise.

Of course, Lura had to ruin it all, "Well, don't we have a temper little one. Didn't think you had it in your bones!" The elf's hearty laughter pierced Danella's pride deeply.

She thinks me a simple weak dote. I'll show her! Dani vowed as she fell in line to head to the mess hall. The king's daughter was so mad that she hardly ate. She left the venison steeped in thick gravy in her bowl, handing the meal over to Huff who gladly ate it. Mar looked askance at her but said nothing. His big wolf dog lay between them. Dani was no longer afraid of his pet. The animal quietly stayed out of the way, usually lying nearby silently watching its master yet never interfering.

After the meal, everyone again headed over to the rec building, but Dani skirted it and headed right down to the practice building. The class' newest pupil was one of the first there and quickly changed into her skimpy outfit not once thinking of her modesty, just stripping and putting the practice clothes on like everyone else.

Ransa started them slowly, having them run in place. Then the corporal moved on to harder exercises. Dani felt every muscle tighten up. They ended with wrestling each other. The princess was the smallest of the group and lost count of how many times her body hit the floor. The entire class ended with the twenty sit-ups. She almost couldn't do it but somehow determinedly managed. Dani had come to realize that the last exercise was the corporal's way of testing if everyone could still manage, if each pupil were up to the training. Danella lay panting, her body covered in sweat with aching sore muscles.

"You need to get some meat on you," Corporal Ransa stood over her. "You need to eat more. Remember, do not skip any meals, eat everything you can get your hands on." The instructor held out her hand giving her a lift up. "I can talk to the cooks and have them give you extra rations."

Panic flooded Dani, "No, please no! My squad will all know. They already think me a useless weakling!" she forcefully blurted out, thinking of what Lura would say, not to mention the others.

The dark-skinned instructor fixed her large brown eyes on her, "Tilly didn't send you, did he?

Danella hung her head, "No, please don't turn me away."

The corporal shook her head, "I'm a fool, but I'll let you stay." With that the combat instructor went over to her bag. She gave Dani a large piece of cheese and some dried mutton tack. "Eat this." Ransa went to leave but turned back, "I will see you tomorrow."

The princess sat down and forced herself to eat the cheese and mutton. Outside, the sky was almost dark when Dani returned to the campsite. This time Lura was again feeding her bird but didn't say anything, yet the elf's violet eyes silently followed her as Dani slid down next to Gorg. Ash sat next to his sibling, seemingly half asleep, with his owl perched nearby. Mar, with the wolfhound at his side and Lar nearby, were once again reading their books as Huff tended the fire. The princess relaxed, as everything seemed so normal, so familiar. Once again, Mar read to her as the tired recruit slowly drifted off to sleep. *Perhaps I do belong...*

Chapter Twelve
Dwarf and Natalia

Huff, once again, spent his dinner in the company of the cooks, scrubbing and washing pans, peeling the root vegetables and any other chores the damn bastards could think for him to do. The Erryian lost count of how many times Tilly had given him extra duty for his insubordination. *I'se gotta shut me mouth,* the dwarf moaned. *Ya might say I's a permanent part of the kitchen now.*

The Iron Ridge dwarf couldn't help himself. As a Erryian, he always had been impetuous and said whatever came into his head. His sister Gertie came to mind, how often had his older sibling cuffed her younger brother when Huff had teased her as a kid. *Tilly picks on me cause I'm from Erry, not from the lower mountains like him. He'd really give it to me if he knew who my mother was!* Everyone knew of the lower mountain half dwarfs' resentment of the prosperous Great Northern Mountains' dwarfs.

Still, he'd opened his mouth once again at the swimming hole snapping back at Tilly when the sergeant had hinted Huff needed to lose weight. The naked Huff had pointed at their squad leader and told Tilly that he also needed to drop some of his bulk.

"Don't talk to me about losing weight, you big fat hill dwarf," Hoffler had exploded, pointing at his sergeant's exposed belly. Of course, he'd gotten kitchen duty again and was not allowed to swim in the pool until further notice.

The other members of his squadron just shook their heads. The she-elf was especially brutal calling him an "overweight dunce that can't keep his flabby mouth shut". *That was an elf for ya,* he angrily thought, *at least her brother is civil.* Despite his dislike of elfs, Huff actually liked the easy-going Ash. The male Hartlander was a great sparring partner, always playing fair. His sister, however, went all out, annihilating any combat opponent that was paired with her. It was like Lura had something to prove.

When Huff had again gotten into trouble, Lar had just shaken his head but said nothing. His light gray eyes implying that the dwarf was acting foolish. The silent desert man said little but let his opinions be subtly known. Hoffler truly respected Mar who had taken on the role of their informal leader. He had actually tried to interject with Tilly on Huff's behalf and ended up getting "chicken" duty. Even Dani had softly said, "Not again, Huff."

Huff had gotten friendly with the small young woman. The two of them were always the last ones to catch up on their daily hikes. She was so tiny and delicate; the chubby dwarf had taken it upon himself to watch out for her, thinking that Natalia would have wanted him to. Slowly, Dani had given up her contempt for everyone and had actually been civil. Huff purposely had stayed back, running alongside encouraging her to "pick up her feet". Still, lately, they had just about kept up with the group. Dani had actually picked up her pace. Often now they were just behind the group, catching up faster.

The young woman seemed to have put on a few pounds, nicely rounding out. *She's not so delicate any more,* his eyes went to her heavier legs and arms, quite noticeable at the swimming pool. Dani had lost some of her modesty to boot, diving right in naked. Even Lura had let up on the girl. In their newly built sleep quarters, the two women seemed to get along well as roommates.

Dani had also become part of the squadron, doing her share of the chores without complaint. Huff remembered the day they had finished their sleeping barracks. How the group had all gotten their sleeping rolls and claimed the inner rooms with Lura and Dani taking the right section while the men took the left portion. A large storage room lay between the two divisions where extra cots, towels, rags and spare uniforms were stacked.

Huff felt great pride in the cabin they had all worked so hard on. Quinn had realized that the Erry dwarf was used to working with wood. The building sergeant had let Huff do much of the design, including allowing the dwarf to add a covered porch to the front of the structure. They were the only building to have a porch. Soon others were mimicking them adding their own.

Despite coming out of her shell, Dani was still somewhat distant. Huff never saw the small woman at the rec hall. Often, she silently and quickly gobbled her supper and then disappeared. At night, she'd reappear at the cabin. He'd often see her sitting on their porch steps, listening to Mar, with his big dog laying next to him. He'd be reading the latest book taken from the camp's library with a lantern shining behind them. Lar stretched out, always close by also listening.

Huff had taken the evenings to building wooden benches that now lay across the porch. He'd even found some chains to make a swing. The Erryian was now building small tables to put next to the chairs. The wood building projects kept his hands busy and his mind off the missing Natalia. Often Lura and Ash were sitting on one of the long chairs also listening to Mar and feeding their owls. The newest recruits had become like family with the same routine every day. Except for at the rec hall, they did not mingle with the other squadrons. Tilly did not encourage it. It was as if the sergeant wanted to keep the six of them separate from the rest of Laren's army.

Why? Hoffler wondered, but the Erryian couldn't come up with a reason. Their group worked just as hard as any of the other camp privates, maybe even pushed more.

If only Natalia was here, his heart ached. He'd only gotten glimpses of her when she was eating her dinner at the far "medical" table. The medics seemed to all hang out together. Another group encouraged not to mingle. None of them ever appeared at the rec hall. They seemed to confine themselves to the med building.

After supper, no one saw any of the medics. Natalia had not once looked at him, not once! The dwarf dared not approach her for fear of what Tilly would do to the entire squad. So, he suffered in silence for a change.

Their days were now fully focused on becoming combat soldiers. Early every day they had full-out marches followed by weapon instructions. Huff hated the bamboo staff and archery lessons. He wasn't crazy about hand-to-hand either. Sergeant Motos was brutal, often pushing them beyond reason. He found his short stature put him at a disadvantage.

He did fine at swordplay and he outrivaled everyone in the axe lessons. The whole squadron had advanced to actual weapons which were sharp and dangerous. His sword, shorter than most, proved quite hazardous if not outright deadly. His over zealousness had nixed a few opponents despite trying hard not to. Everyone in their squadron carried scars from their "practice" sessions.

Huff was better than any in his squadron at throwing and parleying with an axe. He'd even beaten Tilly and Mathie when they had each challenged him. The Erryian missed his magical staff that gave him a large ornate hatchet that would hit its mark every time. *Stop thinkin of it,* he had chastised himself, *it ain't like that any more, youse gotta depend on yar own abilities if I's ever to get outta here.* Hoffler wondered if he'd ever return to his previous life. It seemed like he'd been on the island forever when in reality the time had only been a few mooncycles.

He watched Dani as she was practicing her sword moves. Their instructor, Corporal Mantile, was a no-nonsense half-human/Wild brawny man reminding them of the blacksmith Dohar. The instructor had worked hard with helping Dani. He had gotten the small woman a long-pointed rapier. Dani had excelled in the sharp weapon's use. Huff marveled at how far the small-framed woman had come. No one showed the slightest deference to her now as they had all felt the sting of her rapier. Even Lura, when she'd challenged Dani, had to admit to a draw.

The she-elf outclassed her rivals in just about everything, but archery seemed her favorite. She rarely missed her mark. Only Ash appeared to be her equal often hitting the same target. The male elf proved best in the bamboo staff fighting. Each of them had felt the sting of the man's accurate blows with bruises to remind them.

Lura also excelled in her athletic ability often outmaneuvering her opponents by her dexterity, jumping high forwards and backwards, often fooling her opponents in just her physical moves. Despite her brother's constant chastising her for a bad attitude, she still looked down on all. *If only she wasn't so damn haughty,* the Erryian mused. *She'll misjudge herself one of these days. Then where will Lura be? Someone will come along and be better than she is. It always happens. Good way to get yarself killed.*

One morning after breakfast, an official looking stiff four stripe captain approached Huff. "You're wanted at the command station," he ordered. "Follow me, both of you." The officer also pointed at Mar.

The Erryian shook his head. Now what? Was he in trouble again? He heard Mar order Gorg to stay with Lar. The drylander and the dog stood watching the two leave. Hoffler looked questioningly at the black eyed dark Arthinian that seemed confused like he himself was. Mar shook his head, indicating the man had no idea what was going on.

The command post was near the far entrance of the courtyard. The recruits had passed the low-lying building on their way in, on their arrival. It was a small out of the way structure that housed Laren and his commanders. Although the two had never been inside, the recruits had seen the general and his officers go in and out. The building was not somewhere privates were allowed.

The newest recruits had only seen Laren a few times. Their leader came once in a while to watch his troops' training. He'd once come to inspect their newly constructed sleeping cabin and had complimented them on their good job. Other than that, they rarely saw the general.

This time the command center had two human male guards posted at the entrance. The two sentinels saluted smartly as the captain led them inside. Both guards were attentively standing, their swords held ready, giving the place an official appearance.

Inside were also several regular "at attention" soldiers, stiff in their attitudes. Some sat at several long counters. The group all looked up giving Huff and Mar intense stares as if sizing the two up. The soldiers looked like competent serious officers. The two recruits had never seen them in the proper camp. The captain led them down a hallway to an office that again had two serious soldiers standing guard.

Inside the office sat Yanith.

The old wizard looked up and stood. The head of Mothia appeared haggard with dark circles under his eyes. "Well, Laren reports that you are progressing rather nicely. Although, I do hear you get yourself in trouble, Huff." The powerful mage leaned forward on the desk emphasizing his point. His ornate oak staff lay quietly against the desk within easy reach.

Both Mar and Huff stared opened mouthed. They had expected Laren and were halfway standing at attention with their hands going to salute; a testimony to how they were now proper soldiers.

"Please relax," Yanith sat back down. Neither Huff nor Mar did relax, however. Both wondered what they'd been called to, nervously waiting the *why* of the meeting.

Yanith seemed to sense their uneasiness, "I said relax. You aren't in trouble. I have need of your services. Especially you, Huff."

They both stared wide-eyed at the mage. Hoffler leaned forward, waving his hands in anger, no longer able to keep quiet. "Well, ain't that nice. After all these mooncycles ya finally check on us. Ya uprooted us from our lives and then leave us on this forsaken island. Is that all ya gotta say! Ya need us! How about *how sorry ya are!*"

He heard Mar take a deep breath, "Huff, watch what you say…"

"It's alright," Yanith held up his hand. "I have been keeping track of you. I cannot show any interest in anyone. My attention would put you all at great danger if I did."

It was Marth that spoke up forcefully, anger now coming full forward, "Danger! You need to tell us what's going on, Yanith. Enough of all these secrets. What are you up to? I'm guessing that all six of us were mage trainees. Why us?"

"Ya know they'se done somethin to Natalia," Huff forcefully blurted out. "Ya had no right to force her away from me!"

Yanith put up his hand. Looking at Marth, he quietly explained, "You will know soon enough. Be patient. I am not surprised that you were intelligent enough to put some of the pieces together." The old man looked at Huff and deeply sighed, "Natalia is not forced to do anything. The poor woman is learning to be a healer. Let her be something her own people ostracized her for. Don't stand in her way, Huff. Natalia has a chance to become a great healer, one of the best in the kingdom."

The wizard's remarks hit Huff. It wasn't Yanith or Laren that was responsible for Natalia keeping away from him. It was her own doing. His fiancée did not want to see him. Yanith was right; it probably was her only chance to be something that the Azirran had always really wanted. How selfish Hoffler had been thinking of only himself. A heavy heart filled his chest as the Erryian realized he'd lost Natalia to magic - something the dwarf knew well enough could consume your very being. How could Hoffler blame her when he would do anything to get his magic back!

"I'm sorry, Huff," Mar touched his arm. The Arthinian's black eyes were full of concern. It was then that the Erry Dwarf realized how close they all now were.

"Huff, you know metals, blacksmithing and horses," Yanith interrupted his thoughts.

"Aye, I used to before ya ripped away me magic," he angrily eyed the Mothian mage.

Yanith ignored the sarcasm and continued, "I need you to go to Forge Haven and see Dohar. He is working on something in his blacksmith shop. I want you to take a look and help him. You two can go when the ferry returns to town this morning. Bessie will be looking for you."

"Bessie!" Huff moaned, his mind going to the huge woman seaman's dislike of dwarfs. The thought of another sea crossing turned his stomach.

"What need do you have of me?" Mar stepped forward inclining toward the mage. "I have no blacksmith knowledge."

The old mage let out a hearty laugh. The mirth sounded strange coming from the serious wizard, who rarely even smiled. "Isn't it obvious. I need you to go and watch Huff, keep him out of trouble. You're probably the only one who can."

"Now that ain't fair," Huff spouted. "I's don't need no babysitter."

"It may not be fair, Lord Hoffler," the mage used his Erry proper name, "but it is nevertheless the truth. I'll tell Laren to expect you back tonight on the last ferry run." Both knew the words were a dismissal. Mar turned back as the young lord was leaving.

"Do you have news of my sister? Is Lilith alright?" the Arthinian blurted out.

"Do not worry Marth, my wife Marianna has been checking on her. After all, your sister's healing ability is well known in Mothia. The child will probably be doing her testing early and joining us soon. So, do not worry."

Huff could tell the relief in the Arthinian's face. If Yanith's powerful wife had his sister under wing, the girl was indeed fine. If anyone was a match for anything it was Lady Marianna.

Both men walked down to the beach. Gorg was patiently waiting for his master. How the animal knew where Marth was going was unclear, but the Arthinian was glad to see his pet, rubbing his ears affectionately.

As Yanith had predicted, Bessie was impatiently waiting for them. "Come on ya swagglers, get yar asses down here!" The flatboat was loaded with returning empty crates. There were no other travelers besides the ferry's sailors and the two recruits.

Huff and Mar jumped aboard with Gorg sitting near his master. The boat was violently rocking. The Viamar was not any smoother than the last time they had crossed. As the men rowing headed out, both recruits looked back at what was now home. The island was clouded in mist yet the sun was just peeking through, highlighting Hope Island's lush greenery. How different the misty isle looked to them now.

Both men looked skyward when a flock of the big birds soared just above the clouds. "What are those birds?" Mar asked Bessie who was tending the rudder right behind them.

"Well handsome," the giant shouted over, "they are *youklers*. They be Theror's birds. They watch over the islands. Some say that the god rides them to visit the moons."

"What hogwash," Huff shook his head. "Locals got nothin better to do than make up far-fetched tales."

"Watch yar mouth," Bessie growled at Hoffler. "Youse dumb Erry dwarfs all stink the same, rotten."

"Why ya," Huff jumped up, brandishing his axe. Marth grabbed him, forcing him back down.

"Think ya can fight me with that little axe?" Bessie taunted him. The sea captain reached down and hefted a huge ax that was on the deck by her. The woman's defense was twice the size of the dwarf's weapon. "This here will cut ya to pieces, not that there is much of ya to chop." The large female giant roared with laughter.

"It ain't the size of the axe," Huff shouted back at her, "it's what youse do with it ya giant buffoon!"

"Well, Erryian, when we get to Haven will see what ya can do with that tiny thing." The giant woman with her orange hair flying in the wind, her clothes flapping wildly around her looked half crazy and extremely dangerous.

He heard Marth moan, "Shut up, Huff. We aren't here to get into trouble."

"Hey good looking, Y'ase Arthinian, ain't ya?" Bessie yelled over to Mar.

Marth nodded, "How'd you know?"

"You have the features of their sheepherders. Like them youse black eyes and ya hair, well built and smart too I'd bet. Arthinians is keen bargainers. Always get the best of a trade. Youse wolf is a dead giveaway. Only Arthinians and Wildpeople can handle the wolves and ya definitely ain't from The Wild." The large carroty haired giant smiled at Mar, her sharp long teeth sending shivers down both the recruits.

Mar patted his pet that lay nervously between his legs. Gorg just whimpered, sea travel was not to his liking. All three of the Hope Islanders were glad when the flatboat docked at Forge Haven. Marth grabbed Huff dragging him quickly down the dock and away from Bessie.

"I ain't afraid of her!" Huff unsuccessfully pulled hard trying to get away from the strong dark man's tight hold. The dwarf finally gave up and compliantly headed up the beach toward the blacksmith's shop.

To their surprise, unlike their earlier visit, the shop was quiet. Only Dohar was by the roaring forge melting some ore. None of his workers were at the smaller furnaces. His little boy was sitting close by watching his father work. The blacksmith looked up and then plunged what he was working on in a nearby bucket of water. The steam sizzled and sputtered as the half Human/Wild walked away.

The smithy must have seen the inquisitive looks on their faces, "It's my workers day off." The muscled broad-shouldered man looked at Huff, "I hear you are a blacksmith. You from the Great Mountains?"

"I's was learning, ain't no expert, worked with iron and gems. I worked with wood too," Hoffler answered. The dwarf wasn't sure how good his skills were without his magic. Would the metal feel the same? The Erryian thought of when he was building their sleeping cabin. Wood didn't speak to him like it had with his magic, although his hands still felt the grain. Quinn had been impressed with his wood building skills.

"Come look at this," Dohar motioned him over to a far corner of the shop. Both Mar and Huff wandered over. The two men weren't sure what they were looking at; a large flat leather mat with several rings at the corners. Attached to the rings were thin leather straps. The cords were haphazardly strewn about with several more straps all tied to the ring joints. These straps led to a large hammered out iron shield that lay on the ground. It was a mish mash that made no sense. Attached to the upper part were larger straps shaped almost like a horse's bridle but had no bit for the mouth.

It was Hoffler that spoke first, "Is ya tryin to make a harness for a super large horse?" The Erryian dwarf went over and picked up some of the straps trying to spread the mess out. "Where's the cinch? If that's a saddle," the dwarf pointed to the flat leather seat, "it ain't gonna stay on."

Marth looked at the blacksmith, "You need to give us more information. What is this?"

Dohar shook his head, "Can't tell you much, Laren gave me orders to not tell you anything." The blacksmith looked frustrated.

"Ain't given me much, looks like one big muddle," Hoff shrugged his shoulders, raising his arms in protest.

The brawny white eyed iron worker seemed to shake his head, not sure what to do. Then his thin mouth set in a determined grin, "Come on and follow me." He headed toward the back door. The smithy turned to his son, "Bick, stay here, watch the shop. Come get me if anyone comes."

"Gorg, stay with the boy," Mar ordered his wolf. To his surprise the dog went over to the young lad and rubbed affectionately against him. The albino boy laughed, rubbing the hound on the ears. His thin lip smile showed his long Wild fang teeth.

He's of The Wild, Huff thought, *that damn Bessie was right, they have a way with wolves.* The dwarf watched fascinated as both Gorg and Bick intertwined then sat down contentedly watching the forge's fire. Mar smiled and shook his head.

The two men trailed behind the blacksmith as he went through the back way. The rear yard was filled with piles of raw iron ore and other metal scraps. Huff swallowed hard since the scene reminded him so much of his workshop in Erry where he and his tutor, Yuthiala, spent so much time. The memories seemed so near while the time seemed so long ago.

In the far corner of the yard was a newly built shed; the wood timbers had not even discolored yet. It was there that Dohar went. The half Wild/Human man took a large key from his pocket and opened the door. Both Mar and Huff stopped dead in their tracks when they'd only gone a few steps in. A huge wooden model of a horse – no, it was something else that stood in the middle of the room.

Two sturdy wooden legs supported a huge round wooden barrel, all neatly placed together using thick dark tar to glue it all in place. At one end, a long pole stuck out with what could be an animal's head made by using a bucket. The whole contraption stood much higher than the two men. The wooden statue almost reached the high top of the shed. Extra ropes kept it all in place.

What really astounded them was a copy of the blacksmith's contrivance. It was on the top of the barrel with the straps hanging down and the iron breastplate attached to the front just below the pole neck. Both men stood there, mouths opened, not knowing what to say.

Dohar hesitantly looked at them. It was quite obvious the men thought him crazy. "I've done the best I can. It ain't easy without having one here to test my saddle out."

"What the hell is it?" Huff half laughed. The dwarf indeed thought the blacksmith crazy.

Dohar looked at them, astonished, "Why it's a youkler, of course."

"A youkler!" Mar exclaimed. "One of those birds?"

Huff looked at the wooden statue, "You don't mean that contraption is to put on one of those birds? Is Yanith crazy!"

"You mean Laren, don't you?" the blacksmith's big hands went through his long white hair. "It's the general that come and ask me to help him. Don't know anything about Yanith. He's that famous wizard, ain't never seen him."

Marth grabbed Huff's arm, shaking him lightly. "I'm sure you meant Laren," the Arthinian's black eyes warned the dwarf not to say anything more."

"Yeah, Laren," Huff reiterated.

"Well," the half-breed blacksmith frowned, "the saddle ain't working right." The smithy went and got a ladder, scurrying up the side of the barrel. He jumped on the flat leather seat. "Watch." Dohar reached down taking four of the straps. It was obvious now that they were reins attached to the head harness. The smithy pulled on the fastenings; the head moved left, then right. Huff now realized the large branches full of green foliage were the bird's wings which Dohar had put just behind the saddle. The large wings explained why the flat leather seat had to be so close to the front, near the neck.

Then suddenly the whole contraption fell apart. The rings slid down the reins causing the harness to be off balance. The blacksmith reached forward to grab the excess length, but then the saddle slipped. The front iron breastplate unceremoniously fell, clanging loudly to the floor.

Both Mar and Huff jumped back. "For Theror sake, that mess ain't gonna work right like it is!" Hoffler sputtered. "Youse ain't got the reins hooked up properly. For one thing, the holding rings is too big. On a horse's reins, they is snug with just the right amount of tension. Never mind that youse need a wide tough cinch around the barrel. I mean stomach," the dwarf corrected himself.

"It would help if you had feet holds too," Marth interjected running over to catch the man as the smithy slipped down the side of the barrel.

"Ya need ropes, here and here," Huff going up next to the fake bird, pointing to several areas.

"Laren said you'd help," Dohar sounded relieved. "I've been working on this thing for some time now. My workers are beginning to wonder what I'm doing. I told the general I can't keep it a secret for much longer."

They returned to the shop and spent the rest of the day working on the contraption that they had first seen. Bick and Gorg watched them work, both catching naps together. To Dohar's delight, the saddle started to take shape. Huff enjoyed forging all the new connections, of pounding the breastplate to the right size.

It feels so good to once again work with the iron and leather. Hoffler smiled the entire day. The dwarf fired the breastplate in the forge and then pressed a few quartz gems into it to form a large 'Y' on the front. The men quickly replaced the old saddle with the new one out in the back shed.

"That 'Y' makes it look official," Mar had laughed. "You truly are talented, Huff."

"Ain't nothin," the dwarf remarked. "Ya ought to see me swords!" Huff bragged.

Dohar scrambled up the ladder. The blacksmith looked a lot more comfortable with a wide cinch holding it all in place and footholds for his feet. The smithy tested out the newly configured reins. The bucket moved left and right easily. The breastplate stayed firmly in place.

"I think this is gonna work," Dohar shouted. "Laren is gonna be pleased."

"Well, I don't know how well it's gonna work," Huff laughed. "Youse don't even have a bird."

"That ain't my concern," Dohar pointed out.

Huff's stomach ached. The men had worked all through lunch.

"The ferry just left, Bessie won't be back until close to evening. Go on down to the Rooster, they'll get you something to eat," Dohar told them. "Tell them to put the cost on my account. Take Bick with you. Give the boy something too."

The town was abuzz with activity as they walked leisurely down Main Street. The sea breeze felt cool compared to the hot blacksmith's forge. The summercycle was coming to an end and the chill of autumn lay close by. Shopkeepers were busy tending to customers. Wagons full of recently harvested crops and fresh cut lumber rolled up and down the wide dirt avenue delivering to the various store fronts. The two green uniformed recruits got lots of curious stares, but no one stopped them.

They pushed their way through the swinging saloon doors and were met with a rich aroma of cooking hog and mutton. It all was mixed with the smoke of the large fireplace that roared against the back wall. The sweet tobac smell of the various pipes also filled the room as lots of Forge Haven inhabitants sat at the small round tables that lay across the dining room floor. The loud din of conversation hushed when the three of them and Gorg sundered to a nearby table.

It wasn't long before a half Dwarf/Wild perky barmaid came running over. "Wese have whatever ya got!" Huff almost exploded with hungry excitement. "Bring it all!"

"My da said to put it on his bill, Masie," Bick spoke up getting a big smile from the small lass.

"Ale?" Masie asked.

"I'll take a pint," Hoffler smiled.

"Cider for me," Mar answered. After she'd left he looked at the dwarf, "I'm surprised, most mages don't drink. Sorcerers don't hold well with liquor."

Huff angrily puffed, "You mean ex-mages, don't ya?" Then the dwarf realized what Mar had actually said, "How did youse know? I heard what ya said to Yanith. We ain't supposed to talk about our pasts."

"I have been putting some things together," Mar answered. "I think Yanith's *forgetting spell* is wearing off."

The barmaid came and put their drinks in front of them including a mug full of apple juice for Bick and a bowl of water for Gorg.

Huff looked at his pint of ale, "Dwarfs are brought up on ale. The brew is like our mother's milk. The brew runs in our blood, but you're right, I can't abide any other type of liquor.

Goes right to me head, even a sip." Huff shook his head sadly, "Taking our magic ain't right. What Yanith done, it ain't right."

"Well, I couldn't agree with you more, Huff, but we don't have a choice now do we?" The Arthinian didn't say anymore as their heaping hot bowls of meat and vegetables were put in front of them. Bick got a smaller bowl while Gorg got a bowl full of raw meat. The wolf gobbled it down then settled for a nap in front of the roaring fire with the boy close by.

The spunky little bar dwarf came over to clear up their completely finished plates. She smiled sweetly at them showing her pointed teeth.

"What made ya come to Forge Haven?" Huff asked the perky lass.

"I'se didn't come here, I'se is born here," the barmaid laughed. "We half-breeds don't have much choice. Me parents were mixed. Da is a Dwarf/Wild and me ma is a Wild. We either stay here or we're exiled from the Wild territory completely."

Huff didn't know what to say as both men looked at the woman, astonished by her words. The barmaid looked around and then took a seat next to them. "The Wild don't approve of mixing the races, so they'se offered us this place."

That explains the town's inhabitants, the Erryian thought.

"You seem to do quite well," Mar interjected. "You trade with The Wild and you seem to be prospering."

"Aye," the woman shook her head, "they'se depend on us now. Being by the coast, our weather is good for raising a lot of crops and we supply the entire Wild with lumber products, but they still treat us like second class citizens."

"Ya gossiping, Masie?" A short half-breed dwarf with fuzzy red hair, a big craggy beard with long pointed teeth saddled up to the table. He had big rough furry hands and wore a stained thick apron that almost dragged on the floor. His white eyes shined with curiosity.

"No, Da," the barmaid quickly got up. "I's was just seein if they'se need anythin else." With that the daughter hurriedly gathered their mugs and headed to the kitchen.

"I's Aryute, son of Assla," the short man sat down, "I's

own this establishment. Masie is me daughter. Pay her no attention, the girl likes to talk. Ain't often wese get pure breeds in the town. Me wife was a Wild. She died when Masie was born."

Marth and Hoffler both stood up shaking his hand, "Glad to meet ya," the Erryian spoke up.

Mar shaking his head in agreement, spoke up, "Nice place and great grub."

The flattery seemed to work as the man's features seemed to relax and he took a seat next to Mar. "That's one of the biggest wolfhounds I'se ever seen," the bar's owner looked over at Gorg who was sound asleep by the fire. "Youse from the island," it was a statement not a question. "Wese like Laren's soldiers, good for business. Youse always behave yaselfs. Some of us town people even enlisted with the general. He's a favorite here, he is."

"Glad to hear that," Mar slouched back, seemingly to relax, but Huff knew the Arthinian well enough to know it was the man's way to put everyone at ease. He did it every night back at the cabin quietly reading to them all.

It helped as Aryute also relaxed calling for Masie to bring them drinks. He went on to explain the history of Forge Haven, how the town had grown as more and more half-breeds settled in the coastal town. "The Wild don't like the sea so they'es let us have the coast. They'se have a fear of the Gray Islands. Forge Haveners ain't too crazy about them Islands either. Only Laren dares to go there."

"Why are ya afraid?" Huff asked.

"Wese afraid of those birds," the innkeeper took out his pipe, relaxing as the smoke curled up from his mouth. "Look at me leg." The man lifted his left pant leg. A long scar ran up to his knee. "They'se done that when I wrangled one over a fish I'd caught. They'se have sharp claws, never mind their razor-sharp beaks."

Both Mar and Huff stared unbelievably at the man's deep scar. Both were thinking the same thing, *Is Laren crazy? What was the man even thinking by building a riding apparatus for the monstrous dangerous birds?*

"The general is listening too much to those crazy god myths," Huff muttered to Mar.

Mar just shook his head in agreement.

Chapter Thirteen
A Reckoning

The island's morning had been misty and shrouded in low clouds. It had taken almost to midday before the sun had burned the fog off. Lar's clothes felt soggy. Even during their hike, the drylander felt uncomfortably wet. No one had wanted to swim in the pool as each felt wet enough and the coming autumn winds were cold. Usually the desert man reveled in the abundance of water, but not today.

When Tilly led them to the edge of Hope Island, the sea was raging. It was sending up a cold spray over the cliffs getting them soaked, teasing them with its violence. In the distant horizon, the other islands were completely covered in deep mists. They could hear the screeching of the large birds, but the clouds were too thick to see them. Unlike the norm, the peeking sun felt a coldness that warned of an early fallcycle. Lar felt his body give an unwelcomed shiver.

Back at camp the sea breeze seemed even colder, making Lar shiver as he watched Dani and Lura spar. The two women were both intensely concentrating, trying to out anticipate the other. Although the Hartlander elf was taller and had a longer reach, the smaller woman was extremely quick on her feet, successfully dodging Lura's thrusts.

The drylander marveled at Dani's change. The woman had become agile and strong. Her rapier was a good fit; light-weight but far reaching. Her hand-to-hand combat now matched them all. Most surprising of all was her knife throwing. She always hit her mark and could accurately throw several knives in quick succession. The skill made her a deadly opponent.

The once delicate woman was no longer taken lightly but considered an equal. She easily kept up with the others on their hikes. The squadron no longer had to wait for her to catch up. Dani even looked different. She'd put on weight and had "muscled up" with both her arms and upper thighs appearing much thicker. Unlike the scared spoiled child that had followed them through the Elmwood to The Wild, she was more confident and no longer frightened of her own shadow. Dani was also less condescending, often joining in their cabin conversations over the book Mar would be reading to them.

Lura, on the other hand, just plain fascinated Lar. The Bombian had never seen anyone as swift and capable in her body movements. She jumped the highest, kicked the strongest and wrestled with such intensity. None even came near to beating her at anything - none yet. Lar had come close, but the elf always wiggled out of his holds.

Ash stood next to him, watching his sister battle furiously as Dani frustrated her by dancing quickly away. "Lura will flip over Dani's head and topple her from behind," the male elf commented. Sure enough, that's exactly what Lura did. The small shorter woman could not turn fast enough and Lura had kicked Dani's legs from under her from behind.

The she-elf shouted in triumph. Lura was never happier than when she beat her opponent.

What will happen once someone does beat her? Larandar pondered. *Will the loss devastate her? Who's going to pick up the pieces? Ash?* He thought not.

The Bombian took his place opposite Lura, squaring off with her. His chosen weapon, the scimitar, was swishing in front of his body. The smirk on the she-elf's face told him the woman was already planning to pull some surprise move. The drylander decided to try taunting her. The desert man let his free hand tell her to "come on" and Lar let a thin smile mock the overly proud woman. Anger filled Lura's large slanted flashing lilac eyes.

They circled one another, each waiting for an advantage. Ash and Dani silently watched from the sidelines, as did Tilly. Ash had an anxious look on his face. The drylander felt the absence of Mar and Huff, who usually loudly encouraged him, especially against the she-elf, but the two had not come back yet. Their instructor, Corporal Mantile, intensely watched every one of his pupils' moves. Lar wondered whom the teacher was betting on.

The female elf made the first move, thrusting her sword forward lightning fast, slightly nicking Lar's shirt. "Point for Lura!" Mantile shouted. The drylander had anticipated the move, had planned for the sudden thrust and quickly smacked her hard on her left shoulder with his weapon. "Point for Lar," drifted over the pair. Annoyance swelled in the attacking woman's darkening purple eyes as she gave him another nick on his arm. "Point!" the corporal shouted.

So it went, with each opponent's shirt becoming more and more ripped. "Okay, let's call it a draw," looking at their shredded clothing the instructor called out. Neither Lar nor Lura stopped - the two kept circling. "I said stop," again loudly rang out.

The fight seemed like the recruits were in their own world. The match continued as Lura agilely jumped behind Lar trying the same move she had so successfully done to Dani. The drylander, however, did not even try to turn around but quickly stepped forward out of the elf's reach and then turned.

Lura, surprised, became unbalanced. She tried to move forward, but Lar quickly tripped her. The female elf went down hard but used her strong long legs to bring the desert man down also. The two had dropped their weapons and went full out rolling around, each trying unsuccessfully to pin the other down.

Lura used her knees to hold the Bombian's neck to the ground. He reached back with his own legs and got her torso and brought the elf flat on her back. Lar jumped up using his arms to flip her body high in the air. Lura was so nimble, the woman landed upright on her legs instead of falling down. In a furious rage the Hartland female, head down, ploughed straight into Lar's stomach.

They both went to the ground with Lura ending on top. Her eyes were blazing as she had grabbed her sword and placed it at Lar's throat. The Bombian looked into the woman's crazy unfocused eyes. The elf wasn't seeing anything; her raging emotions were in charge. "Are you going to slit my throat Lura?" the desert man calmly asked her as he felt her knife's sharp edge.

"Oh my god," he heard her mutter as the sword dropped from her hand. Lura's eyes turned back to light violet and tears flowed down her prominent cheeks. It was then that the female noticed the Bombian had a small knife pointed at her stomach. She half smiled, "Draw," the elf conceded.

"Draw," Lar also accepted, taking her outstretched hand to help him up. Dani and Ash stood frozen to the side, each had been afraid to move; the atmosphere had been so tense. Tilly shook his head, "Youse gonna kill each other."

Corporal Mantile strode angrily over, "You both have kitchen duty tonight." The man was not happy. "Don't ever let me see that happen again, save the uncontrolled rage for the enemy."

Who is the enemy? Lar wondered, but kept his mouth shut, as the corporal did not seem open to comments.

At supper, Lura and Lar were put to work. They peeled vegetables and washed pans. "Where's Huff?" one of the cooks asked. "Not used to seeing you two, usually it's that dwarf."

When they finally got to eat, it was after the last mess shift. They sat next to each other alone in the dining hall silently eating their venison steaks and roasted taters. It was Lura who finally spoke first, "I'm sorry I got so carried away. My brother is right, I'm too intense. I could have killed you."

Lar looked at the she-elf. Both of them were frazzled from working so hard in the hot scullery. Yet, the woman was still quite beautiful. Her bright silvery thick hair had escaped her tight bun. It now framed her high cheekbones and large exotic lilac eyes that could flare with such emotion. Her ears, unlike his thick pointy earlobes, were long and gracefully slender, nicely shaped. Her entire body was athletically molded; muscular but still feminine. "You remind me so much of our women in Bombia," he admitted. "My mother would have a great time decorating your violet eyes."

"Decorating my eyes?" Lura looked sideways at him.

"Yes, you see, Bombian women used to cover their faces, so their eyes were the one way into their souls, one way to attract suitors. They would make the most of them. Perhaps, now that our women have uncovered, we will lose that art."

"I noticed Sari's eyes are quite beautifully done," Lura looked thoughtful. "She is quite attractive. Are all Bombian women as striking?"

"Yes," he admitted, "like you elfs, they are head strong and capable. Who knows, maybe we share a common ancestry."

The Hartlander loudly laughed. It was so unusual for the serious female elf to even crack a smile. Lar noticed the smile enhanced her features even more. She was indeed gorgeous and at that moment he saw vulnerability in her. Something or someone had deeply hurt the woman, caused her to draw within herself. Yet he could not imagine what it could have been. Her twin did not share it.

"I would like to know more about your land. My brother and I have traveled extensively with our father, but never to Bombia. It sounds exotically interesting," she told him as they left the mess hall.

"It is very different than the rest of DeLak," he pointed out. "You might find it too harsh compared to your lush Hartland. The air is full of spices. I find the food here so bland compared to our peppery Bombian dishes."

"Who knows, maybe someday I will visit," Lura teased him as the wind played with her hair making the silvery curls fly in the breeze. The wind's wildness gave her an almost mystical look. "Perhaps I will let your mother do my eyes." The female twin headed toward the recreation hall.

"I don't feel like going to the rec building, I've lost my reading partner," Lar told her. "I'm going to take a walk down to the sea. I wonder when Huff and Mar will be back?"

To his surprise she turned around and walked with him. "Tilly said Laren had sent them on an errand to Forge Haven. I don't envy their boat trip."

"Oh, I enjoyed the ride," the desert man admitted. Lar had marveled at the sea's majestic energy. He had enjoyed the feel of the strong winds and the overpowering waves. Like his desert, the intense energy held an element of danger, of unpredictability. One did not know what lay below the sea's watery surface just like one didn't know what lay below the sandy Bombian dunes.

They had gotten half way down the road to the sea when Ash came running up. "I've been looking for you. The owls are hunting in the forest. How was kitchen duty?" he asked his sister. "Lauranna, I hope you learned your lesson!"

"Oh, stop lecturing me. You're not father!" the female elf snapped at her brother then seemed to regret her words. "It won't happen again." Lura once again drew inside herself drawing a veil of no nonsense self-assuredness to her demeanor. The drylander felt her closeness to him draw away.

Lar doubted Lura would change her battle tactics. The she-elf was too high strung for it not to happen again, but then he would not want her any different. It was Lura's high competitive spirit that drove her to be the best. The desert man greatly admired that quality.

When they had gotten down to the beach, the three of them sat in the sand watching the Viamar. The waves were roaring against the beach. Bishi, Lar's pet, came out of his pocket and slithered over the woman elf's legs onto the sand. Lura did not shrink from the reptile, but calmly watched the snake's head plunge down into the loose dry soil.

"Ah, my friend, enjoy the beach," Lar petted the serpent as his pet slithered away. "He misses the desert," the drylander watched thoughtfully while his snake rolled on the beach.

"And do you miss Bombia too?" Lura asked.

"Yes, I miss the solitude that the desert afforded me," Lar's eyes were focused far away as if remembering the rolling sand dunes and huge storms that would suddenly pop up. He could almost feel the dry desert wind brush lightly on his face.

"It is magnificent," Ash broke into Larandar's thoughts. The elf was looking at the massive sea.

"Quite," Lar admitted. He watched three fishing boats dock with a group of local villagers starting to unload barrels of fish. "We never get fish for our meals, where do all those fish go?"

"Good point," Ash remarked and got up. "I'm going to ask."

As he left, Lura shook her head, "My brother is much more curious than I am. He is so like our father."

"I noticed he called you Lauranna. Is that your full name?"

Her eyes went wide, "Oh, we aren't supposed to use our names."

"What is your brother's name?" Lar touched her arm as if encouraging her to tell him. Their bodies were close. Larandar could smell the fragrance of her fine soft silvery hair. Her long curls were now flying loosely with the wind brushing against her high cheekbones. Lura smelled of wildwood and lavender. He breathed deeply; it was intoxicating to his senses.

"Ausanwel," Lura stumbled over it, obviously the name was not something easy to say as Yanith's spell lingered.

Ausanwel, Lauranna. No 'son of' or 'daughter of', he thought. "You're a royal, aren't you?" he asked, knowing that only DeLak royal families, unlike peasants, used their first names like he himself.

She slowly nodded looking inquisitively at him. "Yes, I am too," he admitted. "Larandar," he hesitatingly told her. His mouth went dry trying to say it. He didn't get to pursue their real identities further as Ash had returned. *Is Yanith's memory spell wearing off?* Lar silently pondered.

"They don't know," Ash excitedly told them. "They just take all that fish to a place on the other side of the island."

"How strange," Lura commented. "Look, Tilly's over there. He must be waiting for the ferry, probably for Mar and Huff to return." The lower mountain dwarf was talking with a bunch of waiting soldiers, but his eyes were on the Viamar.

The fishermen headed into the woods, not taking the road to the camp. "Come on," Lura stood up, "let's follow them. We don't have to worry about Tilly looking for us. The ferry isn't even in sight."

Snatching up the black snake, Lar followed the elf twins. The three of them blended into the woods, silently tracking the villagers carrying the baskets of fish. They followed the Forge Haven half-breeds along the southeastern coast of Hope Island. The fishermen obviously often went this way since a well-worn path followed just up from the beach.

They skirted the entire east coast of Hope Island and made the corner at the far cliffs, now heading westerly. The other Gray islands could be seen in the distance, peeking precariously out of the Viamar Sea. The basket carriers kept going west on the northern part of the island. Ash, Lura and Lar had never been in this part of the island before. In all their marches, Tilly had never brought the squadron here.

The three recruits followed slightly heading away from the coast, carefully not letting the leading villagers hear them. The group abruptly stopped when the fishermen approached a small clearing. A looming large barn's outline could be seen in the sunset sky. To their amazement, the town's men started to leave their baskets just outside the front of the barn. They picked up some empty baskets and headed immediately back the way they had come.

"Are they going to just leave the fish there?" Ash whispered.

Just as the three were edging closer to get a better look, Schaller appeared from behind the barn with Okste right behind. Lar put his hand out stopping Lura, she almost had hollered out to their Kazian guide. To their surprise, the two men started dumping the fish all over the ground in front of the barn.

Schaller then yelled out with loud squawking noises. The sky filled with dark shadows as a horde of enormous white birds came flocking downward pouncing on the fish. They were so immense, all three of the recruits stepped back behind a big oak tree in fear.

"They look like giant chickens," Lura said, but then added, "no more like ostriches. Good grief, I don't know what those ugly things look like!"

"Schaller called them," Ash remarked. "The man's an avian seer. He talks to birds. I used to be able to talk to Boris, but I can't now, thanks to Yanith."

So, the twins are not only royals, but like me, ex-mages, Larandar thought but kept it to himself.

"What does Schaller think he's doing with those birds?" Lura's voice was full of awesome wonder. "They are six times his size and look at those outstretched claws!"

"Maybe they tell him of the other islands," Ash commented. "At least we know where all that fish is going."

"We'd better get back," Lar counseled. "The sun will be going down, Tilly will be checking on us. I don't feel like kitchen duty for the rest of our lives."

As they started to leave, the three of them abruptly stopped. Laren had joined the two at the barn. "What's he doing here?" Ash whispered.

They watched as the general took a fish and approached one of the birds, holding the catch out in front of him. The bird sauntered slowly up to him and snapped the large fish from his grasp. The fish disappeared in the bird's large beak as it swallowed the meal whole, then squawked loudly at the three men. The cry was a loud piercing screech that sent shivers up Lar's spine.

Schaller went over to stand next to Laren and loudly squealed at the immense bird waving his hands. "Oviaus," he yelled. The enormous fowl looked curiously at the two then flapped its huge wings and took off. The large shadow circled and then landed again. Laren fed it another fish.

"Are they trying to train that bird?" Ash leaned forward trying to see what exactly was going on.

"That's not possible." Lura took a few hesitant steps around the tree to get a better view of the large creature. "I wouldn't want to irritate those monsters. *By Theror*, look, their eyes are bright bloodshot red and their beaks almost as big as Laren's arm. They don't look real friendly."

"We've got to go," Lar warned. "The evening is getting late. It'll be dark soon. Tilly will have our heads if he finds out we've been snooping. The walk will take too long to go back the way we came. We'll never make camp before dark."

The three recruits headed back into the woods. The forest was thick and the light fading fast. Finding their way was difficult. "Which way is south?" Lura anxiously looked around, trying to see through the thick foliage. "If only we could see the sky!"

They came out on a rocky cliff plateau with the Viamar Sea pounding against the overhangs way below them. The other dark outlines of the Gray Islands were to their right. "Our path circled back around," Lar looked out at the ravaging waves. The sun was almost down; the two moons were just getting to the distant horizon.

"We're still on the northern coast. I never realized how big this damn island is!" Ash threw up his arms in exasperation.

"We could try and follow the coastline, but the walk back could be a long way. We don't know how long the island coastline is," Larandar pondered. "We really need to go straight across. That way would be the fastest."

The three went back into the forest and tried to head south the best they could. "We should be coming across some trail we know," Lura moaned.

The sound of flapping wings filled the air as Boris and Hilda landed squarely on the twin's shoulders. Their pets had returned from hunting. "I wish you could talk to Boris now," Lura told her brother.

"But I can, I just can't understand him. Let's see if Boris understands me." The excited Ash reached up and took the male owl on his arm. Looking straight away into the bird's large eyes, he urgently asked, "Boris, show us the way back to camp."

The bird hooted loudly and then both birds flew off to a tree. As the three approached, they flew to another tree. Their pets were leading them home. The evening was fully dark when the recruits got to a trail that they recognized. Running full out they finally reached the edge of the camp proper. The two moons were now high in the air.

Skirting the quiet courtyard, a low murmur of voices could be heard. The soldiers were getting ready for the night. The posted sentries just waved them on as the three ran past. "They'se gonna get chicken duty," laughed one. The other nodded in agreement.

Their comment caused the three recruits to hurry faster. As they approached their cabin, Lar took the lead heading forward carefully. Voices could be heard. The drylander immediately recognized Tilly's. The sergeant was talking in an urgent almost angry voice with Mar and Huff in front of him. Lura silently pointed at the cabin's porch, Dani was standing there listening, keeping to the shadows as not to be noticed.

"I'm telling ya now to keep yar mouths shut until Laren can talk to ya." Tilly was waving his stubby finger at the two in a stern warning. Their sergeant looked at the defiant men as their faces showed only intense anger. "That damn Dohar wasn't supposed to tell youse anything!" their squad leader frustratingly yelled at them.

"But he did, Tilly," Mar conceded, "and we need Laren to explain this. Where is he? Why were we brought here? Answers!"

"Youse get em when he wants ya to know!" Tilly almost spat the words out.

"Where is Yanith?" Huff interjected, his hands clenched in fists. "Wese see no sign of him when wese get back! That mage was here I tell ya."

"Youse is crazy. What would he be doin here?"

"Yanith!" Lura anxiously whispered in Lar's ear.

It was Tilly that Larandar was focusing on, the man was lying. The desert man's instincts could feel it. "Come on, follow me, let's swing around to the back of the cabin," the Bombian softly said to the elfs. The drylander waved them along.

The tall slim man reached up and opened one of the back window's shutters. "Give me a boost," Lar instructed Ash, but it was Lura who cupped her hands. Using the she-elf's help, Larandar lifted himself up silently, grabbing onto the high windowsill and pulled himself into the dark storage room.

He then reached back and helped Lura climb in. As the Bombian assisted the she-elf through the window, her closeness filled his senses with a strange sexual longing. Her slender body pressed against him. The Hartlander's sweet smell filled his senses; her soft silvery wispy hair enveloped his face. Lar held onto to her for a moment too long. The elf looked into his eyes. There was the same longing in her eyes, made even more beautiful by the light of the moons. Lauranna seemed to quickly catch herself and turned to help her brother in through the window. The moment had passed, but the feeling lingered in his memory.

The three silently went through the middle room, trying very hard not to stumble over the extra supplies.

They stood for a moment looking out of the door. Lar could see the three men still arguing. Dani, standing behind a porch beam, must have sensed Larandar behind her. She turned around to look at him. Her eyes went wide, but Dani kept silent as Larandar put his finger to his lips. He wondered how much she had heard of the sergeant's conversation.

Lar suddenly walked forward stretching his arms as if just waking up, "What's all this noise, can't sleep with all this ruckus!"

"Where's ya been!" Tilly yelled up. "Youse wasn't at the rec hall, neither were those other two! Where's Dani? That woman disappears too much!"

"I came back to the cabin, not feeling well after that kitchen duty you gave us," Lar sarcastically reminded the hill dwarf.

Ash came walking out, "We came with him, been taking a nap. What's going on, Tilly?"

"Youse been here all evening?" Tilly loudly demanded.

"Where else would we be!" Lura came waltzing out, rubbing her eyes. "What is all this racket? You woke me out of a good sleep, you imbeciles!"

Tilly glared at them and was about to dispute their claims when Dani stepped forward out of the shadows, "I can vouch for them sergeant." Dani stood there, her very stance daring him to argue; her hand on her rapier that hung so easily now from her belt.

No, she's not the demur-spoiled scared child anymore, Lar amazingly thought looking at the now confident woman.

Tilly shook with anger but did not challenge her. "Youse better get a good night's sleep, ya all gonna be real busy tomorrow. Count on it!" The hill dwarf stormed off but not before turning to Mar and Huff, "If youse know what's good for ya, keep ya mouths shut!"

All six of them watched Tilly disappear into the night.

"Wese in for it tomorrow," Hoffler said watching the angry lower mountain dwarf leave.

"Yup," came calmly from Ash's mouth. The elf, though a man of few words, always hit the nail on the head. The group was going to feel Tilly's wrath tomorrow.

Then they turned to each other. In that moment, the bond between the six of them was felt by each of them.

"We have a lot to tell you," Mar quietly commented. "You're not going to believe it." His large wolfhound seemed to emphasis his words with a loud bark.

Lura, Ash and Lar looked at each other and the three broke out with huge grins. "I bet we can top you," the she-elf said between fits of laughter.

It was Dani that stepped between them, "What have I missed?"

"Lots!" they all answered together.

Chapter Fourteen
Cohesive Team

Marth sat quietly on the cabin's porch steps looking up at the clear sky above. Gorg was lying at his feet. The wolfhound was lightly snoring. It had been a busy tiring day for them all including his pet. The ferryboat ride coming back had been harrowing as the Viamar had been like a roaring tempest. Bessie had seemed not to even notice nor did the darkening of the evening sky seem to distress the giant at all. "Wese quite used to this, handsome," the giant woman had told Marth. "The sea is the sea, day or night, always the same. I could navigate this boat blind."

When the two had arrived back on the beach, the camp was quiet. Now sitting on the porch's steps his eyes went to the sky. The moons were receding behind the horizon letting the stars stand out. The time was well past midnight, everyone had finally gone to bed after talking late into the evening. The Arthinian was astounded by what Lura, Lar and Ash had recounted. The narrative fit well with what he and Huff had run into at Dohar's blacksmith shop.

What are Laren and Yanith up to? Marth ran everything once more in his mind. *They obviously were planning to try and use one of the youkler birds but to what purpose?*

Neither Laren nor Yanith had been visible when the ferry had gotten back from Forge Haven with only Tilly there to gather his charges back to the cabin. The sergeant would take no questions and had silently led them through the camp.

Marth had enjoyed Forge Haven. The people were friendly despite the variety of backgrounds. It was nice to see the cohesive mixture of all the breeds. The DeLak Kingdom and The Wild could use a few lessons from Haven, especially the elfs. Half-breeds were often looked down upon. Even Yanith was criticized for his mixed heritage, only his immense power kept his critics silent.

The Haven townspeople worked together to make the village prosperous for all its inhabitants. It was as if they had something to prove. Laren's army was the same thing. The large number of hardworking half-breeds had made an efficient militia bringing a wide range of talents. On the island, the soldiers all truly were equal, *especially when it came to dolling out extra punishment duties,* Mar grimaced as the Arthinian remembered his "chicken" duty.

He and Huff had wandered slowly back to the blacksmith's shop after their delicious meal at the Rooster Inn. The tavern's food was a nice break from the 'army' food. Even Gorg had been treated to a large bowl of raw mutton meat. Marth had found the white forest wolves graced many of the stores, especially if the owners were more Wild. It amazed him how much Haven's inhabitants got along with the surrounding environment, even the bears! The Haveners controlled their land effectively, making the Wild have to recognize them through trade.

The shopkeepers were welcoming, many asking questions about the mysterious Grey Island Camp. General Laren was well liked and trusted. The leader of the island's militia had dealt fairly with the town and his troops behaved when the soldiers visited. Everyone in Forge Haven was getting ready for their end of summercycle festival held in just a few days. Mar gathered that many of the Hope soldiers had attended the last festival. Perhaps this cycle would be the same and they'd get to join in the festivities.

The sun had been setting when the ferry returned. The two of them could see the boat with Bessie at the helm. The ferry approached the docks near Dohar's smithy. They could see the flatboat maneuvering into the Haven dock. Huff went straight to the ferry. Marth had taken Bick back to his father, the Arthinian wanting to say one last goodbye.

The hillman found the blacksmith busy at his forge. Mar had learned from the young boy that his Wild mother, Dohar's wife, had died three years earlier of complications with a pregnancy. It was just the two of them now. He liked the half Wild, half human blacksmith. Despite his bulky intimidating build, the half-breed was a kind soul and a loving father - something Marth had never known.

Mar had headed down to the beach. To his surprise, Huff and Bessie were in a heated contest. A good-sized log had been set up on the sand. Each was taking a turn at throwing their axes. A crowd had gathered and were placing bets on who would get their ax the closest to the middle of the target. The Arthinian groaned as both Bessie and Huff were screaming at each other.

The boat's skipper had stripped down to just her skivvies to free up her arms, her black leather sea outfit lay piled on the ground while Huff was shirtless. The big woman was not a pretty sight, but then neither was the pudgy dwarf. Her large body, although mostly muscle, was rippling with fleshy anger. Her fuzzy orange hair was flying every which way. The ferry captain's white eyes were wide and threateningly determined. The giant's huge ax flew through the air, landing squarely in the middle of the upturned log. Her brawny arms flayed in the air accompanied by a loud roar of triumph.

Huff ignored her, taking the same place in line with the target. His axe was much smaller. The dwarf aimed and let the weapon fly. To the crowd's amazement, it not only hit the target but also knocked her axe clean off. The Erryian yelled in victory. The large Wild/Giant woman looked stunned. The crowd went crazy yelling the dwarf's name. Huff became the town's newest hero.

"Howse did ya do that?" Bessie furiously demanded.

"I's is an expert, I'se been throwin an axe since I was a wee toddler," the Erryian laughed. "Like I told ya, it ain't the size, I's knows how to throw." He put his shirt back on and exultantly strove down the wharf. "Wese late, get a move on will ya!" he yelled back at Bessie getting a loud roaring grunt of disbelief in return.

The giant woman grumbled the entire crossing insisting on a rematch. Huff just snickered and ignored her. Marth shook his head hoping that Tilly didn't get wind of the match. They'd both be on kitchen duty forever!

On the porch, Gorg stirred bringing him back to the present; someone had sat next to him. Just from her fragrance Mar knew it was Dani. She smelled of fresh spring flowers. Marth turned to look at her. The woman had taken a seat next to him on the porch steps. She was dressed in an oversized army shirt that served her well to sleep in but unintentionally showed off her shapely legs. The Arthinian looked away as Mar realized how much he was enjoying the sight.

The recruits had all learned how to steal extra clothing and other needed supplies without Tilly finding out. Their middle supply room was full of extra towels, soap, and clothes. Huff had even stolen some left-over apples and bones for Gorg from his kitchen duty.

Dani had cut her long auburn tresses to a short style that curled around her small delicate ears. The style emphasized her perfectly shaped face with her large emerald eyes taking precedence. Even her perky little nose seemed flawlessly shaped to draw your notice to her full-lipped striking smile. It was a smile the group never saw on the trip to Hope Island but now could suddenly appear.

Dani no longer reminded him of his sister. She had grown into a self-assured tough soldier. "Can't sleep?" Dani asked him. "Me neither. My mind is racing over everything that you all related tonight."

"It is a lot to take in," he commented. The young lord noticed her hand had gone to Gorg's ears scratching them affectionately. The two got along very well now. He recalled how frightened Dani had been of his wolf - not any more. The two often lay beside him listening to him read his book, her arms usually around the hound snuggling up to his pet as if drawing strength from the large animal. Like the rest of them, no one feared Lar's snake, Bishi. He'd even seen the black reptile curled up on Dani's lap. Like Gorg and the owls, the snake was *everyone's* pet now.

Watching her snuggle up to his wolf, Marth thought, *I wouldn't mind her doing that to me,* then chastised himself for thinking it. *We are soldiers, not lovers,* the Arthinian reminded himself.

"Yes, a lot to take in," she sighed. "Everything has changed. Nothing seems right anymore."

"Doesn't it?" he lightly touched her arm; Dani sounded so sad, it broke his heart.

"Yes, I was such a fool, Mar," her voice cracked. "Such a spoiled fool."

"We are all fools," he looked up at the disappearing moons thinking of his past disappearing life. His mind went to his books in Arthinia and how his whole life had been centered on his magic. *Lilith had been right. He'd missed the most important things. He had missed the world!*

"My whole life was wrong." It was the first time Dani had really opened up to him. "Everything I valued was so wrong, the people I valued so wrong…"

"It is the future that matters now," Marth lightly touched her hand. "I was just thinking how much the DeLak Kingdom could learn from Haven and Hope. The kingdom doesn't treat half-breeds well. The king needs to change people's attitudes, but then I don't think the king much cares. His family is a bunch of uncaring sheltered idiots. Look what the king did to us!"

"Why do you say that?" Dani's voice filled with alarm. Her hand gripped Mar's tightly. "He does care," she emphatically stated. "It is true how badly half-breeds are treated, but that can change! The king needs only to be made aware!"

"You know him?" Mar looked strangely at her.

"Well, I've heard from others. After all, his sister is the Kazian baron's wife," she quickly answered him. A frown dressed her face as Dani squarely looked at him, "You shouldn't talk, the Arthinian baron is well known for his cruelty and of his isolation. People are frightened of him. I saw him once." Marth noticed her shiver. "He was ugly, all scarred, but worse, the man scared me. Cruelty seemed to surround him. They say that despite his great sorcerer's powers, his royal house is cursed! I would stay away from any of his spawn."

Mar was almost speechless, "Why do they say that? Where did you hear that?"

Dani seemed to hesitate as if couching her words, "Well, from my aunt who lives in Cornia, the capital of Kazia. She told me Baron Arient raped his first wife."

Marth grabbed onto her shoulders in alarm, "What do you mean? You're from Kazia, what is said! Thard Arient's wife, Lady Maria was also from there."

"Yes, she was the daughter of the baron's sister, quite beautiful I'm told. Baron Arient took a shine to her when he visited the Kazian court as Lady Maria was also there visiting her uncle. Arient raped her and got her with child. Then he refused to believe that the child was his. The Kazian baron forced Arient to marry his niece, Maria. When Maria died, her mother cursed the Arient house. She blamed Maria's husband. It didn't help that he would never let their children visit her Kazian family. Arthinia is a very reclusive barony!"

Mar said nothing, just stared into the night. He'd never been told the story but he believed it. The account explained a lot - his father's distain toward him, even hatred, and his mother's unhappiness. Had he raped his mother again and Lilith had been born? Had his father killed his mother? It explained why the baron wouldn't let his children out of Arthinia. It explained his father's reluctance to send his son to Mothia despite wanting to get rid of him.

"Mar," Dani touched his arm. "Where are you? Do you know the Arthinian baron?"

"No, obviously not," he looked towards Dani, but the young lord didn't really see her. His mind was back home as the detestation for his father almost consumed him. The night seemed suddenly cold. *Am I cursed?* Mar looked at Dani. He dared not tell her his real identity, she'd shun him for sure. They all would. Could he blame them?

"I'm tired, we'd best get some sleep," Dani had slowly gotten up, stretching her stunningly toned body. Being in the army had enhanced her muscles to almost sculptured perfection. Once again, he couldn't help but think how beautiful she was.

The Arthinian lay awake; his mind racing with all the day's events vying for attention. However, it was the loathing of his father that forged forward in his thoughts. He worried, once again, for his sister. When Marth finally fell asleep, dark dreams haunted him. He awoke with the dawn filtering in and his body covered in sweat. He moaned, this was going to be a long day. Mar noticed everyone let the nearby stream soak them thoroughly as they washed up. The cold water helped wake up tired muscles and woke up foggy minds.

For the next few days, Tilly worked them hard. He marched them all around the island and then made them work on their combat skills into the early evening until the last call for supper. The sergeant never let up on them, every moment was spent marching, fighting, or doing camp chores. Except for Dani, they all headed straight back to the cabin falling asleep early. No book reading, no discussions, just much needed sleep. Every bone in his body was sore. Marth's torso was covered in small bruises and tiny nicks from weapon fighting. His mind just wanted to sleep. The Arthinian wondered how Dani could still take her evening walks. He'd been too tired to even notice when she had returned to the cabin. *Is she meeting someone? Has she a lover?* Lura thought so.

On the third day, Marth's curiosity got the better of him. After supper, despite being exhausted, he didn't head back to the cabin, but instead quietly followed Dani as she left the mess hall. The small woman headed down toward the barn, but avoided the structure and went into a building across from it. Gorg kept brushing against his master's leg, the wolf disagreed with him snooping.

Is she meeting someone every night? Does she have a lover? Is that why she's changed so much? Despite trying not to, Marth felt the feeling of intense jealousy. *Stop it!* His mind chastised him, *she has better things to do than fall in love with a cursed man. If only she knew who I really am! She'd not even talk to me!*

He quietly slipped through the door, feeling guilty for being nosey, but the young lord couldn't help himself. He instructed Gorg to stay by the entry. Even as Marth opened the entrance, his ears could hear the yelling of a woman. Despite his bulky build, he hid behind a large beam and watched as the intense soldiers were practicing inside. Mar recognized Corporal Ransa who was leading the group. The tall dark-skinned soldier was known as a tough commander, head of all combat training. She instructed the elite ready militia. He'd seen the corporal fight. She was dangerous and strong, often just plain overpowering her opponents. What was she doing here?

His gaze went to Dani who was doing stretch exercises. Her total attention was on Ransa. Every soldier in the group looked fit and resilient just like their instructor. No wonder Dani was so changed; she'd been going to extra practicing all this time! His admiration for the small, once-delicate woman swelled. *So, this is where the woman was going every night.*

He watched fascinated as they paired off and intensely fought. He slipped back outside. Marth was exhausted, *how is Dani doing this?* The recruit sat on a nearby wall patiently waiting for her to come back out. The building was built on a high hill overlooking the practice fields. The sunset was quite striking. He forgot the hatred that had been consuming him since last night and let his mind become one with the sunset's harmony. Mar used to do the same thing when he'd practice his magic spells back home.

Magic, he doubted he'd ever practice being a mage again. *Whatever Yanith had in mind for their group that he'd chosen so carefully, it wasn't short term,* Marth reflected. He wondered, once again, if the six of them were all ex-mage apprentices. *Dani too?* He would not have guessed her a mage but she'd changed and now it was *perhaps.*

"Mar, what are you doing here?" brought him out of his deep thoughts. Dani stood before him. Her angry face told him she was not happy. "Were you following me!"

There was no use lying, "Yes, I was," he simply said and saw the angry blaze of her emerald eyes.

"How dare you!" she spat at him.

"I was worried about you," the young lord half lied, as the Arthinian didn't want to admit he thought she had been with someone.

He saw her eyes soften, but she didn't let up, "I don't need you looking after me! Please do not tell the others, if it got back to Tilly…"

"I'm not going to say a word," he assured her. "We all have our secrets."

"And what are yours?" Dani demanded.

"Beyond telling," he smiled down at her. "How can you find the strength to do this every night?" Marth wanted to change the subject.

"Corporal Ransa expects us here, that means I do it!" she sighed. Despite Dani being tired, somehow, she had kept going. Mar admired her even more.

When the two of them arrived at the cabin, everyone was already there and still awake. "Where have you both been?" Lura teased. *Had they all been waiting for them?* He knew they had, it showed how the group was a family now.

"Walking!" Mar emphatically told the she-elf and got a sneer in return. Ash laughed as the other twin sat on a seat casually putting his feet up. Huff just sighed as if the dwarf was happy they had finally got there. The Erryian also exhaustedly flopped down on a porch chair.

"Youse had us worried," the dwarf admitted.

Lar handed Mar a book, "Well, I took the liberty of stopping by the rec hall and got some reading material. Want me to read for a change? Perhaps we can all stay awake long enough."

It was rather nice returning to the normal. Larandar sat behind him, Ash and Laura on one of the benches. Huff was on a chair, snoring and Dani snuggled next to him and Gorg. When the exhausted recruits all dragged themselves to bed it was with contentment that nothing had changed despite Tilly's efforts.

They got a surprise at breakfast. Tilly announced that practice was ending early and anyone who wanted to attend Forge Haven's Summer Festival was welcomed to do so. Laren had suspended all camp activities to let the soldiers attend the Haven end of summercycle festival. The ferry would be going back and forth until late in the night. Their sergeant informed them that Laren was paying for everything, so enjoy!

"I still expect everyone bright and early tomorrow morning, so keep that in mind as you celebrate! There will be no excuses!" Tilly pointed at each one, but stayed especially long on Huff.

True to his words, the soldiers were let off just after noon. They all rushed and washed up in the stream and got into presentable clean fresh uniforms. The six of them walked down to the beach together. Gorg lightly trotted next to Mar. The two owls were perched on the elf's shoulders, but were hooting loudly at each other. "Hilda doesn't want to go," Ash told them, "but I think Boris is insisting."

To their surprise, two ferries were docked loading up soldiers. Huff tried to steer them toward the one that Bessie was not commanding, but unfortunately the large woman stood imposingly in their way and corralled them onto her boat. The ferry was crowded. "You can sit right next to me, handsome," her long tooth smile was aimed at Mar, her large stubby hand patting a box that was right next to her near the rudder.

Marth reluctantly took the seat as they all snickered. He heard Huff say, "Poor guy." Dani sat nearby stifling a smile, while Lura, who had grabbed a seat by the wooden railing, was just plain laughing. Lar had taken his favorite place by the mast with Ash close by. The boat was packed with excited Hope soldiers. A day off was a rarity.

When they arrived, the six of them strolled down the main road. The town had gone through an amazing transformation. Bright ribbons were tied to every shop; fiddlers and drummers were playing lively tunes along Main Street. The people from Haven were dressed in their best clothes with bright feathers decorating their hair. The straw boots, decorated with good-sized colored beads dangling off the tops, made quite a racket. Every inhabitant had their faces painted with red stripes, every nose a bright pink. Even the wolves had colorful beaded collars, their tails wagging covered in red feathers. The influence of the Wildpeople was very evident.

Marth leaned down to Gorg, "We should have dressed you up." The wolf half growled vehemently disagreeing.

Best of all were the smells of cooked pastries, pies and fresh baked cinnamon sugared bread. Colorfully decorated booths were scattered up and down the street. They held cute little trinkets for the children; wooden dolls, clackers and ribbon sugarcane candies. A colorful decorated garlanded center stage had been erected with several of the inhabitants giving speeches. Mar noticed Dohar with his son up on the platform. The youngster, Bick, enthusiastically waved to them but was quieted by his father.

The young child, however, jumped down and ran over to the group. He had a single rose in his little hand. The boy abruptly stopped in front of Dani and offered her the flower. She knelt down and took the offering. "Well, thank you Bick." Her smile was genuine and warm. As her hand reached for the rose, the woman recruit took the youngster's hand and kissed it.

Bick squealed with delight and put his arms around Dani's neck and hugged her. Mar marveled at the change in Dani as she returned the hug. This was not the same woman who wouldn't even talk to them on their journey to Hope Island.

Dohar joined them. "Bick, leave the lady alone!" the blacksmith chastised his son. "I'm sorry. You look very much like his mother," he sorrowfully explained to Dani. "She was a small human, pretty like you." The Human/Wild man blushed profusely and quickly looked away. Mar noticed the tears that had formed in Dohar's eyes.

"Oh," Dani exclaimed and in a spontaneous moment swept up the small child and swung him around. "Thank you for the rose," she laughed into his ear. "Let's go get some of that ribbon candy." She took his hand and the two went over to the trinket booth and both came back eating the sugarcane treat.

"Thank you," Dohar explained to Dani, "he hasn't laughed like that since his mother died."

The six of them ended up in the Rooster. The place was so lively with music filling the large smoky room. The barmaid Masie waved them over, "I was hoppin ya was comin," she looked directly at Marth. "I got a table over by the fireplace for ya."

"Don't ya remember me too!" Huff pouted, getting a sly embarrassed smile from the flirtatious server.

"Of course," she answered as the perky half dwarf's eyes returned to Mar. "I'll get ya some food and drink."

Heaping plates of aged elk steak, a prized delicacy in Haven, appeared before them along with zesty herbed roasted vegetables. Mushroom pie was the table's favorite. She also brought a large pitcher of their homemade apple mead that was mixed with their popular ale.

Huff immediately poured himself a pint. Taking a big gulp, he sighed. "Now I ain't had a pint of good mead ale in a long time.

"Can we have some apple cider, Masie?" Mar asked the barmaid. "Most of us don't drink spirits."

"You want a sip?" Huff asked Dani. "It's really good!"

"Sure," the small woman grabbed his mug and took a sip.

"I wouldn't," Marth put his hand on her arm as she went to take another sip. "It isn't good for you."

"Stop trying to tell me what to do," Dani snapped at the Arthinian. "You're not my keeper. I'm capable of making up my own mind, thank you!"

Lar spoke up, "Dani, it really isn't good for you. It's intoxicating stuff."

"Both of you, leave her alone," Lura put in despite Ash trying to shut her up. She brushed off her brother's arm, "Dani is a grown woman. She doesn't need you men to protect her!" Mar notice Lura didn't take any of the mead though.

Dani, as if to make her point, grabbed her mug and filled it with the mead then took a big swallow of it. "It's quite good!" she nodded at Huff who was already on his second pint. She completely ignored Mar.

Mar shook his head. To make matters worse, Natalia came strolling in with the rest of the medic group. They took a table in the opposite corner. Huff's eyes followed her, but he made no effort to get up. Instead, he poured another pint and downed the ale quickly.

To Marth's horror, Bessie came waltzing in. The colossal woman roared as she saw Huff. "Come on ya bastard dwarf," the giant waved her large axe. "Let's see what ya can do!"

He heard Huff moan, "Leave me be, you overgrown ox." That only seemed to infuriate the large woman more. She threw her axe against one of the walls as if challenging the dwarf to match it.

"What's the matter, Erryian scum," Bessie screamed at him. "Youse was lucky last time. Afraid are ya! - Typical Great Mountain dwarf. A pock on Erry's baroness."

Reluctantly Huff got up. "Let's settle this once and for all youse witch!" he shook his axe. The dwarf went over to her and then stepped even further back and let his axe fly. It hit her large weapon and spit the handle right in two at the same time knocking her ax completely off."

There was a hush that fell over the room as everyone held their breath. All eyes went to the giant woman. It was Okste that spoke first, "He done beat ya, Bessie. Now concede!"

The big red-headed woman looked over at the male giant then reluctantly nodded and the room exploded in yells of approval. Huff's name was once again shouted out.

The music became quite lively as customers began to dance and sing. A half-Dwarf/Wildwoman came over and grabbed Huff to dance. At first the dwarf resisted, but she insisted and they joined everyone on the dance floor. The tables began to clap as the Erryian animatedly stomped to the music. Huff was quite good. Marth also noticed Maggie and Mathie had joined in. Tilly, Schaller and Okste were clapping and stomping loudly as they watched the dancers circle the floor. Mar looked over at Natalia. She was watching Huff intensely. *She still cares for him,* the Arthinian realized. *Poor Huff.*

Marth was surprised when a three-stripe corporal came over and asked Dani to dance. The Arthinian was even more surprised when Dani agreed. *She's had too much of that damn mead,* he thought, *it has gone right to her head.* He watched as Dani was laughing and trying to stomp to the music. The officer had grabbed her and was whirling her around. Mar felt his face turn red - jealousy flooded his brain. *What is she doing?* anger taking over.

Mar heard Lar ask Lura to dance, grabbing her hand and cajoling the elf to join him. To his surprise, the she-elf took the desert man's hand and let the drylander lead her onto the floor. The two were laughing and seemed to only see each other. *Now that is something,* Mar was taken aback. *I missed that coming,* as the young lord pondered the two. He noticed the frown on Ash's face. The male elf twin did not look happy at the attraction that Lura felt toward Lar. The drylander had his arm around her and was twirling her. Lura was laughing and utterly enjoying the dance. It was totally out of character for the serious woman elf.

Mar got up and went over to the dancing Dani. He pushed her dancing partner separating the two and grabbed Dani's hand. He dragged her over to the table, forcing her to sit. She glared at him, "What do you think you are doing?"

"Putting some sense into your head!" he growled at her. Gorg went over to the small woman whining his agreement. She seemed startled at first, but then her hand automatically went down to the wolf, scratching his ear affectionately. Marth continued, "That guy had his hands all over you!"

"We were dancing!" Dani yelled at him. "I'm enjoying it!" Her words were slurred and her eyes sparkled with the effect of the ale. "I noticed you didn't ask me!"

"Fine, then dance with me!" He took her hand and led her to the dance floor. She was so lovely to hold. At one point she stumbled and Marth caught her. His arm went around her waist pulling her toward him. Her body felt warm and inviting. "Dani, you're driving me crazy!" He felt her well-proportioned muscled body, the curve of her hips fitting nicely in his hands. Her whole body fit nicely against him. He looked deeply into her emerald eyes. To his total astonishment, she looked passionately back at him.

It's the drink, he thought, otherwise she wouldn't even notice me.

When they returned to the table, Dani was giggling, laughing and stomping her feet. The behavior was so unlike the reserved soldier that the female recruit had become. Huff was finishing his fourth pint. The dwarf's eyes kept glancing over at his fiancée, but he made no move to go over to Natalia's table.

This is getting out of hand, Mar looked around the table.

Lura looked at Dani and Huff and said, "You're both drunk!"

"Not me!" Huff exclaimed, "I can hold my liquor."

"Sure you can," Larandar shook his head.

"I'm taking Dani back," Mar announced. He looked at Lar, "Can you see that Huff gets back?" The Arthinian saw the drylander nod, as did Lura. Ash just looked totally annoyed, something extremely unusual for the Hartland male. His slanted, normally lavender colored eyes had turned dark purple when he looked at Lura and Lar, sitting cozily together.

"No, you are not!" Dani slurred her words. She tried to get up but slipped and fell back down. Marth grabbed her hand and dragged her out of the saloon. The slight female soldier tried to fight him, but she was too drunk to really resist. The drink had gone straight to her head.

Well, if I had any doubt that she was a mage, I don't now, Marth thought.

Dani continued to fight him. Finally, he just threw the lightweight body over his shoulder and carried her to the ferry. On the return trip, he sat by the mast balancing Dani on his lap. Gorg put his big wolf body in front of Dani protecting her. She had given up and was leaning against Mar half asleep. His arms easily encircled her. Her hair smelled of fresh cut flowers. Despite her gaining weight, she seemed tiny in his arms.

Notwithstanding the rolling of the flatboat, she didn't wake up. When they arrived at Hope, he once again threw her over his shoulder and carried the woman back to the cabin. As they entered the bedroom, Dani became violently ill. He had just enough time to find a bucket. Her supper came up.

The Arthinian went to put her in her cot, but he had to take off her clothes first. They were a mess. Placing her on the bed, he couldn't help but notice how perfect her body was; firm full breasts, shapely legs, delicate hands and feet, all topped with a beautifully shaped face with wide emerald eyes. Her thick short cut auburn hair just accented all of her as if a final finishing to a painting. He quickly grabbed a blanket and covered her.

She moaned, "Oh, I'm so sick!"

"It's the drink," he tried to tell her. "The sickness will wear off, you need to sleep."

"Thank you, Mar," Dani managed to get out. He could hardly hear her. He bent down to catch her words. Her hand grabbed his shirt, "You were right. You're always right." She pulled him down, her lips lightly brushing his mouth. "Thank you."

The longing for her almost overwhelmed him. The Arthinian so wanted to hold her, tell her how much she meant to him, but he caught himself and quickly stood. He left her sleeping and walked out to the porch, deeply breathing in the cold fresh air. Autumn was definitely close by.

Marth went over to one of the chairs. Leaning it against the wall, he sat looking at the stars. Gorg lay at his feet. He'd keep watch until the others returned. It wasn't that long before Gorg growled and he noticed someone approaching the cabin. It was the damn corporal!

The corporal slowly headed up the stairs looking around to make sure no one was there. "What are you doing here?" Marth came out of the shadows and stood up. He held his knife in his hand.

"I thought, I thought I'd check on her," the officer stuttered, caught by surprise.

"She's fine, sleeping," Mar put as much warning venom as he could into his voice. "I'll tell her you were here! Now leave!"

"Sure, sure," the man backed away, almost running back into the night.

Later when Lar, Lura and Ash returned dragging a drunk Huff with them, Marth helped put the dwarf to bed. Lar and Lura joined him on the porch. Ash went down to the stream to wash up or perhaps just to cool off his anger. "You didn't go to bed, you stood guard over her, didn't you?" the she-elf remarked.

Marth told them about the corporal showing up. Lar just shook his head while Lura stamped her foot in frustration. "Damn, some things never change. How dare he!" she sounded angry.

Ash had returned and snarly remarked, "Look to yourself, sister!" Lura glared at him.

"No, some things never change," Mar commented.

Chapter Fifteen
The Birds

Dani's head felt swollen, her thoughts were a mixed up muddled mess. Slight diffused rays of sunshine were poking in through their cabin's bedroom window. The morning was in a heavy fog. The weather mimicked her thoughts. The day was still very early. Lura was poking and yelling at her to get up.

"Tilly won't let us be late," the she-elf warned. "The sergeant warned us all. Chicken duty is a good possibility if you don't make breakfast. Get up! You should have known better than to drink that stuff." It had completely slipped Lura's mind that the twin had told Mar to let Dani drink the mead.

The warning got Danella's attention. She couldn't miss her classes with Corporal Ransa. There were 'no excuses', the instructor had explained, which included any extra punishment duties. So far, Dani had kept out of Tilly's wrath, doing everything necessary to keep out of trouble. It was not easy to do. She was the only one that hadn't received extra duty. Danella had to keep it that way. The thought got her moving despite her body loudly complaining.

She washed in the nearby stream, immersing her head completely, letting the cold water clear her thoughts. The others were already there. Huff was doing the same thing. Mar hadn't said anything to her. The princess felt herself blush when he had looked at her.

Mar really helped me last night, Dani recalled, although much of it was a fuzzy mess. *He was right, that drink totally was bad for me,* the hungover woman begrudgingly had to admit. Still the resentment of having someone watch over her lingered. The once spoiled woman had worked too hard to become self-sufficient, a capable soldier, of looking after her own self. So, she ignored the Arthinian. *I don't need him to look after me!*

She forced herself to eat breakfast, at least some of it. Her stomach was not a willing participant as waves of nausea came and went. They all seemed out of sorts, although Huff ate every bit of his food. The Erryian dwarf, however, was grumpy and was not his usually garrulous self. His eyes kept wandering around the mess hall. *He's looking for Natalia,* Dani speculated.

"You amaze me," Lura had spat over at the dwarf. "You must have an iron stomach just like those mountains of yours. It matches your brain!"

"Youse just jealous," the dwarf had replied as he ate his second helping.

Lar and Mar were in some deep discussion over sword techniques with Lura trying to interject herself. Ash was very quiet, almost brooding which was totally not like him. Dani said nothing, concentrating on trying to get some of her breakfast down. This was going to be a long day.

Although Tilly marched them to the swimming hole, everyone just sat on the pond's edge or lay down trying to get a quick nap. Tilly had laughed, "Well, did wese all overdo it last night? I's warned ya." They all growled at him, including Gorg. The owls hooted loudly and took off to hunt. Even Lar's snake had poked its head out and hissed. Tilly was not anyone's favorite today.

"You could at least go a little easy on us for a change," Ash complained.

"Ha!" Tilly had exploded. "Is that the excuse you'd give an enemy? *Don't kill me today - I'm not in the mood!"* The lower mountain dwarf stood in front of his squadron, shaking his finger at them. "Youse are a bunch of spoiled babies."

Just to prove his point, Tilly ran them full out back to camp. They all arrived on the practice field sweaty and tired. Their sword instructor, Corporal Mantile, showing a little more sympathy than Tilly, let them mostly just practice. Even the rapier felt heavy in Dani's hand. Despite going easy on them, the entire squadron was exhausted when Sergeant Bunara continued their lessons. The bamboo rods stung; each recruit did not put up much resistance. The recruits worked through lunch. Bunara was not pleased with their performance. No one seemed to mind much except Huff, of course, who loudly complained at missing a meal. Their archery and axe practices were a disaster. Lura's arrows kept missing her target. Huff complained his axe was off balance.

Supper found them picking at their food. The whole table, including Huff, was totally exhausted. Days of Tilly working them hard and a late night in Forge Haven had finally caught up to them. Dani dreaded the evening class with Ransa, yet she had no choice.

Lar left the table, the tall desert man headed toward the kitchen. "Where's he going?" Lura asked.

"What do you care?" her brother sarcastically answered. The harsh disapproval rang loudly. The elf's intense scowl was aimed directly at his sister.

"Ash!" the she-elf looked alarmingly at her brother. "What is wrong with you!"

Mar quickly answered, actually getting up and sitting between the two siblings who were glaring at each other. "I think we are all tired. Let's all settle down before Tilly comes over here!"

That shut everyone up. The thought of extra duty was a powerful deterrent, but Ash angrily looked down at his untouched meal ignoring his sister completely.

Lar came back carrying a large jug of hot strong black tea. "Here, try this. It is an old recipe I learned from my mother as a kid. This stuff will help get our energy back and settle any upset stomachs."

He poured them each a mug full of the dark liquid. Lura put the concoction to her nose, "It smells of cinnamon, mint and maybe berryroot. It smells horrid!"

"Yes, your nose is right, but it also has cardimon root and I found some dandelion stems outside the kitchen door. I had trouble with the cook giving up some of her hot pepper seeds so I stole them when she wasn't looking! Give it a try!" the drylander urged.

They all held their noses and drank. Dani immediately felt a surge of warm vitality filter into her muscles. Her head cleared, her stomach settled down. She looked at the desert man in wonder. All of them were looking at him with grateful eyes as each felt better. Even Ash reluctantly nodded his thanks to Lar. "Great brew!" Huff blurted out as his color returned and his green eyes were once again sparkling with mischief.

Feeling better, they all headed to the rec room together, except for Dani who left for her 'walk'. The princess watched the group go. She then snuck down to the exercise pavilion. Despite her feeling better, Danella was happy when the class was over and she got back into her green uniform. Corporal Ransa had walked over to her.

"You have really come a long way, Dani. You have put everything into your training, including your intelligent mind," the drill corporal acknowledged. "I think I'll have you become a practice leader tomorrow. Perhaps leading to full instructorship."

"Thank you," Dani beamed. It was not something she'd ever thought to hear from the tough teacher. As the princess turned to leave, Ransa spoke again.

"Tilly will have to be told," the instructor's tone was not encouraging.

"I suppose," the princess resigned to her fate, turned back. "I worry that Tilly is going to make me quit," Danella sadly speculated, her heart was beating fast.

"Don't worry, I have some influence with General Laren. I think our leader knows Sergeant Tilly never sends anyone to my classes. That stubborn old-fashioned dwarf never admits he's not in total charge. I suppose Laren had to have a reason for making him in charge of your squadron. Tilly works his people harder than anyone, demands the most. If you hadn't come here, you'd never have survived."

Danella knew the woman spoke the truth. "Thank you, I will be here tomorrow."

"I was thinking you're good enough now to join my special squadron. You'll make a good soldier, Dani; a very good soldier with a chance at getting your own command. Let me get you transferred to under me. Give me a little time to approach Laren."

Dani didn't know what to say. Never had she thought that she'd make a good soldier, never mind actually enjoy it. For the first time, the once spoiled noble had a true purpose in her life.

"Thank you, commander, I would enjoy that!" the enthusiasm rang loudly in her voice.

"Good," Corporal Ransa turned and left, leaving a relieved Dani. *I'll get out from under Tilly. I'll get to show my skills!* It was a testimony to how far the royal had come from her previous court life. Her former pampered life took on a far away dream. She didn't even associate herself with her past any more.

Outside, once again, was Mar sitting on the stone wall with Gorg at his feet. Danella sighed. The king's daughter had to admit she was glad to see the tall dark man. The royal admired him for not only his physical strength but for his intellect. He may be just a sheepherder's son, but he had a maturity that many lacked at court. She wondered if all Arthinians were like him? Perhaps the reclusiveness of their barony had forced them to be self-sufficient and smart.

"What are you doing here?" she bent down petting the large wolf and getting a lick on the hand and a welcoming *woof* in return.

"I thought I'd walk you back to the cabin. Let everyone, especially Tilly, think you're with me. They all think you are meeting someone, maybe that corporal."

The thought had never entered her mind that someone would think her having a tryst with anyone. "Why I never!" she exploded then commonsense took over. *What else would they think? That I'm at extra combat classes? Not likely. And what if Tilly got suspicious?* Mar was right once more. She nodded, looking deeply into his black eyes. *What lies behind those dark orbs,* she wondered? Was his soul just as dark? *No,* she shook her head, *he's too caring to have dark thoughts.* At least Danella hoped so.

They walked back to the cabin. Lar handed Mar a book and they all sat around listening. Lura had passed out the extra brown apples while Huff once again set about making his little side tables. Dani smiled as she took her place next to Mar and Gorg. It all seemed so normal. It had become her existence. For the first time in her life she was actually content.

The book was about the Coorish Wars that were now just a faint memory with only the old mages remembering the battles. It was a time when the Bracaards and their evil allies had ravaged the kingdom. It was long before Dani was even born.

As Mar read, Dani shivered as he spoke of the atrocities done by the weaselworts, border trolls, and the lizardpeople with the help of the evil god Kortis as they ravaged the DeLak people. "How horrible," Danella had commented.

"Yes, it was horrible," Lar commented. "I have dealt with the border trolls, just like the one that attacked us. Although they are dumb, they can be cruel and relentless, especially when there is an army of them. The creatures have no respect for life except for themselves and their masters who needed to pay them in gold to keep them happy. They kill women, children, and old people without an ounce of pity. Remember that when you are fighting them. Show them no mercy - they will show you none!" The desert man's voice was bitter and harsh as if the memories hurt.

"Aye," Huff's voice drifted over them from where he was working on his furniture. "The upper mountain trolls are just as bad. Our army needs to be constantly patrolling the mountain ridges as the bastards come through the northern passes and slaughter everyone."

Once again, Dani shivered. In her former court life, she had never heard of these horrors. Why had not her father educated her about the war, about how terrible it had been? She never knew that these awful creatures still plagued parts of the kingdom. The princess had only heard of these monsters in nursery stories told to her as a child. Her father had been a young prince during the war, yet he did not mention the war once to her.

Why would he have not mentioned it to me? Danella knew the reason, *a spoiled daughter who thought only of what was the best thing to wear at court. Had her father wanted to protect her from such knowledge or did he think she would not care anyway?* The pain of it made her grimace.

"Is this too much?" Mar leaned over to her. "I can stop…"

"NO," she said almost too loudly. "No, we need to hear this, please continue. Everyone throughout the kingdom needs to hear of these atrocities!"

And so, deep into the night Mar read the fascinating battle accounts. They did not go to bed until he had read through the entire book with the overwhelming victory of the king's army that ended the gruesome tale. Everyone's dreams that night were dark and troubling.

At breakfast, Lar made another jug of the dark tea mixture. It helped put a livelier step in their feet as Tilly began their march. The sergeant took them to the pool area. They all swam in the refreshing cold water. Perhaps the group wanted to wash away the previous evening's tale. The story of the book still lingered in their minds.

Tilly then marched them first to the cliffs at the most eastern part of the island. The late summer sea was full of whitecaps. A swarm of seagulls mixed with the large white birds diving after fish that lay below the water's turbulent surface. Their squawking seemed to compete with the roar of the wind. The sun was almost straight overhead. They expected Tilly would lead them back to camp for combat lessons.

The day was clear for once and the other Gray Islands loomed large in the distance. Unlike Hope Island, the outline of the other islands seemed mountainous with jagged sharp peaks; not the least inviting. Then to their surprise, their sergeant headed them on a new northwesterly path.

"He's taking us to where that barn is located," Dani heard Lar tell Ash.

Tilly yelled back, "Keep quiet". They continued the trek in silence as the sergeant picked up the pace almost running full out. The forest became denser, the large banyan trees loomed overhead as the smaller oaks and elms seemed to cower below. Dani thought she caught glimpses of the owls flying among the trees. The squadron was skirting the northern edge of the island getting small glimpses of the Viamar through the forest.

Not long afterwards they came upon the clearing with the barn looming large in full sunlight. Dani couldn't believe how big and sturdy the post and beam structure was. Everyone just stared in silent disbelief. The six of them were winded from running most of the way, even the elfs were breathing deeply. Tilly led them right up to the entrance of the barn doors that lay wide open. Schaller and the giant Okste emerged carrying a large basket full of fish between them.

"Oh, no," Huff loudly blurted out, "don't go callin those damn birds!"

"Shut up!" Tilly hollered at the dwarf, "or ya'll be doin kitchen duty with no supper! That goes for all of ya."

"Enough, Tilly," Schaller snapped. "There will be no threats while I'm in charge here." The lower mountain dwarf glowered at the scout but shut up. "Do not be frightened of the youklers," the Kazian scout looked at the recruits. "The birds will not harm you. They are basically docile but make no mistake, the birds are intelligent beings."

It was Mar that spoke up, "Don't tell us that, it's not true. I've seen the innkeeper Aryute's leg. A youkler left him with a huge scar. I wouldn't call that harmless."

Lura spoke up next, "We saw them the other day. They have huge claws and sharp teeth. We shouldn't be anywhere near them."

"That was Aryute's own fault. He tried to take a fish away from a male youkler. The bird was only defending food for its family; its mate had just had six chicks. The bird could have killed him, but it didn't," Schaller clarified.

Their attention switched to the sky as a large shadow came filtering down. A single bird was approaching. Every one of the recruits looked frantically around and tried to step back but in reality, there was nowhere to go. The noise of large flapping wings filled the air as the immerse bird came to a hopping halt right in front of them. On the back of the youkler was Laren. Schaller grabbed a fish and threw it at the bird. The youkler caught the sizeable fish in its beak gobbling the food right down.

Dani couldn't help but gasp. The sheer size of the bird terrified her. It had red-rimmed eyes with black pupils. It cocked its bushy feathered horse-sized head as if taking them all in. A large squawk came roaring at them as the beak opened and the huge sharp pointed teeth loomed dangerously in front of their faces as the avian bent down to get a better view. Around its face were leather straps that looked similar to a horse's bridle. The neck alone was bigger than a human man; the thick orange legs towered below a white-plumed colossal body. Laren easily fit on the youkler's back.

The youkler flexed its massive wings. The span of the wings took more room than seemed possible causing a mild wind to encircle them. The general pulled on its harness and the bird, with one last squawk, suddenly sat. As Laren jumped down, the soft leather saddle became very evident. The general held the reins that circled the head of the youkler as he walked toward them. He handed Schaller the leash and then stood in front of the six recruits.

"Welcome to Hope Station," he laughed. "I can see that you are all quite overwhelmed. I would like to thank Huff for his help in perfecting my saddle. It was a great improvement over the last one." The Erryian dwarf went bright red as the recruits accusingly looked at him. What had the dwarf been thinking devising a saddle for a bird!

It was Mar that once again took the lead, "General, what do you think you are doing? Those are wild untamable creatures. What do you expect you can do before you get yourself killed! One mistake and you'll fall right off."

"I think I've just proven they are tamable and it is not what *I* expect to do, it is what I expect *you all* to do!" The general stood with his hands on his hips in a determined stance.

"Youse crazy!" Huff blurted out. "I ain't ridin no friggin bird."

Even Dani spoke out, "I'm not getting near that thing! I refuse! I'm leaving! You can't keep me here!"

Laren held up his hand, "Listen, all of you! Each and every one of you was specifically chosen for your magical abilities and for your stubborn resistance to conform to what was expected of you. Each and every one of you has fought against authority. I chose you because of your ability to think on your own. Your uniqueness is what makes you each perfect to become a rider."

"What magical abilities?" Ash plainly told their leader, "Yanith took them all away!"

"Yes, and if you ever want them back you will ride the youklers." Laren looked at each one, "How much does getting your magic back mean to you? This is your final requirement. Are you going to give up now?"

"At least we know what Yanith meant when he said *if we survive,*" Lar stepped forward. "You are playing with our lives unjustly…"

Laren interrupted the drylander, "I am saving the lives of countless DeLak people. These birds are our only hope."

Dani looked at the sitting monstrosity that kept eyeing the recruits as if they were food. *How could these ugly birds save the kingdom, the man's crazy,* she thought.

He must have seen the skepticism on their faces for he continued, "The Bracaard kingdom is training young dragons. They will come across the Viamar and wage war on DeLak and we will be defenseless."

"Dragons!" Lura almost shouted. "How can these birds fight dragons!"

"It won't be the birds. It will be you that will!" The general walked back to the sitting youkler, once again taking the reins. "Let me introduce you to Tura. She's an average female youkler. We only ride young non-mother females not yet mated. The males are too dominant, too protective of their nests and of their mates. The males don't like to travel far from the Gray Islands."

It was Schaller that began talking, "Once a female accepts you, you become the dominant force in their lives. But they must accept you. It took us awhile to learn the techniques of dominance. It will be simpler for you. It's not easy, but then not impossible either."

"Who would like to give a fish to Tura?" Laren looked at them. "Dani?"

Dani backed up, her eyes filled with the old fear that used to consume her.

Mar quickly stepped up, "I'll do it."

Lar also stepped up, "No Mar, I will." But Marth waved him back.

"Sit, Gorg and stay!" he commanded his wolf. The hound growled his disapproval but did as his master commanded. His pet did, however, give one last bark at the bird. The youkler ignored the animal, its red eyes followed the Arthinian as Mar grabbed a fish.

"Hold it out, let her see what it is," Schaller told him, then the scout yelled "Bostrom," and the bird stood up. Laren patted the neck as Mar approached.

The beak opened when the fish left Marth's hand and was quickly snapped up by its enormous beak. One swallow and the catch was gone.

"All I ask for today is that you each give Tura a fish," Laren explained. "Then you are excused until tomorrow."

The twins each managed, despite the return of Boris and Hilda. The owls hooted their disapproval loudly. Huff stayed as far back as possible, heaving his fish high in the air. His fish disappeared into the bird's beak and the dwarf ran back to the group. Lar actually walked up to the bird. His snake had curled protectively around the desert man's neck. The black reptile hissed loudly. Tura calmly took the fish from the dry-lander's outstretched arm, ignoring the serpent.

Dani was last to go. She held back. Her hands trembled. The bird seemed so close. As she looked at the red beaded eyes, the princess felt the youkler seemed to be actually observing her. The bird appeared to scrutinize her from head to toe. *Did the thing actually have some intelligence?* The princess froze, her arms couldn't move.

"Oh, for Theror's sake, get rid of the fish! We'd like to get out of here sometime today!" Lura yelled. "Stop being such a cowardly ninny!"

The she-elf's remarks stung, forcing the princess to take two steps forward. The bird also took two steps forward and grabbed the fish from Dani's hand. Tura seized the fish and swallowed. The bird let out a loud screech causing Danella to fall backwards. From Dani's sitting position the youkler looked even larger, looming high above her. She scrambled to her feet running back to the group.

"Thank you all," Laren once more addressed them. "I ask you not to say a word of this to anyone. If you will agree to ride, then I will see you tomorrow. The decision is up to you."

With a flick of the reins, Laren's youkler once again sat down letting the general mount. Laren quickly turned the bird. The youkler spread its massive wings and they were gone in seconds, their silhouette becoming a dot in the sky. Tilly, Schaller and Okste headed back into the barn carrying the basket of fish, leaving the recruits still staring at the disappearing bird.

"Unbelievable," Lura grabbed onto Lar's arm. The drylander enclosed her hand protectively. Ash reached over and brushed it off.

Lar seemed surprised looking at the male elf, his eyes questioning.

"Leave her alone, don't touch her!" Ash softy told the drylander between gritted teeth.

"I didn't mean…" the desert man started to say, but Lura interrupted him.

"Ash stop it, what is wrong with you!" the she-elf demanded

"Think what father would say!" the male elf spat out.

"What in Theror's sake are you talking about?" she shot back at her brother. "How dare…"

Mar got between them. "Stop, both of you. I think we have more important problems right now."

His words shut everyone up as Tilly returned. The group was silent as their sergeant returned them to camp. The day was already waning; once again they had missed lunch. Tilly dismissed them for an early supper shift.

No one ate much, even Huff. They had shocked disbelief on their faces. Tilly had once more warned them to keep the youklers a secret. Early evening was approaching as all of them, except for Dani, headed back to their cabin. The princess had a heavy heart when she entered the exercise pavilion. The afternoon was still waning; the others wouldn't arrive for a little while. As Danella emerged onto the floor from behind a post, she came face to face with Laren and Ransa in deep discussion.

"This is too bad, she's one of my best. The woman has worked hard," the instructor was saying, "I will miss her. Of course, I am happy she will be on special assignment."

They both turned to see a startled Dani. "What's going on?" the princess managed to choke out.

"The general has personally come to tell me that you'll be unable to attend any future classes." The corporal went over and actually hugged her pupil. "You have worked hard for this promotion. I hope you'll come and visit me when you can."

Danella said nothing. She turned and ran out, not even changing out of her workout clothes. She ran all the way to the cabin, tears flowed down her face. *Once again, my life becomes someone else's.* Dani approached the cabin and saw the group was lazing around the porch. *How did Laren know of me working with Corporal Ransa?* Her eyes went to the Arthinian. *He told him! Mar is the only one who knew!* Uncontrollable anger swelled, flooding her emotions.

As Danella walked up the stairs passing Mar, she pushed him hard. "How dare you tell Laren about my extra combat classes? I hate you!"

She rushed past the surprised man and went into her bedroom flinging herself on the cot. Tears flowed freely. The king's daughter didn't know what was worse, giving up her classes or the betrayal of Mar. Both stung.

"Dani, what are you talking about?" the Arthinian's deep voice was next to her bed.

"You are the only one who knew about my Ransa classes. You told the general or you told Tilly. Laren just kicked me out of it." She turned back over on her side glaring at Mar.

"I didn't, I swear it," he sat down on the bed. "I wouldn't do that."

"Then who did?" she almost screamed at him.

"I don't know," Mar reached down lightly touching her arm. "I just wouldn't do that, I gave you my word."

She looked up into his black eyes. His astonished look told her he was telling the truth. Dani sat up. "The extra classes meant a lot to me. I had gained respect. Ransa was going to make me an instructor."

"I'm sorry. I know it meant a lot. Despite this Dani, you have an important decision to make. Do you want your magic back? Is it worth your soul? Is it worth risking your life?" He looked away as if the thought was too revealing. The Arthinian wanted his magic back no matter what it cost. Now, seeing that he was as conflicted as she was, it was her turn to comfort him.

Dani grabbed on to his hand, "No one will blame you, Mar, if you decide to give in to Laren." Somehow Corporal Ransa's proposal suddenly seemed far away and unimportant to her. She hugged him. "Do what you must, Mar, do what you must."

He turned to her. They both stared deeply into each other's eyes and before Dani knew it, she was kissing him. It seemed so right, so very right. His lips felt soft and warm. As he drew her to him, their bodies seemed to perfectly fit together.

He held her, burying his face in her auburn curls. "Are you going tomorrow?"

"No," she answered and held him even tighter.

Chapter Sixteen
The Decision

Breakfast brought silence. All six of the recruits played with their morning food. No one was eating. Each of their faces were in deep thought. *How many will follow Tilly to the barn?* Marth wondered as he glanced around at all the gloomy expressions. The ex-mage's thoughts went to his earlier suspicions. Yanith had picked the six of them for their magical abilities. He guessed they were all Mothia apprentices awaiting the testing. Had the powerful wizard counted on each of them doing anything in order to get their magic back? Did the Mage leader realize every one of them would likely play with death to get their powers returned?

The Arthinian angrily thought his assumptions were correct. The injustice of tearing their lives apart gnawed at his gut. How many of the group were from the noble houses? Again, Mar guessed all of them but how close were the recruits to the ruling barons?

Didn't Yanith say that all the baronies needed to pay a human price by order of the king? Were the six of them that price? That was the mystery. Were the twins the Hartland baron's children? He thought not. Mar had heard the Hartland baron was selfish and overly proud. The ruler would not send one of his own children. The haughty elf Baron Falsteff would think his children too important to sacrifice. He guessed the twins were more likely his nephew and niece.

How about Huff? The Erryian barony was run by females, surely if the baroness had sent anyone it would have been a woman dwarf. How far down the chain was the dwarf? Mountain dwarfs weren't known for their sorcerers. Marth knew of very few dwarf mages. The Great Mountain inhabitants looked with disdain on magic except if it pertained to their precious ores. Perhaps that was the Huff's key. The Erry Dwarf was one of the few with magical ability.

Lar was a total mystery. Mar knew little of the new Bombian Barony. Then there was Dani. Did she come from a Kazian noble family? Perhaps. The woman was not a typical Kazian who mostly had yellow eyes and blonde hair. But it did not prove anything, as the baron's wife was a Lakelander. Many Lakelanders had married into Kazian families. Was Dani only part Kazian?

He gave up trying to guess and concentrated on himself. There was a good chance he would not survive. Was Dani doing the right thing and giving up? The young lord glanced over the table at the finely sculpted woman. She seemed perfect to him, but then he was deeply in love with her. Lura, concerned, had come into the room last night before he could tell Dani how he felt. The kiss had been too fleeting. The Arthinian was worried - had he gotten Dani when she was emotionally vulnerable and in need of comfort? Mar was afraid he had.

Last evening, they had all gone out onto the porch and pretended everything was normal. Marth had read from a book describing the baronies. Since Bombia was not included, it being too new a barony, Lar had finished the evening by describing his homeland. The drylander had riveted everyone's attention, especially Lura who clung closely to the desert man's arm. Ash had pouted, sitting in a far corner and had asked no questions. Marth was worried about the male elf. The

Hartlander was too possessive of Lura, but then he was her twin.

Now, the recruits were facing probably the biggest decision they'd ever had to make. Marth left the table and headed toward where Tilly met them each morning for their march. No use putting the decision off. The sergeant was waiting with an anxious face. Lar came to stand next to Mar. Then Huff followed suit. Ash and Lura joined the group - no Dani.

Marth breathed a sigh of relief. The Arthinian did not want her in danger. Then unexpectedly, Dani was standing next to him. He looked down at the woman, astonished. "I thought…"

"This is where I belong, with all of you. I've seen it through this far." She lightly touched his hand. Her smile was forced, but her expression said it all. *I won't be left behind.* Danella had indeed come a long way from the spoiled child to a mature caring independently thinking woman.

"Well, well," Tilly looked them over, "glad youse could make it. Let's get a move on!"

The squadron jogged to the cliffs. The Viamar seemed unusually quiet, the waves almost completely subdued. The sun was brightly shining down on the other Gray Islands. No fog today. The sky was full of birds catching the strangely softened winds. The youklers seemed to float in and out of the high clouds. Tilly let the group rest. Not a word was said, but their worried eyes said it all as each of them glanced skyward.

Is our future in those clouds, Marth speculated?

The recruits went north along the coast until they came to the clearing. "Strange, there is no direct route to this area from the camp," Ash had commented perhaps remembering when the three of them had become so totally lost and confused.

"Laren don't want no one comin this way," Tilly explained. "Wese don't need no prying eyes."

The outbuilding seemed deserted, but Schaller and Okste came strolling from behind. The giant went into the barn and returned with a basket full of fish.

A moan escaped Huff's mouth, "Here wese go again!"

Almost on cue, the flapping of wings came floating downward. The sky darkened with the shadows of youklers. Leading the flock was Tura with Laren on her back. Following

Tura were six other youklers. The noise was almost deafening as each bird squawked loudly.

The youklers went quiet when Okste and Schaller emptied the entire basket of fish on the ground. The birds pounced on the catch gobbling it up in a matter of moments. Laren had jumped down leaving his bird to contentedly eat. The general walked around the group of birds. No beak snapped at him, most stepped aside out of his way.

"You see, the youklers do not wish to harm me," the general looked over at the waiting recruits. "Please join me," Laren waved them forward.

Marth and Larandar were the first to do so followed closely by Lura. Ash, after slightly hesitating, caught up with his sister. Huff started forward. Dani didn't move at all. The dwarf turned back, "Come on lass, let's just pretend wese following them on a hike. Wese can do it." To Marth's surprise, the Dani did trail behind the dwarf, keeping her body close to Huff's. Mar could tell Dani was breathing deeply trying to keep calm but not quite being successful, as her eyes were wide with fear. Her face was covered in sweat. In comparison, Dani was tiny compared to the large youklers, looming high above the frightened woman.

Mar walked between the seven birds. The smell hit his nose. All the birds except Tura had dirt on their under bellies as if the flock had been rolling in rancid mud. Laren's bird was sparkling clean. He also noticed each bird, except Tura, had only a head harness with no reins attached; no saddle dressed their backs like the general's ride.

"Slowly stroke their necks," Laren instructed demonstrating on Tura. Marth was surprised at how soft the white feathers were. The bird the young lord was standing next to shivered, its feathers fluffing out. Dirt came raining down into his hair and on his uniform.

"They are filthy," he complained. "Why isn't yours the same?" the Arthinian asked their camp leader.

"Because Tura allows me to wash her," the general matter-of-factly remarked. "You see, when the birds choose to become part of a flock they wash each other. The individual flocks are really quite small by the way. The clean birds are a sign that they belong to that family of youklers. These birds here have chosen to be part of my flock, but it is you that must get their trust. The rider must become part of the flock. If only I or Schaller washed a bird, its loyalty would be to us."

"Ya mean wese gotta wash em?" Huff scrunched his pudgy face in disgust. "I'se hopes ya kiddin."

"No, I'm not. Each rider must gain the trust of one of the youklers. A person cannot ride until the bird trusts them. If they let you wash them, the bird becomes even more trusting."

Lar forcefully spoke up, "That's an impossible task. The youklers are huge! If they don't want us washing them, one bite and we'd be like the fish - dead!"

"No, Schaller and Okste have helped me train these birds. Watch!" he stood in front of the flock. "Omstea," Laren yelled. All seven birds sat obediently down. The general walked up to Tura "Isteia," and the bird lowered its massive head. Schaller threw the bird a fish as if rewarding her. The camp's leader affectionately patted his ride. He went to the back of the sitting bird reaching up pulling on her wing. The enormous wing slowly unfolded. "You see. I can easily wash her," he pointed out.

"I's think ya is crazy," Huff sputtered.

Laren held onto Tura's bridle reins and then yelled "Pomstra". The remaining six birds took to the air with one big "swoosh". The youkler flock was quickly gone, heading back over the Viamar Sea towards the Gray Islands.

The general turned to them. "Who would like to take a ride with me first?" Again, he turned to Dani. Huff stepped in front of her, "Begging yar pardon, Sir, I ain't sure she's quite ready yet..." The dwarf stood his ground as if he was her guardian. The amused smile on Laren's face showed he'd remembered when Dani had flung food at Huff.

The Erryian didn't get to finish as both Lar and Mar immediately stepped forward. It was the drylander that Laren nodded toward. The tall desert man intently watched the general lift himself into the saddle, settling on the flat leather pad, feet in the stirrups. Then Laren reached down and gave Larandar a hand up. The lanky Bombian quickly sat behind the general. "Hold onto to me," he said as the bird quickly turned. With a half running, half hopping motion, the youkler's massive wings unfolded and the two riders lifted.

Mar, amazed, watched them disappear. The Arthinian took a deep breath as he had forgotten to breathe. Lura stood next to him. The elf had tightly grabbed onto his arm. "What if Lar falls off?"

"We have to trust Laren enough that he knows what he's doing," Mar said the words without really believing them. He'd seen the blacksmith, Dohar, slip off the contraption back at Haven.

"Lar won't fall off," Schaller spoke up. "He'll be fine." Everyone shut up and just stared at the horizon.

Sure enough, a black bird silhouette came into view and quickly grew larger. Tura landed right where she had taken off. Larandar jumped down, smiling from ear to ear. Bishi was wrapped around his neck. "That is simply amazing!" the desert man went up to Mar and grabbed his shoulders. "Simply amazing. Try it!"

Mar took Lar's place. The young lord put his arms around the general's waist. Being on top of the bird, sitting in the leather saddle somehow felt natural. The sensation was like riding a horse. Yet that feeling quickly went away as the youkler took to the air. The massive sensation of strength was remarkable. The Arthinian could feel the great muscles of the bird as it lifted itself ever higher. Gorg was barking loudly below. The dog intently watched his master disappear into the clouds. The wolf was not happy.

Marth's stomach tightened in response to the rapid upward movement. The huge white wings flapped causing a whirlwind of twirling air until they had gotten above the clouds. Then the youkler glided. The ride was smooth and totally unfrightening.

The wind flew against his face also whipping at his uniform. The feeling of speed was powerful. The Viamar Sea was soon under them. Mar forced himself to look down. The vast body of water was even more impressive than it had been from the surface. The next Gray Island, which had seemed so far away, came rapidly upon them.

"That is Utipa," the general shouted back. "Most of the birds live there. Look carefully and you can see their nests."

The youkler steeply banked. Marth took a deep breath and held on tighter. He looked down and forward past the neck and sure enough on the various island plateaus were colonies of birds. The general banked again and they headed back to where they had started.

His stomach once again did flip-flops when the bird lowered, hitting the ground and coming to a hopping stop. Marth must have looked as excited as Lar had. The feeling of exhilaration filled his face. The young lord had never felt so alive. He had seen the world in a different light.

Next Ash and then Lura took their turns, leaving Boris and Hilda behind squawking loudly in protest. Their pets could not keep up with the speed of the youkler. Upon their return, the two owls greeted them with loud hoots, clutching onto the twin's shoulders after the elfs each landed. Their pets continued to squeak in the elfs' ears, expressing their disapproval at being left behind.

When Huff stepped forward, it was the giant Okste that lifted the dwarf up. The Erryian pulled himself behind Laren. "I didn't make this saddle with me in mind," the little man told Laren.

"We have a saddle just for you," the general assured him. "Dohar worked extra hard on it."

"Great, just great! Why is I not surprised," Huff spouted, shaking his head in disbelief. Marth noticed the dwarf held tightly onto Laren's belt. His short arms would not fit around the general's waist.

Like the others, Huff loved the ride. "Did ya see the other island?" The dwarf animatedly ran up to the group. His short pudgy arms were flying as he described the sensation. His eyes were sparkling, his bulbous nose bright red.

To everyone's surprise, Dani walked quickly up to the youkler. Grabbing onto Laren's hand, she lifted herself up and behind him. The woman was extremely pale and kept her eyes shut as the bird took off. The two were gone the longest. Upon returning, she too looked excited. Her color had returned, but she said very little. Her emerald eyes, however, were flashing. Her only words were "wondrous, just wondrous".

"I will see you in the morning," Laren told them. "Training begins at dawn, get some rest." The recruits watched him leave, heading back to the other island.

"How does he get back here?" Ash asked Tilly.

"After returning Tura to the flock's nesting area, he has to take a boat back. It's not a pleasant trip," Schaller offered. "He is hoping to make the barn the flock's nest but not until you are trained."

Mar noticed the scout had said, "*you* are trained," not the birds, as if it was the youklers training the riders. The enormity of the undertaking almost overwhelmed the Arthinian. *We are to fight dragons;* the young lord focused on Laren's words. *Dragons!*

It was a quiet hike back to camp. Supper was gobbled down so that they could hurry back to the cabin and discuss the day. Every recruit was now excited at the prospect of riding their own youkler. The atmosphere was so different than the night before. Everyone was up and ready at dawn when Tilly came for them. "Wese have breakfast at the barn," the sergeant informed them. The group headed right out.

When the six of them arrived at the clearing, the birds were already there. The recruits helped Schaller and the giant bring out the fish and feed the youklers. Tilly passed out slices of freshly baked bread and cheese with a variety of fruit for their morning meal. The riders-to-be ate as they worked. First chore was cleaning the barn.

The out building was much bigger than first perceived, the group realized upon entering the structure. The interior went much further back. Twelve immense stalls, six per side, graced the front. The back was a large inside corral. An enormous overhead loft was filled with bales of hay and bags of oats. Small rooms dressed the backside.

"We supplement their diet with high quality grain," Schaller had explained. "Every day, the stalls must be cleaned and fresh hay put down. They get one bag of oats per day and sunflower seeds when we can get some. The plants grow naturally on the islands."

"It's like taking care of a horse," Huff had remarked, remembering his cousin's stables. Schaller had just nodded in agreement.

The chores took to midmorning before the recruits had finished mucking out the last of the stalls. The youklers felt free to wander indiscriminately throughout the barn. The stall doors were wide open and the birds went in and out. The creatures seemed to have a keen sense of curiosity. The six recruits had quickly gotten so used to the large birds that no one paid much attention to their wanderings or their squawking.

After another light mid-day meal Laren assembled his new trainees outside. By the doors were placed two baskets of fish, which had just been delivered. The birds were roaming around screeching loudly at the appearance of their food.

"Each of you get a fish and pick a bird," the general explained. "Get close enough to hand them the fish. If the bird won't take the food from your hand then go on to another bird until one will take it. Let's see how we do."

Marth ordered Gorg to stay in the barn. The Arthinian then headed straight to a youkler. The bird eyed him with its black pupil red-rimmed eyes. It seemed docile enough so he reached into the basket for a fish.

Huff, Dani and Lar each got their birds to take a fish. Ash and Lura ended up switching birds. Marth, however, had trouble with his bird. It squawked loudly at him and refused to take the offered treat. The Arthinian looked around. All the birds had been taken.

Schaller walked up and squawked loudly at the bird. After closely eyeing the two men, the youkler stretched its long neck and slowly took the fish from Mar. "You have got a fussy one there," the scout turned to Marth shrugging. "She'll come around."

"How about getting me another one?" the noble asked.

"This is all there is right now," the scout pointed out. "You'll have to make do."

"What do you mean *that's all there is,*" Marth confronted the bird trainer. "We saw a whole bunch on the island."

"It's not easy," Schaller explained. "We have to find a female, non-mother, who has not picked a mate yet. Then we have to train them. Some are un-trainable. Laren hopes to expand, but with war looming we haven't the time."

"Wonderful!" Mar complained.

Each recruit took a lead rope and attached it to the harness of their bird. They slowly led the birds around the barn. Most went willingly, some hesitated but eventually followed. Mar's youkler pulled at him the whole way often squawking loudly. By the end of the day the Arthinian was exhausted. His arms ached from pulling the reluctant bird behind him.

At one point, the bird had literally run past him and dragged his master-in-training behind with Gorg running alongside and barking loudly in alarm. Schaller had finally caught up with the two and ordered the uncooperative youkler to stop. Mar rubbed his sore scraped knees and blistered rope-burned hands while swearing profusely at the youkler.

"This is not working," Marth complained to the trainer.

"Give her some time," Schaller had responded. What else could be done?

Late in the afternoon, Tilly lined them up and headed them back to camp. At supper, they all excitedly talked about their birds except Mar who just silently listened. He was so discouraged the young lord went right to bed without reading one word to the group. Lar had tried to console him, but the Arthinian just turned over and ignored him.

At dawn, when they were marching to the clearing, Dani had tried to offer some comfort, "You'll have an easier time today," she told him. "Your bird will come around today."

Well it didn't. By late afternoon, all the recruits but Mar had washed their birds. They had named their charges. Dani called her youkler Maylith. Lura called hers Starbeam. Ash called his Moonlight. Larandar named his after a desert flower called Aphil. Huff called his Ruby. Marth, discouraged, called his Wilful.

The next day the new riders, except Mar, put their saddles onto their mounts with the help of Schaller and Okste. To Huff's delight, his saddle had a roll down rope ladder. It allowed him to climb aboard and then tie it back up. When Okste offered to hoist Dani, she refused and took a running jump. It took her three tries, but the small woman finally got the hang of getting up on her youkler. Lar, Ash and Lura easily jumped on.

Mar sullenly watched as Laren instructed them how to handle the birds. "It will happen," the general had assured him. But it didn't happen. Each time Mar approached the bird with a bucket of water, its large beak pushed him forcefully away, often getting the Arthinian soaking wet.

By late afternoon, the new riders were ready to try their first flight. The Arthinian watched as they disappeared into the horizon. Mar helped Schaller and Okste in the barn. When the riders had returned, the group was all excited. There wasn't much that Marth could do but listen to their excitement. Everyone kept telling him he'd also be in the air soon.

This went on for several days. The recruits were just about living at the barn. All meals were now at the clearing.

Laren had an eating-place set up with long wooden benched tables. Maggie cooked for them just like the hill female dwarf used to on their trek to Hope Island with her husband Mathie helping. Finally, the general had moved their cots to Hope Station. Each stall now contained a bed. "For now, the cots in the stalls will let the birds get to know you better," Laren had explained.

He'd also gotten them new uniforms that the youkler riders changed into every day. The brownish gray colored outfits were long canvas shirts with short gilets, knee length tight pants with high riding boots that had slots for carrying knives. Each rider got thick heavy pull-over tie up tops with hoods. Fine sturdy reinforced leather gloves finished the attire. The new uniforms kept the riders warm, as the cool autumn winds were getting chillier.

These outfits remind me of our Mothia robes, Marth noticed. *They are the same color and made of the same material as our former capes.*

Each rider got a good sharp sword, a rapier in Dani's instance, with a fancy handle that had a "Y" engraved upon them; a gift from Dohar. The blacksmith had also made each a shield with the same symbol. Huff had laughed. "I done taught him how to do that," the dwarf boasted. "It stands for 'Youkler Rider'."

Ash and Lura preferred their bows and arrows, which they strapped onto their backs. Huff also carried his axe. The Erryian dwarf had also figured out how to attach bags to their saddles. Despite the awkward looking birds, the riders looked impressive astride their mounts.

Although Mar dressed with the others, he could only watch as they mounted and left. The young lord hated the pitiful looks each of them gave him as they mounted, especially Dani. Every day he tried unsuccessfully to get Wilful to accept him, but each time was a failure.

On the fifth day, he once again watched the riders leave. "Come on, we will go for a walk." Gorg trotted next to him as they headed on the trail leading to the sea. Mar led the stubborn youkler who at least didn't fight him anymore, but trailed stubbornly behind him. Perhaps the bird knew his would-be master carried a couple of fish in his backpack and wanted the treats.

They hadn't gone that far when Gorg let out a deep growl. The wolf hunched his back, warning Marth that something was coming. Out of the woods came four extremely large boars. They stopped, grouping together, snarling at the trio. Green slime dripped menacingly from their mouths. Finally, a giant creature, his size reminiscent of Okste stepped behind them.

"Well, well, my pets, what have we caught?" The monster's blackened teeth poked out of his mouth; his yellow slatted eyes shone brightly against his green scaly skin. A large long snout represented his nose, which snorted loudly. The monster flexed his hands that quickly extended long claws.

Marth had only read about the Lizardpeople, but he had no doubt that this was a prime example of one. The large creature stood on its two hind legs, had a long muscular tail, and its front limbs were more like arms, carrying a club and shield. He drew his sword, holding the sharp blade out in front of his body. He let go of Wilful's reins. At least the bird could fly to safety.

"Go home," he ordered Gorg, but the wolf just growled louder, gnashing his teeth in warning at the wild pigs.

The boars crouched down then advanced slowly. Before they could reach Mar, Gorg attacked. One of the boars yelped as the large wolfhound bit down on the animal's neck. Marth didn't wait, but charged the other three before they could help the first boar. One of the boars' claws raked Marth's chest. His sword cut its head off. As the other two boars went to jump him, a large beak pieced the stomach of one and a sharp claw grasped the other. Wilful had joined the battle, not run away.

The lizard creature roared as it too charged. Mar tried to help the youkler. His sword pierced one of the boar's thighs, but the lizard was upon him and the Arthinian had to switch back to fight the scaly green monstrosity. Gorg had killed his boar and as Marth fought the lizard, the wolf jumped on the green slimly monster's back.

With amazing dexterity, the reptile creature reached back and threw the wolf high in the air. Gorg fell against a tree and lay there, not moving. Mar furiously attacked, ducking the lizard's long arms and aiming at its legs. His efforts were a losing battle as the lizard outweighed him. Its long arms kept trying to grab his sword. It was only a matter of time before the lizard's claws reached him. Suddenly the two owls attacked. With extended talons, the birds attacked the eyes of the reptile man. The evil creature howled and turned its attention to the flying menaces.

Marth surged forward slashing at the lizard's thick green legs aiming high for the leg muscles. The hurt lizard hissed loudly. The fiend fell to its knees. The Arthinian didn't hesitate, the sword swung and cut the long snouted head off. The head rolled, spitting green blood everywhere. The severed face landed at Mar's feet, its long black tongue sticking out. The reptile person had a snake's tongue, forked with venom spilling out of the tip. Mar stepped back as the liquid sizzled on the ground.

Mar turned back to help the youkler, but the two boars were dead at Wilful's feet. The bird, however, was bleeding from several chest wounds. It squawked loudly then lowered itself to the ground. Marth ran first to Gorg. The wolf was hardly breathing; several wounds were bleeding along the dog's back.

He hauled his pet over to the where the bird sat. The beak was wide opened and it seemed to be trying to catch its breath. "It's okay girl," he petted the youkler's neck trying to calm her down. Marth was not only covered in the green blood of the lizard, but also in his own blood as several deep wounds were bleeding profusely from his arms and chest.

The Arthinian sat down near the bird, touching it gently. The noble lord leaned against the soft feathers. He was losing consciousness. Marth grabbed onto Gorg, hugging him. "I'm so sorry, old friend," he was getting delirious. The world was becoming dark.

To his surprise, he felt himself being dragged. The bird was dragging him backwards down the road, holding him tightly in its beak. Mar held securely onto Gorg as the bird pulled both of them. The youkler was amazingly strong despite the bird being hurt. Mar fought trying to keep conscious, but he was just about losing the battle when he heard shouts.

Strong hands encompassed him. His body was being laid down on the ground. It was the last thing Marth remembered before a black void enveloped him…

Consciousness came, but so did terrible pain that forcefully inserted into his thoughts, everything hurt. "Mar, sleep," entered his brain. The hillman tried to focus on who was talking, but awareness slipped away and the hurt man nodded off again. When he awoke, the pain was there, but Mar managed to stay awake. His eyes opened to Dani holding his hand, she'd been crying, her eyes were red.

"Thank the gods you're awake," she croaked. "Natalia, he's awake," Dani yelled. The healer dwarf's face came into view.

She touched him and there was a moment of relief. Although the pain came back, the feeling wasn't quite so bad. "Where am I?" he had trouble with the words. His mouth felt dry, his tongue swollen.

"Youse in the barn. Wese set up a place for ya with Gorg and Wilful to be together. Ya seem to need each other or so me healing sense tells me." It was Natalia voice. "Youse been badly hurt. Yar fever has broken. Ya recovering, but it'll take a while. Sleep as much as ya can." She laid her hands on him, immediate relief. And then again, he slept.

When next Marth awoke he forced his mind to concentrate. Natalia was sitting next to him sound asleep. The moment he slightly moved the female dwarf was awake and bending over him. "Howse do ya feel? It's late, everyone is sleepin," she smiled down at him.

"Awful," Mar clung to her pulling himself up. The room seemed to spin as his eyes took a while before focusing. He was in one of the large stalls. The Arthinian was not on his cot, but they had made him a bed out of thick hay with a pillow for his head. To his right, close by lay Gorg. The wolf was awake staring at him but not moving. His pet's chest was totally bandaged. "How is he?" Marth urgently asked Natalia.

Mar crawled over to Gorg, wincing as he did so. The hound whimpered softly as the dog raised its head to greet him and slightly wagged his tail. "He'll be fine, his stitches will need to heal," Natalia assured him. "Like ya, he's very sore. He drank a little goat's milk today. I'm hoping he'll eat some broth in the morning. Then we'll try some meat."

Marth saw his youkler on the other side. The bird lay sitting, it's head down on the straw. He didn't need Natalia to tell him the bird was in bad shape. The female dwarf helped Mar get over to the bird. "Isn't there anything you can do for her?"

"I'se trying. I'se never worked on a bird before. The creature's thoughts are strange. The youkler needs to eat, but it won't." Her guttural dwarf deep voice was full of worry. "The bird is losing strength from lack of food. Laren and Schaller had tried, but Wilful won't take fish or oats. It does take some water but that's all."

Mar went over to Wilful. "Thank you," he stroked the bird's head. The beady eyes opened, but it didn't raise its head. "Come on girl, if I can make it so can you." The bird slowly lifted its neck. The head cocked one way then looked over at Gorg and slightly squawked. Marth's wolf softly woofed, then settled down again.

"Natalia, get me some fish and have it cut into small pieces," the Arthinian instructed the healer. "I have an idea."

She returned with a plate of cut up fish pieces. While she was gone, Mar had fallen asleep leaning against the youkler. Natalia woke him up. He shook himself, his brain wasn't co-operating. Marth finally managed to kneel next to his bird. The young lord took a piece of fish and held it to the bird's beak. Wilful wouldn't take it.

"Damn it," he loudly swore, "if you don't swallow this fish I'll pry that damn beak open myself. Now eat!" He shoved the piece against the bird's beak. Its eyes looked at him. The mouth opened and took the fish. Then Wilful took the next one, and continued until the entire plate was gone.

"Good girl!" he patted the neck and then collapsed.

Each day brought improvement. Mar could finally stand, although his hurt body limped at first. Gorg was managing to get around. Wilful finally stood and was eating well. Despite Natalia giving him the okay to return to the regular med building at camp, the Arthinian didn't want to leave Wilful. So, he and Gorg stayed at the barn.

Everyone visited bringing him fresh fruit and other small treats. Dani and Lar brought him books to read. He told the twins of their owl's help. The small birds had saved his life. Huff would leave the minute Natalia appeared. Marth felt bad for the two dwarfs. The pair seemed to be caught in one big misunderstanding. He could think of nothing to do about it.

One day, after she had tended to the three of them, Mar couldn't help but say something as Natalia was leaving, "Huff loves you."

She turned around, "Yes, I know Mar. I need to concentrate on my healing. Still even more important, Huff needs to concentrate on what he needs to do. It is better this way."

Marth could see the hurt in the female dwarf's eyes. *She loves him too,* he realized.

Laren had stopped in. "I hear you are all doing much better. You three are lucky to have survived. We have no idea how those monsters got onto the island. I now have regular patrols, especially along the coastline. There is some indication that the lizard and his attack boars were left off by a pirate boat.

I have the riders looking for the ship but haven't found the damn thing yet. The boat may have a Bracaard demon mage on board, helping to hide it." The general had shaken his head, "I would say our bird operation is no longer a secret. War will come soon, I'm afraid."

Finally, one day, Mar put the harness back on Wilful. "Come on girl, let's get out of here and let them clean this stall. Gorg, who had already been going in and out, followed close by as the Arthinian led them out into the sunshine. It was late morning and no one was around. The recruits were probably out flying somewhere.

The sunshine felt good. The air was still warm, but the winter coolness could be sensed trying to intrude. All three of them walked around the outside of the barn. As Mar came back around to the front, Schaller appeared carrying a large water bucket, rags and soap. The guide said nothing but just dropped them at Mar's feet and went back into the barn.

Marth, with trembling hands, dumped the soap in the bucket and soaked the rags. "Omstea" he cried out. Wilful obediently sat. The Arthinian took a deep breath and approached the youkler with the wet cloth. "Isteia" and the head lowered. The Arthinian started scrubbing the bird's neck, getting only a light squawk in complaint. Then he went on scrubbing the entire bird. The washing took three bucket fills, but when the bird was done, Wilful looked great.

He gave her several fish. Schaller, smiling, came out with a saddle. The trainer helped Marth mount and fasten the tack on the bird. They connected the bridle. "Walk her around a bit before you attempt to fly," the Kazian bird seer warned. "I think the group is exploring Utipa today. And then the man left, leaving the Arthinian to cope alone. Somehow, Schaller knew that doing it alone was what the young lord needed.

Marth, his heart pounding, jumped on Wilful and slowly walked the entire clearing. "Ready girl?" he yelled and got a huge squawk. A bark from Gorg made him turn back. "We're a team," he told the youkler. "I can't leave him behind."

The bird seemed to agree. It sat letting Marth down. Running into the barn, the young new rider returned with some rope. He lifted the wolf onto the saddle and securely tied him. "I'll get Huff to help us get a more permanent solution, but this will do," he told his wolfhound as the new rider took a seat behind the dog.

"Okay, Wilful, let's see what we can do," Mar told the youkler. The bird ran and then lifted into the air. Gorg put his nose to the wind letting out a loud howl, enjoying every minute of it. Marth also joined in, yelling loudly into the wind, "Here we come!"

Chapter Seventeen
Youkler Training

Utipa is a beautiful island in its simplicity of jagged mountain plateaus and beautiful white sand beaches. Scores of youklers make their nests on the very tops of the mountain crests. The front side had a view of Hope Island that was spectacular. The backside of Utipa looked onto the open Viamar with several other Gray Islands appearing to the northern side. This back edge was full of green grasses and beautiful sunflower plants. The riders had landed in this section letting their youklers munch contentedly on the flowers.

Lar put down his hood enjoying the feel of the sun on his face. The desert man was now used to not wearing his kaffiyeh. The turban with its large white feather sat in his backpack, a symbol of his past life. *A life before the youklers, before Lura, before...* The drylander stood on the cliff overlooking the sea; he enjoyed the sea breeze rustling through his hair, the feel of the salt water brushing lightly on his face. Bishi was curled around his neck putting its small head to the wind. His eyes caught movement in the sky. Lar excitedly yelled when Mar and Wilful came into view. His arms went up in greeting. The Bombian lord was surprised to see Gorg with the rider.

When Mar landed, the five riders rushed to greet him. Dani hugged the Arthinian saying what they all felt, "So glad you are here."

"Well, Wilful finally decided I wasn't so bad after all," Mar laughed loudly as Gorg barked in agreement. Wilful was already attacking the sunflowers, pecking at the huge flower's middle seeds. As the general approached, Marth gave him a smart salute.

Laren, instead of a salute, shook the Arthinian's hand, "I knew it was just a matter of time. How are you feeling?"

Is he treating us like civilians again? Larandar wondered. *He's been regarding us differently ever since we've been riding the birds. Even our riding outfits are more non-combatant. More like Mothia robes. Will we be under Mothia and not the king?*

"I'm feeling fine." Marth answered, "My leg is still a little sore, but the rest of me healed fine thanks to Natalia." Mar looked over at Huff. However, the dwarf just quickly looked away.

"Well, today we need to practice flying along the coast. This far north, out on the Viamar, the winds change without much notice. A youkler rider needs to handle the upwinds and downdrafts. Riding along the coast will be good practice that will make it easy for you to handle anything that comes our way. When the Bracaards first attack, the war will begin from the sea. The birds must be battle ready!"

"You really believe war is coming?" Ash asked.

"Oh yes," Laren answered. "So, let's get some flying time in. Follow me."

They remounted their youklers and took to the air. Larandar flew next to Lura's Starbeam. Of course, the she-elf was the best rider. The Hartlander's agility was so evident. Her balance was so perfect that she had learned how to stand on the saddle and shoot her arrows. Ash could also manage dexterous movements, but his aim wasn't as perfect as Lura's.

Lura could also sit backwards and shoot letting Starbeam take the lead. The Hartlander's lithe athletic body looked like the moon goddess, Porlis. The elf's pure white silvery hair floated above her as the wind caught her garments, flinging them about like wings. The ashen bow was ready to fire, her owl gripping the proud elf woman's shoulder in anticipation of attacking a foe. It was a picture of sheer beauty to Lar.

The general was right. The winds could be turbulent. The drylander learned to brace himself accordingly using his long strong legs and crouching down near the neck of the bird. The youklers were used to the winds; banking to accommodate the changes. The birds actually anticipated the fluctuating trends of the up currents and downdrafts. The riders learned too and became almost one with their mounts.

The coastline was beautiful. Lar realized how deserted the land of The Wild really was. The Wildpeople did not like to live near the Viamar, did not like the turbulent sea. The inhabitants feared the intense storms that frequented the coast. Only Forge Haven stood upon the shore; half-breeds that had been banished to where The Wild did not want to go. Being pushed to where the weather was harsh and unpredictable had made the Haveners hardy and resilient. Their isolation made them independent from the Wild, becoming their own self-determining populace.

The general took them down to the turbulent Viamar Whirlpool. The huge swirling sea could swallow any ship easily. Even from the air the swirling waters looked danger-ous. The riders stayed far away from the whirlpool's erratic winds. Instead, Laren led them to the Berling Straights. Here, waters and winds were somewhat calm heading down to the southern coast. The water passageway was the only nautical path that ships could possibly follow up along The Wild coast-line.

Laren always turned them around before the flyers hit the elf's Hartland border where the larger ports and the ma-jority of bigger ships were. The seashore was quieter and easi-ly navigable. They could see billowy white sails not far off.

When the riders returned to the clearing, Laren had them practice getting on and off their birds quickly. Even Dani could mount rapidly. She had learned to jump and lift herself onto her saddle with a minimum of effort. Only Huff took a little longer scrambling up his rope ladder, but the short dwarf still was getting the hang of it.

"Your enemy won't give you time. So be quick about everything you do!" Laren had instructed. To emphasize his point both Schaller and Okste had attacked them as they landed. If the riders didn't get down quick enough and have their weapons immediately out, their bodies felt the sting of the scout and giant's weapons.

Most amazing was Huff's ingenuity. The Erryian had spent several days at Dohar's smithy. He had contrived a harness that attached to the back of Marth's saddle that Gorg could be strapped into but could easily get out of when needed. The dwarf also put sturdy straps that Boris and Hilda could hold onto. The twins now always took the owls with them.

Larandar's youkler, Aphil, handled easily and was of good temperament. The drylander had learned to land smoothly, to bank quickly. The tall lank man could dismount running and the bird anticipated his dismounting; being ready and up in the air quickly. Lar also did well in actual combat with the others. Aphil could outmaneuver everyone including Lura. His bird ducked under or over an opponent and had no problem bumping an attacking youkler, getting the other bird off its stride.

Mar was his best opponent. Wilful was a smart bird and easily took to verbal and hand commands better than any of the others. The Arthinian had only to whistle and the bird came. He could yell directions or use hand motions and Wilful quickly obeyed. Marth's bird was also the quickest flyer. The Arthinian was often surging ahead of the other youklers, even Laren. The general seemed content to let Mar lead the group. There were now days when their leader left them to their own devices and the riders did just fine with only the restriction of keeping to the upper coastline. They learned intricate hand signals, a way to communicate to each other while flying.

Hope Station was really growing. Several smaller outbuildings now dressed the clearing. One building had just supplies with Maggie taking charge with several new soldiers helping her. Another structure was a small dormitory that the new additional soldiers slept in. The back rooms of the barn became the sleeping quarters for the riders, each getting their own chamber. *Laren is giving us more respect,* Lar reflected as he looked over his own sleeping quarters. *He's treating us more like officers and less like recruits.*

General Laren, realizing that the whole island now needed defense, had his soldiers build a new large roadway connecting the two island camps. Ox-drawn wagons now arrived everyday with soldiers and supplies. Laren wasn't keeping his birds a secret any more. Often, the off-duty soldiers would come to watch the youklers being trained. The riders became known as the "Youkler Brigade".

One day after they had just landed, Sari and Lori were waiting for them. The two women had just returned to the island. They were fascinated by the youklers. The tiny fairo took off her cape spreading her own small powerful wings. Lori flew all around Aphil, finally sitting on the saddle looking down at Lar who was holding the reins, keeping the youkler quiet. "She is quite intelligent," Lori announced. "The bird has become attached to you. This creature will serve you well." Lar did not ask how the fairo knew, her powers of talking to wildlife were well known.

Sari, skeptical of the birds, kept her distance. "That animal is huge. We have nothing like it in Bombia or anywhere else for that matter." The drylander guide was even more fascinated by the change in Dani. "You have done well," she told her once spoiled recruit. "You have done very well."

The smile on Dani's face told how glad she was to see her old teacher. "Sari, I never thanked you for all you did for me…"

The Bombian woman cut her off, "You have repaid me a thousand-fold by what a great soldier you have become. I get only excellent reports on your progress. Corporal Ransa speaks highly of your skills – and she's a tough critic."

They spent the noon meal reminiscing about their original trek to Hope Island which now seemed so long ago. They were all together; the six recruits and all the guides including the giant, Okste. The difference was that they were all now equals. The inexperienced recruits were now full fledge soldiers and treated as such.

Maggie had prepared a delicious roasted vegetable mutton stew with fresh baked bread. Gorg contentedly gnawed on a bone at Mar's feet. The owls sat serenely on the twin's shoulders carefully watching everyone. Even Lar's Bishi had come out and was curled around the desert man's neck. Their pets had become a regular and accepted part of their lives.

Lori talked of her travels through The Wild. Signs of evil intruders were everywhere, killing indiscriminately as the pirates raided the towns. It kept Sarura, the chieftain's daughter, busy as her guards tried to protect The Wild's shoreline. It was a losing battle as the culprits disappeared quickly.

"Where are all these invaders coming from?" Marth asked the fairo.

"They are coming from the upper Viamar. There must be a Bracaard ship out there and if I'm not mistaken, the captain has a black mage protecting his boat. It is the only explanation for them being able to navigate these treacherous waters and to stay invisible. The pirates want to keep The Wild busy and unable to join the king with the upcoming war."

The mysterious Sari said little of what she had been doing. The Bombian spy just agreed that the Bracaards were testing the waters everywhere, including the DeLak shoreline where pirate raids had increased ten-fold. Many merchant ships now were loading their vessels with fighting men for protection and taking on cannons.

The afternoon brought the riders out on the sea. They practiced fighting each other. Mar did the best, as Wilful skillfully dodged any attempted attack. Laren joined them late in the day. When the birds finally landed in the clearing the sun was low. They headed to the barn leading the youklers to their supper. Okste was bringing out the basket of fresh fish when a ruckus was heard coming down the road. Several soldiers were running toward them. "Fire," they were screaming, "the town is on fire! Smoke from Haven!"

Laren shouted, "Load up!" to the riders.

Okste and Schaller ran back into the barn, coming out with the youkler's battle breastplates. They quickly attached the light protection shields to the front of the birds. Mar and Lar handed out bows and arrows. Long spears got placed in their holders on the back of their saddles. With swords out, the riders quickly mounted. Then the seven youklers flew upwards flying over Hope Island to the Viamar heading toward Forge Haven.

The minute the birds were up, Lar could see the smoke coming from the town. As they passed over the open sea, the ferry full of soldiers was seen heading toward the town. Bessie's huge body was steering the boat straight across, her sail dangerously full open getting the fastest speed possible. The whole ferry looked up as the birds passed overhead and a loud cry of encouragement filtered up. The bell from the town could be heard clanging.

The youklers were at the town in quick order. The whole village was in an uproar as several buildings were aflame; villagers were running around in a panic trying to escape their attackers. The sight of large trolls looting the stores infuriated Lar. The town's wolves were attacking the huge creatures, but the animals were outmatched by size. The few armed brave villagers were no match for the monsters either. The riders attacked the trolls first.

All heads turned as the youklers loudly squawked and dove downward. The surprised alarm in the eyes of the invaders was clearly evident. The pirates had not expected any fight. Lar slashed the back of one troll. The monstrosity turned and roared, swinging its mace, but Aphil was already up and gone.

Turning, this time Larandar went back and slashed at the throat. Green blood gushed everywhere as the giant monster fell. The twins were filling the air with arrows that never missed their mark. The trolls flung their arms in the air to no avail especially handicapped by the owls, Hilda and Boris, attacking their eyes. The elfs aimed for the behemoths' neck. It took several piercing arrows to bring each troll down before they gagged on their own blood.

Huff's axe killed two trolls easily. With several passes, his weapon cut their arms off and they bled out. Dani killed one of the trolls with her spear, which went right through its throat. Bringing her youkler Maylith around, she quickly picked out another spear and did it again to another troll.

It was the Lizardpeople that posed the challenge. Their heavily scaled bodies were hard to penetrate. Several of the villagers lay dead at their feet as did a number of wolves. Marth was the first to jump off Wilful and to attack a lizard that was chasing several Forge Haveners. Gorg ran right along with him. His wolf attacked jumping on the back of the creature biting its neck while Mar kept it busy in the front. When the lizard tried to bend forward to use its arms and grab the wolf, Mar chopped its head clean off.

Lar stood next to Mar as they attacked two other lizards. The drylander flung Bishi at one of the reptile creatures. The snake immediately attacked the slit eyes. The green scaly monster screamed loudly, its eyes began to burn. Lar plunged his scimitar deeply into the lizard's chest, finishing it quickly. Collecting Bishi, he then helped Marth finish the other attacker.

Dani jumped down attacking several large Bracaards that seemed to be in charge of the assault on the town. Two tall humans with orange eyes and bright yellow hair seemed to be directing the onslaught of both the trolls and the lizardpeople, yelling orders at their monsters. Maylith dropped her right in front of the two culprits. They both turned to the small woman and smiled. She looked like easy prey.

Their swords flashed, as the pirates struck straight on. Her shield went up taking the brunt of their swings. Her rapier flashed, cutting both of them on their arms making the orange-eyed humans drop their weapons. Then Dani quickly plunged her sharp blade deeply in each of their chests. The attack happened so quickly the pirates could do nothing but show surprise and fall dead to the ground.

One of the lizardpeople jumped in front of her. It tried to strike her with his large mace. She dodged his attack and reached in with her long rapier, piercing him between the eyes. The creature, stunned, fell dead to the ground.

She then turned to see a third human. The huge human had Dohar's Bick in his clutches with his father terrifyingly watching close by. The evil pirate had a knife at the boy's throat. "Drop your weapons or the boy dies," his wicked smile of black teeth mocked her. Dohar was paralyzed. The blacksmith dropped his sword. Dani didn't hesitate a moment but threw her rapier. The long sharp weapon plunged right between his orange beady eyes. He staggered back, letting the boy go and fell backwards dead. The boy ran to Dani clutching her. The blacksmith fell to his knees crying.

"Go to your father, Bick," she pushed the little boy toward Dohar. She turned and ran down the street. Dead trolls and lizardpeople lay all around. "The rest are escaping," General Laren yelled. "Let's stop them from getting back to their ship."

Lar yelled for Aphil. The youkler immediately flew down, lowered itself letting him jump on. The rest of their squadron did the same thing. The birds were up flying after the fleeing Bracaard attackers. The youkler riders had killed all the trolls and lizardpeople,, but the scum human pirates were fleeing. The brigade, using their arrows and spears, got every last one of the pirate attackers.

"Follow me," Laren yelled, "their ship must be nearby."

The fleeing culprits were heading toward the coast. The birds came upon the coastline quickly, but the riders found nothing. "They have already sailed away," Larandar lamented looking out over the Viamar.

"They have a demon mage," Laren yelled over to him. "He's protecting them."

How will we ever find them? the Bombian discouragingly thought. *We have no mage of our own.*

The town was a mess. The ferry had landed. Soldiers from Hope were helping where the troops could. The fires were being dealt with. The wounded were carried to the Rooster Saloon. Men, women and children had been hurt, some badly. Bodies of dead white hounds filled the streets; almost every Wild wolf had been killed fighting for their masters. Marth, seeing all the dead pets, tightly hugged Gorg.

The riders pitched in with the cleanup, helping where they could. "Where's Huff?" Lura asked. The dwarf or his youkler was nowhere to be seen.

"I saw him veer off on our return," Ash commented. "He headed back to the island instead of coming here."

Suddenly Ruby came flapping down, landing right near the Rooster. Not only did the youkler carry Huff, Natalia was riding behind him. As the youkler lowered itself, everyone helped the female dwarf dismount. The healer was carrying her medical bag.

"The rest of the medics are on their way," the female dwarf informed them. "I'm glad Huff came and got me." The female dwarf hurried into the inn and took charge immediately. Natalia went from wounded to wounded, using her magical powers to heal and comfort wherever she could. Some were beyond help, many weren't. Everyone was doing the best they could, bandaging and soothing. When the medics came on the next ferry, the Rooster Inn became a true medical center.

"Everything is under control." Laren had gathered them outside near their birds. "Everyone back to Hope Station, we have some planning to do."

Dohar had come running up, "Thank you, general." Tears were streaming down his cheeks. "You saved the town. She saved my son," he pointed to Dani. "I am so proud to have helped you with the birds."

"I could not have done it without you, my friend," Laren clasped the large half human man. "We will stop these evil trespassers. We will get revenge. I promise you."

Hope Island was deserted as everyone was helping on Forge Haven. They saw to the birds themselves, giving them as many fish as the youklers could eat. Lar rubbed the neck of Aphil. "You did good, girl," the drylander praised his bird. "You did good."

The youkler rubbed its head against his arm affectionately. The Bombian had become close to Aphil; the bond was complete. The closeness had become both ways. The attachment was thus with all of the riders. Each bird and master had full trust with each other.

After the riders had the birds tucked into the barn, they met in their newly constructed mess hall. Maggie was helping on Haven so Laren had passed out cheese, fruit and bread. Their leader stood at the end of the table.

"We need to find that ship and try to capture it," he told them.

"And how wese gonna do that!" Huff spouted off. "Wese ain't got no mage. Wese can't get past their demon. Wese ain't got no magic!"

"You leave that to me." Laren looked intensely at his youkler team, "That ship has lost a lot of its crew. The boat is possibly lying low right at the moment recovering. It's probably hiding in the fog on one of the Gray Island inlets. There are too many to check all of them. However, with their losses, the ship will have to soon head home. They'll be waiting for daylight. There is only one way the pirates can go or they'll sail right into the whirlpool. The ship has to go through the Berling Straights. We will be waiting for her."

"The seven of us can't beat a ship full of Bracaards," Ash spoke what they were all thinking. "We could burn the boat down perhaps."

"We can't burn the vessel down, not with the demon's protections. We'll have to board the ship and fight them," Laren reluctantly told his riders. "It won't be just you seven, be prepared to take on passengers," the general warned them. "I also want to capture the boat. The ship could be of use in the upcoming war."

It was Dani that exploded, "War! War! That's all you talk about. Look at the town, the people need help now! Forget the ship. We need to alert the king!"

"Yes. War, Dani! War!" Laren shouted back, for once the calm soldier losing his composure. "Do you think the king does not know? There could be many towns just like Forge Haven if we aren't prepared for this war! This ship is the first test of what we can do. Be ready at dawn. Be fully armed up. The pirates will be shooting at us this time." He abruptly left, leaving them silently staring at each other.

That night they sat around finding comfort in each other's company. The horrors of the day had taken its toll, as each face was grim with dark thoughts. Marth tried to bring some normalcy reading from a book of ancient poetry written by one of Mothia's first mages. The manuscript was old and yellow. Lar wondered where the book had come from and how it had found its way to Hope Island. The beautifully written pastoral poems helped ease the tension, but still the riders went to bed early knowing what the morning would bring.

Lar walked next to Lura as they headed toward their cots in the barn. Each youkler was already in its stall, nesting quietly. The drylander gently took the she-elf's hand in his, "Sleep well, we know not what tomorrow brings."

Lura laughed, "You sound like one of Mar's poems. Don't worry Lar, we will all be together. I have faith in us. We can do this." Her violet eyes searched his. Did the Bombian see love in them?

He squeezed Lura's hand and was surprised when she leaned in and kissed him lightly. "See you in the morning, my desert man," the elf whispered tenderly as the Hartlander left him.

Lar stood silently watching Lura leave. The drylander knew then that he'd lost his heart.

Chapter Eighteen
The Pirate Ship

The morning brought deep fog. It was like walking through a thick cloud. They sat at their breakfast table feeling as if the weather expressed their moods. Maggie brought out a hearty breakfast, but the riders just looked at it, all except Dani. The small woman chastised them, "You have got to eat. Corporal Ransa taught me that a good soldier eats when possible because a fighter needs strength. So, eat!"

The whole group took her advice, but they ate in silence as each wondered what the day would bring. *Are we ready for this?* Marth wondered. The thought of attacking a Bracaard's ship was overwhelming. The Arthinian stopped thinking about the attack, *it won't help to worry. It is something that we have to do. Best to just get on with it.*

With the help of Schaller and Okste, the riders got their youklers ready for battle. The birds had been amply fed with buckets of oats. Each bird got their breastplate plus Dohar had fitted their harnesses with eye shields. The Forge Haven blacksmith was ingenious as the Wild/Human made a cage-like covering that allowed the bird's good vision but still protected their protruding eyes from arrows.

The Youkler Brigade loaded up with plenty of weapons; sharp pointed spears, large number of arrows, arm shields and several knifes housed within their clothing. Marth noticed Dani had stuck several more extra daggers in her boots. Their swords were attached to scabbards on their backs. The broad sharp blades were easily and quickly drawn. Each rider had also added a long rope attached to the pommel of their saddle so they could lower themselves down to the ship if need be. They were ready!

"This ain't gonna be no good against a sorcerer," Huff stated the obvious. They all nodded in agreement. If the ship was under the protection of one or more demons, they'd not a fighting chance.

Their passengers arrived, emerging one after the other from the thick fog. All the guides were going. Sari and Lori came together. Maggie and Mathie joined the group. Tilly strode confidently in. Schaller merged quietly into the group. Finally, emerging from the fog was Corporal Ransa - the tough soldier looked formidable. Their mentors, like the riders, were battle ready.

The new arrivals paired off with each rider. Sari stood near Dani, Maggie and Mathie both were near Huff. Ransa joined Ash. Tilly stood nervously next to Lura. Lori went up to Marth, "I will go with you since I'm the lightest and smallest and your youkler already carries Gorg." Schaller obviously was going with Laren as the trainer stood holding the reins of the general's Tura. The brigade was waiting on their leader.

From the fog unexpectedly came Natalia. The healer went up to Huff, throwing her arms around him. The female dwarf hugged him close to her. "Please be careful!" Tears were flowing down her high cheekbones.

Huff, after hesitating slightly, held her tight. "I will," was all the Erryian could manage to get out.

"At least the fog is starting to lift," Lura observed trying to take the awkwardness out of the moment. "I wish the sun would come through and give us some warmth." The breeze was cold and damp. As the birds gained altitude they would really feel the frostiness of the air. Once again, the close absence of summer was evident.

To the riders' surprise, Yanith appeared out of the mist. The old man hobbled over to Tura. *So, this is what Laren meant when their leader had said he'd take care of the magic,* Mar thought.

"Yanith!" Huff loudly exclaimed. "Where is Laren?"

Something is wrong here, Marth mused. The pieces started falling in place. The only explanation was that Yanith *was* Laren. *Why the deception? He truly is powerful if he can physically change.*

"Let's get going," the old mage announced. "I will try and handle the Bracaard mage or mages. Just remember that I will be slower than you. This old body does not move as quickly. So, give me time to get onto the ship before you drop onto the deck. We must reach the ship and attack before the pirates get into the straights. They will have less maneuvering capability. Their ship will only have their front mizzen sails open, leaving it easier for us to get close. The sails being down will be less dangerous for the birds." Yanith explained further again making his point, "The pirates will have less control of their boat if we get them in the turbulent waters before the currents calm down."

"Wait a minute!" Huff was not going to let it go. "Where is Laren? Wese need him. The general knows these birds! We ain't never attacked a ship before!"

"Laren is needed here," Marth decided to help Yanith's deception. The group was more likely to believe him than the wizard. "Someone needs to be in charge of helping the town!"

The old mage looked gratefully at the Arthinian. "Yes, he is needed here. Now, let's go before the ship gets past the Berling Straight."

The riders mounted first and then assisted their passengers. Lori was so small that she fit right behind Gorg. Her arms were securely around the wolf. The fairo had taken off her cape and her wings were flapping in the wind. Huff, Maggie and Mathie all sat nicely on the back of Ruby. Sari, her Bombian gray eyes looking worried, was quite pale as she tightly wrapped her arms around Dani. Marth noticed Tilly, clinging to Lura, had his eyes closed and refused to look down. Corporal Ransa looked stoic behind Ash clutching her sword, ready for battle. They left Natalia and Okste waving goodbye with the cold fog swirling around the pair. Okste had wanted badly to go, but he was needed at the Station, besides the giant wasn't sure of being able to drop safely down to the ship's deck.

Marth noticed Schaller had taken Tura's reins with Yanith sitting in the back. The old mage had his powerful staff clutched in his hand. *So much depends on him,* Marth thought as Wilful headed up breaking through the fog. The air was indeed colder, but the direct sunlight helped take the edge off and the dampness was fading away.

Schaller seemed to know what he was doing. The scout banked Tura and headed what they presumed was southward. The cloud cover was too thick to get their bearings, however, the haze began to thin the further south they went, letting the Viamar come into view. The sky was actually clear when the riders passed close enough to the whirlpool to see the huge swirling waters. The Berling Straight was not far beyond it. As they flew closer, Schaller shouted, letting out several loud squawks.

Numerous flocks of youklers filled the sky. *He's called the birds,* Mar realized. *He's disguising us with the swarm of youklers. The pirate ship will not see us coming!*

The riders flew within the birds, each youkler floated high up, catching the up-drifting winds. *The sea may be less turbulent than by the whirlpool, but it still was something to be reckoned with,* Marth thought, feeling Wilful bank against the breeze's strong push. Then the hillman saw the pirate ship. It was heading toward the calmer waters of the Berling

Straight. The boat was a good-sized frigate with three main masts. As Yanith had predicted, only the front mizzen sails were open as the winds were too strong to open the main canvases.

Good, thought Marth, *it will make the flyby easier for the birds to get close if we don't have to worry about hitting the large sails.* Still, the rocking ship seemed dangerous for the soldiers to drop upon the deck.

Yanith motioned for them to start going lower. Schaller squawked once again and all the birds went lower with them. The brigade passed over the ship, everyone keeping a low profile as not to be noticed. Marth counted at least twenty crewmembers on the main deck. They looked like seasoned fighters and were heavily armed.

Many of the sailors were the small rodent-like weaselworts, furless and blue skinned. Ugly did not do them justice - nauseating was more like it. Although the creatures were a quarter of the size of a human, in large numbers they were dangerous. Although not very intelligent, the vermin attacked viscously, overpowering their enemies always in groups of twos and threes.

Schaller lifted and turned them around for the second pass. The tall scout motioned that the next sweep was the attack. It had been agreed upon that the guides would go first followed by the riders on the next pass. Schaller surged Tura ahead as Yanith would drop first, hopefully coping with the Bracaard's magical protections. *I hope the old man can manage,* Mar worried.

The Hartland riders had their bows notched. The elfs would swamp the deck with arrows, giving the first attackers cover. As the seven youklers quickly dropped, the deckhands alarmingly looked up. Ash and Lura immediately started to shoot, but their arrows missed. The crew was being magically protected. Yanith, despite the rolling ship, landed deftly on the starboard deck, raised his staff and chanted. The next arrows hit their marks as the old man had countered the pirate demon's magic.

As the youklers swooped low almost brushing the deck, the first Hope soldiers dropped down. Schaller had also dropped with Yanith, the bird trainer immediately started to protect the mage, fighting off the crew as they fiercely attacked. The Mothia mage had his staff held high out in front of him. Marth quickly saw why - a dark hooded figure appeared at the helm. From long bony red colored arms a spray of fire was aimed directly at Yanith. The Bracaard's mage had emerged from below and taken high ground at the helm deck!

Mar, taking the lead, turned the youklers and headed down. After jumping, he crashed, hitting the deck hard. Wincing from the pain, the young soldier rolled up quickly. The Arthinian had his sword out and began swinging as soon as he got his footing. Standing was not easy with the rocking of the ship.

Two weaselworts immediately rushed him. The young lord ducked between them and got the weaselworts from behind as the little monsters are not agile creatures. The stout blue bodies had trouble maneuvering nimbly. Gorg had no trouble regaining his balance from the drop. Lori was on the dog holding onto his fur. The wolf started immediately to protect Marth's back. More hoards of the blue tinged rodent beings came flooding up from below deck. Mar and Gorg furiously attacked them.

Dani was close by dueling with two human Bracaards who were wielding humongous axes. She dipped as both axes swung above her, and then she plunged forward stabbing both quickly with her piercing rapier. Both crumpled onto the deck, dead. She then raced forward helping Marth by slashing several weaselworts.

Huff joined Tilly, Maggie and Mathie as the dwarfs also had been attacked by several weaselworts. Their axes made short order of them. The four short mountain dwellers worked well together, methodically attacking and quickly finishing the little creatures. Still more of the persistent rodents came running forward.

Lori was flying, breathing on the few lizardpeople crewmembers that had not been killed during the attack on the town. The fairo paralyzed them long enough for Sari and Ransa to kill them. Lar was fighting with a horde of Bracaards, sizeable beefy men who were protecting the bridge that held the mage and the captain. The skipper was up on the bridge steering the rocking boat and yelling orders. Larandar was aptly fighting his guards, but progress was slow. The desert man needed to get to the upper deck and get control of the ship, but the men were protecting the stairs.

The drylander took Bishi and threw the short thin black reptile over the men. The snake attacked the captain. The venom bite was lethal. The ship's commander screamed, as he clutched his throat, letting the steering wheel turn aimlessly in the wind. The ship lurched, tossing everyone around violently. Lar, who was facing the bridge, saw it coming and braced himself. The four men toppled down the stairs. The Bombian quickly stabbed each one.

Ash and Lura had their bows streaming upward trying to hit the crew that was shooting arrows at the deck from the three-barren masts above. Hitting the lofty pirates was difficult because of the back and forth rocking of the ship, but the twins got everyone. The owls helped as the small birds attacked each pirate bowman making them easier targets for the twins.

Yanith and Schaller were trying desperately to get to the Bracaards' mage. The black clothed hooded man was spiraling waves of fire at the Mothia mage. The old sorcerer was slowly making headway, but most important was that the Mothian wizard was keeping the evil magic from being used against the Hope fighters.

When Lar raced up grabbing the steering wheel, however, the foul enchanter turned to the drylander and sent a fireball directly at him. Yanith fired his own counter magic, but still some of the force of the foul spell reached the Bombian. Larandar went flying backwards, hitting his head on the ship's front railing. The Bombian slumped down unconscious.

The steering wheel spun rapidly, the ship violently tipped to starboard. Mar grabbed onto the railing to keep himself from being flung into the sea. His hand grabbed onto Gorg protecting him from going overboard. Dani banged into the Arthinian as she slid across the deck. Both elf twins were clinging to the tipping masts. Everyone else was flung against the sides. Even Lori, with her wings flapping violently, had trouble keeping her balance.

Many of the crew went headlong into the Viamar. The small weaselworts were flung high in the air with little chance of saving themselves. The demon toppled onto the deck. Yanith, grabbing onto Schaller, managed to get one last spell out.

The incantation hit the mage full force as the evil being went tumbling into the sea.

The ship slowly righted itself. Marth helped Dani to her feet. To their dismay, they saw a second black clothed mage emerge from down below. Yanith was facing the sea and did not see him. The wicked mage lifted his staff ready to attack the unsuspecting Mothian wizard. The demon's hood had fallen back. A red skinned horned figure extended its clawed arms to strike the old mage.

Out of Dani's boot, in rapid succession, came three knives aimed directly at the Bracaard. The evil sorcerer, sensing danger, instantly turned from Yanith, but it was too late as the three knifes struck him squarely in the neck. Still, the demon had time to send a fireball at his attacker. Lori came from nowhere and got in front of Dani taking the blunt of the spell. The fairo went down lying unconscious on the deck; her wings scorched terribly.

"NO!" Danella screamed bending down to the stricken burned figure. "NO!"

Gorg cried softly. The dog went over to the fairo and licked her tiny face. Yanith had come running over, but there was little the magic wielder could do. Schaller was so angry he heaved the body of the dead Bracaard wizard into the sea.

Larandar had regained consciousness and stumbled to the helm grabbing the ship's spinning wheel. The frigate, although still rocking, became stable enough to get their footings.

"We are drifting toward the whirlpool," Yanith yelled above the raging wind. "Get us out of here!"

As hard as everyone tried, they could not get the ship out of the pull of the whirling waters. The swirling intense winds were drawing them towards the turning violent waters of the whirlpool. The forceful currents drew ever closer, spinning them around the center that would swallow the ship.

"Forget trying to save the ship," Schaller told Yanith. "We have to get out of here before even the birds can't escape the pull of the winds." The trainer gave a squawk shout, but the wind was too violent. The ship was doomed with the birds not coming.

"What are we going to do?" Lura frantically urged action.

Mar, using his fingers, gave a loud whistle. Thank the gods, Wilful came flying down. The Arthinian grabbed onto the hanging rope. Swaying violently in the wind Marth climbed himself up to his youkler. The large bird disappeared into the clouds, but then moments later the rider brought Tura down with him. Schaller grabbed the rope and ascended. One after another Marth did the same with each of their birds, until all the riders regained their mounts.

Then came the tedious task of getting their passengers. The twins brought the owls with them. Mathie and Maggie hauled themselves up using Huff's rope ladder. Then, Ransa tied Gorg with Lori's body firmly attached to the dog. Each of the remaining passenger, including Yanith, tied himself or herself securely and were lifted off the doomed ship.

They did not have time to try and get them on the youklers backs, so the birds headed to the nearby shoreline dragging the tied people as they swayed in the wind. It was hazardous going with the figures dangling just above the waterline. The youklers, using their massive wings, at first strained against the whirlpool's pulling winds. It was hard going until the birds neared the shoreline.

The group hadn't even reached the beach before they viewed the ship being swallowed up by the raging whirlpool. As each was lowered to the sand, the thankful escapees collapsed on the ground exhausted, cold and soaking wet. Then the birds landed bringing their grateful riders.

"Youse getting as much fish as ya want!" Huff emotionally exploded, hugging Ruby's neck.

Yanith immediately untied Lori from Gorg. "We need to get her to Hope Station. Natalia is waiting for us." Putting the small unconscious fairo between them, Schaller and the wizard headed Tura into the sky and headed north.

The rest of the brigade slowly followed, as the birds and their passengers were tired. Hope Island was a welcomed sight as the riders all landed in the clearing, quickly dismounting. Okste was there with a basketful of fish, which he dumped unceremoniously on the ground. The youklers immediately pounced on the food, squawking loudly.

The returnees found Lori placed on a cot in the barn. The fairo looked horribly pale. Natalia was attending to the fairy's burns, placing a soothing balm on the sores. Yanith stood over the healing dwarf watching. His face was also gravely pale.

Natalia looked up at the Mothia mage, "I can't heal her. Her fever is raging. Fairy Folk are beyond me. Fairos have their own magic which blocks mine."

"I will help you get past her defenses, but I need warn you that this has a certain risk. Her magic could attack you, may even kill you. I'm weak from fighting those damn Bracaard demons, but Lori will die if we don't do something."

"Then we must do it," the healer took her hands and started to place them on the small winged body.

"NO!" Huff knelt next to his fiancée taking her hands away. "Ya'll only both die! Youse ain't trained properly. I's not living my life without ya!"

Natalia put her hand up to his face, "This is what I do, Hoffler. Healing is what Osiana sent me here for. If ya do not accept that then wese can not have a life together." The Erryian let his hands drop. A tear fell down his check, but the short man nodded.

Once more the female dwarf put her hands on Lori. Yanith took hold of her shoulder with one hand and tightly grasped his staff with the other. "Natalia, you must draw the poisonous spell from her. Then you must quickly rid yourself of the evil. I will give you as much strength as I can, but your body and will is strong. One of the strongest healers I have come across. You can do this!"

Sweat poured down the female dwarf's forehead. A groan left her lips as her body stiffened. The Mothia mage held her tightly keeping her upright. The air seemed to thicken as both figures concentrated. A yell came from Lori as the fairo grabbed onto Natalia's arm. Then both seemed to collapse.

Yanith staggered backward. Schaller caught the old man and lowered him to the ground. The mage seemed totally exhausted. Huff caught Natalia in his arms as the healer sagged against him. Dani rushed to Lori. "She's breathing normally," she cried. "Her fever is down."

Natalia, however, was not. The dwarf was not breathing. Huff cried out in dismay, "Come on," he yelled at his fiancée. "Don't leave me alone. Breathe!" She lay limp in his arms. The dwarf hugged her to him, "Theror, give her back to me!"

Suddenly, the female dwarf gasped, taking in a deep breath. Huff tightly held onto Natalia as her eyes opened. Everyone sighed in relief. The Azirran smiled and then fell into a deep sleep.

Yanith had regained his footing. "The youklers need tending to, then you all need rest. The medics are on their way; let them do their jobs. They'll take good care of Lori and Natalia."

The riders and scouts followed Marth out of the barn except Huff who stayed at Natalia's side. Fatigue circled the whole group. Ransa and Sari headed toward the camp proper while the rest helped get the youklers washed and into their barn stalls. Schaller took care of Huff's Ruby. Supper was a simple hearty stew with cheese and bread. Conversation was beyond them, so they ate in silence. Dani took some supper into Huff. The princess was now quite fond of the dwarf.

Mar followed her to the quickly set up medical room. The Arthinian watched as Dani gave Huff dinner and urged him to eat. Natalia was still sleeping, but her breathing was normal. Lori was awake and smiled at them.

"I owe you my life, Lori," Dani took the fairo's hand. "How can I ever thank you."

"We help each other," the tiny woman winced as she tried to sit up but couldn't. "I owe my life to Natalia. We all owe our lives to each other. It is what the gods intended. Go in peace my daughter," Lori ended with a Fairy Folk blessing and then closed her eyes.

Dani was crying as they left. Marth drew her to him letting her cry on his shoulder.

"I have learned so much," she looked up at the Arthinian. "It was not to become a soldier that Yanith sent me here, it was to become aware of others, not only of myself. I am truly insignificant."

"You're a good soldier, Dani," Mar remarked, "but you're a good person too and you mean a lot to me." The handsome hillman bent down kissing her. The small woman fit nicely to him as her arms went around his neck.

"I don't want to be alone tonight," she whispered, taking his hand. He followed her into her bedroom and shut the door…

The morning brought the riders and their birds together and assembled in the clearing. Laren had called them for a practice run over the Gray Islands. The day was actually warm with the fog having dissipated, so it was clear flying. They spent the day discovering as many islands as they could. Then Laren took them to Forge Haven where they all had a good meal at the Rooster Inn. The birds were now accepted, even revered. The six riders were heroes and treated as such.

Aryute, the inn's owner, would not let them pay for their meal. Masie had brought Gorg a humongous elk bone. The barmaid gave the twins a bowl full of chunks of meat for the owls. Huff got a pint of their best mead. Laughter filled the table as each rider fully enjoyed the feast.

The town was rebuilding, including the construction of a third ferryboat. Throughout the town small white wolf pups were playing. It was harkening to see the Haveners trying to not only rebuild their buildings, but their lives as well.

"There will be regular ferry runs back and forth to Hope Island," Laren explained. "The town needs protection and as the army base on the island grows, so will the traffic to the town. We will station some of our soldiers here for protection."

"You need to convince The Wild chieftain to treat these people better!" Lura spoke up to Laren. "It is not fair that they are treated as outcasts."

This is coming from an elf, Marth reflected. *Dani is not the only one that has changed.* The Arthinian noticed that Ash had also nodded his agreement.

"I concur," Laren nodded. "But I have brought you here to say you have fulfilled your obligations. You'll be going home soon."

Silence, stunned silence as each former recruit looked at each other. "What do ya mean?" Huff blurted out. "What about Ruby?"

"The birds belong to Mothia. You'll have to take that up with Yanith," he told them. The general stood up. "Now, let's get back to Hope Station. We have a lot to do before you leave."

Marth came close to telling them all that Laren *was* Yanith, but one pleading look from the general shut him up. *This is not right, he better have a good explanation!* The Arthinian felt Dani's hand squeeze his. Her eyes were filled with uncertainty. They had been so happy this morning! The entire group had all been so happy. Natalia was much better and so was Lori. Now this!

"I'm sure everything will be fine," Marth assured her, but in reality, the young lord wasn't so sure. *I'm tired of Mothia playing with our lives!*

It was a somber group of riders that flew back to the clearing on Hope Island. After seeing to their birds, each sat alone. The thought of breaking up the Youkler Brigade was painful. They had each forgotten that their one desire had been to not leave their homes to begin with!

Marth walked down to the sea. The young man sat on a large boulder overlooking the tumultuous water which seemed to mirror his feelings. The Arthinian didn't even notice Laren sit next to him. "I have to explain," the general interrupted his thoughts.

"Yeah, I guess you really do, Yanith!" the bitterness was evident in Mar's voice.

"You have to understand what I am doing, then judge me," Laren looked out over the sea. "I was made aware that the Bracaard Kingdom has found a way to train twelve very young dragons. Sari risked her life to get this information by the way."

"Is that why you trained these birds to counter the dragons? The youklers are no match for dragons!" Marth snidely remarked. "The dragons spit fire, for Theror's sake."

"It is not the youklers, but its riders that will counter the dragons. The young fledglings do not yet spit fire, by the way. It takes centuries for a dragon to acquire that skill, but they are fierce and agile with large claws. It is the dragon riders that I fear. They will be Bracaard demon mages."

"That's encouraging," Marth spit back.

"Wait!" Laren encouraged him to listen. "The Bracaards' mages are not soldiers. They know nothing of fighting hand to hand. They are relying strictly on their magic. The dragons are young, not large, so the youklers will match them in physical strength. Also, our birds are underestimated for intelligence. The attackers will think you easy prey, but your soldier skills will give us the advantage. The demons will not be expecting you to fight like soldiers. That is why this was all kept in secret."

"But," the Arthinian glared at the general, "they have magic. We do not! And why are you sending us home!"

"I promised that you would be able to go home," Laren stood up. "I am a man of my word." The general changed into Yanith before Mar's eyes. An old man now stood on the rock, holding his powerful staff. With the other hand, he threw the Arthinian his long-lost staff. Marth grabbed onto the symbol of his magic, feeling the flood of power fill his very being. The young lord had his magic back!

Immediately, Gorg's thoughts came soaring through as the wolf rejoiced in reconnecting with his master. Mar had to calm his pet down just to hear himself think.

"Why?" Marth finally managed to get out.

"Because you will now have to make the decision whether you want to go to Mothia and command the Youkler Brigade or just do the testing and remain a regular mage. The decision is up to you. The choice will be up to each of you. I will not force any to join the battle as a rider. I make no bones that being a Youkler Brigadier will be extremely dangerous. Some will die."

"Me command? Why me?" Mar stood facing the old mage.

"I knew you were always formidable, maybe someday more powerful than I am. My wife, as you know, has the power of sight. Marianna has foreseen that the gods favor you. Her wisdom tells her that you have the potential to rival the king in leadership; that also as a mage, you hold the key to our success. Your pedigree does your skills well, both your father and mother gave you that."

"I think not," Marth countered. "My father does not even acknowledge that I am his. It is Lilith that follows my mother."

"You have more of your mother in you than you know," Yanith smiled. "Now let us go to the others. It is time they all learned what I have told you, but please do not let them know I am Laren. It is my one protection against those that oppose me."

"Why not stay as Laren, young and strong?" Marth asked the old mage.

"As Laren, I cannot wield much magic," Yanith explained. "It is the price of youth. Yet as an old man, my enemies underestimate me."

They walked together back to the clearing. Schaller and Okste were just letting out the birds. The riders were joining them. The sight of Yanith sparked indignation as each of the former recruits accosted the old mage with a barge of accusations.

"Let him explain," Marth yelled above the mayhem. "It's important."

They all shut up as Yanith told his dragon tale. Shock was on everyone's face. But jubilation took its place as each of the squadron got their staffs back. As their magic returned, each rider's spirits lifted. Danella came over to Marth carrying her staff and hugged him. The twins danced around with Lura grabbing onto Larandar and dragging him along. Huff looked at his staff and immediately pronounced, "Approcho" and his large axe was in his hand. He caressed the weapon carefully; tears flowed down his cheeks. "Old friend," the dwarf softly said.

The former recruits all followed Huff's lead. Marth got his magical sword. Ausanwel and Lauranna held their limber ash bows. Larandar felt his staff turn into the beautiful ornate scimitar and Dani was pleased that her staff now turned into a fancy long jeweled rapier rather than a useless necklace. The air was full of joyous celebration. They were mages again.

"You will ride the youklers to just outside Osceta," Yanith explained. "You'll all be provided with ways home from there."

"Wait!" Larandar spoke up first. "What of our birds? Do they not go home with us!"

"No, Schaller and Okste will help Laren get them to Mothia. The mages have housing for the birds there. You each must come back to our fortress for the testing as I promised. After that, you will choose whether you want to be reunited with your birds and become part of the Youkler Brigade," Yanith explained to each of them. "You will all take a full mooncycle to decide - no sooner. Think carefully. I look forward to seeing you at Mothia." The old mage smiled, "Make sure you study while at home. I have no doubt you'll pass the testing."

Yanith left them. They stood looking at each other, each wanting to say something, but the words got stuck in their throats. Mathie and Maggie served them a regular supper and afterwards, the riders all walked down to the regular camp and to the rec hall for one last time. Dani slipped away to say goodbye to Corporal Ransa.

The six of them had first stopped by their old cabin, but new recruits now occupied it. Marth put his arm around Dani as Gorg let out one last bark. Huff broke the mood, as the outspoken dwarf had done so many times before, "Now ain't that somethin, they's usin my chairs!" The riders all laughed, but it was hollow, as each knew how much things had changed. New memories were coming.

Later that evening, back at the barn in the new mess hall, Mar one last time read a book. It was late when they all went to bed, not wanting the new day to come and what the goodbyes would mean.

Mar held Dani in his arms. Their bodies clung to each other, neither wanted to let the other go. The two were loath to break the feeling, knowing that separation was coming. Near dawn, Marth left her bedroom for his own lodging. The Arthinian needed to pack for home.

Chapter Nineteen
The Farewells

As usual, heavy fog shrouded Hope Island. It was thick and soupy. No one said a word during their last breakfast together. Even garrulous Maggie was unusually quiet, just dishing out their oatmeal with Mathie silently helping. Except for Corporal Ransa and Sari, their previous passengers all showed up. Most of the old group was traveling to Osceta with the youklers. Lori, although better, was still too weak to travel. Natalia, however, was going to ride with Schaller who commanded Tura. The female dwarf was going with them.

Laren was not going. To everyone's surprise, the giant Okste climbed up behind Dani. The barbarian looked especially large compared to the small woman. The princess who had been so afraid of him, now easily accepted the Okian. "Hold on tight," she smiled at her passenger. Danella's youkler, Maylith, was the largest of the birds and easily could carry her and the giant.

Everyone was glad that the general came to say goodbye. "Thank you. The Youkler Brigade has reason to be proud of the exceptional accomplishments you've achieved. Remember Yanith's words and study while you are home. No one will be given any preference at Mothia. Good luck!"

The birds swiftly took off. The thick mist had lifted. Schaller took the riders one last time over the Viamar then circled Hope Island. They passed low over Forge Haven. Several townspeople waved up including Bessie who waved her axe high in the air from the docked Ferry. The youklers then headed down The Wild coast.

The seven birds kept close to the shoreline, perhaps Schaller remembered the pulling winds of the whirlpool. As the flock approached the Berling Straight, Gorg barked loudly as if the dog also remembered the harrowing experience. The former recruits and their passengers left the land of The Wild and came upon the elf's Hartland. Merchant ships heading to the busy Osceta port began to appear on the horizon. Just above the port city, Schaller signaled for them to land. As the birds came down in a large clearing, several people appeared. Schaller was expected.

The passengers and riders all dismounted and gathered their backpacks. Each rider stroked their youkler. Time to say goodbye. A somber mood hung over the group as they gathered for the trek into Osceta.

"You're expected at the Ram's Head Inn. Good luck to you all, it has been a pleasure to serve with you," Schaller bowed to them. "May our paths cross again soon! I will see you at Mothia."

As the soldiers left, each turned back for one last look at the birds that had come to be such an important a part of their lives. Schaller and Okste were getting the youklers ready to take to Mothia. The guide was squawking orders to the large white creatures, no doubt getting the birds ready for the rest of their trip.

Marth felt a great sadness descend on him. *What a difference a seasoncycle can make,* he pondered. *How are things in Arthinia? Will my father welcome me? I doubt it. He probably hoped I'd be killed. Lilith, how is she?* Mar had missed his sister; she was the only reason the young lord was looking forward to home.

The port city of Osceta looked the same. The dock area was jammed packed full of sailors of the different breeds of the DeLak Kingdom. Elfs, dwarfs and humans mingled easily. The town buzzed with purpose as everyone was selling or buying. Several large ships were anchored at the wharf. It was near high noon when the group approached the Ram's Head. A fancy good-sized carriage was parked just outside the inn. Four large magnificent matching horses were hitched to the reins; their shiny roan coats glittered in the mid-morning sun.

This is strange, a visiting royal? Marth reflected, *given the clientele of this place. I wonder whose it is?*

The Hope group sat at a long table. Unlike last time, the scouts sat with the six former recruits. Despite their imminent departure, light banter circled the table. Laughter surrounded them as each rider reminisced about their training bungles. They even laughed over Dani's throwing of her meal at Huff.

"It was a waste of a good meal," Huff teased her. "It sure smelled good on me!"

All was forgiven, all wrongs forgotten.

Gorg's amusement entered Marth's thoughts. The wolf missed Lori. His pet was fond of all of them, even the owls. *We will see them again soon,* Marth assured the hound. *They will all be at Mothia in a mooncycle.* At least the Arthinian hoped so. His eyes went around the table. Would the twins leave their homeland again? Would Huff come? *A lot depends on Natalia,* Mar thought as his eyes went to the female healer who sat next to her fiancée.

Lar was sitting next to Lura. It was pretty obvious the drylander was in love with the female elf twin. It was also pretty obvious that Ash disapproved. Could the Bombian leave his beloved desert for Mothia? Marth was sure again that it depended on his feelings for the elf. Would Ash have something to say about it?

Marth's eyes settled on Dani. Would she be at Mothia? The young lord had tried so hard to tell her who he actually was last night. As his arms so desperately clung to her, the thought of losing Dani stopped him. She would not like him being the son of the cruel Arthinian baron. Could the heir to the Arthinia Barony convince a Kazian that he was not like his father? Kazia had plenty of reason to hate the reclusive Thard

Arient. They thought him responsible for the death of one of their own.

The entrance of the most beautiful woman he had ever seen interrupted his thoughts. She was tall, exquisitely shaped with a perfectly sculptured ivory colored face. Her delicate pointed ears just barely poked out of her long blonde curls. Marth looked into large mauve eyes that sparkled with intelligence. Despite her tall stature, she was delicate with a litheness that expressed strength and agility. Her pure white clothing was simple, but it seemed the most stunning gown the noble had ever seen. It was as if the woman walked in light. Her smile brightened the entire room. Everyone was staring, openly admiring the most powerful healer in the kingdom. Outside of her husband, the lady was the most powerful wizard in Mothia.

The elf twins had jumped up, "Marianna!" The Hartlanders both bowed low followed by everyone else. The owls fluttered over, landing on the beautiful woman's shoulders. "Well, hello. They are glad to be returning home," she told the elfs in a melodically hypnotizing voice as their owls returned to their masters.

She's Yanith's wife! Mar was stunned. *What is she doing here?*

Looking at the elfs, Lady Marianna announced, "How nice to see the two you once again." Her voice was beyond lyrical, harmonizing within itself, a typical mage elf. "Your father will be here shortly. I look forward to seeing him," she informed the twins. Both their faces lit up in excitement. "Please, everyone sit." Her long tapered fine shaped hands waved them down.

Who is the twin's father? entered into Marth's thoughts. *How does she know their father?*

Lady Marianna took the seat at the head of the table. "I am glad to see you all. I feel like I know each and every one of you. My husband has told me so much about your team. He has praised you immensely." Her bright eyes went to Natalia, "He has told me of your great gift, my dear."

Natalia blushed profusely, "It is nothing compared to your ladyship."

The lady just smiled, "Do not underestimate yourself. Now who do we have here?" Her penetrating gazed fell on the wolfhound.

Marth had not noticed that Gorg had his paws on the table and was intensely looking at Yanith's wife. *She is fascinating,* the wolf told his master.

"He is quite a stunning wolf," the lady looked at Marth. "How do you do, Gorg?" she pointedly aimed her remarks at his pet. The Arthinian hound barked loudly.

The innkeeper had the meal brought out. The plates contained his best elk meat, fresh vegetables and fruits. Freshly baked biscuits with honey butter accentuated the meal. Even the cider was freshly made, sweet and with no aftertaste. Tasty fruit-filled pastries followed.

Lady Marianna talked to the group as if the lady personally knew them. Each conversation was individually tailored and each felt that they were most important to her. Marianna's violet eyes settled on Dani, "You are looking well, my dear. Your mother is anxiously awaiting you."

"Thank you, your ladyship," Dani replied but looked immediately down at her meal saying no more. Marth felt he had missed something, but what? The young lord wasn't sure. Something had passed between Yanith's wife and Dani, but he couldn't fathom the reason.

"I wish you all a most pleasant trip home." Yanith's wife turned to Marth. "I have stopped here to offer you a ride home. I have business in Arthinia."

The offer had taken Mar completely off guard. Of course, he couldn't refuse. "That is most kind of you, your ladyship. You need not trouble yourself..."

She lifted her hand, "No problem at all. There is plenty of room in my carriage. Now I will leave you to say your goodbyes. I hope to see you all at Mothia."

When she left, the room seemed dull. Each stared at each other knowing it was time to head home.

....

Huff was going north with Tilly, Mathie and Maggie, at least until the lower Great Mountains. All four stood outside the Inn getting their gear together. It was a long trek and their backpacks were full. "We're just waiting on Natalia," Hoffler told the other dwarfs.

Natalia emerged from the Inn without her bag. "I'm going to Mothia with Lady Marianna. We are first going up to Arthinia, then continuing on to the mage fortress."

"NO!" Huff exclaimed. "You have to come home and marry me." He grabbed onto his fiancée, "You can come with me to Mothia when I go for the testing."

Natalia stepped back, "Hoffler, you don't know what your mother is going to do. The baroness will probably order you not to marry me. I disobeyed her by following you. She does not like disobedience."

"I don't care what the baroness thinks," he shouted. "She cannot prevent me from marrying you!"

"It's not only that, Huff," the normally soft-spoken woman raised her voice, "Lady Marianna thinks I have a chance to be a great healer. I can't pass up that opportunity."

"I will go with you!" the Erryian forcefully said. "You're not leaving me behind!"

"Yes, she is," it was Yanith's wife who had come out of the Inn. "You have to go home Hoffler. Natalia, are you sure you want to marry him?"

"Yes," the female dwarf told her, "but his mother will prevent us from marrying, my lady."

"Hoffler, are you sure you want Natalia for your wife?" Lady Marianna turned to him.

"Yes, I will marry her no matter how long it takes," the dwarf firmly told the powerful female mage.

"Then I pronounce you man and wife," Lady Marianna held her hands above the two. "No one now can pull you apart, no one!"

Hoffler and Natalia looked at each other and immediately embraced followed by a long tender kiss. "I will miss ya," Huff held her tight. "I will be at Mothia next mooncycle. Await me."

"Oh yes, I will be anxiously looking for ya," Natalia gave him one last hug. As he left with the other three dwarfs, tears flowed down the female dwarf healer's face. "Thank yee, my lady. I will not disappoint ya."

"I'm sure you won't," Marianna broadly smiled.

....

It was Ash that first sighted the Hartland ambassador walking with Marianna up the road toward the Inn. "Father!" he yelled dragging Lura away from Lar. Both twins ran to meet Eranwel Falsteff. The tall distinguished looking elf hugged both his children, drawing the twins close to him. Marianna bid him goodbye.

"I am so glad to see you," he told his offspring. "And you too, Boris and Hilda." He reached into his pocket bringing out two long worms that the owls immediately snatched up.

"We're glad to see you too!" Lauranna squeezed his arm. "It seems so long since we've been away."

"I have a carriage awaiting us. We'll head right to El-vasor. All your friends will be so excited. Everyone is so anxious to hear what you two have been up to. Did you meet any interesting people?"

Lauranna started to speak up, but Ausanwel quickly interrupted, "Yes we have, Father. We'll tell you all about our training when we get home." Ash then glared at his sister. Now was not the time to bring up Lar.

When she is away from him, she'll see how foolish this whole affair is! Ash assured himself. *If she doesn't, Father will convince her.*

Ash saw Lura look back and saw the disappointed frown on her face when she noticed that Lar was no longer where she had left him. The drylander was no where to be seen.

"Come, let's get home!" their father sounded so excited. Lauranna said not another word as the twins followed the ambassador to his carriage.

....
..

Larandar had watched as the twins had run to their father. His eyes widened when he realized who the man was. *That's Ambassador Falsteff! I've seen him at my father's court. He has the ear of King DeLak.*

His heart sunk as he realized who the twins really were. He didn't imagine the ambassador, the brother to Hartland's baron, would take kindly to his daughter's affection toward a Bombian, given the pride of the elfs.

Lar thought back to the tender goodbye he'd just had with Lura. She had held tightly onto him, passionately kissing him, a promise of more to come. Her assurances that they would be together in Mothia in a mooncycle's time, now ringed hollow. The desert man had seen her excitement as Ash had interrupted them when their father was sighted. Obviously, there was a close parental bond. What of her mother? He did not know.

"We have passage on a ship," a familiar voice with a Bombian accent interrupted his thoughts. He looked up and his cousin Sari was standing in front of him. "The route will take us along the coast as far as Barta at the mouth of the Issla River. There we can catch a boat home to Kimla."

"I wondered where you were this morning when we took off," Larandar told his cousin.

"I had to come to Osceta for a couple of days," the exotic woman stated to him but said nothing else. Lar guessed she was a spy for Laren or an "information gatherer" to be kinder. Sari came and went like the wind. "It will be good to go home for a bit," her voice sounded cheerful. The Bombian baron's son wondered how long Sari had been away. "I need to talk to your father."

He speculated what Laren's spy was going to tell his father, but he did not pursue it since Lar knew his cousin would not give secrets away. "Well, let's get going," he picked up his backpack. As the desert man went to close it, he saw his turban lying on top. His hands grabbed the kaffiyeh, looking strangely at the turban. The cap seemed out of place somehow, as if the head covering no longer belonged to him.

Sari took the kaffiyeh and placed it on his head. "Now you look more like my cousin. A true Bombian." She stood back scrutinizing him. "I'll be right back, Dani is coming to the wharf with us." The female Bombian disappeared into the Ram's Head Inn.

Larandar felt the white hawk's feather that so prominently lay in the middle of his forehead now. As Sari emerged with Dani in tow, he thought no more about it. Lar could not fight that he was Bombian, no more than the desert could fight the sand. At least Dani would be on their journey for a while. The former recruit was going to miss them all.

Dani had looked strangely at him but had said nothing. The three of them headed down the street toward the dock. Home awaited!

When they had reached the port's opening, several large ships were tied up. At the very end was a huge ship flying a flag - it was the colors of the king! "Look, someone important must be in Osceta!" Lar pointed the ship out to his cousin and Dani. It was quite elegant, quite richly adorned. The rest of the ships looked grungy in comparison.

"Yes, someone important," Sari dryly commented. The female Bombian hugged and then bowed low to Dani. "Good luck Princess Danella, you're ship awaits you."

To Larandar's shock, Dani hugged Sari back, "Thank you once again, Sari, for all your help." Dani came over to Lar, "I will miss you, fellow youkler rider." And embraced the drylander then quickly turned with tears in her eyes and fled to the king's ship.

"Princess?" Larandar half shouted it. "Does Mar know?" *No,* the desert man knew he was right, *the Arthinian sheep herder has no idea. Poor Mar. A shepherd's son will never get the hand of the king's daughter.* A great sadness descended on the Bombian. Once more he thought, *Poor Mar,* then came, *poor me too!* His snake stuck its head out of his pocket. "We're going home, Bishi, going home."

....

As Dani walked up the long plank of the big flagship her mind wandered back to the castle. *Did my mother or father send the ship?* she wondered wishing her parents had not done so. Guards standing at the bottom of the ramp almost stopped the princess. Who was this gray uniformed armed woman? The sentries were going to stop her, but Kethi, her maid in waiting, had come running down the walkway and bowed on one knee to Dani.

The guards immediately backed off. Her maid's eyes went extremely wide when the lady-in-waiting looked closely at Danella. What had happened to the royal daughter? Short cropped hair that barely curled around her unadorned ears. What was her mistress wearing? A plain, hooded shirt with loose fitting pants, not to mention the boots. Was that a long blade hooked to her rope belt? Were those knives sticking out the sturdy worn boots?

Dani knew what the maid was thinking and laughed. "It's me, Kethi." The Hope soldier lifted the servant up. Bowing was not any longer a welcome greeting. "Tell them I'm aboard so the captain can set sail. I'm anxious to get home." The princess looked back at the town. Sari and Lar were no long visible. "There is now nothing here for me."

"Yes, my lady," the maid ran back up to the deck.

Danella watched the ship slowly leave the dock. The king's flag ship was not far out to sea before the sails were unfurled and the boat picked up speed. The Viamar looked quiet and peaceful. *So, different,* she reflected. *Now my life is the one in turmoil.* Her mind went to Mar. *Surely my father will see the great man he is.* The Princess had so wanted to tell Mar who she was.

Last night, the Arthinian had tenderly asked her to marry him. Dani had cried in his arms, but wouldn't tell him why. Mar had also told her of Laren's wife's future prediction. Wilful's rider was to be made commander of the Youkler Brigade and that great things were in store for the talented rider. Although Marth had great doubts, Danella believed Marianna's prophecy. The king's daughter believed in Mar.

Surely my father will not stand in our way. Her mind could not conceive of a life without the Arthinian. *I care not that his father is a sheepherder.* Her maid, Kethi, interrupted her thoughts.

"I have a bath drawn for you. Your gown is put out. We must do something with that hair!"

"Please, Kethi, give me a few more moments," Dani turned back to watch the sunset. She wondered where Maylith was, had the birds reached Mothia yet?

Her maid stood close by. The servant's eyes were carefully watching her distressed mistress. The maid's face said it all, *this was not the king's daughter, had Danella actually said "please"?* There was something very different about her mistress. Where had the spoiled immature child gone and the new self-assured considerate woman come from? No, Princess Danella Louisa was not the same!

....

Marth had given his backpack to Lady Marianna's footman and then climbed into the good-sized carriage. The two facing seats were soft and comfortable. Gorg settled next to him with his large head on his lap. He sat across from Lady Marianna and Natalia. The four large carriage geldings were well matched and strong, so they were traveling at a good clip. The horses' coats gleamed in the fading sun as the impressive stagecoach left the coastal city, heading up into the elf's Hartland.

The Arthinian hadn't realized how tired his mind and body were. The rocking of the coach quickly put him to sleep. He awoke when they arrived at the city of Yontia on the shores of the deep cold Marsh Lake. The carriage had crossed the border to Arthinia while Marth had slept. They were spending the night at the lake city. His home of Arianta was less than a day off.

They ate a quick supper at a large clean inn with the owner fussing over them. The beds were thick goose down and spotless. In the morning, the owner's wife had packed a picnic basket for the coach's occupants. Yanith's wife did not want to stop, but to hurry on to Arient castle.

The lady was a fascinating person. She quizzed them about the youklers, not only getting Mar's opinion but Natalia's medical opinion. The dwarf healer explained how she had helped heal the bird. Her ladyship was fascinated, asking many questions. Yanith's wife also listened intently as Marth recounted the attack on the town and pirate ship battle. Marth noticed how intent she became when he mentioned Laren's name.

After a quick lunch, they headed toward the capital city of Arianta. Despite Marth missing his life on Hope Island, he welcomed the rolling hills of Arthinia; the sight of the sheep grazing with the trained wolf hounds watching guard. The young lord hadn't realized how much he had missed the simple tranquility of his former life. The scholar looked forward to his books and of seeing his sister.

"What is it that you need of my father?" he boldly asked the lady. Arthinia's heir saw the startled look on Natalia's face when the dwarf realized who Marth really was.

"I have something I want to trade with him," Marianna's eyes took on a wary look. "I want him to let me take Lady Lilith to Mothia…"

Marth jumped up almost hitting his head, "The baron will not let my sister go," he said as he once again settled down. "She is too valuable to him. My father knows Lilith has great power."

"I think he will." The powerful mage put her hands on her lap as if confirming her decision was not negotiable. "If I give Thard what he wants, the baron will let your sister go. He will release her to me."

Marth stared at Yanith's wife, but she was not going to say anything further on his sibling. *Your father will not let Lilith go,"* Gorg penetrated his master's thoughts.

I do not know what she is going to offer him, the young lord told his wolf.

They rode in silence through the streets of Arianta. When the carriage got to the castle, several burgundy uniformed servants came out to carry their luggage. Marth grabbed his own, waving away the help. The Hope soldier was used to serving himself, he preferred life that way.

"Your room is ready, Sire." One of the domestics led the way. The servants bowed to him now, so different from the day the heir had left Arient Castle. Gorg followed closely at his feet, *they are glad you are home,* entered into his head from his pet.

His room was just as the lord had left it, but with his books were now back on the desk and his clothes hung neatly in the closet. His shoes were all shined. They had a bath ready for him. A loud knock and then his door flew open. Lilith came running in. The small girl jumped into his arms hugging him tightly.

"I'm so glad you are home," she squealed with excitement.

Coralla followed closely behind her student. "Lilith, let your brother get some air."

His sister dropped to her knees and hugged Gorg. The wolf licked her face with great enthusiasm. *The child has grown since you left,* his pet acknowledged.

"Did you know that Lady Marianna is here?" his sister was so excited at the prospect of the great healer actually being in the castle.

"I know, I rode here in her carriage all the way from Osceta. That is the elf's big sea port on the Viamar Sea."

"I know that!" she laughed at him. "Coralla has been teaching me geography. I wish I could see the city for myself."

"You will someday," Marth assured her.

"What are you wearing?" Lilith touched his gray clothing. "You look strange!"

"It is my army uniform…" Marth started to tell her, but they were interrupted.

"Your presence is required, my lord," a burgundy uniformed male informed him. "The baron would like to see you in the Great Room."

The returned home Hope soldier saw the alarm in both Coralla and Lilith's eyes. "Father's not going to send you away again?" his sister clung to his arm.

"No, I'm here for at least a mooncycle," he assured his sister. "I think we should plan a picnic tomorrow. Don't you think so, Coralla?"

"Certainly Sire," the tutor took hold of Lilith. "Come we have lessons to do." She dragged the little girl out leaving Marth to quickly dress, grabbing his staff as he left to meet his father.

Thard Arient was pacing when Marth and Gorg walked into the main meeting room. The audience room was austere as far as most cathedra rooms went. A lone ornate throne-like chair was all by itself in the center of the room. While his father sat and decreed, everyone else stood.

The baron abruptly turned facing his son. The scarred face of his father seemed even more ugly than ever; his eyes even more cruel. "Well, you are home. I see you somehow survived."

"Yes," Marth forcefully stared at his father. The mage apprentice clutched his staff, letting his magic calm him down. It would do him no good to lose his temper with the baron.

"Yanith has sent word that you are to take your testing on the next new moon. Is that your plan?" The statement was sarcastically said.

"Yes," again Mar would say no more. He wasn't sure what his father was conniving, but he'd not help him with it.

"I think you should plan on staying there. You are not to return home." It was a challenge, one that Marth was not going to take.

"Fine," he replied and said no more.

"For Theror sake, speak up for yourself. Are you such a coward you cannot face me?"

"And what good would it do, Baron?" he glared at his father. "I'm well aware of your feelings. You do not even think I am your son!"

"How dare you talk back to me," Arient shouted. "You sniveling bastard. I only kept you because of your mother…"

"Don't bring my mother into this! You've never done anything for anyone but yourself!" Marth screamed back at him. He saw his father raise his staff. Before the spell could reach him, Mar chanted, "Okteina," and his body and Gorg's became surrounded in light. The baron's spell flowed around him, but did not touch the inner ring. Mar heard his wolf growl. The large hound was crouching, snarling, his sharp teeth showing.

Baron Arient looked shocked at the strength his son had and started chanting again. A loud, "Stop it! Stop it immediately, both of you," interrupted his spell. Lady Marianna stood in the doorway. Anger encompassed her face. The power that the lady mage emanated was commanding. Both men were frozen in place.

She walked calmly, standing between them. As she let them go, both fell to the floor. Marth got up quickly, the baron not so fast.

"My lady, this is between me and my son." Arient half snarled, but took a step back when she glared at him.

"You will stop or I will take back my sighting. I will make sure that my blessing will be rescinded. I will talk to the king canceling the whole agreement. Do I make myself clear?"

"Yes," now it was the baron's turn to say little.

"What is she talking about?" Marth looked over at his father.

"I have agreed that your sister is going to Mothia. It will be the best thing for her." The baron was lying, he wouldn't willingly let Lilith go, but Marth didn't care as long as his sister was leaving. Thard Arient was not finished though, "The king has agreed that I will have his daughter in marriage. Lady Marianna has seen that an heir will come with the Princess. I will no longer need you!"

Marth just looked at him, relief flooded his thoughts, both Lilith and he were free, were safe. "Well congratulations, Father, I wish you both the best."

Little did he know how he'd come to regret those words.

To be continued…

Full Graphics for this book can be found at
http://pjbelanger.com/mages

Thank You!

Thank you for taking time to read
Mage Riders – The Recruits.

If you enjoyed it, please consider telling your
friends or posting a short review. Word of mouth is
any author's best friend and is much appreciated.

Also by Pj Belanger:

The Houses of Storem - Epic Fantasy
The Thunderstone
The Treachery
The Triad
Space Detective - A Skip Brown Adventure
Murder on Nestor – Race to Death
Murder on M.O.S.S. – Medical Mayhem
Murder on Hilda – Slippery Slopes
Murder on Casey – Plains on Fire
Collections of Sci-Fi/Fantasy short stories
Sci-Fi à-la-mode
Soldiers One – Warriors of Misfortune
Soldiers Two – Warriors of Courage
Soldiers Three – Warriors of Strength
Mage Riders - New Fantasy series
Vol I - The Recruits
Vol II – The Riders of Mothia

Available at all major online retailers
See more information at
http://www.pjbelanger.com